# Not My People

# Not My People

## A Historical Fiction (1976 - 1986)

## By Ben Jakob

# Not My People

---

## A Historical Fiction (1976 - 1986)

## By Ben Jakob

www.theprodoodler.com
Cover Design by The Pro Doodler

# ACKNOWLEDGEMENTS



The Pro Doodler
198 Halpine Road, Suite 1177
Rockville, MD 20852
www.theprodoodler.com

Ordering Information:
Quantity sales: Special discounts are available on quantity purchases by corporations, associations, and others. For details, contact the publisher at the address above.
Printed in the United States of America

First Edition
14 13 12 11 10 / 10 9 8 7 6 5 4 3 2 1
ISBN #978-0-9905891-8-1

# NOT My People

## A Historic Fiction
## (1976-1986)

# Ben Jakob

# **ACKNOWLEDGEMENTS**

No book of this magnitude would be complete without expressing thanks and appreciation to certain individuals.

First and foremost, I would like to humbly express my never-ending gratitude to the Big Boss, without whose help I would not be anything or have anything.

I would also like to thank my dear wife whose patience with me is unending. I thank her for allowing me the time and space to be able to write this book and bring it to the light of day.

Thank you to my honored parents and in-laws who have raised me and encouraged me and without whom I would not be the man I am.

Finally, I would like to say thank you to the following people.

L. Marcus for her encouragement and numerous suggestions.

The first time a historical figure is mentioned, there will be an asterisk (*) by their name.

Except where noted, the Torah thoughts in this book are original thoughts from the author.

# DISCLAIMER

This book is intended for entertainment purposes only.

This book is a work of historical fiction. The main characters of the story never existed and are purely a product of the author's imagination. However, some of the episodes are based on historical events. The book is a historical fiction by virtue of the fact that the lives and deeds of the fictional characters have been melded into actual historical events. Although the dialogues involving historical figures recorded herein never took place, I have attempted to reflect their true personalities and philosophies, in character for the individual.

For your convenience, an alphabetical index of the historical characters contained within can be found after the novel.

Despite the fact that numerous episodes in this book are based on history, overall it is a work of fiction. Names of fictional characters were chosen at random and are not meant to represent any historical figures.

Names, characters, businesses, places, events, and incidents either are the products of the author's imagination or used in a fictitious manner. Any resemblance to actual persons, living or dead, or actual events is purely coincidental.

# DEDICATION

This book is dedicated to:

Our great rabbis and leaders throughout the generations who have shown us how to live by their very actions. I have had the privilege of briefly meeting a few in our generation.

# **OTHER TITLES BY BEN JAKOB**

- <u>Doomsday Bunker Book</u> – On being prepared for a disaster
- <u>Doomsday Bunker Book</u>, Underground Edition – On being prepared for a disaster
- <u>Addendums for Doomsday Bunker Book</u> – On being prepared for a disaster
- <u>CADD Manual for House Location Drawings</u> – Written for a specific company, but adaptable for any company that uses CADD for house location drawings.
- <u>Viduy</u> – A translation of the Viduy Written by the Chida, ZTL.
- <u>The Quality of Light</u> – A manual for photographers on lighting
- <u>Kitchen Guide</u> – tips and tricks for the kitchen
- <u>The Late Great Who</u> – Sequel to <u>Not My People</u>

# APPROBATION

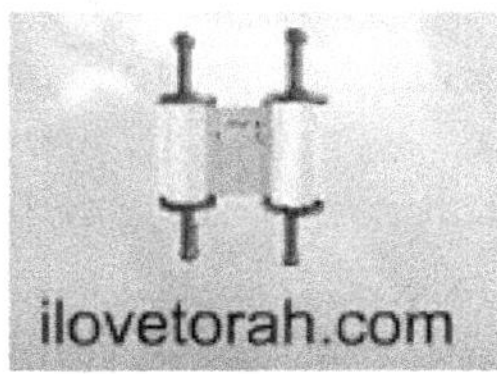


*Haskamah* for my dear friend Rabbi Ben Jakob:

We know that the entire *Torah*, written and oral, was given at *Har Sinai*; Since Shlomo HaMelech said that there is nothing new under the sun (Koheles 1:9).

We know that we aren't allowed to add to Hashem's praises beyond the words already given since that would imply that Hashem's greatness has a limit. Similarly, one might think that adding to the *Torah*, which is complete, would indicate a lack of appreciation for its perfection--but we see it's not this way. The greatness of *Torah* is revealed when someone seeks the *emes,* truth, and tries to uncover, through toil and arduous work, what is hidden inside. The true *Torah* of Moshe shines forth from the desire to reveal what is hidden and to clarify it, thereby sharing the detailed understanding the person acquired from their toil.

Even though the *Torah* is perfect, it was given in such a way that a human being can bring forth new insights, a fresh perspective to what is already given. The desire to reveal the *Torah* to others and illuminate it in practical ways through *chiddushei Torah* is what the oral *Torah* is about. Sometimes the way to a person's soul is through stories and fiction written in a *Torah* perspective. I see Rabbi Jakob's desire to show people a way to find Hashem in our generation. Each soul at *Har Sinai* received its own revelation; no two have the same spiritual experience because no two people are exactly alike. Rabbi

Jakob shares the experience through his *chiddushei Torah* written in fictional stories. I hope that Hashem gives him the strength to continue spreading to the world the holy words of *Torah* to inspire us to bring the best out of ourselves.

Rabbi Jakob is a *tomim* (pure-hearted one) in the most flattering sense of the word.

I wish Rabbi Jakob much success in all his endeavors.

With blessings,

Rabbi Moshe Steinerman

Jerusalem, Israel

www.llovetorah.com

# **TABLE OF CONTENTS**

# PROLOGUE

## November 5, 1985
## Brooklyn, New York

**Barely** five weeks ago, Hurricane Gloria devastated the east coast of the United States, and things were still not back to normal. New York was still cleaning up from the historic storm. It was a massive and concerted effort for everyone: city workers were clearing debris, and the Sanitation Department was cleaning up the trash strewn about in the storm. The Red Cross was assisting displaced people and the newly homeless, while charity groups were helping as best they could with ensuring that everyone had food and clothing. Even every-day citizens were helping one another cope with the devastation.

Those prepared for emergencies with stocks of food and water fared better than those without. However, there were no castes, no hierarchies; communities and individuals came together to share whatever resources they had. They happily shared what they had with their friends and neighbors. After the devastation of this hurricane, more people decided they would start to prepare for disasters.

To add insult to injury, today the heavy clouds had emptied themselves into the already saturated streets of New York. The temperature was also about ten degrees below average for this time of year. People were scurrying to and fro trying to avoid being soaked from the downpour and from the cold. Raincoats, umbrellas, and ponchos were the dress code of the day, although they afforded little protection from the elements.

Most did not dare venture out of doors; others with something important to accomplish were not as fortunate. The intrepid Asher was not among the lucky ones. He bundled up tightly and resigned himself to walking the few blocks to his destination; at least, while walking, he could review the situation and predicament in which he found himself. He had something important to achieve; something was bothering him and he needed to discuss it with the rabbi. He needed advice, and in his mind, there was no one better to discuss his issues with, than Rabbi Mishovsky.

Asher Siskin had enormous respect and admiration for Rabbi Baruch Mishovsky. Truth be told, everyone felt that way about the great Rabbi and *Mekubal.* Aside from his tremendous erudition in all aspects of the Torah, he seemed to have a special connection Upstairs that gave him insight beyond the ken of most people. He was charismatic and empathetic; he understood people and their hearts. Rabbi Mishovsky was five-foot-ten-inches tall, svelte, with sparkling blue eyes that saw right into a person's soul and gave him the appearance of being some kind of angel. As a child, he had lived through the horrors of the Holocaust and survived the murders to which many Jews had succumbed. These living nightmares made him sensitive to his people and he always had time, day or night, for any petitioner.

Asher was of average height with dark brown hair and brown eyes; with his height and well-kept physique, he was an impressive figure when he opened his well-appointed shop. He was clean-shaven and always wore a suit to work. Asher owned a hat shop and haberdashery on Eighteenth Avenue in Borough Park, for men and boys. His store catered exclusively to the Orthodox Jewish community where he earned a good living. He was fair to his clients and paid his employees well. In actuality, the only employee he had was his younger brother Danny who could easily pass for his twin.

Asher was dating a young woman and wanted the Rabbi's advice and insight. Laura Feld was a kind and empathetic woman. Asher was impressed with her intelligence and wit but was concerned that she was not as observant and committed to Judaism as he was. They had recently started dating and the relationship seemed to be progressing well, but there was a shared concern over their differing levels of religiosity. He had mixed feelings and needed someone to advise him before investing more time and commitment into the relationship. He was troubled and unable to sleep, as he did not want to string her along if they were not going to be able to build something lasting.

Asher felt that Laura had good *middos*: she was caring, intelligent and gentle. She kept *Shabbos* and kosher and even worked as a server in a kosher restaurant, where they first met. However, she was a bit more liberal in her observance than what he wanted in a future spouse. She was more modern Orthodox while he was more *yeshivish*.

"Would Laura's anticipation of welcoming the *Shabbos* Queen be as exuberant as mine?" he thought to himself. "Would she be careful with checking vegetables and other *mitzvahs* as I want in my home? Should I compromise or look for someone else? But she is so amazing. Every time I am with her, I want to grow and be a better person. Maybe she is willing to do these things for me, but is it right for me to ask her?" He felt so torn and confused.

Laura felt the same and was not sure if she wanted to become more observant, but she was willing to consider it, especially for someone like Asher. She was vacillating on continuing to date him or not. Considering others she had dated in the past, Asher was a gem and worth her time and effort and it did not hurt that Asher owned his own business. She vividly recalled dating Moshe, and the nightmares of trying to end the relationship: he did not know how to take "no" for an answer and eventually she had to get an order of protection against him. Instinctively, she felt Asher was different and would always treat her with respect.

Asher was feeling good about himself. Despite the turmoil that was tearing at him, he had worked out his questions in detail and was ready to present them to Rabbi Mishovsky. He knew he was allowing his emotions to cloud his judgment and wanted an unbiased opinion. He wanted to talk with the *Rav* about the dating situation. These were some of his thoughts while carefully making his way, in the storm, to see the *Rav*.

When Asher walked into the *bais medrash* and saw the diligence of the Rabbi studying Torah while wearing *tefillin*, it was awe-inspiring. He did not want to disturb Rabbi Mishovsky so to be respectful, Asher stood there, imperturbably, waiting to be noticed by the *Rav*. While waiting, Asher took in the room he had been in before. There were a number of people studying different tomes, the walls were lined with *sefarim* of all sorts, and a humble *aron kodesh* and *bima* occupied places of honor in the unpretentious *bais medrash*. A moment later, the *Rav* felt someone's presence, looked up and saw Asher standing there patiently waiting to be acknowledged. Immediately, a smile appeared on the *Rav's* warm face, but it lasted only a second.

The *Rebbetzin* just brought down some tea for the Rabbi from their upstairs apartment.

"*Rebbetzin*," the *Rav* addressed her urgently, "please call 911 immediately. Asher needs to go to the hospital."

"טייקעף, right away," *Rebbetzin* Shulamis Mishovsky said as she raced to the *Rav*'s small office to make the call.

Asher was shocked and thought, "When someone tells you to call 911, you don't hesitate. When someone with the *Rav*'s vision, tells you to call 911, the urgency is even more pressing."

"What's wrong?" Asher asked suddenly unnerved and shaking with fright not even sure he wanted to hear the answer. He could not imagine what was wrong, as he felt perfectly healthy. This was far from what he expected from his meeting with the *Rav*.

"You need to go to the hospital, now. Your life depends on it. Don't fear, in the meantime, I will say Tehillim." The *Rav* was already murmuring the holy words by heart while reaching for the *sefer*.

Confused and disconcerted, Asher went outside and sat down on the cold stone steps to await the emergency medical technicians; *Rebbetzin* Shulamis went outside with Asher to ensure he got safely on the ambulance and to be there for moral support. Within minutes, Asher heard the wails of several emergency vehicles approaching. As he heard the rapid approach of the ambulance and the increasing decibel levels of its sirens, his anxiety increased proportionately. In short order, an ambulance, police car and fire truck arrived blocking traffic on the street. Asher was still not sure what was wrong with him and he was equally concerned that he did not know what to tell the EMTs.

Six days a week, Asher would *daven* at an early *shacharis minyan* and go for his daily three-mile jog while listening to a Torah lecture on his Walkman. *Shabbos* was the exception; he would *daven* at a later *minyan* since he could not jog on *Shabbos*. It was important to him to stay in good shape, as he believed in the importance of maintaining a healthy body as well as mind and soul. After his jog, he would return home for a quick shower and then he was off to his store. Every evening, Asher attended a *daf yomi shiur* and he knew how to learn.

The paramedic asked Asher, "What seems to be the problem?"

"I was visiting the Rabbi who lives here and he had his wife call 911. I inferred that something is seriously wrong with me, but I don't know what it is."

"Do you have any symptoms?"

"Just a headache, nothing serious; I'm also feeling slightly hot, but that may be due to my nervousness."

"That doesn't sound serious, but let's take some vitals."

At that juncture, Rabbi Mishovsky came running out of the *bais medrash*, "Get this man to the hospital, now!" he said emphatically as he pointed in the general direction of the local hospital.

Startled, the paramedic turned and saw the fiery look on the rabbi's face and quickly gathered his gear and Asher and retreated into the ambulance. With lights and siren, they took off immediately to Maimonides Medical Center on Tenth Avenue and Forty-Eighth Street, just a few minutes away.

Once they arrived at the hospital, the triage nurse also did not understand the urgency. The paramedics were only able to provide his vital signs, which were normal (except for slightly elevated blood pressure, which was to be expected under the circumstances). Asher was made to sit and wait in the waiting room for several hours. Several times, he considered leaving and returning home, but recalling the look on Rabbi Mishovskys face, he stayed rooted in place.

Siskin was feeling disquieted on several levels. He still was not sure why, but if Rabbi Mishovsky sent him to the hospital, there had to be a compelling reason. However, the medical staff was doing their jobs and triaging based on observable symptoms. It was as if he was not sent to the ER for anything but a hangnail and he was just wasting their time. Frustration and worry kept battling for the top spot in his mind. He tried to close his eyes and take a nap while waiting, but the noise and frenetic activity in the ER, in addition to his nervousness, kept him awake.

Asher tried to be patient while sitting in the uncomfortable hard plastic orange chair. He thought to himself that maybe someone should donate more comfortable chairs to the hospital. He could not detect anything seriously wrong with himself so how could he expect the nurses to feel differently. The triage nurse was acting as a guard protecting her domain by following protocol and making sure the most serious cases were treated first. Asher understood that in an ER, people were not seen on a first-come-first-served basis.

Despite the morbid atmosphere, it was a fascinating scene as he looked around the drab yellow ER waiting room. Asher watched as a moaning woman in labor was brought in and taken straight back through the double doors to the ward. After a serious car accident, a man and his son were brought to the ER in critical condition: they were stabilized and whisked off to the operating rooms. A man had been doing some construction and partially sliced off a finger: not life-threatening, but also needed an operating room. Surprisingly, the man seemed quite calm despite the gruesomeness of the damaged hand he was holding with his good hand. "It must be the pain medicine," Asher thought to himself.

All these and more came in and were advanced to the front of the line. Their cases seemed more emergent during the seemingly never-ending length of time Siskin was kept waiting. Even a bawling child was taken while Asher waited.

Sitting two seats from Asher was another man who seemed to be in a similar situation as he. Asher decided to inquire, "Hi, my name is Asher." He proffered his hand and continued, "If you don't mind me asking, what brings you here today?"

"Stewie." He shook the extended hand and said, "The sclera of my eye is bloody and I just want to make sure that nothing is wrong."

Asher noticed the bright red in the whites of Stewie's eyes. "Wow! Is that painful?" he asked concerned.

"No, not at all, in fact, I only found out there was something wrong when one of my co-workers mentioned it to me."

"I hope you'll be okay," Asher said sincerely.

"Thanks so much. It's probably just a burst blood vessel in the eye and will heal by itself. Just wanted a day off from work," he joked. "What brings you to this exotic vacation resort?"

"Honestly, I am not really sure. It's a strange story how I got here."

"I'm not going anywhere. Do tell."

"I went to my rabbi to discuss something. He is a great man and he sent me here with no reason or explanation. I still have no idea why he would send me to this fancy resort, as you call it." They both smiled at each other.

In short order, Stewie was called back to see the doctor. After a while, he was released and went on his way. As he left, he and Asher wished each other well.

As he watched the receding back of Stewie, Asher wondered to himself, "Will they ever see me? This is ridiculous that I've been here for several hours already and I don't even get a t-shirt." He was uncomfortable and could not decide if his stiff muscles were due to him sitting in incommodious chairs for so long, or was indicative of something more foreboding. Feeling a bit warm, Asher removed his jacket, tie, and hat and rubbed his sore legs and arms.

About an hour later, Siskin started to feel uncomfortable and realized he was probably running a high fever. The pain in his muscles was increasing and he was now experiencing sudden chills and nausea. He was beginning to notice his chest simultaneously feeling raw and itchy and his eyes seemed damp. Asher went to the bathroom and removed his shirt and *tzitzis*. He lifted his undershirt and was shocked as he stared at his reflection in the mirror. His entire torso was covered in angry red marks like a clown's nose and he now saw the wetness in his eyes was blood. Suddenly he was shaking and his heart had an irregular, frantic beat. Now he was scared. "How did the *Rav* know? What did he see?" he wondered to himself.

Siskin lowered his t-shirt and with his shirt and *tzitzis* in his hand, quickly made his way to the triage nurse. Without looking up, she said, "We will get to you in short order. Sir, I need you to have a seat, we will get to you as soon as we can but we have more critical cases that need to be handled first." His pressing for attention exasperated her when clearly there was nothing wrong with him. "Why do I get all the hypochondriacs?" she wondered to herself as she continued to review a patient file. "It's not even a full moon."

Without saying a word, Asher just lifted his undershirt revealing the horrible blemishes on his trunk that seemed to want to reach out and bite someone. The nurse looked up and gasped when she saw his red chest and bleeding eyes. Without hesitation, the triage nurse went into high gear; this was serious. She immediately paged the ER physician who came over and identified himself as the head ER doctor. Suddenly the emergency room was abuzz with high activity with everyone running around frantically like a swarm of ants. Asher was suddenly so ill that he was unable to process all the frenetic activity: everything seemed to move in slow motion for him and was making him dizzy.

The next thing he knew, Asher was in an isolation room that had a special air filtration system. He was feeling alone and scared; no one was telling him what was going on and he did not completely understand the situation. Asher was an intelligent person who normally was in control of his surroundings, but now he felt disconcerted and as if everyone else was controlling him. The staff removed Asher's clothes, hooked him up to an IV and donned facemasks. They also connected cardiac, pulse and oxygen monitors to him. The doctor asked him about any travel abroad, to which Asher responded in the negative. Not knowing where he could have contracted any serious disease, they were taking precautions because of his symptoms, which were getting worse. The doctor said he had a maculopapular rash that was indicative of one of the forms of hemorrhagic fever or something similar. Tests were needed to determine the diagnosis more accurately and to decide on a course of action. Asher was glad that Rabbi Mishovsky had demanded he go to the emergency room. He doubted if the triage nurse would apologize to him, but now, that was the least of his concerns.

Asher was scared as he heard terms bandied about that sounded serious, but more testing was needed. Maybe he had malaria or typhoid fever; either one was frightening. One of the questions being asked was if the contagion was airborne or just transmitted via bodily fluid or blood contact. If it were airborne, that would probably rule out the hemorrhagic fever.

The entire medical staff was on high alert and running around in near-panic. The head doctor of the ER called the Public Health Department and the Centers for Disease Control and Prevention. The entire hospital was immediately locked down: no one was allowed in or out. The police and hospital security guards blocked the entrances to ensure containment.

"Do you have family we can call for you?" a concerned nurse asked Asher gently.

"My parents may be concerned about me. Please call them," and he proceeded to give the nurse their phone number.

Despite the lockdown, a few other people showed up exhibiting similar symptoms to Asher's.

Asher wanted to call Rabbi Mishovsky, but he doubted they would allow him into the isolation unit. Still, Asher longed to hear his mentor's words of comfort. No one was allowed to make phone calls as the CDC was trying to prevent widespread panic. That was ironic because the doctors on staff at the hospital and those from the CDC were wearing environmental suits with specialized breathing apparatus. "That must be provocative to others on the unit," he thought to himself. He felt that he was losing the ability to focus on anything as if he was looking through a heavy fog.

From his bed in the isolation room, Siskin called to his doctor, "I feel so horrible. I've been vomiting, having chest pains and diarrhea. What's going on with me?" He was frightened by what was happening and needed reassurance that he would be well.

"We don't know yet. You are very sick and we have to find the underlying cause. Are you positive you have not recently traveled abroad? Or maybe had contact with anyone who has?"

"I cannot speak for my customers, but I deal with a very exclusive clientele of only Orthodox Jewish men. I have not traveled anywhere." He was speaking slowly and having a difficult time following the conversation: his mind was shutting down.

The doctor felt bad for his patient. He knew Asher was probably dying and there seemed to be nothing he could do to help him.

PROLOGUE

With more infected patients arriving by the minute, it was clear that an epidemic was at hand.

The paramedics who brought Asher to the ER were recalled to the hospital to be quarantined. By the time they returned to the hospital, they too, were exhibiting symptoms of a rash on their faces. Doctors from the CDC arrived at around the same time as the paramedics and took over management of the outbreak.

Asher felt a warm dampness on his cheek. He touched his face and found his hand covered in fresh blood; he screamed out in panic. The doctor returned, "I'm sorry to say this, but you are bleeding from some of the orifices of your head."

"Doctor, I am in serious pain, is there anything you can do for me?"

"I will order something for you, but since we do not yet know what you have, we have to be cautious."

"Okay, thanks, doc," he sunk back into the sheets of his bed and felt as if he was falling into an abyss. He was terrified and wished he could reach out to his family for succor and comfort.

The doctor ordered analgesics to soothe his aching patient. Until they knew his exact diagnosis, they could not give him anything but the most basic of medications. The doctor felt completely powerless and wished he could do more.

Asher felt as if he was dying and tried to say Tehillim, but was unable to concentrate. Just in case his end was nigh, he struggled to say *vidduy* and *shema*. It was all but impossible to get the words out and keep his mind focused.

Eventually, a kind nurse had sympathy and the decision was made to permit the call to Rabbi Mishovsky, but Asher was too far gone to be able to hear the rabbi's words of consolation. He was already unconscious and barely alive. Asher lay motionless as doctors consulted with CDC experts and secretly prayed for an answer of their own.

All the staff and patients in the ER who were not already in hazmat suits were issued facemasks. There were people of all ages in the ER and most were cooperative with the lockdown. Some scared and unruly patients tried to exit the hospital but were forcefully prevented from doing so. They were removed from the waiting room. Visitors to the ER who had been healthy moments ago began to exhibit signs of the now telltale hemorrhagic fever. No one bothered guessing anymore if it was airborne.

Many questions had to be addressed: what exactly was this? Where did this start? How did it happen and from where did it come? When did this begin? Who, if anyone, created this virus? Who was

23

patient zero? Most importantly, was this the work of terrorists? Could it be the Russians, who were against the Biological and Toxin Weapons Convention of April 10, 1972?

Answers were needed.

# 1976

## September 10, 1976
## LaGuardia Airport

**Charles** Outterridge had recently graduated high school and had matriculated into college to be a nutritionist. He was a tall, black man with broad shoulders and a gentle disposition. He had a break before the next semester and decided to fly to Chicago to visit extended family. His flight left on Friday evening September 10, from LaGuardia Airport.

Charles was disappointed to be missing the *bar-mitzvah* celebration of Yaakov Applebaum, but it could not be avoided. He had limited free time between semesters and had to use it wisely. Charles had not seen his extended family in a while and this was the only time he had available. He had given Yaakov a generous gift for a man his age and means. He would have enjoyed the celebration, but a check would have to suffice for now.

Charles recalled a conversation he had had with Yaakov a week before the *bar-mitzvah* celebration. "I will have to save you a nice sugary piece of cake," Yaakov joked with Charles.

"Make sure it has plenty of sugary icing on top to throw off my blood sugar chemistry."

"With plenty of sprinkles," Yaakov rejoined, with a twinkle in his eyes.

They smiled at each other; Yaakov knowing that Charles

would never eat anything like that and Charles knowing that Yaakov was only teasing.

He embarked on a Boeing 727, flight number 355. The flight time should have been a brief two and one-half hours. There were over eighty passengers plus crew destined for Chicago's O'Hare airport.

Zvonko Bušić* was a thirty-two-year-old, thin, Croatian man wearing a black suit and tie with a checkered shirt, sporting a closely cropped beard with a noticeable mole on his cheek. He was a fanatic fighting for the independence of Croatia from Yugoslavia. He had his wife Julienne Bušić* (an American) and three cohorts with him on the flight.

Calling themselves "Freedom Fighters for a Free Croatia," they wanted to spread the word of the plight of their country.

Ninety-five minutes into the flight, Zvonko called over a flight attendant and handed her a note. "Please deliver this to the captain. It's important," he said in a soft and even tone.

She looked at the folded piece of paper and was completely shocked and petrified by what she read.

> On behalf of the Freedom Fighters for a Free Croatia, we are hereby hijacking this plane. We have five bombs on board.

The suddenly disconcerted flight attendant glared at the passenger/hijacker and was rooted in her place. Unblinking, she stared at the man who had handed her the note and could not move.

Zvonko coughed to awaken her out of her reverie and reminded her to take the note to the cockpit.

Quickly, the captain went to the stranger to apprise him that they do not take hijack threats lightly. Zvonko Bušić informed him that the airplane was hijacked, that his group had five gelignite bombs on board, and that another bomb was planted in a luggage locker across from The Commodore Hotel in New York City with further instructions. Through the captain, they told officials, where at Grand Central Station, they could find the bomb. The bomb in the locker was to strengthen the impression that the bombs on the airplane were real. They had planned well.

Gelignite, also known as blasting gelatin, is an explosive material consisting of collodion-cotton (a type of nitrocellulose or guncotton) dissolved in either nitroglycerine or nitroglycol and mixed with wood pulp and saltpeter (sodium nitrate or potassium nitrate).

The principle demand contained in the instructions in the

locker was that an appeal to the American people concerning Croatia's independence is printed in many of the local and international media. If the instructions were followed, the bombs would be deactivated.

People were nervous and scared as one of the terrorists faced the passengers while making an announcement. "We will be stopping briefly at Montreal's Mirabel International Airport for refueling and then continue on with a slight diversion." He was trying to keep the crew and passengers calm while maintaining control. "Sorry for any inconvenience this may cause you. We don't want to harm anyone, so please just cooperate with us." As he was making this announcement, the plane started to bank toward its new destination across the border to the north.

There was murmuring among the passengers about what would be their fate and what would happen to the plane. Tension filled the air as the quintet paced the narrow aisles of the aircraft. There was talk about what would happen in Montreal and if anyone would be released or if all were ill-fated. Apprehension was high and much speculation abounded as to possible outcomes and what the authorities were going to do to protect them.

Charles was concerned and nervous about the situation. He was surprised that no one on the plane seemed to be panicking. He motioned to one of the flight attendants, an attractive blonde woman, and asked for a drink. With a smile, she filled his request.

"I'm scared," Charles mentioned to his seatmate, agitated and not able to sit still.

"So am I, but if you are religious, pray to your God for help."

"Have you ever been in this situation before?" he asked trying to relax in his seat.

"By 'this situation', if you mean a hijacking, then no."

"Will we get out of this alive?"

"There's no way to be sure. It helps that the crew seems calm and willing to do whatever is needed to secure our safety."

"That's a good thing. I guess I will not get to Chicago tonight."

"Probably not. I don't know where they are taking us. Just try to stay calm and you should be Okay." He felt bad for the lad but there was nothing he could do for him.

Charles felt the man was being polite, but curt, and decided not to bother him again. Ruefully, he thought to himself, "If I were given to nail-biting, I would have no nails left."

After landing and refueling, a brief static sound came over the PA system before the captain announced they would continue their unscheduled trip. At ten p.m., the plane started to taxi. The five hijackers placed themselves strategically throughout the plane. A blonde-haired man was constantly patrolling the aisle, while an oily-skinned man was in the cockpit bent over the captain. There was another terrorist in a black leather jacket who sat in the stewardess chair facing the passengers holding a black pot in his lap. A big man was standing at the back of the plane, while the fifth man was sitting in the back cradling another bomb.

# September 11, 1976
## Borough Park, New York

*Shabbos* morning has always been a special time for Torah-observant Jews. Throughout the millennia, Jews have always held the seventh day of the week as sacrosanct: it was, and is, a special gift from HaShem.

The particular *Shabbos* of September 11, 1976, appeared particularly regal, almost as if HaShem Himself was shining down from Heaven with a smile. The weather was perfect with barely a cloud in the blue sky and the temperature seemed to be favoring the celebrants. It was almost as if the whole world was celebrating the event with them.

When a family gathered to fete a family *simcha*, it was an even more special *Shabbos*. The family was gathered together in *shul* for the special event of a boy becoming a man. This was always a reason to rejoice, especially for someone as special as Yaakov.

Yaakov Applebaum was a studious junior high school student who took his studies seriously and always had a *sefer* in his hands. He had stellar role models in his parents' who taught their children to always be considerate of others' feelings and needs and Yaakov exceeded his parents' expectations in particular with excellent *middos*. Yaakov was an unassuming, thin, young man with deep blue eyes, and dark brown hair, who was well-liked by everyone. The only person who seemed to have a problem with Yaakov was his mother. On occasion, Elana would become exasperated with her first-born and his absent-mindedness; he often got lost for hours in a book. He was a mature, introspective and well-adjusted young man.

Yaakov's father, Yisrael Applebaum, made sure to set aside time every day to study Torah. He knew how to learn and made sure to instill a love for Torah and its beauty, in his four young children. There was nothing more important to Yisrael than the Torah: his whole life revolved around serving HaShem and studying His Torah.

He could have taken, and passed, the exam to receive his rabbinic ordination, but he saw no reason to do so.

By profession, Yisrael was a chemist and had a Ph.D. in chemical engineering, specializing in quality control within the food industry. He received much of his education while serving in the United States Army. Whenever there were developments in his field, he traveled across the country lecturing about the innovations. He knew how to disseminate complex topics and distill them into easily understood information.

Yisrael conducted research to develop new and improved manufacturing processes for the food industry, troubleshooting problems and applying principles of chemistry, biology, physics, and mathematics to solve those problems. He was passionate about his work and respected in his field, although, like his son, he could be a bit absent-minded.

Yisrael was five-foot-nine-inches tall with broad shoulders and an impressive bearing. Because of what he did for a living, he was health-conscious and always considered nutrition, sometimes to the consternation of his children. He often consulted with eighteen-year-old Charles Outterridge, an amateur nutritionist. Although Charles was not Jewish, he was mindful and appreciative of *kosher* laws. One of Charles' siblings had diabetes and he was fascinated with how the body utilizes nutrients and how sometimes it does not work properly. He wanted to learn how to use nutrition to redirect the body to work properly instead of always having to rely on drugs. He planned to study nutrition in college, as he wanted to make a vocation of his forte. In the meantime, he enjoyed the camaraderie of the Applebaum family. Charles was an admirer of Yisrael and over time, they developed a kinship. He was impressed with the Applebaum family and their Torah way of life.

There were always words of Torah on Yisrael's lips and there was never a *Shabbos* meal without *zemiros*. Every evening, *Reb* Yisrael went to the Yeshiva to study and awoke early every morning to attend a *daf yomi shiur* before *shacharis*. Except when traveling to lecture, or for research, which was not more than once every few months, Yisrael Applebaum was always home for dinner. He was a loving and caring father and devoted husband who, although a bit aloof, was always helpful with the children's homework. He valued this time at home as much as he did his Torah study, work and his personal relationship with HaShem.

Mrs. Elana Applebaum was an elementary school teacher in a local *cheder* where she was an excellent teacher who was loved by all of her students. Her goal was to make her students want to come back the following year to study Torah. Elana was a petite, high-cheeked woman and a perfect partner to her husband and always made sure he had time to study Torah. On occasion, she would feel distressed that Yisrael was not home when she needed his help with the children, but she knew his time studying Torah was most important. Her kith often commented on her sensitive hazel eyes that seemed to sparkle when she smiled, which was constantly. She was a sensitive woman who understood the nature of people. This was what made her an excellent teacher and which she imbued to her own children.

They were a family who embodied *chessed*, always having guests for *Shabbos*; they also made sure sick and poor families had food. If there was a *mitzvah* to be done, it was probably done surreptitiously by the Applebaum family. They were not rich, but what they had, they shared with those less fortunate. Emulating our forefather Avraham, their door was always open to anyone in need.

The Applebaums lived in a nondescript red-brick townhouse in Borough Park, Brooklyn, with a small garden in front of the house. The house was cramped for their family, and that was often a topic of distress in the home as the children were often getting in each other's space.

The *bar-mitzvah* celebration of their oldest child was a simple affair, but pleasant. Many *bar-mitzvah* parties were elaborate and ostentatious, but Yaakov wanted something modest: unlike most, he preferred low-key events. Most of the guests were either members of his family, close family friends, or his classmates. Yaakov Applebaum read flawlessly from the Torah and gave a beautiful *d'var* Torah.

Before starting his *d'var* Torah, Yaakov looked around the well-lit room at those who came to celebrate his becoming a man. He was touched by those who joined the family and was appreciative of their presence and encouragement. Everyone anticipated hearing deep words of wisdom from the budding scholar. He smiled nervously as he began his *d'var* Torah:

"Rosh HaShana is in two weeks, so I would like to say something apropos to those special days of awe.

"During the entire month of Elul and beyond, we say a special chapter of Tehillim; chapter 27. In it, we say something that needs explanation, or clarification if you will. 'אם תחנה עלי מחנה, לא יירא לבי, אם תקום עלי מלחמה, בזאת אני בוטח.' Though an army would besiege me, my heart will not fear; though war would arise against me, in this I trust.'

"What is the word 'זאת, this' coming to teach? What is 'this' referring to?

"We also say in *davening,* from Tehillim 92, וכסיל לא יבין את' 'זאת 'And a fool will not understand this.' Again the word 'this'. What is the connection? What is 'this' coming to teach? To what is it referring?

"There is something interesting in part of the *davening* that we do not experience during any other time of the year. I would like to explore it briefly with you.

"There is something fascinating in our *machzors*. We see it three times every year but never question it. But, it's very unusual.

"The נתנה תקף (Let Us Cede Power) is one of the most emotional and stirring prayers of these special days. This special *tefilah* was composed by Rabbi Amnon* of Mainz, Germany, about a millennium ago. Rabbi Amnon recited this before *kiddusha* of *musaf* and then passed his holy soul to heaven.

"Three days later, Rabbi Amnon appeared in a dream to Rabbi Klonimos *ben* Meshullam*, who was a great *talmid chacham* and *mekubal* in Mainz. Rabbi Amnon taught the prayer to Rabbi Klonimos and asked that it be included in the prayers for all Jews around the world. Obviously, it was.

"In our *machzors* are the words 'ותשובה ותפילה וצדקה' 'But repentance, prayer, and charity...' powerful words in our supplications before our Maker. What is unusual is that above these three words are three other words. 'צום קול ממון' 'Fast, voice, money'. It is as if rabbis were translating these words for us. No other words, just these. Why? What is the reason these words need a special translation? Don't we already know that repentance is with fasting? Prayer is with our voice? Charity is with our money? What is the big secret here that our great Rabbis of yore had to tell us with these words?"

Yaakov paused his monolog and glanced around the room at his family and friends. He noticed that some people were nodding their heads in understanding while a few others were confused. He also noticed his two youngest siblings, Michal age seven and Yochanan age three, scampering around quietly at the back of the small hall - that brought a smile to his face as he remembered himself doing such things when he was their ages.

Yisrael discretely tried to get Yaakov's attention to continue his speech. With a shudder, Yaakov noticed his father's gesticulations and quickly returned to his allocution.

With a nervous smile, Yaakov continued; "I believe the answer may be explained as follows. The word of *tzom* (fast) has a *gematria,* numeric value, of 136. The word of *kol* (voice) has a *gematria,* numeric value, of 136. The word of *momon* (money) has a *gematria*, numeric value, of 136. Interesting. All three words have the same numeric value. Coincidence? I think not.

"Since there are three words, let's multiply the 136 X 3 and we come up with 408. The number 408 is the *gematria* of *zos*, this.

"What I think this all means is that we can always believe in these three things (repentance, prayer, and charity), to save us from war, as in the first *passuk* we discussed.

"It's also clear that a fool will not understand, or do, these three things: repentance, prayer, and charity.

"This is what I think the rabbis were teaching us with their enigmatic message. We have to constantly be aware of these three things in our lives to prevent ourselves from becoming fools: also in order to be able to find our salvation and stay committed to our purpose."

Yaakov concluded his speech with acknowledgments and thanks to his parents, Rabbis, and others who helped him reach this pivotal time in his life. He looked up from his paper, smiled and lowered his shoulders clearly relaxed that the task of his speech was over. He smiled, took a deep breath and looked up at his Rabbi and parents who were all looking at him with *nachas*. His mother was practically in tears as she eyed her eldest child.

Everyone was impressed that such a young man was able to have such a deep understanding of the prayers. Yaakov had seen and noted something unusual. It bothered him enough to find an answer that was well thought out and researched.

His parents and family were *shepping nachas* from him.

After *davening*, there was a small *kiddush* in *shul* with a modest spread of cakes, drinks, and simple *nosh*.

After *kiddush*, Yaakov walked with his family the three blocks back to their home, for a pleasant *Shabbos* lunch. It was a short walk; everyone was happy, joking around, and convivial with Torah discussions on everyone's lips with the younger two children running around. They were all talking about how proud they were of Yaakov and how grown up he looked in his new suit.

As the Applebaums walked home, still feeling inspired by Yaakov's speech and the earlier events, they felt what seemed to be a strange and significant tension, almost albatross, in the air. It was not the family, but something was clearly wrong. There was an added rush and excitement among the non-Jewish community members. Police were scurrying around with their radios hushed but active; they were running amuck. Something was afoot and it seemed as if all first-responders were on high alert. There was stress written all over people's faces.

"Thank you for your service officer, but can you tell us what's going on?" Yisrael inquired of a haggard police officer.

"I guess you haven't heard, there's a terrorist attack going on right now. All law enforcement and first responders have been mobilized. You're not in any danger." He said quickly and rushed away.

Yisrael turned to his family, "When we get home, we will all say Tehillim for the salvation of whoever needs this from HaShem."

Upon their return home, the younger children were hungry and did not want to wait. Elana gave the youngsters some food while the rest sat and said the holy and comforting words of King David, and then put the tension out of their minds. They would not let the apprehension in the air mar their euphoria. They finally sat down to a scrumptious *Shabbos* lunch interspersed with Torah discussions and *Shabbos zemiros*. It was a wonderful experience and an extraordinary time for family and friends.

When young Master Applebaum celebrated his becoming a *bar-mitzvah*, he received what he considered a significant amount of money as gifts. Before and after that special *Shabbos*, envelopes of gifts came in the mail. He took judicious notes of who gave which gifts and made sure to send thank you notes. "Recognizing the good" was something inculcated in him from an early age. However, he was feeling a bit lazy and it took him a while until he completed sending out the notes. Exasperated, his mother kept reminding him of his responsibilities.

As with everything, his parents' raised him according to the dictates of the Torah, so he immediately gave ten percent to *tzedakah*. Well, immediately may have been a bit of an overstatement as he was not overly excited to part with the money. There was no question in his mind; this was what HaShem expected from him, so of course, it was what he did.

He was a young man who was always looking to the future, so he resolved to invest the largess he received. Immediately after *Shabbos*, Yaakov decided to meet with David Anderson.

David was a member of the *shul* where Yisrael Applebaum *davened*. He was five-foot, five-inches tall at 175 pounds and always made sure to dress well. He was sensitive about what he considered his diminutive size, so he used his apparel to draw attention away from his short stature. He was an investment broker and a caring man. David was a conundrum as most investment brokers and financial wizards were not given to show their emotional side, but he was. His was a busy office in Flatbush. Yaakov's parents also used Anderson for their retirement and investment planning.

Yaakov felt mature when he discussed his investment needs with Mr. Anderson. Being proud of his actions, he could not help but smile to himself. He was only thirteen but he was planning for his future, and this was the behavior of an adult. When Yaakov looked around Andersons' office, he was astounded at the frenetic pace. People were on the phones talking rapidly, periodicals and investment brochures were well-thumbed, notes and ledgers were constantly consulted. The office itself seemed to exude order and discipline: the walls were an oyster-shell-white with a worn beige carpet on the floor.

"I like the idea of investing in a company that is going to be in the needs of people's homes for the foreseeable future and beyond. I think Kodak and Fuji Film are two such companies. What do you think?" Yaakov asked Mr. Anderson. He had done his research and was proud. He tried not to let that pride show on his features, but it was not easy; he could not suppress the smile that came to his face.

"That is very wise and perceptive of you. They are both good and strong companies. They are positioned to grow and they have a strong history. They are both poised to take advantage of upcoming technological advances. I'm also going to suggest a few other companies for you to consider."

David pushed his glasses up on his hooked nose and then proceeded to discuss a few other companies he felt would be wise investments for the young investor.

"I want any dividends and returns to be reinvested back. For the foreseeable future, I don't want to touch the money."

Impressed, David responded, "You are wise beyond your years. I would imagine that most people your age would just squander the money. To be honest, many adults would also be frivolous and spend their largess." They continued to discuss the merits and demerits of a few companies. David also showed Yaakov how to check the newspaper for the stock market fluctuations and how to interpret them for his particular needs.

"Investing is basically putting your money to work for you," explained Anderson. "Essentially, it's a different way to think about how to make money. Growing up, most of us are taught that you can only earn an income by getting a job. Additionally, that's exactly what most of us do. There's one big problem with this; if you want more money, you have to work more hours. There is a limit to how many hours a day you can work, not to mention the fact that having a bunch of money is no fun if we don't have the time to enjoy it.

"You can't clone yourself to increase your work time; instead, you need to send an extension of yourself - your money - to work.

That way, while you are putting in hours for your employer, or even mowing your lawn, sleeping, reading the paper or socializing with friends, you can also be earning money elsewhere. Quite simply, making your money work for you maximizes your earning potential whether or not you receive a raise, decide to work overtime, or look for a higher-paying job."

Yaakov was amazed at this concept and now understood the basics of investing, but had not associated making use of his money to replace the possible need for a higher-paying job. This excited the young man and grabbed his attention powerfully.

"A common joke I have heard is that the word 'job' stands for 'just over broke'. Having a job is no way to make a living. As I just said, you want to have your extension, money, which earns money.

"True investing doesn't happen without some action on your part. A 'real' investor doesn't simply throw his money at any random investment; he performs a thorough analysis and commits capital only when there is a reasonable expectation of profit. Yes, there still is a risk, and there are no guarantees, but investing is more than dumb luck. Economics is how people respond to incentives and disincentives. The rest is opinion and makes no difference to the reality of how the stock market will go. This differs from 'economy' which can be influenced by what individuals or groups while 'economics' cannot be controlled except by how people react to what is going on in the world. Always remember that people will act in their own best interest.

"By planning ahead, as you are doing, you can ensure financial stability for the rest of your life, and especially during your retirement," he said, beaming with pride over his young investor.

To himself, he thought, "He really is a smart kid. He is going places when he grows up."

Yaakov was able to grasp the fundamentals of investing quite easily and he realized that if HaShem had things go the way he hoped, he would be set for life. If he kept his vision clear and followed through, he imagined he would be able to live comfortably off the interest and dividends. He also understood that the stock market was risky and he could lose everything. When the time came, he wanted to have a job and not deplete his investment income; maybe he would even open his own business in the future. In this way, he would be financially secure for the rest of his life. He had heard, "The wealthiest people have multiple streams of income." In the end, Yaakov left with a diversified portfolio that anyone would be proud to own.

This whole event made Yaakov Applebaum realize that we are not in charge of our future: only HaShem is in control and is the

Boss. We have no say in the stock market, all we can do is our homework and hope we make the right decisions. Because of this, Yaakov decided he would refer to HaShem as the "Big Boss". He prayed for HaShem's blessings on the decisions he made. He felt good.

# September 11, 1976
## Atlantic Ocean

With an accent, the oily-skinned man announced, "We are going to pass out papers for you to read. Read them, please. You should not worry. We do not intend to kill anybody. All we want is for our declaration to be published in the American newspapers. We are not asking for difficult things. We want the world to recognize the injustices against our people - the People of Croatia."

The plane was then flown to Gander, Newfoundland, where thirty-five passengers were released. The old, women, children and infirm were allowed to deplane. Charles remained onboard, a captive. He was scared, alone and wished he were among those discharged. His hopes did not come to fruition and his life was still in danger, but he held onto the hope of safely returning to his family. He desperately wanted to talk with his parents and hear their comforting words. "Maybe they should put phones on planes," he thought to himself.

"Am I pinning too much hope on the announcement of that nasty man that they don't want to hurt us?" Charles thought to himself. "They don't look so bad. Maybe they will let the rest of us go soon." He was feeling cautiously optimistic but desperately wanted to go home. Charles looked at his seatmate and was shocked to find him asleep. "How can he sleep in this tension?" he continued to think to himself. All he wanted to do was go visit some family, and here he was being taken to who-knows-where. He wondered, "Maybe I should have gone to Yaakov's *bar-mitzvah* celebration."

From Gander, the plane was shadowed by a larger TWA 707 plane, which guided it to Reykjavík, Iceland. The hijackers' initial European destination was London, but the British government refused them permission to land.

The terrorists wanted the plane to drop leaflets from the air over both London and Paris. The leaflets contained their manifesto and were to be used to spread the word of the plight of the Croatians from Yugoslavia. The plan was for the 707, which was geared for trans-Atlantic flights, to drop the flyers while the hijackers on the 727 were watching. Because the 707 had a swept-wing design with podded engines, any leaflet dropping would have clogged the engines.

Bušić had not anticipated this snag in his heretofore carefully laid plans. Quickly, he had to come up with a different strategy.

IN THE MEANTIME, OFFICERS FROM the New York City Bomb Squad went to investigate, and they discovered a bomb in a luggage locker at Grand Central Station. Carefully, they transferred the bomb to an explosive secure truck for transportation. With a police escort closing off streets, they gingerly drove to the department range at Rodman's Neck in the Bronx. Once there, Officer Brian Murray* (age 27), along with three other officers, began their attempt to defuse the bomb by remote control. After setting a cutting instrument on the two wires attached to the device, the officers retreated from the bomb pit for several minutes.

The bomb pit was made of a hardened and reinforced cement block (to protect people should an explosion occur) built deep underground. Brian thought about the brilliance of its construction and appreciated the safety precautions as he went to work on the device.

At a distance, and from behind a barricade, the technicians used a remote control to cut the wires in order to defuse the bomb. After significant effort and time, nothing happened; it did not work. When they were unsuccessful in disarming the bomb by remote, they cautiously drew near. During their approach, the bomb suddenly exploded, instantly killing Officer Murray and seriously injuring the other three officers.

(Sergeant Terence McTigue* lost an eye in the explosion, while two other officers, Henry Dworkin* and Fritz Behr*, were wounded but not as seriously. They were all heralded as heroes.)

AS SOON AS THE PLANE entered French airspace, a Dassault Mirage III fighter plane escorted them. When the hostages saw the fighter plane pacing their plane, they became excited with the prospect of a peaceful rescue in the immediate future. When the terrorists saw the excitement among their captives, they immediately ordered the shades closed. The hostages were suddenly feeling even more tension than before. Their hopes of a quick resolution were quickly dashed as they slumped further into their seats. Charles was fidgeting in his seat with his tension mounting. His mouth was dry and he kept asking for more to drink. The anxiety among the passengers was so high, one could practically see it floating like a heavy fog.

The plane landed in Paris, France, at Charles de Gaulle Airport and several hours passed with no apparent action. The concern and apprehension among the hostages was mounting in spades. Eventually, the passengers were herded to the rear of the plane.

One of the passengers, named David, collapsed. Charles watched as another passenger identified himself as a doctor and rushed to the fallen victim. The doctor declared that David was in diabetic shock and the terrorists allowed the man to be released to the hospital.

"I think that man may have been faking his diabetic shock to get out of here," Charles thought to himself. "He didn't show signs of dizziness, shaking or sweating. The first thing the doctor should have done was to give him some orange juice. Maybe the pair was colluding to get off the plane." Since he was not sure, and it would not help anything, Charles kept his observations to himself, mindlessly avoiding his own fear with obsessive thinking of how to escape.

After receiving information that their demands were met, the group surrendered to the French police. At eight p.m., after direct talks with the U.S. Ambassador to France, the hijackers capitulated. They were transferred to the custody of the Federal Bureau of Investigation. Their onboard explosive devices were revealed as fakes: they were just pressure cookers. The episode had been resolved peacefully with no injuries to the hostages.

"Well, that only put me about thirty hours behind schedule, not including getting back to New York. I can't wait to go home," said Charles to himself.

The only fatality was Brian Murray; none of the hijacking victims was harmed. Charles was shaken but unharmed and felt confident about his future and the impact he would make for people to live good and healthy lives.

Zvonko Bušić was convicted of air piracy resulting in death, which carried a mandatory life sentence with parole eligibility after ten years.

# 1977

## February 1977
## Brooklyn, New York

**Yehudis** and David Anderson had not always been the most religious couple. They were proud of their Jewish heritage, but being observant did not come easily to them. They married in 1967 and were financially comfortable, but there was something significant lacking in their marriage. David was an investment broker and Yehudis was a nurse. They had a nice home and a comfortable life. The main point of contention and strife in their home was the lack of progeny running around; they had not been blessed with children.

Over the course of time, the Andersons started exploring the observant lifestyle. The Applebaums were one of the families who had a positive influence on the couple.

Another couple, the Benjamins also showed the couple how beautiful Torah observance could be. As they grew in their observance, the Andersons often spent *Shabbos* meals with these families. It was always a wonderful experience.

By the beginning of 1977, the Andersons had reformed their lifestyle, keeping *Shabbos* and had converted their kitchen to kosher. Things seemed to be going well for them and *Shabbos* often found David and Yehudis with guests of their own for meals in their stately home. They also had first-hand knowledge and experience with returning to the fold and they were able to help others do the same.

One Friday night the couple invited two friends, Rena, and Michael Pasternak, for dinner. There were nice *zemiros* and words of Torah over the course of the delicious meal: the friends all enjoyed each other's camaraderie. Rena was eight months pregnant and there was talk about the upcoming *simcha*. There was banter about the possibility of either a boy or a girl. All agreed that as long as it was a healthy child, everyone would be happy and thankful to HaShem. Although after ten years of marriage the Andersons did not have any children of their own, they still were happy for their friends. They would not let their own pain get in the way of their friendship or excitement.

Rena was feeling a bit under the weather, "I need to lie down," she said softly. She was a slight woman and this was her first pregnancy. She hobbled over to the sofa and tried to relax. She assumed her weakness and tiredness was due to her pregnancy and the typical third-trimester weight gain and pressure. With foreboding and apprehension, Yehudis watched her friend amble to the sofa.

Yehudis tilted her head to the side and furrowed her brows as she watched Rena squirming on the sofa. Something was not right with the pregnancy or the mom-to-be.

Being a nurse, Yehudis was concerned for her friend and went to sit on the sofa next to her. "Rena, you seem flushed. I want to feel your forehead." She placed the back of her hand on Rena's forehead and was shocked at what she felt.

"How long have you had a fever?" She was concerned; this was not good.

"I don't know, probably since Thursday, not long, why?"

"A fever during pregnancy is very dangerous. I suspect you have a fever of over 101. David, get me the thermometer."

David was unsure if he was allowed to use a thermometer on *Shabbos*, however, he knew that when it comes to matters of life, he should do what was needed and ask his rabbi later. He immediately retrieved the requested instrument.

The foursome was concerned and alert with all eyes focused on Rena. Michael began pacing back and forth nervously in the living room. "What if something is wrong?" he asked out loud to no one in particular. "What will be with my wife and the baby? What should I do?"

As the thermometer was placed in her mouth, she sat up in a panic, "My water just broke!"

"David, call 911. Now!" Yehudis urgently called out.

Not comprehending the reason, but understanding the exigency, David knocked the phone off the hook with his elbow, to honor the *Shabbos*, and called for emergency services.

The ambulance arrived in short order and rushed Rena to the hospital. The medical staff made heroic efforts while both David and Michael said Tehillim the entire time. Unfortunately, there was nothing that could be done: the fetus had self-aborted. There was nothing anyone could say; at that point, they all felt devastated by the loss.

# June 1977
## Micheaux State Forest, Pennsylvania

When growing up, Yisrael Applebaum was a member of the Boy Scouts. It was something he enjoyed and he wanted to pass the experience and closeness to nature to his own progeny. He looked forward to taking them camping and teaching them about the outdoors. The experience would give them skills they could use for the rest of their lives. He fondly recalled the overnight camping trips and the excitement of waking up in the forest and davening to HaShem in nature.

"What type of camping are you planning for?" Elana asked her husband. Elana was not as keen on the idea as was her husband, but the children would enjoy it immensely. She was willing to go with whatever his plans were and she would enjoy herself or at least pretend to do so. It would be a peaceful and relaxing time for the family to become closer.

"Well, there are different forms of outdoor camping. The light of heart campers go camping in a recreation vehicle with all the comforts of home. In my opinion," Yisrael said, "that's not real camping. Then there are those who enjoy state parks where within about an acre or two of property, there are dozens of campsites about ten feet wide by thirty feet long. Campers are within arm's reach of their neighbor. In addition, within walking distance of the camping spots are comfort facilities and showers. They even have electricity and phones in the campgrounds.

"However, the diehard campers go to state forests. In a state forest, each camper is given a campsite that's about an acre in size or larger. The next closest neighbor is several miles away - not even within shouting distance. There are no comfort facilities: if one needs a bathroom, one has to dig a hole in the ground or set-up a lean-to. It's not the type of camping for the faint of heart or someone with a delicate constitution. This is often called primitive camping."

"What's a lean-to?" Tziporah asked.

"A lean-to is just a tarp that is set up at an angle to shield from the elements. In our case, we will set up a tarp for our bathroom area." Elana was less than enthusiastic about this part, but she would go along for the sake of her children. Elana would prefer roughing it in a hotel room.

"A more extreme form of outing is backpacking. This is where the camper puts all his gear in a backpack and is dropped off at one location. If he can't carry the gear or food, he doesn't take it with him. Several days and dozens of miles later, the camper is retrieved at a distant location and goes home. They have to be at the rendezvous at the appropriate time as there is no way to confirm or change the time. It's very rare that a backpacker goes out alone; they generally go in pairs. We are not ready for this, it takes much more experience."

"What about in the future?" Yaakov asked hopefully.

"Yeah, that sounds exciting," Tziporah chimed in.

"Maybe."

Micheaux State Forest is almost 86,000 acres and located in south-central Pennsylvania. It is crossed by the Appalachian Trail and is a lush and beautiful forest.

In order to accommodate their crew and supplies, the Applebaums rented a large van for their camping trip. Elana and the children went with the luggage in the family van, while Yisrael drove the rest of their gear and food in the rented van.

In anticipation of the trip, Yisrael and Elana went to an army surplus store for all the camping gear they would need.

The family left early on a Sunday morning in June, in tandem, for the scenic six-hour drive. It was a long trip, but it was worth the effort. Between Boy Scouts and his military service, Yisrael had plenty of experience camping, they were not expecting any difficulties. It was going to be a wonderful adventure, which they planned to do many times in the future.

When the family pulled into the reserved camping spot, the parents were unable to contain the excitement and enthusiasm of the children. As soon as they alighted from the van, the four children ran around exploring nature. It was wonderful! With broad smiles on their faces, Yisrael and Elana watched their children's exuberance. The area designated for their excursion was perfect: they were in the middle of the forest at the edge of a clearing that was about one-hundred feet long and about fifty feet wide. Near the middle of the clearing was a singed area that had been used many times for a fire-ring.

With an impish grin, Yaakov cupped his mouth with his hands, took a deep breath and shouted at the top of his lungs, "Hello!"

"What are you doing," Elana asked him, while Tziporah mimicked her brother in an echoing, "Hello, hello, hello."

"Abba said that there would be no one within shouting distance. I want to make sure."

Everyone laughed while Yisrael ruffled his son's hair.

"What's that smell?" twelve-year-old Tziporah asked.

Yisrael inhaled deeply through his nose and smelled. "Ahhh, that wonderful smell is nature. We don't experience fresh air while living in the city."

"Oh, I love it! I can get used to it."

In vain, Elana tried to stifle a laugh.

Yisrael gave the children age-appropriate jobs to aid in setting up their campsite. The youngest two were tasked with gathering kindling, while Tziporah was to gather the heavier logs for firewood. Tziporah was a small-boned tomboy and enjoyed the ruggedness of the outdoors. She preferred to keep her brown hair short as she felt it complimented her thin face, and it was more her style as a person. She loved climbing trees and riding her bike everywhere.

Yaakov helped his father pitch the tents and set up a fire ring while Elana set up the kitchen area. In the end, they had a great layout for their camping site. There was a large tent for food preparation and eating. They had another large tent for the parents that also had space for the family to sit together. There were two smaller tents for the children, one for the boys and one for the girls. The layout had the four tents forming a loose circle around a central fire ring.

Off to the side, about twenty yards west from the tents, was a lean-to for use as a bathroom. It was a tarp strung between four trees at an angle to prevent any leaves and rainwater from accumulating.

To the east of their tents, they designated a place for *davening*. Further to the east was a wide rushing stream with fish. The sounds and smells they experienced on their camping adventure were unique and thrilling.

About two-hundred yards to the north, beyond a copse of trees, was the Appalachian Trail going up a hill. The Applebaums were looking forward to exploring part of the trail.

After several hours of setting up their campsite, Elana made dinner while Yisrael and the boy's *davened mincha*. It was an exciting and highly spiritual experience for them. It may have been the first time the holy words of *davening* were heard in this environ. They each took a little bit longer to say the ancient words to their Creator.

After *mincha*, the family had dinner around a roaring campfire.

After eating, no one was in any hurry to move, so Elana and Yisrael sat with their children while reminiscing about the past fifteen years of their familial life. With such pleasant thoughts and reverie, after *davening maariv*, they contentedly went to sleep. The exertions of the long drive and setting up camp exhausted the weary travelers and they were fast asleep.

The Applebaums were woken early the next morning to the mellifluous sounds of nature. It was different from waking up with an alarm clock compared to the birds chirping and singing praises to the Master of the world. The children were exhilarated by everything they saw and heard. From the chirping birds in the trees, the breeze rustling the green leaves, to frogs croaking and the gentle rush of the nearby stream, all assailed their senses. Yisrael and Yaakov *davened* side by side in nature and it was the most inspirational *davening* Yaakov experienced in his life. After *davening*, while still wearing their *tefillin*, father and son sat and studied Gemara for an hour. They learned twice every day for at least an hour at a time. During this camping trip, father and son became even closer than they were as they forged their spiritual bond. Yisrael missed his morning routine at *shul* with a *minyan*; however, this was also something special that was well worth his absence.

"Even when on vacation, we are expected to set aside time to learn Torah." Yisrael always emphasized to his children the importance of following the dictates of HaShem. "Unfortunately, some people think that when they aren't home, they can leave the Torah behind. This is not what HaShem wants. The Torah is not a part-time activity; it's something we commit to twenty-four hours a day, every day," he explained to his son with passion and zeal blazing in his heart.

"We say in *davening,* 'הנותן לשכבי בינה להבחין בין יום ובין לילה'. We praise HaShem for giving the rooster the knowledge to know the difference between day and night. It is a beautiful thought and blessing, but the obvious question is why is that the first *beracha* we say every morning? What is so important about a rooster knowing the difference between day and night? I mean, who cares? Don't we all know when the sun is shining or the moon is out? It's so obvious for anyone to see.

"The reason is simple," he said answering his own question. "It's to teach us a lesson about what HaShem wants from us. He gives us so much and continues to give us everything we will ever need. It's His Divine plan that the rooster can tell the difference between day and night and announce it to the world. He set up His Majesty and Glory in everything we see and do. It is there for us to find and see. The science, chemistry, and biology that He set up in this world are for our benefit. This *beracha* is to teach us that it's our job to look for and try to understand the rules of nature. We have to discern His plan and how things were set up in motion to work." He looked at his family who were paying rapt attention to what he was saying, and in his heart, was thanking HaShem for his wonderful family.

"This is one way we can become closer to HaShem. By the beauty of nature, HaShem is extending His Hand to us, so to speak. By trying to understand how and why nature works, we are clasping that proverbial Hand.

"This is why I think it's great that Yaakov refers to HaShem as the 'Big Boss'. He is the Boss over everything and when Yaakov says that, he is acknowledging this fact. It's beautiful. I am very proud of you son."

Yaakov blushed at the parental compliment as he looked out at the trees. Elana looked at her son with motherly love.

"This is the first *beracha* we say to teach us how important it is for us to look for His ways and try to understand them."

Elana was listening to Yisrael and she smiled at her husband. "That was so profound. Thank you so much for sharing that with us."

During the course of their camping trip, Yisrael showed his children the intricacies and significance of a spider web. They found a rabbit warren. There was a large anthill several feet tall. Yisrael explained how an ant tunnel has numerous branches and could be ten feet deep or more, and just as wide. However, different types of ants form different styles of tunnels. He explained why in the Northern Hemisphere, moss grows mostly on the north side of a tree, in the shade. He was knowledgeable of many things and eager to share what he knew. They learned how to track the sun and how to navigate by its position in the sky and even tell the direction of the compass by the position of the sun and a watch. Everything was discussed and explored with an eye to the perfection that HaShem placed in this world. From their trip, the whole family grew in Torah and *yiras* HaShem. They all had a better appreciation of the world in which they lived.

Yisrael was able to show his family some other wonders of HaShem. "This is an amazing tree called a mountain maple. The sap from this tree is often used to make maple syrup. The bark is used to tan leather. The twigs and roots can be used to treat eye irritation and as a stress reliever," he explained, honored he could use his passion to both entertain and educate his family.

"Here is a really nice experiment. How can we get a can of

soda to be ice cold, out here in the forest with no electricity?”

Receiving only stupefied looks from his family, he continued, “If we soak a sock in the stream, put a can of soda in it and hang it from a branch overnight. The cool air of the night causing the evaporation of the water causes the temperature in the can to drop significantly.”

“That is so ‘cool’,” Tziporah said while making quotation marks with her fingers when saying the word cool.

Everyone laughed at the cute pun.

He continued, “This creeping vine is called cleavers or goosegrass. Notice the hairs that grow out from the stem or even other leaves,” he touched the leaves gently admiring the colors and textures of the leaves. “This helps the plant grow and cover almost anything. All parts of this plant are edible but the hairs can make it less palatable when eaten raw. The plant can be used instead of coffee, although it has less caffeine. Ground up and made into a poultice, it can be used to treat minor cuts, burns, bug bites and stings.”

“Ewww,” the younger children chorused.

Yisrael smiled and continued his pedagogy, “In order to use plants for medicinal or seasoning purposes, most of the time they need to be dried. There are many ways to dry plants, including special devices that are built for that purpose. The easiest method is just to lay it out in the sun. However, this does not offer the consistency that is preferred in the commercial use of these plants. Many herbs and weeds can be ground into a paste or poultice and used for different medicinal purposes.

“This tree is called the American ash. If you ever play baseball, you are probably handling it. It is very common in baseball bats, furniture and flooring.”

Over the next several days, he went on to show them many more trees, edible grasses, and herbs, and explain all of the ways they were given by HaShem to serve humanity. His contribution and the grand tour of the forest was fulfilling to him and his family. Everyone was amazed at the breadth of Yisrael’s knowledge. They never knew that plants had been used for medicinal purposes. The younger children were bored by his elocution and decided to explore their environs instead.

“This is a weed that we have even in Borough Park. It’s called purslane and it is high in vitamins and nutrients. All parts, except the roots, are edible and can be eaten in many forms, including raw.”

“If I make a salad from it,” asked Elana, “then we will be eating ‘weed salad’?”

Yisrael laughed at the insinuated double entendre, while the children were blissfully ignorant.

After breakfast on Tuesday, the family went for another hike. They geared up, headed for the Appalachian Trail and started to ascend the mountain.

Yisrael carefully kept his family on the main path. As they climbed higher up the mountain, they passed several offshoot paths and considered taking a few to explore further. Elana suggested they do so later, on their way down.

They came to a sign indicating a lookout point down a path to the right. Elana thought it would be a good place for them to take a break and have a snack.

Because they were walking in the forest, it took them longer to walk the mile than if they had been in an urban setting. After about a thirty-minute hike they finally arrived at the lookout point. Everyone was tired after the long hike up the mountain and then to the expanse that lay before them.

Their weariness could not deter them from being astounded by the breathtaking vista they saw in the valley below.

When Yaakov saw the scene, his jaw dropped and said, "The Big Boss really knows how to create beautiful scenery." The overlook provided a front-row seat to the most beautiful mountain range, as if hand-painted, it reflected all of the colors of the rainbow, blended to express pure majesty.

"Yes He does," everyone exclaimed in wonderment.

'מה רבו מעשך ה' " How wondrous is Your creations HaShem." Yisrael said in awe.

The entire family observed in amazement the panoramic landscape before them. They were at the top of a cliff protected by a natural wood cross-post fence that almost blended into the scenery.

They estimated they were about three hundred feet up from the valley below where they could clearly see a wide blue stream, with lush green banks, wending its way through the green forest. As far as the eye could see, were green trees of various shapes, sizes, and species. Far below, they could see what could only be a family of brown bears ambling near the stream. There was a flock of birds singing their songs while hovering over one section of trees. The quietness of the moment seemed to stretch forever into the horizon.

Everything in their purview looked as if it had not been touched since the beginning of creation. The only thing slightly marring the view were the dark nimbus clouds at the horizon. It looked as if there may be a storm brewing in the distance. They were not going to let a little rain sully their camping trip.

Not My People

After enjoying the beautiful blue sky, fresh clean air, the waves of the majestic mountains, and the frolicking animals below, they ate some GORP (Good Ol' Raisins and Peanuts), which Elana learned to make back in her youth in the Girl Scouts. Before partaking of the snack, they discussed the different *berachos* for the food. A canteen of water was also passed around. Well-rested, they continued on their hike. When they returned to the main path, they turned to head in the direction of their base camp, ready to relax and reflect on the day. After a while, they came to one of the smaller paths and turned right to explore.

Shortly they came to a massive pile of large boulders. The children were enthralled as they climbed up and around the mountain of megaliths. The pile must have reached up at least fifteen feet high, and about fifty yards wide. It was fun.

Tziporah was the first to reach the pinnacle and saw a shanty in the distance. "I want to explore that shack up ahead," she exclaimed. When Yaakov reached the peak with his sister, he joined in her desire to explore the structure.

Elana and Yisrael were hesitant, but after conferring, they acquiesced. They would go around the pile of rocks, join their children and briefly explore the building in question.

A few minutes later, four excited children were at the broken wood cabin door, with their parents. Elana had a sense of foreboding, but was not sure why: however, due to the exuberance of her children, she resolved to hide her apprehension.

The cabin was a one-room shack in deplorable condition. It stood, if you can say it was standing, about seven feet tall, twenty feet wide and about twenty-five feet long. There were holes for windows but no panes of glass occupied the space. The roof was partially caved in. In front of the closed door was something that was reminiscent of a porch. There was a nearby stream flowing down from a higher elevation. In front of the cabin was a fire ring that looked as if it had been recently used. There were some ropes strung among a few of the trees.

Before either parent could stop them, their children had flung open the door and let themselves in to explore the interior.

Yisrael and Elana quickly joined their children inside the cabin and what they saw shocked them. Their instincts told them to run away as fast as possible but seeing the excitement of their children made them hesitate.

The large dank room held a threadbare cot, burnt out blackened wood stove, a wood table that was barely standing and two rickety chairs. There were items around the room that made it look inhabited. There were pots on the stove, a dirty plate with some cutlery on the table, clothes were strewn about, and animal skins and meat hanging from the ceiling. There were flies buzzing about dirty clothes and dishes.

"Someone's living here," Elana declared almost panicking. "We had better leave at once!" Her voice was shaking in fright as she was instinctively reaching to protect her children.

"Someone **is** living here," a deep and unfamiliar voice declared from the doorway.

The family turned to face a dirty and disheveled man of average build and height with a ruddy complexion. His entire being seemed to match the rundown shack in which they were standing.

ALEX NORTON WAS FROM PITTSBURG, Pennsylvania, and he was on the lam hiding out in the shack, sheltering himself from the weather and the law.

Norton was twenty-one years old and had been living with his parents in Chambersburg, Pennsylvania. They moved from Pittsburg two years prior, for his father's job. His parents liked living in the urban setting of Chambersburg, where everything they needed was nearby. Alex had a decent job working in an orchard but did not like most of his co-workers. The orchard stood on over two-hundred acres of land.

Alex preferred living in the big city and often talked about returning home to Pittsburg. Everyone knew of his penchant to return east. He was very vocal about his dislike for country living and wanting to live back home. He considered his sojourn in Chambersburg as a temporary layover until he could return home.

Alex was a proud American, as were most people who lived in the area, but the several orchards in the vicinity hired mostly illegal immigrants. He did not mind immigrants at all; in fact, though he was born in the United States, he was a second-generation American. He would have preferred to be working adjacent to people who were in the country legally. To him, illegal immigrants were lawbreakers. Most of them worked under-the-table and did not pay any taxes, sending their incomes home. The only thing he had against his coworkers was that they arrived in this country by breaking the law.

Alex often went to a local bar, as alcohol helped to alleviate his tension.

He felt better about the situation when he drank himself into a stupor. He knew that he should not drive home after leaving the bar, but he did not live too far, so he deluded himself thinking he would be Okay. "It's a straight shot east on Lincoln Highway followed by only two turns. I'll be fine," he told himself. "I will just drive slower than usual and I won't get into an accident. It's no big deal, I've done it before." Even after receiving two DWI citations, he still thought himself able to drive home safely.

One fateful night, Alex was returning home from the bar. He was no more inebriated than usual, so he did not anticipate any difficulties. Of course, things did not go as planned. Alex ran a red light at a high rate of speed and swerved into oncoming traffic. He had a head-on collision with a van, doing serious damage to both vehicles. Arriving on the scene, first responders were shocked to find anyone still alive.

The young mother, who was driving the van, and her two children, were rushed to Chambersburg Hospital. Fortunately, the children were in car seats; their injuries were serious but not life-threatening; however, their mother was not so lucky and had head trauma, internal bleeding, multiple broken bones, and numerous severe lacerations. Her injuries were life-threatening and she remained in critical condition.

Several hours after the accident, Alex awoke from his drunken state, to find himself handcuffed to a hospital gurney. He had only a vague recollection of the accident; most of it was a blank. There was a stranger sitting near his bed in the hospital, reading a book.

"Who are you? What's going on?" Alex was barely able to enunciate his words as he tugged on his handcuffed arm. His mouth was dry and his mind clouded. The alcohol was still coursing through his body and he was feeling dizzy and could not think coherently.

The uniformed officer read Alex his rights and informed him of the charges: three counts of vehicular assault, reckless endangerment, and DWI. He also told Alex about his victims and possible additional charges that might be added in the future. Alex remained mute; he was shocked. He started crying and was remorseful for having hurt a family.

After several days in a coma, the young mother succumbed to her injuries, and the charges were amended to include vehicular homicide. The widower and young children were devastated.

Alex was upset and knew he was going to prison. He did not relish the idea of spending time behind bars, although he knew he deserved worse for having killed someone and destroying the lives of the woman's husband and children. The enormity of what he did was beginning to hit him and he realized there was no coming back from this and nothing he could say or do could change the situation.

"I really shouldn't have been driving," Alex thought to himself repeatedly. "Those tickets in the past should have taught me something. I'm just too stupid to learn from my mistakes. Now it's too late and I really blew it." He was scared and not sure what was going to happen to the rest of his life. How would he be able to live with himself now that he had killed someone and ruined a family?

When the widower learned that Norton had several DWI tickets and was still driving, he was shocked and angry. During a victim impact statement, he asked the judge to send Alex to prison for the maximum time allowed. "For all we know, my late wife was suffering in pain after the accident. Now my young children are without a mother and I am without a wife. How do I pick up the pieces from this?" he asked rhetorically as he wiped away the tears falling down his face.

Alex's parents were at the trial to support their son, although they were angry with him for getting behind the wheel when he was drunk. Never the less, he was their son and they loved him, albeit, not his actions.

The widower was depressed and now needed help to raise his children. Life became difficult for him and his children because of a three-time drunk driver. He was angry about it and would rather have meted out revenge himself, but could not do so. He would have to let the justice system mollify that need.

Because there were young people who were also victims of Alex's drunkenness, the judge sentenced him to the maximum of ten years - no time off for good behavior. When Alex heard the sentence, he collapsed into his chair, stunned and shaking with fright, overwhelmed by the truth of his poor decision-making. He knew that he had no one to blame except himself – he had royally messed up. Norton felt that his life was over. Spending the next ten years in prison was a daunting thought. "How will I live through it? How will I survive? What can I do?" he wondered with a frightening thought.

His father was stoic at the verdict, but his mother burst into loud sobs and nearly collapsed to the floor.

Alex was housed in the Franklin County Jail awaiting transfer to a supermax state prison. He was in a gray six-foot by nine-foot concrete cell he shared with another convict. Alex realized he would be spending the next ten years in a similar cell for twenty-three hours a day. He would only be allowed out of his confinement for one hour each day for exercise. Meals would be delivered through a narrow slot in the cell door.

He had a few weeks until he would be moved by the Department of Corrections, so he had to plan quickly. While at the county jail, he heard a train air horn in the distance that planted a seed in his mind, "There must be train tracks nearby." While chatting with one of the correction officers he was able to confirm the presence of train tracks not far from the prison.

While waiting for the transfer, Alex, who was bright and resourceful, carefully watched everyone's routine, looking for breaks in the usual day-to-day activities. He was particularly interested in people who came and went from the county jail. He formulated a detailed plan of escape from the prison, and how he would live off the land. Eventually, he was able to hide by jumping into a large prison laundry basket. He hid there waiting for the prison guards to wheel the basket outside, providing him access to his freedom.

Alex was feeling so nervous that he could barely breathe in the claustrophobic confines of the basket. He knew that if he were caught, five or more years would be added to his sentence; he felt it was worth the risk. While in his concealment, he felt his heart racing and his blood pressure skyrocketing. As the laundry basket was being wheeled across the cement of the loading dock, every inch felt as if it were a mile; he could not get out of the compound fast enough. When the basket bumped over the transition into the back of the laundry truck, his hands flew to his face and he almost called out from the impact of the jolt.

"I gotta get hold o' myself," he thought. "This'll be over soon, I hope, and I'll be out-a-here in a few minutes." He dreamed of living anywhere but in prison. His head was pounding and his mouth was dry. "What I would give for a bottle of water right now," he thought. His mind was racing and he needed to calm down, so he thought about the slop that was served for lunch in the prison. It was so innocuous that he could barely recall eating.

His basket, with many others, was put on a prison laundry truck and he was soon outside of the prison. By the time prison officials did a roll call and realized Alex was not there, he was far from the prison.

Just to the north were railroad tracks and authorities thought he hopped a train trying to return to Pittsburgh. He had told his friends he longed to return to his hometown where he still had many friends, so the authorities started their search in the direction of the Steel City.

Alex assumed the authorities would look for him in Pittsburgh, so he did not make his way there. He went into the vast expanse of Micheaux State Forest. Eventually, he found a cabin well-hidden and had been living there for several months before encountering anyone.

WHEN ALEX ANNOUNCED HIMSELF FROM behind the intruders

who happened into his adopted domain, the Applebaums froze in their tracks. They were not expecting anyone at this shanty since it was so far off the beaten track and behind a huge pile of boulders. Here was a dirty man who appeared out of nowhere who claimed to be living in the dilapidated cabin.

Instinctively, Yisrael stood in front of his wife and children to protect them. The children were scared of the stranger who looked like a bedraggled ruffian.

Elana and the children cowered behind Yisrael, in his protective shadow. The children were never exposed to someone from this type of lifestyle but instinctively knew their father would do everything to protect them. Elana tried to comfort her children by hugging them close to her.

"Who are you?" demanded Alex in a coarse voice. He was not sure who was invading his hideout and he was very concerned. Since there were children present, he was sure they were not law enforcement. He did not want to hurt more people, he just wanted them to leave and forget his existence. He did not want them to turn him in to the authorities and then spend the next fifteen years or more in prison. He liked his freedom, despite his living on the lam in this ramshackle hut in the middle of nowhere.

The two youngest children were quietly whimpering in fear cowering behind their mother. Maintaining his position between the stranger and his family, Yisrael addressed the man, "We were hiking and came across this cabin. We were just exploring. We didn't mean to intrude on your, uh, space." Yisrael was being cautious and did not want to mention that they were camping just a few miles away. Every fiber of his being was on high alert in order to find a safe escape route for his family and protect them from any possible danger. In the back of his mind, he quickly said a short prayer to HaShem for His help.

"How did you find my home?" Alex was thinking that he was probably safe. "Maybe they just think I am a homeless man and not an escaped convict," he thought to himself. "This is just a coincidence that they are here."

"This man is delusional," Yisrael thought. "This is not his home; this is a ramshackle cabin that he is squatting in." Addressing the stranger, Yisrael said, "The children were running around exploring and saw the cabin. They convinced my wife and me to let them explore the cabin. We had just walked in when you arrived. We are sorry for intruding into your home. We did not realize someone lived here.

"We will just be leaving now." He started to hustle his wife and children toward the door while maintaining his position between the interloper and his family. Yisrael was keeping a close watch on the stranger, lest he make any sudden moves.

They were scared and trying to exit the building. The family was uncomfortable and instinctively did not like Alex.

Suddenly Alex noticed the Bowie knife hanging from Yisrael's belt and reached for his own large knife. Alex quickly wielded his knife in his right hand before Yisrael could react. Yisrael raised his arms a bit away from his body to indicate that he was not a threat.

"Please let my family go, and we can talk. We are no threat to you. There's no reason for violence."

Alex was dubious and contemplated his options. Yisrael noticed the hesitation and took advantage of the moment of hesitancy.

IMMEDIATELY AFTER HIGH SCHOOL, YISRAEL served in the military. His own father was a highly decorated Colonel in the Marines and both men excelled in hand-to-hand combat training. He was proud of his service to his country was grateful for the opportunity and the skills he had learned. He had not practiced his fighting techniques for a long time, but now that training would enable him to protect his family.

Yisrael lunged forward and grabbed Alex's right hand with both of his. He moved his right knee forward to check Alex's right knee. Yisrael then twisted Alex's arm out to the left and pulled it down hard and fast to meet his upward-moving left knee. Alex's arm was broken forcing him to drop the knife.

Yisrael called out to his family, "Run! I'll catch up."

"You broke my arm, you buzzard," Alex cried out in pain.

"You threatened my family," he said simply. Without turning his back on Alex, Yisrael kicked Alex's knife out the door and quickly retreated from the cabin and found his family out of breath at the pile of boulders. His left leg was sore from the impact with Alex's arm, so he was limping a bit. Without stopping, he quickly directed his family back to the main trail.

Immediately prior to heading down the trail, Yisrael took a leafy tree branch and did his best to obscure his family's footprints. He did not want the deranged man tracking them.

The concerned parents herded their children down the mountain trail as quickly as possible and returned to their encampment. "Elana," Yisrael said breathlessly, "you take the younger children and the van and go to town and bring the sheriff. I'll wait here with Yaakov and Tziporah to secure our site and gear."

"Good idea," she said and quickly jumped in the van with the two younger children. It would probably take a few hours to make the round-trip.

Yisrael employed the help of Yaakov and Tziporah and proceeded to set up some traps. They wanted to protect themselves in case the man found them – Yisrael did not want to take any chances in protecting his family. If this stranger who was hiding out in the woods was dangerous, he wanted to be prepared.

With some fishing line, they strung up several tripwires between various trees. They dangled fishhooks from the trees to cut any intruder. Yisrael also set a heavy log, high up in a tree that when tripped, would release the log and bowl down whoever did so. He also arranged several weapons, including knives and heavy branches, around the campsite in case they were needed.

There was no time to dig trenches and camouflaged holes, so they made do with what they had. After the physical labor was completed, the adrenaline wore off and the reality of the situation started to set in.

Yisrael sat with his children and said Tehillim until Elana returned with the Rangers. The family gave their testimony and divulged Alex's last known location.

WITH A BROKEN ARM, THERE was not much Alex could do for himself. With great difficulty, he made a splint for his arm and packed up the best he could, then headed in the opposite direction from the family. He did not want anything more to do with those people, and he was sure they would tell the authorities. He was in tremendous pain and needed medical attention, but could not go to the hospital. He was not sure where to go or to whom he could turn.

In short order, the Rangers caught up with Alex and arrested him without further incident. A small reward was forwarded to the Applebaums for the arrest of Alex Norton. Alex would be spending the next fifteen years in a super-max prison. He was not going anywhere for the foreseeable future.

All that night, everyone recounted the events about the perturbation during their exciting day. They agreed it would have been better to have not encountered the vagabond, as they thought of him, but it did lend some adventure and excitement to their camping trip. It was not until late that night that everyone was able to fall asleep. Yaakov decided he wanted to learn martial arts when they returned home, to be able to protect his future family.

For dinner Wednesday evening, they ate freshly caught fish from the nearby stream. It was the first time they ate fish they had actually caught. Yisrael showed his children how to check for fins and scales. He also explained that if you see fins, there are scales.

"Freshly caught fish does not smell. It's only when fish sits that it develops that common fishy odor. You can also tell the freshness of a fish by the eyes. Fresh fish, the eyes are clear; fish that is not fresh, the eyes are foggy."

Afterward, Elana showed them how to kill and prepare the fish. This trip was destined to be a series of first experiences; a priceless opportunity to connect, share and create wonderful memories.

On Thursday afternoon, the Applebaums sadly packed up their campsite, making sure to leave nothing behind except for their footprints. They took several rolls of film to remember the wonderful experience. Maybe next year and every year thereafter they would go camping. However, they all agreed to be more careful about exploring decrepit cabins.

They returned home with plenty of time for *Shabbos* preparations.

# July 13-14, 1977
# New York City, New York

## New York City Blackout

Various News Sources:

Wednesday, July 13, 1977, 8:37 p.m. EDT. There was a lightning strike at Buchanan South, an electrical substation on the Hudson River, tripping two circuit breakers in Buchanan, New York. Buchanan is about forty miles north of Manhattan on the Hudson River. It is fed by the Indian Head nuclear power plant half a mile to the west.

A second lightning strike caused the loss of two transmission lines and the loss of power from the nuclear plant at Indian Point. Because of the strikes, two other major transmission lines became overloaded. Per procedure, Con Edison tried to start fast-start generation at 8:45 p.m.; however, no one was staffing the station, and the remote start failed.

At 8:55 p.m., there was another lightning strike, which took out two additional critical transmission lines. As before, only one of the lines was automatically returned to service. This outage of lines from the Sprain Brook substation (in Yonkers, Westchester County, N.Y.) caused the remaining lines to exceed their capacity. After this last failure, due to problems at the plant, Con Edison manually had to reduce the loading on another local generator at their East River facility. This exacerbated an already dire situation.

At 9:14 p.m., more than thirty minutes after the initial event, New York Power Pool Operators in Guilderland, called for Con Edison operators to "shed load." In response, Con Ed operators initiated a five-percent system-wide voltage reduction and then an eight-percent reduction. These steps had to be initiated sequentially and took several minutes to complete.

At 9:19 p.m., the final major interconnection to Upstate New York at Leeds Substation tripped due to thermal overload, which caused the 345kV conductors to sag excessively into an unidentified object.

At 9:22 p.m., Long Island Lighting Company opened its interconnection to Con Edison to reduce the power that was flowing through its system and overloading submarine cables between Long Island and Connecticut.

At 9:24 p.m., the Con Edison operator tried and failed to manually shed load by dropping customers. Five minutes later, at 9:29 p.m., the Goethals-Linden interconnection with New Jersey tripped, and the Con Edison system automatically began to isolate itself from the outside world through the action of protective devices that removed overloaded lines, transformers, and cables from service.

Con Ed could not generate enough power within the city, and the three power lines that supplemented the city's power were overtaxed. Just after 9:27 p.m., the biggest generator in New York City, Ravenswood 3, shut down. With it went all of New York City.

By 9:36 p.m., the entire Con Edison power system shut down, almost exactly an hour after the first lightning strike. By 10:26 p.m., operators started a restoration procedure. Power was not restored until late the following day.

Rioting and looting ensued and more than 3,800 arrests were made and there was more than a billion dollars in damage.

Because of the power failure, both LaGuardia and Kennedy airports were closed down for about eight hours, tunnels were closed due to lack of ventilation, and 4,000 people had to be evacuated from the subway system.

FOR SOME PEOPLE, THE BLACKOUT of '77 was fun, for others not so much. Esther Weiss was a teenager of fourteen living in Queens when the lights went out. Esther was a creative and inventive young woman, with blond hair and whose hazel eyes exuded warmth and wisdom, with a bit of mischief. She was excited, never having experienced anything such as this. It was spooky and she took advantage of that feeling and told scary stories to her younger siblings. Her parents laughed at her ability to find the good and fun in any situation. This ability would serve her well in the future.

For others, the blackout was a wake-up call. Nineteen-year-old Tuvya Justin lived with his widowed mother Atarah Justin in Queens and this catastrophe had a major impact on them. Tuvya was a handyman who did odd jobs for people, and his mother was a piano teacher. They came to the realization they did not want to be caught unprepared so they decided to stock up on food, water, and medical supplies.

Many Jews thought it humorous to give their Italian neighbors *Yahrzheit* and *Shabbos* candles for light.

Two close friends spent a couple of days in excited camaraderie. Rivkah Somers and Emily Archer were twelve and thirteen years old respectively. They were brilliant and highly creative young women who were also excited by the blackout. They spent the time studying and entertaining their siblings.

Most people were not affected by the blackout beyond being discomfited by the lack of electricity for two days. Fourteen-year-old Yaakov Applebaum was not bothered at all; he just went to his *Rebbi*'s house and spent the time learning Gemara. The budding *talmid chacham* did not need electricity to grow in Torah.

On the other hand, two young men in Brooklyn thought they would have some fun with the blackout. Mordechai Samuel was a redhead who loved to clown around; his friend, Henry Davis was his collaborator and confidant. They were both eighteen-years-old and had just graduated high school.

The pair got their hands on a megaphone and headed to the tallest building in the area: the northeast corner of Fifty-Seventh Street and Fourteenth Avenue where there was a seven-story apartment building. They went up to the roof of the building and stood at the edge where they looked down and saw some people walking on the street and others milling about: it was perfect.

They held up the large megaphone and Mordechai said in a deep booming voice, "Attention Earth!"

They laughed so hard, they could barely catch their breath as they ran away from the site of their mischief.


# July 13, 1977
## LaGuardia Airport

Mr. and Mrs. Weinblatt, a newly married young couple, were in LaGuardia Airport waiting for their connecting flight, they planned to live in the Holy Land. They were returning from a pilot trip to find a good *Yeshiva* and an apartment.

Their trip went well and they were excited about their upcoming *aliyah*. Zev Weinblatt was planning to join Rabbi Horowitz in his Jerusalem *Yeshiva* and continue working as a *sofer*.

Rabbi Shimshon Horowitz's *Yeshiva* was prestigious and not the easiest into which to be accepted. The Rosh HaYeshiva was a world-renowned *posek* and *talmid chacham*. He was erudite with all of *shas* and *poskim* at his fingertips. No matter what subject one discussed with him, everything seemed fresh in his mind as if he had just reviewed the material. Despite his renown, he was a very humble man who lived a very simple life.

Zev was accepted into the *kollel* and had shown the Rosh HaYeshiva a sample of his writing; the Rosh HaYeshiva was pleased with Zev's work. They found a small apartment close to the *Yeshivah* and everything was looking up for them.

It takes a special person to become a *sofer*. One does not become wealthy from being a scribe, but something a person does in order to have a business that involves working with the Torah. To become a *sofer*, a person must study not only how to write but also be fluent in the relevant Jewish laws. It usually takes one to two years of studying and apprenticing before one is ready to start writing. Most often, budding scribes will start their writing with a Megilah since one is allowed to go back and make corrections, unlike other holy works.

The main reason Zev liked being a *sofer* was that the writing of the holy letters is infused with holiness and he felt surrounded by the purity and the divine in his work. He took this work seriously and wrote in diligent concentration while writing each letter pristinely and carefully. In order to infuse the process with extra holiness, prior to writing the Divine names of HaShem, he went to the *mikvah*.

Zev was always reviewing the applicable laws and practicing his skills, to improve himself and the quality of his holy work. He understood that his job held the key to the recipient's health and blessings from Above. One mistake on his part could mean a disastrous outcome for one who received and used his productions.

Miriam Weinblatt was knowledgeable in Torah and was an excellent teacher who was going to teach at Shlomit Women's Seminary in Jerusalem. Miriam loved to teach and share what she knew. She was humble enough to know that she had much more to learn and she continued to do so alongside her husband.

Before they were even able to board their connecting flight home to Chicago, the entire airport was suddenly plunged into darkness.

While looking around and seeing light only from the moon and stars, plus a few lights from aircraft and motorized vehicles on the tarmac, they had an eerie feeling. They both had experienced blackouts, but nothing to this magnitude. It was both exciting and scary at the same time. When the lights extinguished, some people screamed and went into a panic. Within a few moments, the airport's backup generators came on and with it the emergency lights, with a shimmering amber hue.

The couple, perplexed and confused, later found out the entire region was blacked out. All of the flights were delayed, including their flight to Chicago; numerous flights were canceled. It did not matter to the young couple, they had so much about which they wanted to talk. They found a quiet corner and said Tehillim together. It was too dark for him to learn from his ever-present Gemara, so they also talked about their future and their upcoming move to Israel. They discussed their goals, their new neighborhood, and the *Yeshiva*. They were so excited and inspired that the inconvenience of being delayed in the airport during a blackout for over eight hours did not matter to them.

They returned to Chicago and resumed their planning and packing. Zev and Miriam decided what they were going to bring in their lift to help them settle in Israel. The quality of products in Israel was not what they were used to and importing new items could be costly. They were intent on bringing as much as they could in their container. They dreamed as they talked, of the day they would be permanent residents of the Holy Land. They could already feel the holiness of the soil beneath their feet.

# August 1977
## Al-Awja, Iraq

It was a hot and dry day: this was typical weather in Al-Awja, Iraq for this time of year. People would sit around waiting and pining for even a slight breeze; a rare occurrence. Paper fans were standard issue for almost everyone who wanted to feel some minor comfort and relief.

Fifteen-year-old Ahmed Yousef al Rashim and fourteen-year-old Mohamed abu Sharif were the best of friends and inseparable. They were also dirt poor and envious of their well-off neighbors, which made them angry about their situation. The teens were troublemakers and rabble-rousers. They enjoyed causing mischief in the frowzy neighborhood.

The teens got a thrill from throwing stones at people and animals as they passed. Immediately after releasing their projectiles, they fled with shouts of jubilation. They threw dirt and mud onto people's clothes hanging out to dry and stole food from street vendor's carts and grocery stands. When they were caught, they were often severely beaten for their reprobate behavior but did not care. They loved the thrill and excitement of their adventures; besides, they had nothing else to do.

To wile away the time, they often played backgammon on a communal board; they could not afford their own game board. Most of the time, they just wasted the day and did absolutely nothing. They were both from destitute families and had nothing of any real value. Most of the stores in the poor section of town were just holes-in-the-wall and there was no real business done as no one could afford to purchase anything beyond their daily bread. Even that was often beyond the financial means of most people in the neighborhood.

Having heard rumors of how the rich lived, but never seeing it for themselves, the pair ventured to the east where the wealthy lived. It was the first time they ever saw an automobile and were amazed to see a mode of transportation that did not require an animal. The roads were paved, unlike the dirt roads where they lived and they had never experienced electricity or indoor plumbing before. They watched with incredulity the scene before them with mouths agape and disbelieving eyes.

They were amazed to see such a plethora of stores and eateries. In their limited experience in the world outside of their small enclave, they were completely overwhelmed. As they walked past a bakery, their olfactory senses were enthralled and their mouths watered at the sight and scent of the different confections. They had no idea there was such an amazing divergence of foods that could be had, compared to the sabulous foods they were used to.

"Let's go around back and see if we can find some discarded cakes," Mohamed said to his friend. Mohamed was fair-skinned, lighter than most of the people he knew. His father would often deride him for looking so much like his mother, Sarah. His father clearly disliked her, and one time in anger mentioned that she was not a 'pure Muslim'. Mohamed asked his father what that meant, but no answer was forthcoming. This gave Mohamed a complex and he became self-conscious about his appearance. All of his friends had dark eyes and black hair while he had light-brown eyes and brown hair, as did his mother. He inquired about their differences but his mother chided, "We mustn't speak of these things." He could not help but wonder.

They found some discarded moist cake with a soft white, buttery frosting; they had never tasted anything so delectable. They thought they were eating a bit of heaven. They headed back home, but wanted to return as often as possible to eat some 'real food'. The trash of the wealthy could feed them well, so they pledged to each other to bring some food back for their friends.

"When is your father martyring himself? Do you know what his plan is?" Mohamed asked his friend. They both knew that this was the ultimate sacrifice and any martyr was considered holy.

"He's already in Palestine. It should be any day now," he said excitedly. Ahmed was proud of his father; however, he did have his reservations. When his father became a suicide bomber, Ahmed knew he would be without parents and this concerned him. Ahmed was an independent, dark-complexioned young man, with black hair and dark eyes, as were both of his parents. Even though Ahmed considered himself an individual and self-reliant, he still needed his father.

Jafar Yousef Al Rashim had been recruited by Saddam Hussein's* minions to be a martyr for the cause. For some Muslims, this is the ultimate and greatest achievement one could attain.

Jafar, Ahmed's father, was sick of his life and had been angry for years. His wife died in childbirth and left him alone, when his good-for-nothing son, Ahmed, was born. Jafar hated Ahmed for killing his wife and for the longest time took his anger out on Ahmed. Now, fifteen years later, he was honored to be a suicide bomber, to end it all, and get the seventy-two virgins he was promised and felt he deserved.

Jafar took a plane to Egypt where he spent a few days touring and praying in a Mosque. It was the first time he had been on a plane and was not prepared for the change in air pressure upon takeoff and landing; nevertheless, he was excited and a bit apprehensive. To enter Israel, he used one of the many tunnels other terrorists used to sneak weapons into Israel. He made his way to East Jerusalem and quickly found the local cell and enthusiastically presented himself to the Imam.

"*Alssalam ealaykum w rrahmatih w barakatih* (Peace be upon you and his mercy and blessings be upon you)," Ahmed said to the Imam.

"*Wa-Alaikum-Salaam.*"

"I'm here to provide my service as a martyr for our cause," he said, bowing toward the Imam."

"Welcome honored guest," the Imam smiled.

Jafar spent the next several days in prayer, fasting and preparing for his ultimate task. The night before his mission, he gorged himself on a large and scrumptious meal. He knew this would be his final meal before his killing himself and many Jews. He was both scared and excited for what he considered a sacred mission. He was also happy that he would finally be rid of his miserable life and go to his just rewards. Ahmed was aware that his son was not happy about his mission, but he did not care enough to write him a letter. Jafar wanted out of this life and this was the best way of accomplishing this goal.

# Friday, August 12, 1977
## Jerusalem, Israel

On late Friday morning, when Jews were rushing around and preparing for *Shabbos*, Jafar set out on his mission of destruction, mayhem, and murder. His plan was simple, while on a bus, detonate a bomb strapped to his chest, and kill as many dirty and despicable Jews as possible. He had a demonic smiled on his face while he relished the thought.

Despite the August heat of the Middle East, he wore a light, bulky, mud-colored jacket to conceal the explosive vest he was wearing. He took the nineteen bus bound for Center City, Jerusalem. He planned to wait until the bus reached Mercaz Ha'ir, Center City, before initiating the explosive vest, in order to cause as much carnage and murder as possible.

Jafar looked out of place wearing a bulky jacket in August, and he immediately aroused suspicion. A few of the passengers were concerned and approached the bus driver, Eldad. "We are concerned. There's an Arab wearing a bulky jacket in this heat, sitting near the rear door. Something doesn't seem right."

"I'll call the police and check it out," Eldad said, with a concerned look on his face. He was not given to rash actions but was very deliberate in everything he did, especially when it came to possibly saving people's lives. He had never encountered a terrorist threat, but he knew what he had to do.

Eldad immediately radioed for help, pulled the bus over to the side of the street, and preemptively tried to get passengers off the bus to safety. Nervously, Eldad walked down the bus aisle toward Jafar. When he saw the would-be terrorist and the maniacal look in his eyes, he realized the man was probably a terrorist with the common mission to kill as many as possible. Jafar was not a hardened terrorist and was unable to control his raging emotions. He was sweating and clearly nervous; his eyes twitched and his hands shook, like a frightened and cornered rabbit.

Eldad was now convinced that the stranger was up to no good and had to be stopped. He had to act quickly and decisively or many would be hurt or killed. Eldad did not consider himself a hero, but he was also not a coward.

As Jafar saw Eldad coming toward him he knew he had been discovered and he panicked. The bus was already half empty when Jafar blew himself up murdering twelve Jews and injuring more than twenty others. The bus was destroyed. Eldad was hailed as a hero as he saved many lives while giving up his own in the service of his country and people. Multitudes attended his funeral and mourned the loss of a hero. Separately, both the Prime Minister and President of Israel called the family with condolences and gave them a "Certificate of Thanks" as an appreciation for their sacrifice and the courage and bravery of Eldad.

# 1978

## February 5-7, 1978
## East Coast United States

Various news sources:

The Northeastern United States was hit by a massive blizzard from Sunday, February fifth, through Tuesday, February seventh, 1978.

A catastrophic and historic nor'easter brought blizzard conditions to the New York metropolitan area. It was the worst blizzard in recent history. According to some reports, the New York metropolitan area received up to three feet of snow. It paralyzed the entire state of New York and the surrounding areas for a week.

The storm had hurricane-force winds of approximately eighty-six miles per hour. A strong Canadian high-pressure system kept the storm in place over the New England area.

The storm killed approximately one-hundred people and injured about 4,500. The damages were estimated at over 520 million dollars and countless homes were destroyed.

**Initial** predictions of snowfall were calling for just a few inches. Never trust a weather forecaster; prognostication is not an exact science.

Some people love snow. It is beautiful and there are those who find it romantic, exhilarating and rejuvenating. Children love snow - no school, building snow forts and snowmen, having snowball fights and much more.

Other's hate the frigid white powder. It is backbreaking work to shovel snow. After finishing shoveling, a bit of wind comes by and blows the snow right back onto the area just cleaned. So a person grudgingly clears the snow again, but then the city plow comes by and packs the snow tightly against parked cars. Of course, that only happens minutes after extricating one's vehicle from behind a pile of the stuff. Parents of small children often do not like snow because it is more difficult to entertain young minds locked indoors.

Due to the massive snow piled up around the entire region, children of all ages enjoyed the forced vacation from school, and work.

The more industrious children had fun digging igloos and snow tunnels; the younger children made snow angels. Some parents pulled their children in makeshift sleds: garbage can lids were great for this. One could find a myriad of snowmen of different shapes, sizes, and styles all throughout the neighborhood. One family even made a snowman upside-down: it was funny to see a snowman on its head. Some people had snowball fights.

Many families ran out of food and other supplies, while others were concerned for their safety and survival. Everyone shared their provisions to help their neighbors in any way they could. Unfortunately, there was looting in some areas by unsavory people. It was almost funny seeing thieves struggling to wheel a brand new refrigerator down the street. The police did not think it amusing and arrested the hapless perpetrator.

# February 21, 1978
## Borough Park, New York

Walking down the busy Avenue in Borough Park, Brooklyn, one would see disparate people. One would see everything from Chasidic, Modern Orthodox to the non-observant, black hats to no hats. One would also see all nationalities including American, Mexican, Israeli, Russian and many more.

It was impossible not to notice a plethora of shops doing an assortment of business on the Avenue. The various signs, lights, sights, and smells coming from every direction assaulted the senses. There were bakeries, bookstores, candy stores, clothing stores and much more. There were also banks, photography studios, hat shops, and small businesses. A large choice of restaurants of every description and type; some larger, some smaller, available to tempt everyone's pallet. Many of the stores were owned and operated by Orthodox Jews. Most of the shop owners lived within walking distance of their stores while some even lived above their own establishments.

Despite the snow still piled around, some shops were open and doing a brisk business; particularly those stores dealing with food and basic supplies. No matter how one tried, snow shovels or salt could not be found for sale. People did not want to be caught in another storm without these and other necessities. Many people were even considering purchasing snowplows and attaching them to the front of their cars. It was impractical, especially in the city, but many flirted with the idea.

Jake Benjamin was one of those small business owners who had an office on Thirteenth Avenue in Borough Park, Brooklyn. Drafting and design are an art form. Everything that is constructed or manufactured, at one point, has to have blueprints. Making blueprints is often called "detailing" due to the detail required to draw them. Blueprints tell a manufacturer the size and shape of each part or element of the product. For example, mortgage bankers use house location drawings to know the exact shape and size of a piece of property they are financing for a purchaser.

Originally, Jake started his drafting business in the basement of his Borough Park home. He was very successful as a one-man operation and loved the commute. Due to the quality of his work, his clientele increased and he had to expand both in space and employees.

Jake employed a few drafters in his busy office. He was a fair employer and always made sure to pay his employees well and treat everyone with respect. His wife, Tikva, was his secretary and bookkeeper as she had excellent eutaxy skills and was as dedicated to the business as was her husband. They were a loving couple with four young children. The couple was busy doing mechanical, electrical, and architectural drafting. Jake also engaged an apprentice engineer.

One day, a client with an unusual request entered the busy office. "My name is Phillip Rush. I have a few real estate holdings: I buy and sell houses. I'm also a doomsday prepper." Phillip was urbane and sophisticated; he was dressed in a nice three-piece suit with a conservative tie.

"What's that? I've never heard of a doomsday prepper," Jake asked, his curiosity piqued.

"Basically, this means that I'm concerned that a major

catastrophe may strike sometime in the future and I want to be protected and prepared. Remember the snowstorm of two weeks ago?"

"I sure do," Jake responded with a shudder, it was something he would rather not have lived through. "I was concerned that if we couldn't get out to the store soon, we might run out of food. There is still snow piled high from it. I also remember the blackout a year ago." Jake could not decide which one was the worse experience, but the cold of the snowstorm seemed to make the decision easy.

"That's exactly what this is about," the client responded. "I want to hire you to design an underground concrete bunker for me. This is an unusual project." In the back of his mind, Phillip was concerned that Jake would consider him a fool or psychotic. However, this was something that was important to him and his family.

Jake studied his new client for a moment. He had intelligent eyes, a high forehead and did not appear to be the type given to panic or craziness. He seemed calm and collected. Jake replied, "I'm completely unfamiliar with this concept. I'll have to research it." Jake was scrupulously honest. He was intrigued by this idea.

Rush looked around the busy office. There were a few draftsmen busy working at elevated desks that tilted to about forty degrees: the tables were two-feet deep and three-feet wide. The drafters were working on some architectural and mechanical drawings. It was amazing what a talented person could do with some pencils, rulers, and triangles. There were numerous books around the office depicting the rules and regulations for construction and building anything in the Tri-State area. There were also some *sefarim* in the office.

"That's exactly why I want to hire you," he responded. "You are deliberate and don't rush into anything. Your reputation precedes you."

Humbly ignoring the compliment he said, "Please tell me more about your needs." Jake was no stranger to atypical jobs.

ONE TIME JAKE WAS HIRED to recreate, on paper, a crime scene for the FBI. A special agent came to Jake's office with some hand-drawn sketches of a crime scene. The sketches were rough; however, with skill, he was able to turn those rough sketches into an exact layout of a crime scene. Jake created isometric drawings, along with plan and elevation views of the scene. The drawings were helpful in the court case as they showed the jury exactly what had transpired at the crime scene.

"MANY PEOPLE AROUND THE WORLD are concerned about a possible doomsday or similar situation." Philip Rush continued, hoping he was not coming across as a complete lunatic. "They're not talking about the possibility of the world coming to an end; they are more concerned about a major war, financial collapse, horrific weather, public services being cut off or some other significant event. More people are just concerned that their utilities (gas, electric and water) may be cut off for a while. We have all experienced this to one extent or another.

"Even the United States government has concrete bunkers around the country. The most well known is the top-secret bunker under the White House in Washington D.C. It's actually located beneath the East Wing. There are several ways to get to the underground emergency command center. There is even a trap door under the Resolute Desk in the Oval Office that leads to the Presidential Emergency Operations Center (PEOC).

"The PEOC was built six stories below ground under the East Wing to provide the President with a secure hiding place in the event of an emergency. Access to the PEOC is by an elevator located behind multiple vault-type doors with state-of-the-art biometric access control systems. While the exact specification of this emergency Presidential bunker is classified, it is built to withstand a direct nuclear hit.

"This part is what we know about the PEOC, however, the exact specifications are not known.

"The largest underground bunker in the world is under the Greenbrier Luxury Hotel in White Sulphur Springs, West Virginia. Construction began in 1958 on the 112,544 square-foot bunker, which was built 720 feet into the hillside. It was completed in 1961." Phillip was knowledgeable about prepping and relevant trivia. He could converse in-depth about prepping and wilderness survival.

"Very interesting. I never knew any of this," Jake interjected. He was fascinated with the information. It sounded wise to him and made good sense to be cautious to make sure to be completely prepared for any eventuality.

"The most infamous underground bunker was Hitler's bunker. Most people don't realize it, but it was actually two bunkers built in two stages. The first stage, the *Vorbunker*, was constructed in 1936 was about five feet beneath the cellar of a large reception hall behind the old Reich Chancellery at Wilhelmstrasse 77. The *Führerbunker* was located about twenty-eight feet beneath the garden of the old Reich Chancellery, 390 feet to the north of the new Reich

Chancellery building. Besides being deeper underground, the *Führerbunker* had significantly more reinforcements. Its roof was made of concrete almost ten feet thick. About thirty small rooms were protected by approximately thirteen feet of concrete; exits led into the main buildings, as well as an emergency exit up to the garden. The *Führerbunker* was built in 1944.

"Most people don't know about much of this," he said. "Getting back to our main topic, many people prepare for emergencies by stocking up on food, water, medicine and more. These people are preppers.

"The basic prepper will stock enough food, water, and medicine to last their family or clique for a month.

"Some people go as far as sectioning off part of their house as a bunker. Some will go to a further extent and build an aboveground or even an underground bunker. The latter is what I want. I want you to design an underground concrete bunker for me. I'll be purchasing a piece of property about ten acres in size for my bunker."

Jake and the client had a long and detailed conversation about what he wanted: Jake took copious notes. As he was listening to the description of what Phillip wanted in his underground bunker, he came to realize that is was going to be a fortress. This project was going to take significant effort and planning to bring to fruition.

"We have all experienced a loss of public utilities or have been snowbound for a few days," explained Phillip again. "At the very least, everyone should have a month's supply of food, water and medicine stocked up for emergencies."

"Yeah, that makes perfect sense to me. I'll have to start doing that myself. I'm sure my wife will agree." Jake was impressed with his client and his meticulous planning. Jake recalled the Mishnah that states, "Who is the wise one? The one who sees the future." No one can see the future, but we can anticipate it and plan accordingly.

The client added, "Part of what I want you to do for me is the research I will need for electricity, water reclamation and storage, food, and air supply and filtration. I know this will cost extra, but that's okay. I'll pay."

"You do realize this will take a while for me to research and design your bunker properly?"

"Yeah, that's fine. There isn't any rush. I just want a complete report. I'm not someone who believes the world is coming to an end tomorrow or that some catastrophic event is imminent. I just want myself and my family to be prepared because I'm concerned something may happen in the future. And even if it's not in my lifetime, my children will have a safe place to go in case of an emergency."

They sat down and worked out the details for the bunker. It was going to be a major project and take considerable resources to plan and then implement. Jake was excited about this project and looked forward to the challenge it represented. He knew his staff was up to doing what was needed for this unusual client.

After leaving a deposit, the client left confident his project was in good hands. Jake and his wife sat down to discuss this bunker and its ramifications for the business and their personal lives. This new client was going to require a significant investment of time, probably six months or more, much of it in the library doing research. This would require innovative technology with the ability to adapt as mechanization and electronics changed over time.

"I would also like to start stocking up a month's worth of supplies for our family. What do you think?"

Jake's wife was practical and this was one of the many reasons he loved her. She was able to keep everything and everyone in the office on track. The children, well, they were a different story.

"I completely agree," his wife said. "Especially after that nor'easter, it's very important. I was really concerned about having enough food, water, and any needed medical supplies, especially for our family. Any idea how we should get started prepping?" She was already considering practical ideas for supplying her family for any eventuality.

"Philip suggested that every time we go to the store to buy groceries, we buy one or two extra cans of something. When we finish a gallon container of a drink, we wash out the bottle, fill it with water, and store it. When we buy things like bandages and toilet paper, we buy a few extra for an emergency supply. Over the course of time, we'll have a good stock which we rotate so nothing gets stale." Jake smiled at his wife; they were always of the same mind. They would be prepared for the next major weather event and not have to worry about running out of supplies for their family.

"I will start with the next shopping list. Do you know how much water we should store?"

"He told me, one gallon per person per day is a good start. If we plan for a month, it would mean one-hundred and eighty gallons of water."

"We can do that. We can get four water drums and store them in the backyard. Maybe we can even collect some rainwater."

Jake decided to call Tuvya Justin and bring him in on Philip's project.

Justin had done some construction, remodeling, and repairs for several of Jake's clients. Tuvya knew how to read blueprints and would be a valuable asset to this project. That is if he was not high - thankfully, he did not get high often. Tuvya had done work on Jake's home and helped partition his office. He would need to consult with Tuvya on a few ideas for this project. Jake would also have to hire someone to help with the research and cover the extra time Jake would be busy.

"I also want to bring in Yona Glick. He's an engineer and will be able to help with the design and construction of the bunker. Being underground, I am concerned with how thick the concrete would have to be in order to withstand the pressure of the dirt.

"I'm also curious to know how far below ground the bunker would have to be in order to protect its inhabitants from any contamination."

# October 1978
## Borough Park, New York

"How does one store so much water without it taking over the bunker and making sure the containers don't leak?" Tikva asked her husband. The question was insightful and typical of her ability to analyze situations. Jake derided himself for not having considered this question much sooner but now was ready with an answer.

"The water barrels that we are using at home are great, but he will need more water storage than that. I've found something called an IBC, (Intermediary Bulk Containers). This is a food-grade plastic container and can hold about 330 gallons of water in less space than the equivalent in barrels. A few of those in the bunker would hold enough water for an indefinite amount of time; add to that a rainwater reclamation system and the water can last indefinitely. In fact, we could probably convert our water barrels to IBC's and store more water in less space," he explained.

"Electricity could be a bit of a challenge. Solar panels are not strong enough to collect enough electricity for any significant length of time. However, with a large battery bank, this could be overcome to an extent. My research tells me that technology is improving and over the course of time, he can make upgrades to different components of the system I'm designing for him."

It took eight months to complete the project and write the reports for the design of the bunker. Jake Benjamin was proud of the finished product.

After speaking with his engineer Yona, they were able to come up with a unique design for the bunker. At first, they considered making the underground bunker rectangular and about three feet below the surface. After doing research into nuclear weapons and fallout, they determined that the roof of the bunker would have to be ten-feet below ground. That depth would prevent radiation from penetrating into the bunker but would translate into several hundred tons of dirt above the bunker. How could they design a bunker to withstand that weight? How thick would the concrete have to be? What about reinforced concrete? How many support-beams would be required? Would the support beams take up too much space inside the bunker?

Yona had an unprecedented idea for the shape and construction of the bunker. The concept was a round bunker with a monolithic dome for the roof. After doing a significant amount of research into building design, Yona concluded that using this configuration, he would only need four inches of concrete for the walls, roof, and floor of the bunker. The curve of the dome would have to be 0.33 the diameter of the bunker, or greater. The shape of the monolithic roof would distribute the weight and pressure of the tonnage of dirt over the round walls. He made the diameter of the bunker thirty feet. The dome would have to be ten feet high at its apex with no need for support beams. Jake was amazed by the new design that was completely singular, unlike anything else he had ever seen.

In order to better allocate the space, he divided the bunker into three levels. The top level would be the main floor followed by the bedroom level. The basement would house the storage, emergency equipment, and basic supplies.

On the surface would be a small shed that would camouflage the entrance of the bunker.

The shed would have gutters that fed downspouts that would be routed to bring rainwater in through a filtration system and then into the bunker.

There would be pipes running from the surface down to the bunker for air, where it would run through several, multiple stage biological filtration systems.

Solar panels would be attached to the roof of the shed and wired to a DC converter inside the bunker. There would be a large battery bank to store electricity. The whole system was planned as modular in design to accommodate technological advances in the future. In this way, components could be swapped out as needed to update or upgrade the system.

There would be plenty of storage space in the basement for food and other supplies.

| Main Level | Bedroom Level | Basement Level |
| --- | --- | --- |
| 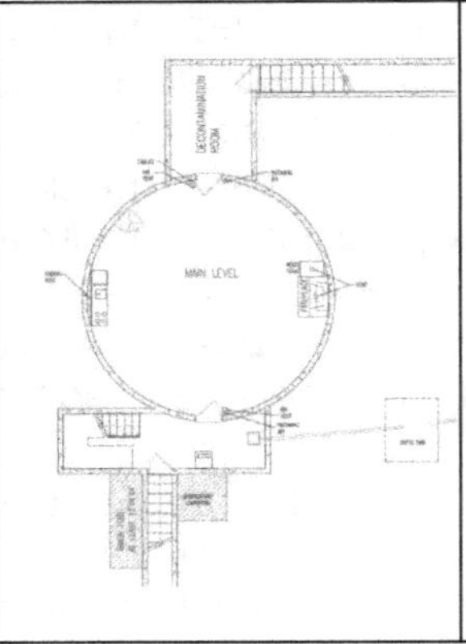 MAIN LEVEL (DECONTAMINATION ROOM) | 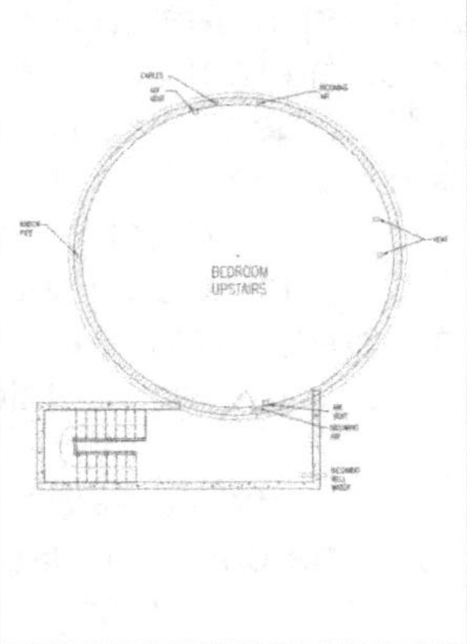 BEDROOM UPSTAIRS | 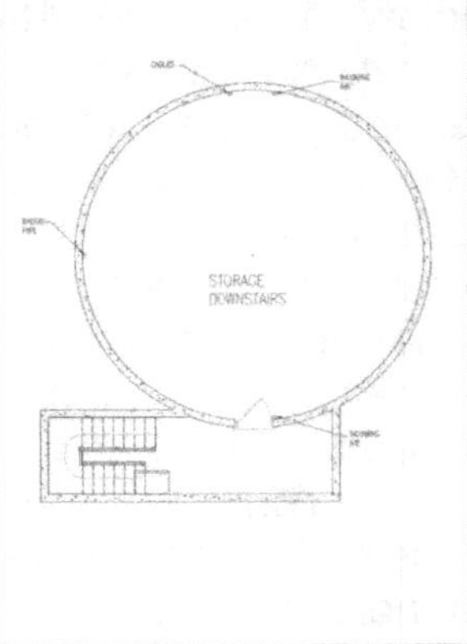 STORAGE DOWNSTAIRS |

Jake delivered seven "E" size blueprints to the client with isometric, plan, and elevation drawings. There were also sixty pages of notes on his research, which included a complete list of suggested foodstuffs. Everything was well documented and referenced. The client was happy with the finished product: it was exactly what he wanted.

"I still don't have a property for the bunker, but that will come in time. At least this step is completed. Thanks so much," Phillip said happily. He was very impressed with the results as he flipped through the booklet that Jake gave him. He was excited that this project was progressing in a positive vein. Phillip smiled to himself as he considered the ramifications that soon he would have a place to escape to in case there was an emergency.

"You're quite welcome. By the way, my wife and I already started prepping."

"That's great! Welcome to the 'prepper' club." They smiled.

"Let me know if I can be of service to you in the future." Jake walked his client to the door.

After delivering the finished product of the bunker designs, with all the attendant research, to his client, Jake wrote a book. After a few more months redesigning the blueprints to make a more generic bunker and expanding on his findings, he called the book, Doomsday Bunker Book.

Jake designed two bunkers - one aboveground and another underground. He included several blueprints of his new designs of both bunkers in the book along with information on air and water filtration, solar power, food storage and much more.

He hired Alexander Bently to design the book and the cover. Alexander was a talented graphic artist who did great work. Alexander used his talents to design a high-quality book that sold well.


# November 1978
# Borough Park, New York

Fifteen-year-old Yaakov Applebaum was normally a happy, even-tempered young man with a penchant for telling puns. There were not many things that bothered or agitated him; however, as with everyone, he had his good and bad days. This was one of those bad days; he was bemoaning his troubles and wondering why things sometimes seemed so difficult. He applied himself to his studies which were getting progressively more difficult, causing him angst. He did not like these feelings; however, they were part of his life.

Whenever young Applebaum was feeling down, he would check his stock portfolio and excogitate what his money was doing. He knew not to rely on just a couple of days of reporting, he was concerned with the long-term growth of his portfolio. Financially, he was doing quite well and he was glad. He was also taking note as to how much money he should be giving to *tzedakah*. Like clockwork, every three months, he would withdraw the appropriate amount and give it to Rabbi Daniel Starr who would distribute it to the appropriate places and people.

Rabbi Starr was a tall black man with eclectic interests. His expertise was in *shaatnez* and in writing *gets* but was not averse to exploring other avenues of Torah. Those subjects were diverse, but they interested him greatly and he made them his forte. *Shaatnez* was a subject many people ignored and therefore he made it his business to educate others. Most people just assume that their clothes do not contain *shaatnez;* especially women's clothing. The problem with this assumption is that it is factually incorrect. Everything one wears needs to be checked for the forbidden mixture. Rabbi Starr also did whatever he could to help women who were *agunahs*. He could not stand to see anyone suffering, especially for no reason save the angst of a recalcitrant ex-husband.

In order to get to *Yeshiva* every day, Yaakov had to walk several blocks to catch a city bus, which dropped him off about a mile from the school. From there, Yaakov walked up a hill to the school.

He did this every morning in order to make it to *shacharis* at school: inclement weather or not.

On one particularly cold and rainy day, there were already two inches of snow on the ground. The mercury registered just above freezing; add the wind-chill factor and it barely broke twenty degrees. Not the type of day someone would want to be outdoors, but Yaakov still had to walk in the slush to catch the bus while bundled against the bad weather and trying to keep from falling. After what seemed an interminable length of time, he arrived at school, he proceeded directly to the *bais medrash,* shirked his extra winter gear and sat down to wait for others to arrive for *shacharis.* He was feeling cold and depressed and thought that maybe he should just get up later, *daven* at home and catch a carpool to school. He was sitting on the bench in the school *minyan* room with these depressing thoughts coursing through his mind. Yaakov was feeling agitated and confused by his thoughts. He was conflicted because he knew he should be at *shacharis* at school, but especially on days like this one, he did not like the trek to get there. He questioned if it was worth the effort.

Suddenly there was a gentle hand on his shoulder. Standing to his left was Rabbi Ginsburg with a warm smile on his face. Rabbi Meir Ginsburg, in his congenial way, said, "Just think of all of that cement piled up on your scales when you get to *Shamayim.*" Then Rabbi Ginsburg walked away to prepare himself for *davening.*

The mystified and stupefied Applebaum was left wondering how Rabbi Ginsburg knew what was on his mind. How did Rabbi Ginsburg know his thoughts and understand what was bothering him and then convey the exact message he needed to hear? Yaakov recommitted to make the early trip to *shacharis* with a smile. Never again did he complain about the long cold peregrination to school for *shacharis.* This was Yaakov Applebaum's first encounter with rabbis who seemed to have prophetic abilities; it was not to be his last rendezvous with people who seemed to be transmundane.

"I want to surround myself with people like Rabbi Ginsburg. Rabbis like him are perfect role models. No wonder everyone loves him," Yaakov thought to himself.

It was not long after this incident when Rabbi Ginsburg decided it was time to open his own *Yeshiva.* He was a master educator and a phenomenal *talmid chacham.* Rabbi Ginsburg knew he had much he could impart to his students to inspire them. He would be in a better position to do so from his own *Yeshiva*: the time was ripe.

The following year, he started his *Yeshiva* in a *shul* located on a busy street in Flatbush. His *Yeshiva davened* with the *shul* and used the *bais medrash* and basement for their classes.

Rabbi Ginsburg was a wonderful *rebbi* and became a sensational and awesome Rosh HaYeshiva. When he gave his *shiur,* he would stand for the entire time without shuffling his feet. He had a tremendous influence and effect on his students. All his *shiurim* took many hours to prepare and were delivered with eloquence and clarity.

YAAKOV APPLEBAUM WAS TIRED OF being perceived as a nerd by his high school classmates and friends. He had no interest in sports, but he did have an interest in being able to defend himself and take care of his health. If the need ever arose, he wanted to be able to protect his future family. He vividly remembered the recent encounter his family had with a convict while camping, and he did not like feeling helpless. On the contrary, he felt safe while watching his father jump with alacrity to action in order to be palladium for his family. He wanted to fit in with the crowd.

After doing some research and making inquiries, he decided on Kenpo karate; it is a practical system and was famous because of several celebrities who had studied this form of martial arts. Elvis Presley* was the most famous and there are videos of Ed Parker*, the founder of Kenpo Karate, with Bruce Lee*. There was a *dojo* a few blocks from Yaakov's house which he could attend regularly. The first few karate classes were awkward for Yaakov, as he was not used to the coordinated motion and the purpose of the movement. "I must admit," he thought to himself as he spied himself in a *dojo* mirror, "I like the way I look in the *gi.*"

He enjoyed watching the *sensei,* whose movements were so graceful and yet powerful at the same time. *Sensei* looked sharp in his black *gi* with a black belt and numerous patches. He had such poise and his bearing alone commanded respect. At the entrance of the *dojo* were numerous awards, certificates, and trophies. The student-teacher, Bert Sobol was just as noble in his aspect. In some ways, it seemed to Yaakov that Mr. Sobol was even more knowledgeable in martial arts than was the *sensei. Sensei* had one wide red band and two narrow red bands on his belt indicating a seventh-dan black belt. Mr. Sobol only had four narrow red bands, indicating a fourth-degree black belt.

Applebaum thought to himself, "Either of these men knows more ways to kill me than I know how to die. Physically, they are powerful men, but they don't act haughty in any way. It's amazing that the power and strength they command does not go to their heads. It's almost as if the aptitude makes them humbler. Mentally, they are also very strong."

Bert had been taking karate at the same *dojo* for a number of years. In reality, this was not the first place he had studied martial arts: Bert started taking karate when he was only five years old. He was an expert in several forms of martial arts and had achieved high *dan* in many. He was accomplished despite his young age of seventeen. Ed Parkers Kenpo was his favorite since it was the most practical form he had ever taken. He was not impressed with people being able to kick above their own heads, although it looks cool, it is completely impractical.

Now he was a student teacher in this *dojo*. He lived and breathed martial arts.

When Yaakov achieved and was awarded his yellow-belt, he was proud of himself and excited. He was intrigued by the awards ceremony and liked all the symbolism. He tried to be humble about the advancement, but the reward still went to his head and he felt flush. He chided himself knowing he should not be proud of this first level advancement, but he admitted to himself that he was proud of his accomplishment.

After the testing, the student placed his old belt folded up directly in front of him. The sensei placed the new belt to the left of the old belt in the shape of an "L". The new belt was folded just like the old one. The "L" shape stands for learning.

The student then bows and touches his head on his old belt, to symbolically soak in the knowledge from the old belt. He then stands and puts on his new belt. The *sensei* and any other student instructor or higher belt student comes by and kicks the student in the stomach. The kick represents the pain of childbirth and the associated pain: the reward for receiving such a cherished, lifelong gift. Then in order of rank, the other students go and shake hands with the instructors and fall-in side by side with them. In this way, everyone shakes each other's hands. The instructor, then hammer-fists the person next to him in the gut and it is "passed down" to the lowest ranking student. The lowest ranking student, then "sends it back" up the line.

When the next ranking student hit Yaakov, it hurt and he almost doubled over. He did not want to show his pain. Yaakov took control over his emotions and did not let the achievement go to his head. He had a sense of accomplishment and now he had an incentive to advance further. He hoped that next time the hammer-fist would not hurt nearly as much; he had to toughen himself. With his newfound skills and abilities, Yaakov also was anticipating more accord with his classmates. This was an additional reason for him to celebrate and be happy with his accomplishments.

SEVERAL TIMES DURING THE YEAR, *Sensei* would give demonstrations of his speed and skill in order to attract more students. He would do these presentations in schools or public libraries. Everyone who witnessed these events was impressed with the *sensei* and his students who also participated.

"I need a volunteer," *Sensei* announced to the curious but reluctant spectators. No one in the crowd was interested in being hurt, so there were no takers. The *sensei* was prepared for such an eventuality. Looking over the group, he quickly assessed the person who appeared to be in the best physical shape. "You," he said pointing to a well-built young man, "Please join me up here. This won't hurt, too much." *Sensei* had a smile on his face as he delivered his practiced line.

After some heckling by the spectators, the young man came forward.

"What's your name?"

"Stan."

"Hi, Stan. I want to demonstrate speed and accuracy."

"Okay," Stan replied hesitantly.

"Don't worry; this won't hurt me at all," he smiled and surreptitiously surveyed the room for a response.

The crowd laughed.

"You are going to stand here and I will stand all the way over there," he pointed to a spot twenty feet away. "I am going to count down from three and when I say 'one', I am going to give a flying roundhouse kick and flick the tip of your nose with my toe; don't worry, I washed my feet this morning."

Cackling was heard from the onlookers.

"You will have ample warning. You will try to block, move or deflect. Try to protect yourself."

"Uh-huh." Stan was nervous, but he knew how to handle himself, especially with the warning. "I should probably tell you, I am the captain of the wrestling team. I am no stranger to fighting."

"That's why I chose you. I could tell from your physique that you are in good shape and take care of yourself." The group of teenagers cheered their friend as *sensei* walked about twenty feet away from Stan.

"Stand ready," the *sensei* called while cupping his mouth to make the distance seem even further.

Stan struck a defensive pose in anticipation of the

forthcoming strike.

"Three," the *sensei* struck a fighting stance.

"Two," everyone called out together.

"One!"

In the blink of an eye, the *sensei* leaped forward leading with his left foot. He placed his left foot to three o'clock while he turned in a clockwise direction. His arms were balled into fists in a defensive position. He continued to pivot on his left foot while bringing his right foot up to a horizontal position preparing for the strike.

*Sensei* continued his rotation while leading with his right foot and struck Stan on the tip of his nose with barely the edge of his toe. All of this happened before Stan was even able to react or move a taut muscle.

Even with the warning, the young man, the captain of the wrestling team, did not even have enough time to recoil, let alone defend himself. Everyone was shocked and amazed at the speed, agility, and accuracy of the *sensei*.

Over the years, Bert helped Yaakov grow in belt level, stopping just shy of achieving his black belt.

# 1979

## March 28, 1979
## Middletown, Pennsylvania

**Three** Mile Island is situated on the Susquehanna River, just south of Harrisburg, Pennsylvania. Located on the island are two nuclear reactors that became operational on February 8, 1978.

Two bridges lead to the island, one on the north end, which is the main entrance, and one from the south.

On March 28, 1979, there was a cooling system malfunction in one of the reactors, that caused a partial meltdown of the reactor core.

In the nighttime hours preceding the incident, one of the reactors was running at ninety-seven percent efficiency. One was shut down for refueling.

The initial cause of the accident happened at approximately 5:30 p.m. on March 27, 1979, during an attempt by operators to fix a blockage in one of the eight-condensate polishers, the sophisticated filters cleaning the secondary water loop. These filters were designed to stop minerals and impurities in the water from accumulating in the steam generators and increasing corrosion rates on the secondary side.

With the steam generators no longer receiving feedwater, heat and pressure increased in the reactor coolant system. This caused the reactor to perform an emergency shutdown. Within eight seconds, control rods were inserted into the core to halt the nuclear chain reaction. The reactor continued to generate heat and, because the turbine was no longer using steam, the heat was no longer being removed from the reactor.

The relief valve stuck open due to a mechanical fault. The open valve permitted coolant water to escape from the primary system and was the principle mechanical cause of the partial meltdown that followed.

Many people in the Harrisburg and Hershey, Pennsylvania areas were concerned they had been exposed to radiation. Subsequent analysis showed that there was no need for concern, as readings taken by both lay and professional in the entire area showed no measurable radiation. That did not stop people from panicking and fleeing the area.

For a long time, many impacted people would tease each other saying that they did not need lights at night. They just glowed in the dark. Or people would jest that they would point their radioactive finger in an offender's direction.

It was because of this accident the Nuclear Regulatory Commission established tighter rules and controls for nuclear power plants and facilities.

This was just an accident. Or was it?

# September 1979
## Borough Park, New York

It was a typical *Yeshiva* high school class. The eighteen boys in the junior class were from diverse families: all of them were good students and were respectful. Boys will be boys and sometimes they could be rambunctious and mischievous. All of them loved their *Rebbi* who treated them as adults and equals and encouraged them to grow and become the best they could. It was part of this respect shown them by this unusual *Rebbi* that drew his students closer to him. The Rebbi could have easily started his own *yeshivah,* but that did not interest him; he would rather be merely a teacher in a *yeshiva.* He was soft-spoken, gentle and always had a smile on his face.

Rabbi Meir Ginsburg was a one of a kind high school *Rebbi.* He was short in stature, but he was a great man. Rabbi Ginsburg was humble and he seemed to anticipate his students' thoughts before they did. *Rebbi* loved his "boys", as he called them, and he looked after them, and dotted on them, as would a parent. He himself had been through World War II, although he never talked about what happened to him or his family. Over the course of time, there had been a few hints dropped that Rabbi Ginsburg had lost his wife and children to the murderous Nazis. The rumor was that he had learned in the *Mirrer Yeshivah* in Mir, Belarus and went with it to Shanghai, China, at the beginning of World War II. Rabbi Ginsburg was a big *talmid chacham* and was always accessible to his boys for any of their needs.

RABBI DOV SINGER WANTED TO be a *rebbi* in a *yeshivah,* but not just any yeshivah would do for his charismatic personality. He had just married the previous year and set up his home in Borough Park. He was studying part-time in Rabbi Horowitzs Brooklyn *yeshivah*, going to college and taking some educational courses. He was also teaching alongside Rabbi Ginsburg trying to learn as much as possible from this great rabbi and educator. Dov often consulted with Rabbi Ginsburg about his students and curriculum and appreciated the guidance he was offered.

Mrs. Zahava Singer was teaching in a girls' Jewish day school where her students loved her and would do anything for their teacher. She was also taking educational classes alongside her husband. Because they were taking concurrent classes, it made their schedules easier and they were able to do their homework together.

They were both dedicated to their students and to growing in Torah. However, they had their eyes set on moving to Baltimore, Maryland for the next school year. They were tired of the fast-paced New York and preferred the more docile community of Baltimore. Dov had already been accepted into the local *kollel*. They also submitted their résumés to the local schools and everything was in place for their move.

Before making their monumental move, Dov went to Rabbi Ginsburg for a *beracha*. The rabbi had an enigmatic message for Dov. "Shabbos should be a strengthening for you and your wife. The left arm is the weaker one, but that is where we put on *tefillin*, even when it is powerless. Always keep the faith."

Dov looked askance at the rabbi and was confused by the strange *beracha*. He had no idea what he should infer from Rabbi Ginsburg but decided he would keep it in the back of his mind. He left Rabbi Ginsburg very confused and could not ratiocinate what he meant.

YAAKOV APPLEBAUM WORE HORN-RIMMED glasses and button-down shirts with an ever-present pocket guard and pen. He dressed plainly as would a typical high school nerd, preferring a good book to physical activity. His large glasses, which he was perpetually pushing back up his nose, were stereotypically characteristic. He was the perfect straight-A student. Yaakov was not into sports but could play a great game of chess. He was taking Kenpo Karate but was trying to be a humble young man. However, since he started taking martial arts, his peers noticed his demeanor was calmer than it had been in the past.

For the most part, he got along with his classmates but was not in a clique. In addition to being smart, Yaakov had a good memory and gladly helped anyone who asked, with homework. He was respectful to everyone, although shy when meeting new people.

Yaakov often consulted with Rabbi Ginsburg about his actions and more specifically the *tzedakah* he was expected to give. Rabbi Ginsburg was proud of his student and the direction he was taking.


# October 1979
## Brooklyn, New York

In our era, computers are ubiquitous and no one would even consider being without one. This was not always the case. This story recalls a time when the term, "desktop computer" was not in the lexicon and few people had any idea about computers or what they could do or would be able to do in the future. Only the largest companies could afford a computer and few people had them in their homes. The concept of a "desktop" or "personal" computer was unknown, but this was about to change. This was the dawn of what would be known as the computer age.

Rivkah Somers and Emily Archer were brilliant and inseparable, and the best of friends. Emily was more analytical and Rivkah the more artistic, but they were both adroit.

They even looked similar, both having brown hair and blue eyes. The compatriots were of average height and weight. The only way quickly to distinguish them was that Emily wore contacts and short hair while Rivkah had glasses with long hair framing her face.

They spent all their free time in each other's company playing, studying and doing homework; well, as little homework as possible. Topics that were difficult for others came easily to the pair, while their personalities complemented one another as did their shared sense of humor. Because of the closeness of the pair, their families became friends: Miss Archer spent quite a bit of time at the Somers' house.

For her birthday, Emily received an Apple II computer and started to play around with it. She invited Rivkah over and they were both intrigued and excited by the new technological device.

It was bulky and clunky, but it was a computer and a new toy for the duo to explore.

In order to understand how it worked, one of the first things they did was to carefully dismantle the computer and put it back together. They also started to learn how to program it. There were few formal computer classes, so they learned through experimentation, mostly on their own. They read books in the library and any other resources they were able to access. On the downside, they were so engrossed in the new hobby that they ignored many of their friends. Recess and breaks often found them huddled together with pens poised over some graph paper for making notes.

They even wrote a program for doing artistic drawings on the computer. The two close friends were excited and realized they already had a direction for the rest of their lives. Many said that computers were just a passing craze; the two friends argued that computers were part of the wave of the future.

The excited duo submitted their program and they became known among the earliest computer programmers. They did not make much money, but that was not their objective. They felt they had something to contribute to society with programming. All the signs indicated that they were on their way to the goal they had envisioned for their future.

# 1980

## March 1980
## Israel

**For** Israel, 1980 was a year of a bad drought and many were suffering from lack of food and water. Farmers were losing crops and money and water was being rationed across the country. Everyone was saying extra Tehillim and the special prayer for rain thrice daily in *Shemoneh Esray*: it was not helping. Unfortunately, the Merciful One was withholding the life-giving precipitation. This was the worst drought anyone had seen in Israel in recent memory. It was already the beginning of March, the end of the rainy season in Israel, and there was not enough rain for the year.

From Jerusalem, Rabbi Shimshon Horowitz suggested to the Jewish world to institute a public fast and do *teshuva* to beseech the Master of the world for mercy. Because the Rosh HaYeshiva, Rabbi Horowitz, was respected worldwide and his request had merit, the *yeshivas* and lay people willingly complied. The Rosh HaYeshiva said, "We should not suffer like this. Not my people." Everyone was feeling the pressure and suffering of this drought and not a single person liked what everyone was going through. It had to end soon before more people suffered and died without life-giving water.

The assembled *minyan* consisted of some of the greatest rabbis and *tzadikim* in town. In a city like Bnei Braq, that was not difficult as there were so many great rabbis living within walking distance of everything. The *minyan* was scrupulous in making sure they *davened* at sunrise (*naitz nireh*) every day, slowly and deliberately, with deep feeling and intent. One day, uncharacteristically, forty-six-year-old Rabbi Baruch Mishovsky asked to lead the *davening*; he was the youngest rabbi in the *minyan* but was well respected by all.

Despite his young age, Rabbi Mishovsky was already known for his erudition in *Gemara, halacha, Rishonim,* and *Achronim.* There were rumors of him studying *kabalah* before doing *tikun chatzos* in the middle of the night. Some said he was prescient in his advice and counsel and he had helped many people through their trials and tribulations.

Baruch Mishovsky was an orphan having lost his entire family in the Shoah. The only other person in his family alive from that nightmare was a maternal great-uncle who moved to America before the war.

Baruch was born in 1934 to Rabbi Avraham and *Rebbetzin* Braindel Mishovsky. The young boy showed an incredible grasp of everything he was taught by his learned parents. He was a prodigy and there were high hopes for his becoming a future leader of his people. Rabbi Avraham Mishovsky was a well-known *posek* and *gadol* renowned for his insight and the open miracles he performed. Rabbi Avraham's father was known as a great *mekubal* and *chasidic* master. The *Rebbetzin* also came from a long line of great rabbis who performed mirabilia and together they had nine children, of whom, Baruch was the youngest. As did some great rabbis of the day, Rabbi Avraham Mishovsky foresaw the coming destruction of Europe and tried to influence as many people as possible to flee the carnage that was to be World War II. A number of the *Rav*'s students took heed and tried to migrate to far-flung places out of the reach of the Nazi killing machine. However, many did not want to leave their beloved rabbi. A few survived, most did not since obtaining visas was near impossible. Even if one was able to obtain an exit visa, finding a country that would take Jewish refugees was all but futile. Unfortunately, most of the Mishovsky family did not make it out in time.

In a brutal attack on the Jewish community, young Baruch's entire family was taken. There was no warning before the Aktion Reinhard when suddenly all the Jews were rounded up and stuffed into cattle cars. The train cars were so tightly packed with the suffering Jews that there was no room to breathe. Many died in transit; there was no way to know how many, as there was no room for them to collapse. The surviving hapless Jews were sent to Auschwitz where most of them were murdered by the Nazis. Baruch was only ten years old and was able to hide for a time, alternatively in the bunk or the laundry sorting building. In 1944, in Auschwitz, Baruch met a young charismatic and angelic man. This thirty-nine-year-old was the Klausenberger *Rebbi, HaRav* Yekusiel Yehudah Halberstam*. The *Rebbi* was familiar with Baruch's holy lineage and family and took the young orphan under his wing. The *Rebbi* studied Torah together with the young boy and influenced him to live up to his potential and his family's great standing in the worldwide Torah community. Baruch tried to stay close with the *Rebbi* and learn from his ways. He wanted to stay warm by the fire that was the Klausenberger *Rebbi*'s personality in his oasis of holiness in the in which they found themselves. After the Holocaust, he threw himself into studying the Torah, to make up for lost time. Through his own actions, the *Rebbi* showed young Mishovsky that the Torah is life and without it, we wither.

After the war, Baruch attached himself to the *Rebbi* and stayed with him in Feldafing Displaced Persons camp. The Klausenberger *Rebbi* taught him to say *kadish* for his family and he treated the young orphan like a son. In 1947, when the young Baruch became a *bar-mitzvah*, he joined the ranks of adulthood. The war had just ended and *tefillin* were impossible to obtain. The *Rebbi* had a precious pair and every day, Baruch would don them. The young man noticed that the *Rebbi*'s *tefillin* seemed to emanate some special radiance and he decided he wanted to find out what that meant. Eventually, he was able to get hold of a pair of *tefillin* that had belonged to a holy martyr, checked them to make sure they were kosher and started wearing them. Even as a young man, he decided that the straps from the *tefillin* would never touch the ground and that he would never speak anything but Torah while wearing *tefillin*. He wanted to be as holy and righteous as possible to make his late parents proud of him. Instinctively he knew what his parents would have wanted from him and how he should live his life. He was not going to let them down but follow in the holy ways of his mentor, the Klausenberger *Rebbi*. Even more so, this would please his Maker. That was to become his ultimate goal and mission in life.

The Klausenberger *Rebbi* moved to America in 1947 and then to Israel in 1960; Baruch Mishovsky went with him. While in America, in 1956 (when Baruch was twenty-two), Baruch wed and as a wedding gift, the *Rebbi* awarded him *semicha*. Through the influence and encouragement of the *Rebbi*, Rabbi Baruch Mishovsky went on to become a great rabbi himself. He became known for his erudition and even more so, his humility. When Rabbi Mishovsky arrived in the Holy Land in 1960, he was only twenty-six years old. However, he already knew all of Bavli and Yerushalmi by heart. He had all of the Rishonim, Acharonim, and *poskim* at his fingertips.

While living in Israel, Rabbi Mishovsky went to meet with Rabbi Yitzchak Kaduri*, and Rabbi Baba Sali Abuchatzayrah* and talked with them in Torah. They were the greatest kabalistic rabbis of the time, and in due course, Rabbi Mishovsky became close with these great rabbis and learned from them. They, in turn, treated the young rabbi with love and respect. Over the course of his sojourn in Israel, he stayed at the feet of the Klausenberger *Rebbi* but also went to learn from and become close with other great rabbis and Torah leaders in Israel.

Rabbi Mishovsky constantly studied Torah with all his might and deep concentration and continued to grow by leaps and bounds. After crying through Tikun Chatzos nightly, the *Rav* slept only four hours and was abstemious barely eating enough to keep his soul in its earthly container. His *Rebbetzin* doted over him and made sure he ate; however, he still fasted every Monday and Thursday. He went to the *mikveh* every day before *davening* at a *naitz minyan* with other great rabbis.

*DAVENING* LED BY RABBI MISHOVSKY was always inspiring, although an infrequent occurrence. One could not help but be moved by his entreaties before his Maker. Even when he did not *daven* from the *amud*, if you stood close enough, you would hear him crying and talking to his Father in heaven. It was as if he was standing in the very Presence of HaShem holding a conversation. Although he was only forty-six years old, he was already acknowledged as a great rabbi and future leader of his people.

While leading the *davening* that particular day, when he arrived at the part of *Shemoneh Esray* containing the prayer for rain, he cried out and begged his Father in heaven for rain. He had tears staining his angelic face; everyone was moved and felt the sincerity of his entreaties.

Matthew Greene was a real estate developer who was visiting and touring Israel at the time. It had been some time since he was able to tour the Holy Land. When he heard the entreaties of Rabbi Mishovsky that morning, something in him was stirred. For a fleeting moment, Matthew considered that maybe he should be more scrupulous with his business dealings. Unfortunately, those feelings did not last long enough to make a lasting effect on his unique way of doing business.

As usual, after *davening*, Rabbi Mishovsky sat down for a few hours with his beloved holy books. He was always the first to arrive in *shul* and the last to leave, preferring to spend his time plumbing the depths of the Torah. With his *talis* and *tefillin*, he looked like an angel delving into the precious world of Torah. He continued to learn diligently for several hours and then prepared to walk home. His *Rebbetzin* would have something small for him to eat when he returned home before he would return to his studies.

The *Rav* opened the door of the *shul* and expectantly looked up at the sky. It started to rain. "Not my people, they suffer enough," the *Rav* thought to himself. With all of his heart, he loved the Jewish people and he took on the suffering of his people as if it were his own.

# July 1980
## Borough Park, New York

On a brisk Sunday morning, Tziporah snuck out of her parent's house and rode her bike with a goal and an adventure in mind. She was a curious teenager who loved to explore her neighborhood and its goings-on. A hotel under construction on Twelfth Avenue was calling her name, begging her to explore it.

"Today I'm going to explore that new hotel. The weather is perfect," she thought, as her short brown hair blew back from her face while she pedaled quickly to her destination. She loved the sound of the playing cards clacking against the spokes of the wheels of her bike.

She parked and chained her bike behind the wooden barrier of the construction site. Tziporah quickly glanced around to assure herself that she had not been noticed as she ducked behind the safety barrier.

A construction crane was towering over the unfinished five-story hotel building that intrigued the intrepid explorer. It appeared as a long arm reaching up and over to touch the hotel. She was impressed and giddy with excitement, wondering if one day she would be able to climb that crane. For now, she would content herself with exploring the bowels of the new construction.

Tziporah quickly mounted the front stairs and squeezed herself between two planks of wood that unsuccessfully tried to prevent her entrance into the half-built building. With a smile on her face, she began to explore the future hotel and its armamentarium for construction.

She felt briefly uncomfortable but she attributed it to her trespassing in the building. She shook her head to ward off the feeling that was trying to intrude on her excitement.

The intrepid adventurer began her exploration at what would eventually become the first floor. "Next time I will go upstairs and explore there," she said aloud to herself. The reverberation of her voice as it slightly echoed in the building startled her. She laughed at herself uncomfortably and her echoing laughter surprised her.

There was quite a bit of construction that she stepped over and around: wires, tools, cut lumber, HVAC equipment, and other miscellaneous job-related implements.

Suddenly, a cool zephyr blew through the unfinished building sounding strangely eerie to Tziporah. The wailing of the wind sounded to her like a screeching cat and made her shudder. She quickly shook off the feeling and resumed her exploration of the unknown building.

Carefully, Tziporah descended a partially finished stairwell, "It's very dark and scary down here," she thought to herself. Using her flashlight, she peered around with apprehension and excitement. Briefly, she considered returning to the upper level to get out of the darkness but decided to forge on instead.

In one particularly large room, Tziporah noticed some wooden planks laid across some rickety-looking saw-horses surrounded by some chairs. "This must be where the construction crew eats," she thought, noticing the discarded remnants of food.

Tziporah jumped and let out a small yelp when she spotted a rodent eating something on the table. She took a breath and noticed the small ears and a thick tail. "That's a rat, he won't bother me," she said trying to calm herself. Turning to the rat, she said, "Sorry I scared you, but you scared me too. I won't bother you while you eat your lunch." The rodent tilted its head as if trying to understand what the stranger was saying, and then promptly returned to filling its stomach.

The penumbra of Tziporah's flashlight cast ghostly shadows on the walls and ceiling and made her ill at ease. Suddenly, she heard a noise that seemed to be coming from upstairs. Quickly looking around and not seeing anything untoward, she told herself, "I better go upstairs quickly; it's not safe down here."

She returned to the main floor and again heard a strange sound that made her nervous.

Suddenly, a black pigeon flew across her path startling her and causing her to scream out in fright. She spun around quickly and her foot became entangled in something rope-like that caused her to fall to the ground and scrape her hands. At first glance, she thought she was entangled in a snake and she cupped her hands to her face and screamed. However, it was only an orange extension cord that was interlaced in her legs, so with a nervous laugh, she extricated herself from her bindings and decided it was time to exit the building and return home. She felt she had had enough excitement for the day, maybe even the week.

Tziporah stood up and was suddenly standing in front of a strange, stout man and she screamed again and stepped back. "Who, who are you?" she nervously asked the stranger.

Daud Albaf was a Middle-Eastern man who was the watchman for several construction sites. He would patrol the different sites for which he was responsible and usually sleep in the buildings when no one was working. Daud would often eat the food left behind by the construction crews in the different buildings he canvassed. The sudden noise of the interloper woke him from his nap and he came across Tziporah on the floor.

"I'm Mr. Albaf and I'm the watchman here. Who are you and what are you doing here," demanded a deep voice with a slight Middle-Eastern accent.

"I - I, my name is Tziporah," she stammered, "I was just exploring. I was curious. I'm sorry, I will leave right away."

"You were screaming, are you OK? Were you hurt?" he asked indifferently.

Tziporah did not think the man was being sincere and she wanted to leave as quickly as possible. "I'm fine, I wasn't hurt, a pigeon frightened me and I tripped," she said instinctively rubbing her scraped hands together while trying to edge her way to the exit.

Then she dashed past Albaf, ran down the stairs, and practically tripped on a hare. She quickly unlocked her bike, jumped on it and exited the premises as if running from a flaming building. Emerging from behind the barrier, she almost ran over another girl coming down the sidewalk.

With adrenaline still coursing through her body from her recent experiences, she let out another screech when she collided with the pedestrian.

"Hey Tziporah, what's going on?" the newcomer asked, herself a bit frightened.

"Libba, I did not realize it was you. Don't do that! You will scare me into the middle of next week."

"Don't do what?" she asked while raising one eyebrow.

Catching her breath, she said, "Let's go get some pizza and I'll tell you all about my adventure."

# August 1980
## Baltimore, Maryland

Rabbi and Mrs. Singer recently moved from New York to Baltimore. He planned to teach Torah studies in a local boy's Jewish day school while his wife was going to teach in a local girl's Jewish day school. They were happy and things were going well for them: they had a nice, albeit small, apartment, good jobs, family, and friends, and he was learning in the local *kollel*. Most importantly, she was expecting their first child in a month: it was an exciting time for the young growing family.

It was a pleasant Friday night in August and the couple had a wonderful *Shabbos* dinner with some friends. There was great camaraderie, *zemiros,* delicious food, and inspirational words of Torah. The Singers left their friends' apartment after Friday night dinner and were walking home to their apartment a few blocks away. They were in a great mood; this was not unusual, as they were always in good spirits as their lives' events seemed always to be favoring them.

As they walked down the street, the young couple was chatting contentedly about their lives and their future. From out of the dark night, a thug, Mark Franklin, mugged them for the money he was sure they were carrying. One small problem with that assumption, they were a *yeshiva* couple and they would never even consider carrying money on *Shabbos*. If Franklin had been privy to that information, he would have considered a different course of action on that fateful Friday night.

Mark Franklin was a large black man who lived in a neighborhood just south of the Singers that due to reverse gentrification, was once a nice area.

Franklin dropped out of high school, as he knew that public school could not teach him anything he did not already know or anything he would need to know for the life that he was going to live. He did not have a job; he did not need or want a job. If he wanted or needed something, he would just take it. He already had a few encounters with the police but until recently, since he was a juvenile, he was not concerned with any legal ramifications. He had already spent a few nights in jail and felt it was not so bad.

He was now in need of some money for his drug habit, cash to procure his fix.

Several blocks to the north of where he lived, if you can call it living, was a predominantly Jewish neighborhood. Mark was confident that all Jews were rich, so on Friday night he walked up the Avenue and passed a large white synagogue on his right that bespoke wealth. The synagogue had an arched white façade, red-carpeted steps and looked elegant with its glass doors. However, since his only experience in his heretofore short life was his decrepit neighborhood, it did not take much to impress him.

He continued walking and saw an imposing old stone building on his right that was a synagogue. Despite its age, this building looked regal and cared for by the community. He was convinced that he was in the heart of Jewish wealth. He turned left onto a tree-lined and dark street, the perfect cover for a mugging. He justified his actions by considering it "borrowing" the money as opposed to stealing it. Besides, Jews had so much money they would not miss the little he was about to pilfer.

While walking up the quiet street, he saw a couple walking. "They be dressed good," he thought to himself, not knowing they were dressed in their *Shabbos* attire. "They must got money."

He quickly advanced on them from behind and brandished his knife. Without warning, he quickly thrust his knife to the heel into the back of Rabbi Dov Singer. Dov buckled from the force of the penetration. The pain had not yet registered as he was felled forward to the ground while Mark maintained his hold on the knife. At first, his wife, Zahava did not comprehend what happened. Mark quickly slashed at Zahava, who started to scream, but Franklin struck her hard in the face with the butt of the knife. She was knocked to the ground and clamped her hands over her mouth in pain.

"Give me all yo' money! NOW!" Franklin demanded vociferously.

"It is our Sabbath, we don't carry money," she cried out. "Please, we need an ambulance." She was having a difficult time enunciating her words, as a tooth was knocked out from the blow. Her mouth was bleeding and her face was already beginning to swell angrily from the impact. She tried to crawl to her husband to help him. Being eight months pregnant and bleeding, that proved to be difficult. Dov was not moving.

"SOMEONE PLEASE HELP!" She screamed at the top of her lungs in desperation. "HELP!" she repeatedly screamed, hoping someone would hear her.

"I don't believe you," Mark seethed. "All Jews got money. You be dressed all fancy and stuff. You be either comin from or goin to somtin fancy like. Give me yo' money or I'll kill you both."

"Honestly, we don't have anything." She continued screaming

for help. Her husband was barely conscious, and his blood was spilling out onto the pavement painting it red.

The assailant was furious. He was scared and started to panic. He jumped on the young couple and brutally stabbed both of them repeatedly. Someone must have heard the commotion because suddenly others came to the defense of the hapless pair and restrained the attacker. Someone ran to call the police and an ambulance.

Someone in the crowd was able to administer first aid, but the situation appeared dire. A man tore off his shirt and applied it to Dov's wounds as a compress to attempt to stave off the bleeding. Another removed his tie and used it as a tourniquet around Dov's upper arm. The Good Samaritans were doing everything they could to save the unfortunate couple.

It was only minutes until an ambulance and the police arrived on the scene. The couple was immediately rushed to the emergency room at Sinai Hospital just a few miles away.

Stabbed seven times, Dov was in critical condition requiring many surgeries.

Zahava was stabbed four times and was also in critical condition. Unfortunately, she lost the child she was carrying.

While waiting for the police to arrive, several people forcibly detained Franklin. He was arrested and taken to Central Booking.

Once in the emergency room, one of the wounds on Dov's back ripped a little farther and started sucking air into his lung cavity resulting in a collapsed lung. The medical staff immediately sprang into action and placed a tube into that side of his chest: his lungs then returned to normal function. He had received a stab wound in the upper section of his left arm partially severing his radial nerve. As a result, he had little to no feeling in his left hand and had little mobility in his arm below the wound.

Rabbi Singer was in the Intensive Care Unit for several weeks and had to stay in the hospital for an additional month and required significant physical therapy and rehabilitation after release. Because of the permanent damage to his left arm, he would also require occupational therapy to learn how to do things differently. Unfortunately, he lost partial use of his left arm and hand.

Mrs. Singer was in the ICU for a week. Her wounds were not as bad and she was released after only a few weeks. She also needed physical therapy and rehab. Sadly Mrs. Singer would never be able to carry another child.

The physical scars would take some time to heal while the emotional ones would take much longer: the couple was devastated.

They had a better understanding of the enigmatic *beracha* from Rabbi Ginsburg. It was on a *Shabbos* they were mugged and his left arm was of little use, and by some miracle, he did not lose it. At least he would still be able to put *tefillin* on the arm. Maybe, due to the rabbi's *beracha*, it was not worse.

The Jewish community banded together to help the young couple through this onerous time. The entire Baltimore community said Tehillim on their behalf and helped them in many ways. People came to visit the couple in the hospital and offered physical and emotional support. If the couple needed food or even just some company, friends and neighbors were available. Several days a week, Rabbi Singers *chavrusah* came to the hospital to study with him, while Mrs. Singer was visited by several women who read to her.

Mark Franklin pleaded guilty to two counts of first-degree attempted murder and two counts of assault with a deadly weapon. If he were to have gone to trial, he would have gotten twenty-five to life with no possibility of parole for twenty years. As a result of the plea bargain, he was sentenced to fifteen years to be served with no possibility of parole. After being released, he would be on probation for ten years.

The Singers were beside themselves with depression. They were angry about what happened to them. Their complete faith in HaShem was shaken, but they heroically tried to remain steadfast to their commitment to and the strength they derived from the Jewish faith.

# 1981

## January 1981
## Flatbush, New York

**In** 1981, Rabbi Ginsburg officially moved his growing *yeshiva* to a house he purchased in Flatbush on East Fourteenth Street near Avenue P. Rabbi Ginsburg lived upstairs with his family above the *Yeshiva*. A few of the *talmidim* lived in the basement that was set up as a quasi-dormitory. The quarters were tight, but the students did not care as long as they were close to their Rosh HaYeshiva. Tuvya Justin was hired to remodel the first floor into one large room for the *bais medrash*. In addition, a small room served as the Rosh HaYeshiva's office and the kitchen was made into a classroom. Also in the basement was the kitchen and dining room for the *Yeshiva* where the *Rebbetzin* cooked delicious and nutritious meals.

Nachum Weiss was born in 1961 and was one of the first students in the new location. Nachum was a troubled young man and the Rosh HaYeshiva tried hard to influence his young *talmid*. He knew that Nachum had a bad temper, but with some guidance and *musar*, that could change.

Nachum came from a good family, but as was often common with the first-born, he was controlling and oftentimes impatient. If things did not go his way, he immediately blew his top at anyone and anything within his purview.

The Rosh HaYeshiva tried to maintain a mentorship role with Nachum to be a source of strength and grounding to counter his harum-scarum attitude. Rabbi Ginsburg often said that there is no such thing as a bad *middah*, but what we do with it, can be. For the most part, while in the *Yeshiva*, Nachum was in control of his temper. However, it was difficult to fight with a *stender*.

Every *Shabbos* afternoon, the Rosh HaYeshiva gave a *shiur* for the community which was popular and regularly standing room only. Most every *Shabbos*, the Rosh HaYeshiva spoke on issues of *shalom bayis* as he felt there could always be more *shalom* in the world, especially in families. He often tied his *shiur* to the weekly Torah portion or current events.

He often spoke of the relationships of Adam* and Chavah*; Avraham* and Sarah*; Yitzchak* and Rivkah*; and Yaakov* and his wives. Rabbi Ginsburg said that he was mostly talking to himself but everyone could listen in as he was just trying to improve his own *shalom bayis* and to emulate the holy ways of our forebearers.

The *Rebbetzin* was in full support of her husband and she was as great a woman as he was a Rosh HaYeshiva. She not only made sure there was good food for meals for the *talmidim;* she was also available in case anyone needed her sagacious, motherly advice.

# January 1981
## Al-Awja, Iraq

For January, it was unusually warm in Al-Awja, Iraq. Normally, the temperature was in the forties (Fahrenheit) for that time of the year; however, this year it seemed to be perpetually ten degrees warmer. The warm weather may have had something to do with the unrest some people were feeling. This was especially so in the poorer areas where there were fewer distractions and only a smattering of people had jobs.

Nineteen-year-old Ahmed Yousef al Rashim was frustrated and angry. He failed at everything he tried and felt like a loser. He had only one friend in the world, eighteen-year-old Mohamed abu Sharif. They both were raised the same way - in squalor, and to hate Jews and all they stood for. When they were growing up, they were fed the hatred of Jews with their breakfast, lunch, and dinner. Well, that was when they had food to eat, otherwise, they just ate just animus of the Jews. Ahmed knew that all of his problems were the fault of the Jews. He had never met any Jews, but he knew they had horns and controlled everything - banks, newspapers, the United States, Palestine, drug companies and hospitals. Mohamed was not as vitriolic as Ahmed was, but he wanted the Jews to stop controlling the world, expecting he would then have a better life.

He was destitute and that was the Jews' fault. Ahmed was trying to improve his situation, but it was the Jews who controlled everything, and for that reason, he lived in this dirty, crime-ridden and impoverished part of Iraq. It was a self-fulfilling prophecy that he felt he never stood a chance to make anything of himself.

They lived in Al-Awja, a city about eight miles south of Tikrit in Iraq on the western bank of the Tigris River. One might have thought it would be a thriving city, since, in 1937, Al-Awja was the birthplace of the president of Iraq, Saddam Hussein Abd al-Majid al-Tikriti*. But alas, the living conditions were far from ideal. There were two sections of the city: one section close to the river for the elite who lived in nice homes with plenty of land. More inland, across the main road to the west, was where the rest of the population lived in squalid conditions. This was where Ahmed and Mohamed lived. They shared a small, filthy, one-room hut with a shared outhouse. They had only one table, two rickety chairs, and slept on straw spread on the floor.

Ahmed was born in 1962. His father was a suicide bomber who killed himself in 1977 while blowing up a bus in Jerusalem murdering twelve Jews and injuring twenty others. His mother died in childbirth and Ahmed felt that if it were not for the Jews, his mother would have had better medical care and would not have died. If not for the Jews, his father would not have had to martyr himself to kill Jews. Ahmed had been alone ever since and was depressed and angry. He had four older siblings and all five of them were ne'er do wells. He never knew his mother, but he remembered his father as being a disciplinarian raising him as a strict Muslim.

Mohamed was as poorly dressed in tattered clothing as was his friend. He was a year younger than his friend and his father was a religious Muslim. His mother was not actively observant; she just seemed to go along with her husband. It was as if she did not care about her husband's religion at all. His father was a brute and abusive to him and his mother. Mohamed had fourteen half-siblings. His father had three wives, all of whom were abused and abusive. His older brothers also beat him, frequently to a bloody pulp.

His mother, Sarah, did not talk about her family. In fact, all she said about her parents was that they died a long time ago. However, one time, she let it slip that her parents were still alive and Mohamed was confused and did not know which version was true.

When he asked his mother about it, she just turned around, ran to her room and cried, never answering him. Mohamed felt there was more to his mother's parents' history than she was telling him. She was clearly not happy and looked as if she did not belong, somehow always out of place.

Mohamed wondered why his father kept her on a tighter leash than his other two wives. It was almost as if his father did not trust her, but then why would he have married her? What was so different about his mother from his step-mothers, or the mothers of his friends?

Mohamed was a religious Muslim, but only because he had to be. His parents, specifically his father forced religion down his throat and he greatly resented it. He was not sure how religious he was going to be when he would be completely on his own. With his rudimentary reading skills, he had read some Western stories and fantasized about living a better life.

As with most of their friends, they had not gone to school and had no real education. As a result, they could only do menial jobs, and even those jobs were few and difficult to find. Most often, they could only get a job collecting trash. This was the lowest of low jobs one could have since in their world, it was the most humiliating work. As soon as they had saved enough money to last a few weeks, they would quit that job and look for something else. The problem was there was no other employment to be found.

They had just quit their job, again, and decided to go to their favorite coffee shop, which was also the local hangout. The coffee tasted like swill, but it was the only coffee shop in the area so they did not know any better.

They were sitting there one day expressing their anger and at that moment, they had an epiphany and came up with an idea: become terrorists and take revenge on the infidels, but since they were both utter cowards, they would not commit suicide. They started to formulate plans as they fed on each other's rage.

After a few meetings at the coffee shop, they felt as if the proprietor was watching them. They became paranoid and decided to continue their scheming and planning in an open field. Ahmed and Mohamed went further west of town into the fields to do more strategizing. They had some ideas and made detailed plans over the course of the next month. However, they hit a snag, as guidance and significant money were needed, of which they had neither.

In the field, they saw in the distance a large mound of dirt that was about one-hundred-ten yards long and seventy-five yards wide. It was an unspoken secret that it was a mass grave of people who had disappointed the "Butcher of Baghdad."

"We need help. We need the advice and support of someone bigger and smarter than us," Mohamed said.

"I agree," Ahmed said. "But who's going to help us? We are just teenagers with a plan." He wondered as he looked out over a mound of dirt that was almost the size of a soccer field. That was when inspiration hit him, "We should contact Saddam Hussein. He can probably help us, but I don't know if he will."

"How do we reach him?" Mohamed asked. "If he would be willing to help us, and give us money, we can do this."

"I don't know how to reach him. We'll have to put out feelers that we want to talk with him. Before that, we need to write down our plans. That will show Saddam Hussein that we are serious and have definitive plans."

"Okay," Mohamed said. Neither of them had much of an education, but they were able to do basic reading and writing. They would have to collaborate on the effort to transcribe their plots onto paper.

In order to improve their rudimentary educational skills, they found a tutor who was willing to teach them *pro bono*. They did not divulge the rationale behind their need to increase their language skills and to learn English. Over the next several months, they did well and wondered why they had dropped out of school; they were intelligent men.

They decided to call themselves the "Palestine Freedom Group." It did not matter that they had never been to what some called Palestine. Both knew that Palestine was mentioned in the Koran and therefore belonged to the Muslims. They never opened the Koran, so they did not know the reality - no such mention is found. They were angry and planned to take vengeance on the deplorable Jews. That was all that mattered to them, and that is what they were going to do – they were now on a mission and with enough planning, they would not fail.

Part of their plan was for Mohamed to attend a *Yeshiva* and learn how to mingle with Jews. It would be easier for him to masquerade as a Jew since he was not as swarthy as was Ahmed. However, he did have a serious concern.

"If I go to a Jew school, how will I hide my horns? I mean my lack of horns. You know all Jews got horns." Mohamed innocently asked his friend.

"Why do you think they wear those Jew caps on their heads? Just make sure you are always wearing a cap and you'll be fine."

"I don't know," he shook his head. "What if it falls off or blows off in the wind?"

In exasperation, Ahmed said, "Let's ask Saddam Hussein when we see him. I'm sure he'll have some good advice."

"Okay."

"We can always just nail it to your head," he teased.

Mohamed just laughed, but in the back of his mind, he wondered if there was a bit of seriousness to the tease. Due to his familial abuse, he was rather sensitive.

They let everyone know that they wanted to meet with Saddam Hussein and that they had grandiose plans. They started at the coffee shop where they had initiated their project and hoped their message would reach its intended destination.

# April 1981
## Al-Awja, Iraq

The compatriots were conspiring to become terrorists starting in New York. While they were working on improving their rudimentary education, they were doing everything they could to get word to Saddam Hussein about needing his help. They were rebuffed many times and were derided even more for their efforts. They were almost ready to throw in the towel and give up on their hopes since no one was willing to help introduce them to the dictator. It did not help that everyone was afraid of the Butcher of Bagdad.

Eventually, word reached Saddam and he was curious. What could these two losers say that would be of interest to him? For some reason that even he could not identify, his curiosity was piqued.

After a complete background check on both Ahmed Yousef al Rashim and Mohamed abu Sharif, Saddam Hussein agreed to meet them in one of his bunkers in Iraq. The two were extended an invitation. They were both excited and petrified at the same time. Would they persuade the man or be killed by him? Were they heading to greatness or their demise? Would Saddam Hussein approve of their plans or laugh in their faces? They were now heading down the path of their own making and did not know where it would lead. They felt as if they were about to enter the lion's den.

The pair were told to go to a specific obscure café at the other end of town. To get to this cafe they had to find a small arcane side street in the middle of a poor neighborhood. It was not in their normal environs so they were not familiar with the area. Walking down a cobblestoned street, they almost missed the turn to go down another narrow alley. The path did not really qualify for the term alley: it was not labeled and could easily be missed. After walking in the heat of the day and almost getting lost twice, they finally found the café that was just a hole in the wall.

When they entered the establishment, a bell over the door tinkled announcing their arrival into an eatery that had more paint peeling than what was still on the walls. There were a few rickety tables and mismatched chairs around the small floor with the proprietor standing at the counter overlooking the one patron holding a glass containing a clear liquid. Ahmed suspected that the patron was really a guard. They approached the proprietor and asked for a glass of water with lime: recognizing the code, the shopkeeper prepared them for the next stage. They had to go through careful scrutiny in order to be able to pass: they were patted down to make sure they were not carrying any weapons, then interrogated to make sure they were whom they claimed.

From here, they were escorted out the back door of the café. Their escort considered the possibility these men were plants to ensure he was doing his job well. Knowing Saddam Hussein, one could never be too sure or too careful. They entered another building that housed the entrance to an underground bunker. Ahmed and Mohamed were getting more nervous as they went through more and tighter security. Nervously, they looked at each other and thought to themselves, "Are we really going to see Saddam Hussein, or is this going to be our end?" Were they headed to their deaths by the hands of the butcher? Were they going to get out of this alive? They were petrified of the uncertain future. However, there was no backing out now.

This second building was so dilapidated and small that it was barely more than a one-room shack. Here, they were subjected to a full-body search. They imagined that it would have been easier to get to see the infidel President of the United States. The escort led Ahmed and Mohamed into a closet on the far side of this hut where there was a hidden panel inside of a closet that doubled as a metal detector. The escort pressed a hidden button and the panel yawned open to reveal a poorly illuminated elevator. Ahmed and Mohamed looked at each other; they were impressed and quite surprised as the elevator descended six stories to an underground bunker. They had never been this far underground before and never experienced an elevator and were a bit shaken by the experience.

When they exited the elevator, they were again inspected and searched. Saddam Hussein was not taking any chances with his security.

The two friends were escorted down a short and poorly illuminated hall to a conference room. There was a soldier armed with an AK-47 rifle (also known as a Kalashnikov) standing on the side waiting for them. There were some refreshments on the side breakfront, from which Mohamed wanted to partake, but Ahmed slapped his hand and hissed, "Don't you dare take anything, it'll look really bad." Instead, they sat down and waited for Saddam Hussein to join them. Comfortable executive chairs surrounded the fifteen-foot oval conference table. At one end of the table was a luxurious executive chair they assumed was for Hussein.

Saddam Hussein had many doppelgangers around the world including in Iraq. One never knew if one was actually talking with him or a proxy. In either case, the man was treated with deference as if he was royalty.

Saddam Hussein, or his double, walked into the room as if he owned the world. The soldier snapped to attention and saluted. Both Ahmed and Mohamed jumped to their feet in abject fear of the Butcher. Simultaneously, they both said, "Allah hu akbar."

Saddam Hussein just nodded his head. He took his seat at the head of the table and waved his hand to indicate to his guests to sit.

They knew that if they did not impress Saddam Hussein, their life would not be worth a plug nickel. However, they came prepared to give it their best. They had their notes and sketches prepared for the meeting.

They were nervous; no, they were scared out of their minds and could practically hear their own hearts beating in their chests. They had never met someone who could easily have them killed. Slowly, in detail, the young men spelled out their plans to the dictator. At a few points, Mohamed became tongue-tied and had a difficult time finding the right words, so Ahmed took the lead, and did most of the talking. He showed Saddam Hussein their notes, drawings, and plans.

They were going to wreak havoc in New York and set the stage for other attacks they would carry out over the course of time and in other locations. They would start with poisoning the water treatment plants, bombing the subway system, then cut communications and finally the electrical system. Their plan was flexible leaving room for adaptation. They gave a detailed five-year plan and a long-term plan for an additional ten years. They would start in New York and work their way to Washington D.C.; subsequently, they had grandiose plans for more terrorism in Israel.

"I do have a concern," Mohamed wanted to sound intelligent

and important in front of Saddam Hussein. He sat up straight in his chair and asked, "My role would be to infiltrate the Jewish community. I would go to a Jew school to learn their ways. If I go to a Jew school, how will I hide my lack of horns? I don't have horns."

Saddam Hussein guffawed. "You idiot! Jews don't have horns." He shook his head in wonder and thought to himself, "How can some people be so stupid. But I like their plan."

Mohamed lowered his head in shame. "I wonder who started that rumor," he asked himself. "Now I feel like a total fool. I hope he will not kill me and still help us. What did I get myself into?" He was struggling to keep his composure and not shake with the freight he was feeling.

Despite Mohamed's ludicrous question, Saddam Hussein was mildly impressed with their plan and agreed to give them five million dollars. It was more than what Ahmed or Mohamed could have hoped for and they were ecstatic. They had no idea how much money that was, but for them, just the number was practically enough to make them jump out of their seats. They looked at each other credulously and wanted to dance with joy.

Before they left, the dictator also shared with the young men some other tips, including suggesting they find an additional person to join their team and possibly even two. "However, be very careful who you add to your cadre. Not everyone can be trusted, so vet them well."

Saddam Hussein told them to go to South America and meet with a man who could give them valuable help. They were to look for the "Old German" in the city of Mar Del Plata, Argentina in the Andes Mountains. "When you get to the town, you are to go into the local pub and ask for the 'Old German,' Adolf Leipzig*. You are to give the code 'The Painter', or you will be killed. This man is a recluse, is secretive and always has bodyguards nearby."

"Okay, we will see this 'Old German.' We could use all the help we can get."

Saddam Hussein added, "I have another job I want you to do for me. I want you to go to Harrisburg, Pennsylvania."

Nervously, Ahmed asked, "Why?"

"Just south of Harrisburg, about ten miles downriver, there is an island in the middle of the Susquehanna River called Three Mile Island. On March 28, 1979, there was a nuclear power plant meltdown. Everyone thinks it was an accident. I know better. I sent someone to sabotage the cooling system. It didn't work as I had hoped, as there were no injuries or deaths. However, had it been successful, the entire plant would have exploded and hundreds of infidels would have died immediately and tens of thousands would have died a slow and painful death. The United States government hushed it up as an accident." Saddam Hussein smiled viciously while wringing his hands with delight as he thought of what could have been.

Mohamed cringed. It was one thing to want to kill people quickly, even to cause them suffering by ruining their water and communications. It was entirely different to cause people to suffer and die a slow and painful death. He was about to say something, but he suddenly remembered in front of whom he was sitting. He kept his thoughts to himself.

Ahmed, on the other hand, was ecstatic. It was exactly his type of thing and he liked the idea. He wondered if there were similar 'projects' he could do. "I know nothing about nuclear power plants, but I will have to find out more. When I get to the United States, I will do more research," he thought to himself. "There is so much more I have to learn if I want to become the head of our cell." Aloud he said, "We can try to add something with that place to our plans. What was it called?"

Angrily, Saddam Hussein pounded his fist on the table and said, "Three Mile Island. It's south of Harrisburg, Pennsylvania. And don't try, you had better succeed!" He shook his head in frustration. "Some suicide bombers are so stupid," he thought to himself. "I guess that is why they are so willing to kill themselves."

Aloud Saddam Hussein said, "The martyr I sent in '79 was a fool and messed up my plan. I expect better from you!" He was so exacerbated that he was practically frothing at the mouth.

They looked at each other and back to Saddam, and nervously responded, "We won't let you down! We'll make you proud," they enthused as one while nodding their heads.

Before leaving, they were curious about the bunker. Saddam Hussein offered them a tour, which was gratefully accepted. He picked up the phone and called one of his underlings for the peregrination of the main parts of the bunker. He could not be bothered to do it himself and was glad to conclude the meeting and be rid of these nuisances.

The pair was amazed at the size and scope of the underground shelter. Clearly, it was secure and more luxurious than anything they had heretofore seen. The bunker had sufficient stock of food, water, and other supplies to last for several years. It was built far enough underground that it could withstand a direct hit from any conventional missile. On the roof of several surrounding buildings were solar panels and rainwater reclamation systems, and there were several air vents with filtration systems in place. The bunker was designed in luxury and Saddam Hussein, if it really was him, lived in an underground palace.

Sitting on the dictator's desk was a book, _Doomsday Bunker Book,_ which was used to design his bunker.

The structure of the bunker was constructed from concrete and was round with a monolithic dome. The bunker had five main levels below the dome and three smaller levels inside the dome. On each level of the bunker was a sophisticated air filtration system that vented air to and from the surface. It was a completely self-contained city in a fortress with enough space to comfortably house over fifty people. In an emergency, it could hold more than double that number.

There were bathrooms and showers on all levels. There was also a recreation room, library, mess hall, game room and more. The bottom level was for storage, food, water, and other supplies.

There was an elevator on one end of the bunker and a staircase on the other, leading to the surface.

The would-be terrorists thought they would want to build a bunker in the United States. They made a mental note to look for the author of _Doomsday Bunker Book_ and have him design their bunker. They did not need something so elaborate, but if it was good enough for Saddam Hussein, it was perfect for them.

They were off to South America.

# August 1981
## Buenos Aires, Argentina

Ahmed Yousef al Rashim and Mohamed abu Sharif traveled to South America. This was not a pleasure trip, although they planned to enjoy themselves. Argentina is a beautiful country in South America. While there, they took a few days to tour Buenos Aires, the capital of the country. They were enthralled by the sights, sounds, and smells of this city. They had never been exposed to anything like in their prior life.

They had a wonderful time and enjoyed the many tourist attractions. They could have spent a month or more just touring the capital city, but they had an agenda: more, it was a mission. Reluctantly, they tore themselves away from being tourists to embark on the first leg of their mission.

# August 8, 1981
## Mar del Plata, Argentina

Ahmed and Mohamed had to get to Mar del Plata to find the elusive Adolf Leipzig, and the only way to get there was a five-and-a-half-hour bus ride. Mar del Plata is an Argentine city on the coast of the Atlantic Ocean, about 250 miles south of Buenos Aires and at that time was the second largest city of Buenos Aires Province.

Once in Mar del Plata, they asked around trying to find the "Old German". Ahmed and Mohamed went to numerous cafés and bodegas trying to cull information about where to find Adolf Leipzig. At first, no one wanted to help them find the recluse and they were considering abandoning the effort and continuing on their mission in the United States.

After a few weeks of futile searching, they finally found someone who was willing to help them, for a "gift." This stranger directed them to a café in a different part of the city. They had a difficult time finding the café as it turned out it was, in fact, a pizzeria at the other end of Av Pedro Luro, called Pizzeria Castel Franco, not the best section of town.

Once inside the pizza shop, they started making inquiries for the painter. No one seemed to know any painter. They offered the proprietor a "gift" and Mohamed said, "We are not looking for **a** painter, but '**The** Painter'."

Suddenly, the owner of the shop knew about whom they were talking and demanded their IDs and told them to return in a few days. Mohamed and Ahmed were taken aback by the demand and the reticence of the shop owner, it reminded them of when they tried to meet with Saddam Hussein. Reluctantly, they handed over their passports, otherwise, they rightly assumed they would get nowhere, or more likely, killed.

After walking around Mar del Plata for two days and enjoying the sites, they decided it was time to return to the pizza shop.

Upon their entry, the proprietor immediately recognized them and returned their ID's. The men had passed the scrutiny and for an additional gift, he had the information they wanted. Before leaving, they had some more pizza and drinks.

After paying their tab, the proprietor gave them clear directions to the villa for which they were looking.

When they finally arrived, a petite older black woman greeted them at the door. "What do you want?" she asked cautiously.

Ahmed responded, "We are looking for the 'Painter'."

The woman was cognizant that few people knew the codeword. These men did not look old enough to be Mossad (Israel's equivalent of American CIA) agents. Her woman's intuition told her that these men were no threat to her. She said, *"Buenas tardes.* I'm Cutinga*, the lady of the house. Please show me some identification."

They looked at each other and then, with a shrug, handed her their passports. Cutinga carefully scrutinized the proffered documents and returned them to the men. Having heard from the pizza shop owner, she was expecting them and knew they were safe.

"Please come in and call me Cutinga," she said with a strong Mexican accent, as she stepped to the side to allow them entrance. Out of respect, they doffed their kufis and could not help but noticed the opulence of the furniture and lavishness of the well-appointed house. There were also some old paintings on the walls that were probably originals - rare and expensive.

Cutinga escorted Ahmed and Mohamed down the hallway with dark, rich wood paneling, to a study that seemed to exude power. Cutinga opened the mahogany door into the study for the young men, who upon entering, noticed it was richly appointed and stylish, just as the rest of the house and they were afraid to sit on the plush chairs as they were unaccustomed to seeing such affluence. A polished mahogany desk occupied the center of the room, old paintings framed in fancy wood-gilded frames were displayed on the walls, rich curtains hung over the windows, plush beige carpet on the floor silenced their steps, and upholstered elegant sofas hugged the walls. Curiously absent from the trappings of the room were family portraits. There was a large red, white and black Nazi flag behind the desk and a large portrait of Adolf Hitler* mounted in an elegant gold-leafed wood frame on a sidewall, immediately drew their attention.

When Adolf Leipzig sauntered into the room, Ahmed and Mohamed snapped to attention and immediately noticed his uncanny resemblance to the portrait of Adolf Hitler hanging on the wall. They found it disquieting that they could not help looking from the man to the portrait and back.

However, Leipzig was a frail old man walking with a cane, he did not have a mustache and he had a baldpate. Maybe he was a brother, but then why would he have the same first name and a different surname? Besides, Adolf Hitler and his recently married wife killed themselves and others in 1945. Their bodies were carried outside, doused with fuel and burned, leaving only a part of his mandible.

This man had a paunch and when he talked, it was clear he had asthma as he wheezed with every breath. He was slightly stooped but of average height and there was an air of power and charisma about him.

He bade his guests sit, which they did reluctantly at the edge of the chairs. They were afraid to ruin the expensive and luxurious chairs.

"I heard you were looking for me. What do you want?" Adolf rasped to his guests. His voice was guttural and his accent was clearly of Germanic origin. His eyes were piercing and demonic: he had clearly seen more than his share of evil.

Ahmed nervously took the floor and hesitantly stammered, "Mr. Leipzig, my name is Ahmed Yousef al Rashim and this is my good friend Mohamed abu Sharif. We just came from Saddam Hussein in Iraq. In fact, he told us how to find you, sir. We are planning a series of terrorist attacks on the United States and then eventually Israel. Our main target will be the Jewish population with collateral deaths to infidels, I mean, non-Jews." He was concentrating with all his might on his words so to seem important and smart. He did not want to stumble nor hesitate with what he had to say.

"What do you want from me? I'm just an old man living out his life in retirement. I don't get involved in stuff like this."

Confused, the two would-be Muslim terrorists looked at each other and Ahmed raised his eyebrow at his friend. This was not what they were anticipating, "We were hoping that maybe you could give us some advice or help us financially. We thought that is the reason Saddam Hussein sent us to see you."

"Give me all the details of your plan. Don't leave out any of the minutiae." Adolf was non-committal although curious.

Ahmed was cautiously buoyant. "We want to wreak havoc against the Americans and more specifically the Jews." The pair laid out their plan in detail, showing Leipzig the sketches and charts for their plots. Mohamed produced a written timetable they had prepared for the occasion.

Leipzig was attentive, carefully reviewing the supplied documentation and asking pertinent questions. He was moderately impressed and thought they had a good chance to accomplish something. He gave them valuable advice and even some financial support, for which they were grateful. Leipzig sent them to a counterfeiter to make fake identifications for them. They now had US passports, driver's licenses, and birth certificates. They even had Social Security cards and GED's so they could obtain employment. They made two sets of fake IDs in preparation for their journey to the belly of the beast, the United States. The trip had been productive and worth the effort.

Cryptically, Leipzig added, "Before you leave, I want to tell you something." Leipzig was wheezing and having a difficult time getting his message across. He took a sip of water from the glass at his elbow and continued, "This is not well known, but I think you and your plans have potential, so I want you to be aware of something. After you have established yourselves and accomplished some devastation, go to a place called Roswell, New Mexico. Back on July 8, 1947, it was reported that a flying saucer crash-landed on a ranch on the outskirts of Roswell. However, that is not what really happened..."

Adolph gave them some incredible information that they had a difficult time comprehending. However, they took copious notes and promised the eccentric old man that they would use his information wisely.

They felt completely prepared for the next stages in their plan.


# September 1981
## Jerusalem, Israel

During his junior year in high school, Yaakov Applebaum already knew he wanted to go to Israel to learn in a *Yeshiva* for at least a year or two. He knew that if he lived frugally he could allow his investments to continue to grow. Financially, he was already quite comfortable, but he knew that it was all in the hands of the Big Boss. After spending some time in *Yeshiva*, he would get a degree, but there was still time for that. While still a senior in high school, he had taken some college-level courses, so he was well on his way. He was a planner and this was his method, being deliberate and not rushing into anything. Unfortunately, this methodical approach often led to him having a difficult time making decisions.

Before Yaakov even left the United States, he went to *HaRav* Shimshon Horowitz's New York branch *Yeshiva* for an admittance exam. The Rosh HaYeshiva's son delivered the exam and the young man did well. During the summer, before going to Israel, Yaakov started learning in the New York branch to get a head start on his learning. Soon after joining the *Yeshiva*, Yaakov became known as a *masmid,* always being in the *bais medrash, schteiging*; growing in leaps and bounds. He woke up early, was on time for every *seder* and stayed late being quotidian in his routine. After a short time, Applebaum became close with the Rosh HaYeshiva.

Rabbi Shimshon Horowitz started his *Yeshiva* in 1958 on

Forty-Fifth Street in Borough Park, New York. In 1975, he moved his *Yeshiva* to Yerushalayim but left the New York branch under the auspices of his son. Rabbi Horowitz wore *talis* and *tefillin* all day and was acknowledged by all as a *gadol* and was a world-renowned *posek*. He had five children; all married, and he was grooming the oldest two sons to be next Roshei HaYeshiva. His oldest son ran the *Yeshiva* in New York and his second son helped run the *Yeshiva* in Israel. His three sons-in-law gave *shiurim* in the *Yeshivas.* There were about 500 students, including *kollel,* learning in the Israeli branch in Jerusalem and about one-hundred in Borough Park.

The *Yeshiva* was built into the side of a mountain, which allowed the dormitory and dining room to be built below the entrance level. The main level had the *bais medrash* and *Yeshiva* offices, while upstairs were classrooms and the library.

A few days after Yaakov arrived in the *Yeshiva*, he noticed a chair outside the Rosh HaYeshiva's office door. This seemed aberrant, as no one ever had to wait more than a few minutes to see the Rosh HaYeshiva. The *shamash* was efficient in making sure everyone was able to meet with the Rosh HaYeshiva expediently. The Rosh HaYeshiva was available to everyone at all times of day and night. Yaakov asked another of the students about the chair.

"It's the *fahair* chair," he was told.

"What's that?" Applebaum asked, his curiosity piqued.

"When you get into the *semicha* program, you'll find out," he said with a light laugh.

Yaakov was befuddled; however, his *mussar* training taught him not to ask further. Every so often, he noticed different *bachurim* sitting in the *fahair* chair, seemingly totally spent. Yaakov curtailed his curiosity and did not inquire further.

One of the lessons Yaakov learned is that from the actions of our great rabbis, we can learn Torah. However, that learning must be coupled with book knowledge. One has to know what the *halacha sefarim* say in order to understand what is being done by the *talmid chacham.*

However, sometimes the actions of the rabbis can be confusing and the student has no choice but to approach and ask for clarification. This is part of the meaning of the Mishneh, which states, "A shy person cannot learn."

Overcoming his timidness he approached Rabbi Horowitz, "Begging the Rosh HaYeshiva's pardon, but the Mishneh states, ' אין הבישן למד (A shy person cannot learn),' I have a question." Yaakov was respectful but he wanted to understand and grow from the actions of this great and humble man.

1981

Rabbi Horowitz smiled at Yaakov and nodded his head to give permission for the question.

"Whenever the Rosh HaYeshiva walks into the room, we all stand. However, the Rosh HaYeshiva says, 'Sit down, sit down.' I'm confused. Why does the Rosh HaYeshiva tell us to sit down?"

"Why do you stand?"

At first, Yaakov was a bit confused. Then he realized the Rosh HaYeshiva was trying to encourage him to think. It was not necessarily the job of the Rosh HaYeshiva to directly answer questions, but to guide his students and teach them how to learn. "The Rosh HaYeshiva teaches us Torah. He is a living embodiment of a Sefer Torah. When a Sefer Torah is brought into the room, we stand in honor of HaShem and the holy Torah."

"You can stand," the Rosh HaYeshiva enigmatically responded with a smile. He knew very well that the young man in front of him was now even more bewildered than before.

Yaakov was perplexed. "Now I'm even more confused."

The Rosh HaYeshiva smiled. "Most people stand for me. I am not worthy of the honor. I am just a simple man. However, if you are standing in honor of the Torah that I teach you, then you are not standing for me, you are standing to honor HaShem and His Torah. That is a beautiful thing."

Yaakov understood. He was amazed at the humility of the great man. "I must try to emulate the Rosh HaYeshiva," he thought to himself. In a number of ways, he already was trying to copy the diligence of Rabbi Horowitz, but it was not easy. True humility is a very difficult and elusive attribute to acquire, but it seemed to the young man that his Rosh HaYeshiva had integrated the attribute into the very fiber of his being.

Shortly, Yaakov applied for and was accepted into, the *semicha* program. Rabbi Horowitz gave him the assignment to study Chulin 91a and attendant commentaries. However, he was to concentrate on learning the *sugya* according to *halacha*. He threw himself wholeheartedly into the study and after about three months, Applebaum was ready for his first *fahair* and he went to the Rosh HaYeshiva's office for the *bechinah*. It was a warm day and the Rosh HaYeshiva had the fan blowing gently.

The pale yellow office was sparsely furnished with a plain desk and an armchair for the Rosh HaYeshiva. There were also two simple chairs for the myriad visitors or petitioners who came for advice, a *beracha* or *shailah*. Next to the Rosh HaYeshiva was a bookcase overstuffed with sefarim that he might need at any given time. A lamp on the desk illuminated the sefer Rabbi Horowitz was using, while a dim ceiling light did little to displace any darkness. During the day, the only light was from a window that looked out onto the expansive Jerusalem Mountains. At his elbow was a simple glass of water.

The *bechinah* seemed to be going well and Yaakov was feeling comfortable and quite sure of himself. Suddenly the Rosh HaYeshiva threw a question at Applebaum to which he was not one-hundred percent sure of the answer and he struggled to find the resolution.

"A young man comes home carrying a piping hot pizza for dinner on Thursday night. His mother is cooking for *Shabbos*. There is food on the stove, the oven door is open with food baking or cooking inside, pots and pans with raw ingredients or remnants are all over the counter and table and in the sink. The young man steps on a roller skate as he walks into the kitchen. He loses his balance and falls backward and the pizza flies up, the box opens and the pizza lands in pieces all over the table, oven, stove, counter and sink. What's the *halacha* regarding all of the dishes and foods?"

Yaakov stammered and he was unsure where he should go with this multi-faceted and complicated question. Hot foods, cold foods, wet foods, dry foods, dairy, meat, probably *parve*; cooked and raw foods were involved. Pots, pans, and utensils were in question and he probably had to take into consideration the amount of money enmeshed. There were so many issues to be taken into consideration. Suddenly he was scared and stumped, and he knew it. He froze and did not know what to say.

In order to buy time to formulate his thoughts, Yaakov said, "The first thing that comes to my mind is the welfare of the young man. I hope he's Okay." Yaakov then paused without a clear direction in which to go with the question, and the Rosh HaYeshiva recognized the delaying tactic of his young student. Yaakov was at a loss and struggling, concerned that he would be expelled from the *semicha* program.

The Rosh HaYeshiva immediately perceived weakness and honed in on the lack of assuredness.

Before Yaakov could even grasp the entire situation, the Rosh HaYeshiva threw another wrench at him.

The pressure was on.

"Your mother is cooking a meat casserole in her oven. It's in a closed dish. In the same oven is a pizza. The oven is set to 350 degrees and everything is hot. While taking the pizza out of the oven, it brushes against the closed casserole dish. Discuss the different issues involved."

Yaakov started to sweat under the pressure. All of a sudden, he noticed that it felt quite hot in the Rosh HaYeshiva's office. Yaakov wanted to take off his jacket, tie, and hat but knew it would not be a good idea or even appropriate. His mouth was dry and he could not wait until this ended. After more than half an hour of this additional intense pressure, the Rosh HaYeshiva dismissed Yaakov and told him to study the relevant material again, along with additional material assigned. More pressure. He still had to maintain his regular learning schedule in addition to the material he had to absorb for the *semicha* program.

Hesitantly, with unsure steps, Yaakov stood up and went to exit the Rosh HaYeshiva's office while remaining facing him. Out of respect, Yaakov did not turn his back on the Rosh HaYeshiva. Yaakov shuffled out of the office completely spent, while loosening his tie, exhausted and sweating. Yaakov found a chair immediately outside the office and sat down completely worn out from the *fahair*, grateful for whoever thought to put the chair there right when he needed it.

Suddenly, it dawned on Yaakov that this was the meaning behind the *fahair* chair and he no longer needed to ask someone for clarification. No wonder *semicha* from his Rosh HaYeshiva was such a rare and valuable commodity. It was something to be treasured, as it was difficult to earn; it was a daunting task he set for himself. Yaakov wondered if he would be able to achieve the level needed to attain such a precious award from Rabbi Horowitz.

# October 1981
## Jerusalem, Israel

The Rosh HaYeshiva taught that it is a great *mitzvah* to pick up the *mitzvahs* others leave behind or ignore, and that intrigued Yaakov Applebaum. The last *mitzvah* in the Torah is the writing of a Sefer Torah and is often neglected. Because of some of the events in his early life from not fitting into the clique and its attendant loneliness, he found himself interested in helping the underdog. *Mitzvahs* that were ignored, he felt, fell into that category. He decided to commission someone to write a Sefer Torah on his behalf.

Yaakov knew that this was going to be a major financial undertaking and was concerned that it might drain his resources. He thought that if he were to spread the payments out over time, he should be able to manage without difficulty. He really wanted to do this *mitzvah*. Yaakov asked around for information about different local *soferim* and hearing great reports of the quality of *Reb* Zev Weinblatts work, he asked the Rosh HaYeshiva who gladly gave a glowing approbation.

Before he commissioned *Reb* Weinblatt to write the Torah, Yaakov wanted to see the family first hand, so he invited himself for a *Shabbos* lunch. This was easily accomplished as Zev learned in the same *Yeshiva* and always invited men from the yeshiva for meals on *Shabbos*. Yaakov noticed that Zev *davened* with deep *kavanah* and learned diligently: this was important to Yaakov.

The Weinblatts were a sweet family who loved to host guests for *Shabbos* in their modest apartment. *Reb* Zev and his wife, Miriam, were big *ba'alei chessed*. They were all soft-spoken and gentle people, the epitome of a Torah family. *Reb* Zev was a skilled *sofer* who was extremely conscientious with what he did; his work was excellent and exquisite. He was deliberate when he wrote or made *tefillin* and *mezuzos* and his work was in high demand, but since he wrote slowly, everything took him an inordinate amount of time. This was great for his clients, as they loved his work; however, it was a problem for his growing family: he would never consider rushing these holy tasks. *Reb* Zev had three young children and one on the way, as a result, he needed an additional infusion of money. Zev and his wife Miriam figured they needed an additional one-thousand dollars per month to cover the mounting debt and feed their growing family.

After meeting the Weinblatts, Yaakov was impressed with them and their dedication to the Torah. He also wanted to count the Weinblatts as friends and Yaakov decided to engage Zev to write his Sefer Torah.

Nervously, Yaakov approached Zev in the *Yeshiva* one morning, "I would like to commission you to write a Sefer Torah for me. You come highly recommended by the Rosh HaYeshiva and others." He could not figure out why he was feeling apprehensive but at least some of this he attributed to the amount of money involved in this undertaking.

"Thank you so much," he replied humbly while lowering his eyes, "you do know that writing a Sefer Torah can be quite expensive." Weinblatt was appreciative of the forecasted income; however, he was honest and skeptical if this young man could afford what he was asking.

"I know. That won't be a problem."

"I'm not a fast writer. This will take time."

"I'm not in any rush. In fact, I am figuring that if it takes you two years, I can pay you one thousand dollars every month until I have paid for it. Does that work for you?"

Weinblatt was incredulous at the fortuitousness of the possible earnings. He was desperate for money and here was HaShem throwing in his lap a good solid commission for the exact amount he needed. "Sounds perfect."

Applebaum had some minor experience in business, he was not going to leave things open. "I want to put this in writing."

The two men wrote an agreement that was approved by the Rosh HaYeshiva. They signed and dated their agreement in front of two witnesses. In a little more than two years, Yaakov would be the proud owner of a brand new high-quality Sefer Torah. At the same time, Zev had a guarantee of *parnassah* for the next biennial.

# 1982

## February 1982
## Flatbush, New York

**Winter** in New York: people say if you do not like the weather, just wait a few minutes, it will change. Honestly, that is said about most places on our planet. As usual, at this time of year, the weather was fickle. It had just started to rain and the road was just beginning to become slick due to oil on the road interacting with the ice. If not careful, one could skid as if on a sheet of ice, so most motorists knew to slow down and be cautious. Yona Glick was an engineer and thought he knew better. He was driving up the Interboro Parkway East toward Queens. He had just gotten onto the Parkway when the vehicle in front of him lost control on the slick road. Glick neglected to take other drivers into consideration: no matter how good a driver he might be, he had no sway over other motorists. He also had no say over the condition of the roadway.

Most people who live in New York will attest that there are two types of people: those who have been in a car accident, and those who are **yet** to be in a car accident; it is just a matter of statistics. Sometimes the accident is just a small fender-bender that hardly warrants pulling the car over, except it is the law. Then there are the car accidents requiring the Jaws of Life and evacuation by helicopter. Yona's car accident was somewhere closer to the latter. It was a serious collision by any standards, one that could not have been avoided.

Yona was a cautious person in everything he did: he exercised often and was careful with what he ate. Born in 1948 and of average height and build, he was deliberate. He was a prudent driver, however, once the car in front of him hit a slick of oil and started to spin out there was nothing Yona could do. Thankfully, he was wearing his seatbelt or the accident could have been much worse. It was as if time slowed down for him and he saw the accident happen on a movie screen - in slow motion. Then everything went blank.

The next thing Yona knew, he was waking up with his wife, Devorah, looking down on him laying on a hospital gurney. He was disoriented and confused; it took him a while to focus or even become cognizant of the beeping sound he was hearing. It had been almost twenty-four hours since the accident, but he had no recollection of anything since driving on the Parkway. Except for the minor aches and pains throughout his body, he was not aware of anything at first; later realizing that this was probably due to the morphine drip. He was connected to a heart monitor and had a nasal cannula tube to aid his breathing.

He had a few broken bones, a fractured rib, some lacerations and a concussion - nothing too serious. Thankfully, the other driver was not badly hurt either and no one else was hurt in the accident. A few days of recovery in the hospital for both of them, and they would be fine. Yona would need some physical therapy to get back to normal. Both vehicles were totaled.

After Glick got out of the hospital, he went to see his doctor for some painkillers. The broken bones from the accident were bothering him along with the whiplash and his weakened lower back. He was not used to living in pain so his doctor prescribed the standard dose of Tylenol-3.

Devorah had longanimity and was sensitive to his needs, helping him in every way she could. She understood he was living in pain and would take some time to heal even after the casts were scheduled to come off in a few weeks' time. She had caring eyes and a gentle manner but did not know what it was like to live in constant pain.

Over time Devorah harbored doubts about her husband. Her pathos was sincere since she knew he was in pain, but she questioned if he was exaggerating or if it was authentic; maybe some of it was psychosomatic or just in his mind. However, his pain was real. She tried hard to be understanding of Yona and his pain, but sometimes it frustrated her. He saw the frustration on her face and hated the way it made her feel. It was a difficult time for the family.

Yona was faithfully taking his medicine and going to physical therapy. He was doing everything he could to help deal with the pain and lessened mobility since the accident. The problem with Tylenol-3 was that it put him to sleep day and night. He could not work; he could not help around the house; he could not assist with the children. Since Yona could not function, he returned to his doctor for something else, something stronger.

The doctor prescribed 5mg of oxycodone twice a day. This was not much better as it barely took the edge off the pain, and still made him drowsy and gave him constipation. He was afraid to drive because of his inability to concentrate, while his ineptitude on the job resulted in him getting laid-off making his depression even worse.

After about eight months, the pain had slowly increased as his body became used to the medicine. The efficacy of the drug had diminished and he was miserable.

He needed more medicine; he could not live like this and could not continue. He was in agony when he went back to the doctor for more medicine to lessen the pain. His physician doubled the dose.

He did not want to admit it, but Yona was addicted to the painkillers. Over the next several years, his doctor changed his medicine and dosage several times. He also tried Percocet and Vicodin but nothing helped. He needed more and the doctor was unwilling to give him more than the recommended dosages. Living in constant pain was making him angry and testy and he did not like that. His wife and children were taking the brunt of his bad moods and irritability caused by the pain.

Yona could not live with this pain and he had to do something: it was debilitating and exhausting and he could not function; he could not work. He was in a downward spiral with no way out. Surgery was not an option in his case and he feared it could leave him crippled. He needed more and stronger drugs than his physician was willing or able to prescribe. He had to find another resolution to his pain, and quickly.

Because his life was spinning out of control, and he needed to get out of pain, Yona decided to resort to illegal means. The first time was frightening: he recognized the unknowns and the risks: robbery, bad drugs, poor dosages, getting caught, to name just a few.

Right next to the cemetery on the corner of Fort Hamilton Parkway and Thirty-Seventh Street, Irwin Thatcher hung out and ran his drug business. The clandestine business was known to the police, but he was never caught since he never kept the drugs on his person, preferring to keep them in the trunk of a car or in the hollow of a tree just inside the cemetery. He was less likely to be arrested if he did not have any contraband on his person.

One late evening, Yona walked down Fort Hamilton Parkway looking for someone who fit the bill of his preconceived notion of a drug dealer. There were a few other men hanging back who Yona assumed were his bodyguards.

Nervously, like a shy dog with its tail between its legs, he approached a thin man who looked shady with low hanging pants. Before he had a chance to say anything, Irwin called out, "Are you lost?"

Yona looked over this strange man: he was lanky and had deep dark set and shifty eyes. Apprehensively, with a shaky voice, he said, "I need some painkillers." More than anything, he was afraid of the police, or even worse, getting beaten up

Irwin looked the interloper up and down. "This must be a cop," he thought to himself. "So what do you want from me, man? I'm not a doctor or pharmacy. Get lost!" his comrades laughed.

"Please help me. I need something for this constant pain."

"I don't know you."

"I have cash. I need something to help me. I need something to take away this pain." Yona was desperate and was grasping for any hope. This man was his only prospect, "You've got to help me."

Furtively, Irwin looked around and did not see anything amiss, no one who looked as though they were law enforcement or did not belong on his street corner. He decided to take a chance on this unexpected potential customer, "Okay, what you want?"

They had a brief conversation that concluded with a mutually beneficial exchange of cash and drugs. The arrangement became mutually advantageous for some time as he became a regular visitor to this particular part of town.

Yona continued to take the prescription from his doctor, which partially mitigated his complete dependence on illegal drugs. However, as he perpetually needed more than the medical practitioner prescribed, he often found himself on Fort Hamilton Parkway where Irwin became his secondary, although illegal, pharmacy. He also did some doctor-shopping to obtain more legal drugs for his pain. He was smart, making sure to use different pharmacies for the different medications, and did not submit most claims to his health insurance company, preferring to pay cash.

Devorah was an intelligent and perceptive woman; after a while, she realized what was happening. She was not angry with her husband but demanded he sought help. She understood his not wanting to, or willing to, live in pain and discomfort, but she also did not want to live in this fashion, with a drug addict as a husband. She did not want her children exposed to this way of life. She knew it was not his fault; the accident was just that, an accident. It was no one's fault that he got hurt but he needed to take responsibility for his subsequent actions.

At his wife's behest, Yona sought drug counseling, but he did not take it seriously. The drug counselor talked with him about understanding and overcoming the addiction while taking steps to overcome his destructive behavior. Yona needed to learn how to avoid his triggers and deal with the pain. He did not want to be influenced, he was not sure he even wanted to change.

As a result, much to the consternation of his wife, Yona continued his drug habit. She was angry with him for his behavior and for not taking her seriously.

A common refrain of hers was, "Which is more important to you, your children or the drugs?" or, "How can you look at your children and then do drugs?"

Finally, Devorah had enough and threatened him: either he went into a rehab facility and take it seriously, or he gave her a divorce. No more games or scheming, her endurance was at its limits and she put her foot down.

Yona finally capitulated and went into rehab. He also consulted with Charles Outterridge who was able to help him with some dietary suggestions to help with his addiction and pain.

Yona went into a facility for about three months to help him with his drug problem where he studied cognitive behavior therapy. He faithfully attended both the individual and group therapy sessions and learned how to avoid a relapse, his triggers, and to deal with his anger.

After he completed the program and graduated, he was released from the rehab facility. He returned to live with his family and slowly tried to rebuild his life and family.

All these efforts and ministrations helped for a few months, but he slowly returned to his old habits. He relapsed and went back on drugs for the pain.

Devorah had had enough. Her patience was stretched beyond its limits and she demanded a divorce. He complied, realizing it was better for his two children if their parents were to go their separate ways, amicably.

He arranged the divorce and *get* through Rabbi Starr. Yona moved out of their house and into a small studio apartment in Borough Park.

It was a difficult time for Yona and his broken family. It was particularly difficult for the children being without their father at home, and Yona felt alone without any support system. It was depressing just looking around his small studio apartment, at the bare walls, with nary any furniture.

After a while, Yona was fully back on the licit and illicit drugs and unable to function, and he lost his job. He started to spiral down again and this time he did not have his wife or any friends to help him. He was depressed and getting worse - he felt he had no reason to continue.

Since he lost his job, he could no longer pay rent for his small studio apartment. His landlord saw what was going on and felt bad for his tenant and gave him a break on the rent for a time.

Soon enough, Yona was in penury, living on the street, homeless and in constant pain. He was able to get some assistance from a homeless shelter so he did not have to always sleep on the street and was able to get something to eat. He was not too concerned about eating kosher food, as long as it was something in his stomach. He rationalized that it was a matter of life or death, so he ate what he could get. He was too embarrassed to go to Jews for help. He had no one and felt so alone.

# Purim 1982
## B'nei Braq, Israel

Purim can be either a time of tremendous personal spiritual growth or just base lewdness and being a drunk. It all depends on the person and their priorities. The Gemara says (Eiruvin 65a), "Wine goes in, secrets come out." When a person imbibes and becomes inebriated, their true personality comes to the fore.

Purim particularly draws this tendency out: many become highly inebriated. Some will show their lofty side, while most will make complete fools of themselves and act inappropriately.

Yaakov Applebaum was on a mission to grow spiritually and become close to those who were able to help him achieve and develop the lofty goal of spiritual growth. He felt that *HaRav* Baruch Mishovsky was one such person. Yaakov heard wonderful stories about the Purim *seudah* and festivities at the *mekubal's* place and he wanted to experience spiritual emprise.

Yaakov went to *Rav* Mishovsky's humble apartment in Shikun Hay, Bnei Braq. It was already packed with men eager to see his angelic face and hear words of Torah from his holy mouth. The *Rebbi* sat humbly at the head of the table conducting the Purim meal as a conductor would his orchestra. The shine on his face was radiant and he looked regal while the words of Torah and *zemiros* flowed like water. Other great rabbis also came to soak up the spirituality of Rabbi Mishovsky. There was plenty of food and drink, of which, the *Rav* partook none. It was almost as if the *Rav* sustained his body by filling it with Torah.

"We say the *kriyas shema* thrice daily. It's the affirmation of our faith in the One above. It is the last thing we say before retiring for the night. It is the last thing we say before we return our souls to our Maker. We say the first *passuk* on many occasions, including *Shabbos* and *Yom Kippur*. Obviously, there is more here than just what plainly meets the eyes. When we say the *kriyas shema*, it needs to be said with the utmost *kavana* and we need to understand completely what we are saying.

"The word *shema* stands for שאו מרום עיניכם, lift up your eyes to Heaven. Why is that? What is the point? It is obvious that we have to raise our eyes up to Heaven to see and acknowledge the One who created everything. However, why is it part of the *shema* when we are extolled so? There are other places where, due to humility, we are advised not to lift our eyes. There seems to be something else going on here.

"The Vilna Gaon in Likutai Hagera says that the *shema* is representative of all the *karbonos,* offerings. In order, they are as follows: שלמים, מנחה, עולה, אשם, חטאת, ד' מינין דתודה. *Shelamim* (peace), *mincha* (meal), *olah* (elevation), *asham* (guilt), *chatas* (sin) and the four categories of the *todah* (thanksgiving). The *chachamim,* rabbis of yore, told us that in place of the offerings, we have our prayers.

"Parenthetically, many people call them 'sacrifices', however, a better translation would be 'offerings'. When we bring the *karbonos,* we are not sacrificing anything. Sacrificing implies giving up something of ourselves for nothing in return. The *karbanos* are not that. When we bring the *karbanos* in the Bais HaMikdash, we are not giving up anything. We are offering of ourselves to our Maker, to become closer to HaShem, hence the work *karban* literally means 'to bring close'. In this respect, we are actually gaining and not losing anything at all. This would be a better translation.

"Returning to our subject, now we can understand a bit better what this means. When we say the *shema*, in addition to everything else, we are also mentioning the offerings. By doing so, we are in essence bringing the offerings on the holy altar. We should do so with proper *kavanah* and intent. By having the proper thoughts, we are elevating our *karbanos* to a much higher spiritual level on the holy altar in the Bais HaMikdash, may it be rebuilt speedily in our days."

Everyone answered Amen.

After a short period, the *Rav* had something else to say.

"The question has been posed: why is it that the fourth finger is also known as your ring finger? Most women will put their engagement and wedding rings on their fourth finger. Some men too wear wedding bands; they also wear those rings on their fourth finger.

"The fingers of your hands represent different people in your family. Your thumbs represent your parents; your index fingers represent your siblings; your middle fingers represent you; your fourth fingers represent your spouse and your pinkies represent your children.

"When we bind the *tefillin*, it's the middle finger that gets all the attention. In all customs, the straps wrap the middle finger three times. There are more pressure points in the middle finger than any other finger. The middle finger is a small cataclysm of us; it represents us.

"Try this..." The *Rav* demonstrated and continued, "Put the heels of your palms together. Next, bend the middle finger of both hands and put them together, knuckle to knuckle. Now put the other fingertips together with the matching fingertips. The folded middle finger is us.

"The thumbs, which represent your parents, are easily separated. This is because you are eventually going to leave and be separated from your parents.

"The index fingers, which represent your siblings, are also easily separated for the same reason.

"The pinkies, which represent your children, also separate fairly easily as your children will move on.

"Your ring fingers, which represent your spouse, cannot be separated. This is to teach you that you are one with your spouse and cannot be separated. Divorce should not be an option - not my people."

Other rabbis spoke just as eloquently as did Rabbi Mishovsky. There were always people talking in Torah near the *Rav*. It was a beautiful and inspirational Purim.

After several hours spent in the presence of the *Rebbi*, Yaakov left feeling inspired and uplifted. "I want to do whatever I can to become close to the *Rebbi*," he thought to himself. He made efforts to visit the great rabbi as often as possible.

Rabbi Mishovsky was an atypical man: he was humble and

treated everyone as if they were better than he. He was tall and thin with sparkling blue eyes and the proverbial broad shoulders to help ease the burden of anyone who came to him. With everything he did, the Rabbi tried to emulate his mentor the Klausenberger *Rebbi* and to honor his holy martyred parents.

One of the most unusual characteristics of Rabbi Mishovsky was that he rarely gave a "yes" or "no" answer to a petitioner. He was reticent and usually talked in cryptic messages; most often just quoting an obscure *passuk* from somewhere in TaNaCh. He was short with his words, but every syllable was weighed carefully.

Rabbi Mishovsky's door was always open: he was available twenty-four hours a day, seven days a week. If someone was in need, Jewish or gentile, it did not matter. All were welcome to bring their questions and petitions, and everyone left with a warm smile and knowing that someone loved them dearly and unconditionally. The *Rebbi* never took any money; however, if someone wanted to donate to his *bais medrash*, he did not reject the offer.

After this Purim experience, Yaakov returned on many occasions and became a regular visitor to the humble home and *bais medrash* of Rabbi Mishovsky. It was a small building with his home being three small rooms in the back for the family and the front being the *bais medrash*. The *bais medrash* itself was a plain room with no airs or ornamentation. The *Rav* would explain, "The Kabalah says that a place for davening should be plain and simple to carry the *tefilahs* on High, and where one can *daven* without distractions."

Yaakov would sit in the great rabbi's *bais medrash* to learn; there was an almost surreal aura that was filled with holiness. It was discernible as soon as one entered the *bais medrash*; it might have had something to do with the *Rav* restricting frivolous conversation: only words of Torah and *davening* were permitted in his *bais medrash*. Yaakov was able to learn on several levels. Of course, he was able to study Gemara or any other subject he desired. He was also able to learn diligence in Torah study just by watching the rabbi. There were always *sefarim* in his hands or next to him and he was constantly perusing them. However, it seemed to Yaakov that he was just glancing in the holy works to confirm what he already knew was written.

On a few occasions, Yaakov had a question about what he was studying, which he would bring to the *Rav*. It did not matter if it was an obscure Ketzos or Meiri. The *Rav* seemed to have it all at his fingertips and was easily and succinctly able to answer Yaakov's questions. The *Rav* was pleased with the young man.

In a city like Bnei Braq, few people could afford air

conditioners and even fewer actually had them. *Rav* Mishovsky was no different, and invariably, the windows were open to let in the fresh air. As is known to happen with open windows, bugs entered. Yaakov noticed that there were never any bugs within about six feet or so of the great man.

Rabbi Mishovsky came from a *chasidic* dynasty of which he remembered nothing. The Nazis murdered the vast majority of his family when he was just a young child. However, the Klausenberger Rabbi made sure he was aware of his holy and illustrious lineage. Rabbi Mishovsky knew about his parents and grandparents. He wanted to emulate them and please them in Heaven. Every Friday night, Rabbi Mishovsky held a *tish*, which were times of spiritual growth and heady words of Torah. They met all the desires Yaakov had to help him become a greater *ben* Torah.

# June 1982
## Borough Park, New York

Rivkah Somers was serious about growing in Torah and the service of HaShem, as it was the most important thing in the world to her. Her long-term goal in life was to serve HaShem with every facet of her being, so Israel was where she wanted to study. Thus, she went to study in a top-notch women's seminary in Jerusalem. Shlomit Women's Seminary was considered one of the best women's seminaries in the world and Rivkah was up for the challenge. She quickly advanced and became one of the top students in the seminary.

Her close friend, Emily Archer stayed in America and continued her computer learning and programming. As much as her friend was growing in Torah, she was growing in computer knowledge. Emily kept up a correspondence with Rivkah to keep her abreast of programming updates and news. At the same time, Rivkah made sure to enclose words of Torah in each letter to Emily. Emily proceeded to learn Lotus1-2-3, and she kept up her Torah studies. This was important to her, but computers were her calling.

She upgraded her computer with the latest Intel 80286 chip and bought the new Sony Trinitron monitor.

Emily also learned FORTRAN, COBOL, and Multiplan for Apple. She was learning everything she could about computers and programming.

WordPerfect released their word processing program

WordPerfect 1.0 and she devoured that too.

One of the reasons that Emily threw herself completely into her computer studies was because she felt lonely.

EMILY'S FATHER, RICHARD ARCHER, GRADUATED from Yale Law School in New Haven, Connecticut, in 1963 with high honors at the age of twenty-six. He became a highly sought after lawyer and advanced rapidly. A fit five-foot-ten-inches tall and broad-shouldered Richard posed an impressive figure. He quickly obtained a job at one of the largest and most prestigious law firms in Manhattan. They occupied the top fifteen floors of a large office building and had a few satellite offices in other boroughs. The firm handled all forms of legal cases and Richard worked in every department to become well rounded in all genres of legal cases.

While in college, he met Susan Silverstein who was a fellow student in several of his classes. She was a great student, but she needed a bit of help so Richard started tutoring her. They started spending quite a bit of time together in and out of the classroom. Eventually, they began a romantic relationship and married during their junior year. She graduated in 1964 and immediately landed a great job with a high-power Manhattan law firm. They bought a nice home in an up and coming neighborhood in Glendale, Queens. Many upper-class families were moving into the area. Theirs was a red brick three-story home with a nice front and back yard. Over time, they furnished it nicely and in good taste.

Richard was a cigar aficionado. He had several humidors, cutters, and punches, and when he was feeling adventurous, he would even roll his own cigars or stogies. He would never light his cigar from a butane lighter but would use a long match to avoid contaminating the flavor of the cigar with the butane.

Richard only smoked in his home study or on the back porch. Susan was not enthusiastic about the smell of the cigars, but it was his one vice, so she ignored it as long as he restricted his smoking to his designated areas. Sometimes he felt as if he were in exile, but if it pleased his wife, he was willing to endure the banishment.

Together Richard and Susan begat two beautiful children: Emily was born in 1964 and Bob in 1966. They were both good children; although Bob was a bit of a rebel, they both developed an aversion to the smell of cigars. Although Richard was not home much due to his work, he did try to spend quality time with his children and be available to them. Richard tended to be gentle but firm with his children, making sure they were well behaved and followed the rules set up in the house.

The couple worked for different law firms; however, that was never a problem. She worked for a corporate law firm and he did mostly criminal law.

In 1977, when Richard was only forty, he was appointed to the bench of the Circuit Court of Manhattan. His salary increased commensurately. In 1982, he was appointed to the Federal criminal court system as an Article III Judge. He was one of the youngest ever appointed to such a prestigious position. The family purchased and moved to a beautiful piece of property in East Islip just off the Bay in Long Island. They had almost an acre of land and a large sprawling home with manicured front and back lawns.

Because both parents worked so many hours, they were rarely home and the children became latchkey kids spending a significant amount of time home alone. From a young age, they learned to fend for themselves after school and they became independent. Every day the children came home, had a snack and did their homework. If time and weather permitted, they would go for a bike ride or a similar outdoor activity. Although different from one another, they were close. Due to loneliness from her absentee parents, Emily threw all her energies into her studies.

Because Bob was feeling abandoned by his parents who were always at work, he developed obsessive-compulsive disorder to compensate. He ended up in psychotherapy and using medication to help deal with the symptoms. Lithium was the antidepressant of choice, but he did not like the side effects of the medication.

Over the course of time, Richard and Susan slowly grew apart and when their children were still young teens, the couple amicably divorced but remained friends. Richard moved to Flatbush with his daughter, while Susan remained behind on Long Island with her son and resumed using her maiden name.

Later, after her friend, Rivkah, went off to Israel to study in Shlomit Women's Seminary, Emily missed her friend and felt lonely without companionship. She contemplated joining Rivkah in Israel, but that was not what she wanted for her life. Emily wanted to remain in America and continue teaching computers. Instead of making *aliyah*, she decided to get a pet.

She decided against a dog or cat for practical and emotional reasons and instead decided to adopt a rabbit.

Rabbits are social animals and the right breed would perfectly meet her needs. If necessary, she would also be able to leave a rabbit alone for a day or two.

She went to a rabbit rescue in Brooklyn and found a young Flemish Giant rabbit. The doe would grow quite large to about forty-five pounds, she was friendly and craved human contact. She took the rabbit home and named her Bessie.

A few years prior, Richard Archer added a second story to his garage and converted the second story into an apartment. Emily was living there giving her proximity to her father but also affording her some privacy. This way she was also able to avoid the cigar smell.

Bessie was not going to be confined to a pen or a hutch. The rabbit instead had the run of Emily's apartment and with little effort, she was litter box trained. Bessie had a great personality and regularly started grooming Emily by licking her. When Emily was studying, Bessie would come over and lie all stretched out, next to her. They loved each other. Emily was happy with her decision to get a pet, especially a rabbit. She enjoyed spending time with Bessie and Bessie was always excited to see Emily when she returned from teaching or errands.

BERT SOBOL WAS SITTING IN Glatt Chow Restaurant enjoying a pleasant dinner, delighting in both the ambiance and his meal. Due to his martial arts training, his favorite seat was with his back against the wall to remain aware of all who entered.

Bert was unable to earn a living doing karate, but it was his passion and he excelled at it. He was good with his hands and loved working on cars and their engines, so he opened an automotive mechanic shop in Borough Park, not far from Glatt Chow Restaurant. He was well aware of the stereotypical mechanic who always found problems with cars and gouged their clients. He was different and treated all his customers fairly and honestly and his shop became busy and successful. In part, this was because, with any dealings with active or retired military personnel, he would only charge fifty-percent of his labor charge. It was his way of thanking military individuals for their service.

At the restaurant, Laura Feld was his server and she was dedicated to her customers. She handed Bert a menu and said, "Hi, I'm Laura and I'll be back shortly to take your order."

Laura was a *quidnunc*, always interested in the latest gossip and news. Working at Glatt Chow, she was able to satisfy that need. She knew that it was not right, but she had a difficult time resisting the temptation.

Glatt Chow was a nice kosher restaurant on Thirteenth Avenue in Borough Park, Brooklyn, where the ambiance was perfectly enhanced by the décor: there were nice paintings on the walls; the lights were dimmed; soft music played subtly in the background. Bert, as did many people, liked the restaurant which he patronized regularly.

One day, while Bert was enjoying a delicious dinner at Glatt Chow, two men walked into the restaurant. Bert noticed them and immediately the hairs on the back of his neck stood up; suddenly he was on high alert. His senses were honed from more than a decade of intensive martial arts training. He looked closely at the two men and realized there was a telltale bulge in the small of each of their backs. The convexities were too small for guns, but they could easily be knives. Just as these thoughts were flittering through his mind, the men brought their knives out and brandished the glinting steel at the manager, demanding money.

Stealthily, Bert quickly approached them from behind and raised his hands in order to smash their heads together. One of the interlopers heard someone coming and he turned to protect himself.

In the blink of an eye, Bert repositioned himself into a right neutral bow. He redirected his right hand around the back of the offender's head to bring his head forward to meet Bert's forward-moving left elbow. This completely disoriented the first man.

Simultaneously, Bert took his left knee, brought it up, and forward into the small of the second man's back. He made contact with the man's kidney, forcing the man's stomach forward and head back. Bert turned to his right and repositioned into a left neutral bow, cocking his right hand by his waist, and brought his left elbow down hard breaking the second man's nose. The man went down to the floor begging for mercy.

Bert turned to the first man and with his right hand, delivered a heel-palm to his chest, causing him to bend backward. Bert took advantage of this and delivered a right foot sword chop to the man's left knee, shattering the knee. The intruder was in no condition to put up any resistance.

The whole fight lasted just a few seconds and except for a bit of scuffling noises and grunts from the intruders, most of the patrons did not notice anything until it was over. However, the manager and Laura observed everything and could not believe what they saw, or more accurately, did not see. They were about to be robbed and this patron became a Good Samaritan and protected them. They had never seen anyone move with such proficiency and force and were incredulous and appreciative.

Not that he had to, but Bert made a citizen's arrest of the two incapacitated criminals and waited for the police. Officers Liam Conners and Peter Jackson arrived on the scene put the would-be criminals in handcuffs and read them their Miranda rights. They took statements from those in the restaurant and took possession of the weapons as evidence. The police were not used to arriving at an armed burglary crime scene with the perpetrators already in custody and with no one else injured. They were thankful to Bert for the quick and decisive capture of the would-be robbers.

As a show of gratitude, the manager of Glatt Chow, Menashe Mendelssohn, said that from then on, Bert's meals were vouchsafed by the restaurant.

The adrenalin coursing through his body felt good: he liked the rush of helping people and that feeling went to his head. This could be the culmination of all those years of martial arts training. Maybe this would be his calling and he had the skill and ability to make it happen. Glatt Chow restaurant was where Bert Sobol started his vigilante work.

# August 2, 1982
## Jerusalem, Israel

It was a beautiful Friday just after the fast of the Ninth of Av: the weather was perfect. Many people love to go to the Kossel before *Shabbos* to prepare themselves for the holy day. It is spiritually uplifting and inspirational to d*aven mincha gedolah* at the Kossel and then prepare for *Shabbos*. After *davening mincha,* some men sing Shir HaShirim before leaving the Kossel.

Yaakov Applebaum loved to go to the holiest place in the world, in preparation to greet the *Shabbos* Queen. For Yaakov, this was a highly spiritual experience that filled him with ardor. The first time he saw the Kossel was emotional: he broke down and cried. He approached the Wall with awe and did something not many people do; Yaakov tore his shirt in mourning. Every subsequent time, he approached the Kossel with trepidation and could not understand how some people joked around and ran about in front of the Kossel. It is a holy place: the Holy Shechinah is there and it is a place deserving reverence, not frivolity. It did not matter how many times he went to the Kossel; it was always a special occasion to him. If he did not go to the Kossel on a particular Friday, he felt a significant lacking in his *Shabbos*.

Yaakov had a distinguished appearance in his black suit, white shirt, dark tie, and black hat. He was dressed as a typical *Yeshiva* student.

He had a spiritually uplifting time *davening mincha* at the Kossel, and afterward, he sat down to say some Tehillim for a bit.

The timeless words of King David always soothe the soul. Yaakov always felt more relaxed going into *Shabbos* having sung Shir HaShirim, as he was wont to do, close to *Shabbos*. He resolved always to try to take the last half hour before candle lighting to sing Shir HaShirim. He knew it would mean he would have to take on extra responsibilities in the home once he would get married, but that was Okay. He liked the idea, especially if his wife would join him.

As Yaakov was leaving the immediate area of the Kossel, a man approached him. The stranger was nondescript and could have passed for any well-dressed tourist, wearing a jacket and a button-down shirt. Obviously absent was a *yarmulke* and he seemed a bit out of place.

"Would you be interested in exploring the love of Jesus Christ?" the stranger asked. It seemed, this stranger was a Christian missionary who was intent on proselytizing a *Yeshiva* student. The situation was so strange it was laughable. It was idiotic that this man would want to try to convert a *Yeshiva* man to Christianity before the Kossel.

At first, Yaakov was taken aback. "What is this man thinking, if anything?" he thought to himself. He could not believe what he had just been asked. "Have the Jews not been persecuted enough throughout the millennia with Christians trying to forcibly or coercively convert them?" Then he had another thought, "Maybe I can have a bit of fun and teach this man a lesson at the same time."

"Actually," Yaakov said aloud, "I just have one question. Maybe you can help me."

"Sure. What do you want to know?" the stranger asked.

Yaakov said, "It says in your bible, 'Ask and it will be given to you; seek and you will find; knock and the door will be opened to you.' What does all that mean?"

The missionary thought to himself, "This is going to be easy." Aloud he responded, "That is a verse from Matthew 7:7. Encapsulated, it means that we are a religion of love. We happily share what we have and gladly give to others. When someone asks something of us, we gladly and happily give it over. It shows us that all is in the hands of God." The stranger was smiling. He was happy to be able to answer Yaakov so easily. It was a simple question with an easy answer.

"Wow!" said Yaakov. "That is beautiful. You mean to tell me that if someone asks you for anything, you will give it over to them?"

"Sure." He said, happy this lesson was going so well. He was confident this man was going to be easy picking.

With a straight face and in a deadpan voice, Yaakov said,

"Your wallet," as he proffered his hand to accept the gift of a wallet.

It was at this point when the so-called ecclesiastic realized he had been caught in a carefully laid trap. He knew he would have to give up his wallet, but he would hope for the kindness of this smart man who had just fooled him and would thus return his wallet.

Reluctantly, with a frown, he handed over his wallet. Before the man could even think of a response, Yaakov put the wallet in his pocket and quickly said, "Supplemental income. Your jacket," as he again stretched out his arm to accept the forthcoming gift.

"Wait a minute..."

With a disarming smile, the young *Yeshiva* student interrupted, "You are trying to teach your religion. A teacher must follow up on his words. Your actions have to follow your words or your words are meaningless."

Unwillingly, shaking his head in desperation, he removed his jacket and handed it to Yaakov. Yaakov draped the jacket over his arm and said, "Supplemental wardrobe. Your shirt," as he again reached out his arm to accept the bestowal.

This was all going too fast for the stranger; he had to slow the pace. He could not think. He knew he had fallen into a quagmire and that this quick-thinking Jewish student had bested him, but what was he going to do?

"There is no way I am going to give you my shirt!" He exclaimed emphatically.

"You just told me that you represent a religion of love. Your religion requires you to give up something requested of you. I want your shirt. You are trying to proselytize to me. You can't be a hypocrite. You have to live up to your own words. Give me your shirt!" Yaakov demanded decisively.

With great distress and reluctance, realizing he had lost, he unbuttoned and removed his shirt and handed it to Yaakov.

"Thank you, have a nice day," Yaakov said and turned to walk away laughing to himself.

"Wait a minute," the shirtless missionary called after him.

"Yes?" Yaakov asked with an innocent expression and smile.

"I thought you were interested," he said trying to salvage what little dignity and self-respect he had left.

"I never said I was interested. I never even gave that impression. I just had one question, which you answered so well," he said, his voice dripping with sarcasm.

"So why did you take my wallet, jacket, and shirt?"

"Because, perhaps, maybe now you will stick to people of your own religion and stop bothering my brethren. We've suffered enough for two thousand years of people trying to convert us to your religion. Maybe this will teach you a lesson; enough already."

"Give me back my stuff," he demanded.

"You gave these items to me of your own volition. They now belong to me." Yaakov turned and walked away leaving a discombobulated missionary standing there with his mouth agape. He wanted to run and hide and was so angry, he was practically crying.

As he was walking away, Yaakov Applebaum turned around just in time to see the missionary being arrested for indecent exposure in front of the Kossel.

When Yaakov returned to the *Yeshiva*, he gave the property to the Rosh HaYeshiva and told him the story. The Rosh HaYeshiva gave a hearty laugh, "That was wonderful!" he said with a smile as he clapped his hands. "Maybe it will teach that one man. Too bad it won't stop the rest of them."

# August 2, 1982
## Jerusalem, Israel

It was a Friday in the early afternoon and the sky was azure with only a few wispy clouds to break up the blueness. Mohamed abu Sharif was not used to the hustle and bustle of Orthodox Jews getting ready for *Shabbos*. Jerusalem was not what he expected. He was not sure what he should have expected, as he was from a small backward town while this was a thriving metropolis with all the modern conveniences.

Several days before, Mohamed took a flight from South America to France, where he stopped over for a few days to get his mind ready for his mission of going undercover as a Jew. He was excited but scared knowing Israelis were ruthless and if he were found out, they would show no mercy and would torture and kill him; at least that was what was going through his mind. He would have to watch his every step as he had a vital mission to accomplish. He checked his forged passport repeatedly and kept reviewing his new name, Moshe Sharf: he must not forget his new identity.

Once he arrived in Lod airport on Thursday morning, he was well on his way to infiltrating the Jewish world and there was no turning back. He passed through customs with nary a glance, which surprised him, and when he stepped out of the airport, the dry heat of Tel Aviv hit him like a sandstorm, reminding him of home. When he heard Hebrew for the first time, it sounded like *galimatias*. He took a taxi to Jerusalem where, near the Central Bus Station, he found a hostel to stay in overnight. He wanted to travel light so he did not have much in the way of luggage. Mohamed/Moshe was not used to the clamor and commotion of Jerusalem: people were running around at what he considered a frenzied pace, horns on vehicles were announcing the anxiousness of their drivers, and vendors were vociferously hawking their wares to passersby. He was used to his backward town, but this was a modern thriving city and it scared and confused him. He was overwhelmed by the frenetic activity and cacophony of sounds all around him. He walked around for a bit, bought a falafel, watched the people, was amazed at the varied cars and busses, and finally returned to the hostel and retired for the night.

With everything he had just witnessed, he was having second and even third thoughts about his mission. He was unsure if he could succeed without getting himself killed.

MOHAMED WAS SCARED AND RUNNING for his life. He was panting heavily while running down a dark alley; someone was chasing him and yelling something unintelligible from behind. As he was running, he quickly glanced around and did not recognize his surroundings. Mohamed was lost and did not know where he was or how he got there. He was not used to this much exertion and was perspiring profusely.

He was running at full tilt and was short of breath. He was barely able to call out to his pursuer, "What do you want from me?"

His nemesis shrieked to him, but again, he could not discern the balderdash being spewed in his direction, but somehow it seemed a bit softer than before.

He did not understand what was going on, why he was being chased and harangued, where he was or from whom he was running. He stumbled and found himself sprawled face down in a puddle in the alley. He was now in pain from the scrapes and bruises sustained from the spill. His clothing was torn, he was dirty, wet and bleeding. He did not understand how he was bleeding so much with such small abrasions.

He turned over and suddenly saw an ogre standing over him and taunting him. The pursuer was larger than life and appeared to be a behemoth ready to attack him. Suddenly the apparition changed to a wisp of smoke and then appeared to be his mother. He called out in tears, "*'Um*?" (Mother)

He heard what sounded like someone calling his name, but it was not his name. "Moshe, Moshe." Mohamed was startled.

The apparition pointed her finger at the frightened man on the ground, opened her mouth to speak, but her mouth grew larger and larger until it engulfed him. Suddenly he felt trapped, immured inside an enclosure from which he could not find an exit. He started flailing his arms and screaming for his mother.

Suddenly, there was a pounding coming from far away. From the back recesses of his mind, he heard someone calling and did not understand what was happening. While he was thrashing around, his arm encountered something and he heard a loud crash.

Abruptly, with a flash, he sat up and realized that he was in bed in the hostel. It was all a nightmare, a horrible and vivid hallucination. He was breathing heavily and shaking like a leaf. His pillow and bed sheet were soaked with his sweat. His nightmare unnerved him and some doubts about his success in the mission started to creep into his mind.

In the morning, he took a long shower enjoying the luxury of hot water cascading over his body. As he left the hostel, he started the next phase of his adventure: he was scared and excited at the same time. Despite his fatigue, he considered himself a soldier on a mission.

He took the Number One bus and was dropped off just inside the wall of the Old City. There were so many people milling about, but he was easily able to maneuver himself to the Western Wall. As he walked through the courtyard leading up to the plaza itself, Moshe Sharf passed several security officers arresting a shirtless man who was pointing at a young man who looked like a rabbinic student who was walking away. The man being arrested was saying that the young man took his jacket, shirt, and wallet.

Ignoring the unquiet, and wanting to avoid an encounter with the police, Moshe stepped into the plaza of the Kossel and was amazed by what he saw: wads of paper tucked into the crevices in the stones of the Wall were defying gravity; birds were soaring above like messengers taking the prayers on High; shrubberies were growing above adding a bit of green to the spectrum. There were men of all stripes and modalities of dress standing silently in front of this ancient Wall. A man over there was crying silently. Another man was swaying back and forth. A third man was sitting in a chair and reading something quietly with his lips. There was a separate section for the women where the entire scene was repeating itself.

"Moshe Sharf", he kept repeating to himself his newly adopted name, was in a world of his own while observing what the goings-on around him. He was caught off guard when there was a gentle tap on his shoulder. Surprised out of his reverie, he turned to face someone who he assumed to be a rabbi. This man had the most gentle features and eyes he had ever seen that seemed to look right through to his soul.

"Do you have a place for Friday night *Shabbos* dinner?" The stranger asked thinking Moshe was Jewish.

Befuddled, Moshe said, "Um, no - no, I don't." He was not even sure what he was being asked.

Handing Moshe his card, he said, "Show up tonight at this address about 7:30 and you will join me and my family."

Before he knew what happened, Moshe had taken the proffered card and the stranger was off in search of his next guest. Moshe did not know it then, but he had just been, "Picked-up." He was exactly where he wanted to be - on his way to learning how to act as an orthodox Jew. The card said…

Mayer Sherman
63 Arzay Abira Street
Jerusalem, Israel
02-879-885

He joined the stranger, Rabbi Mayer Sherman, for Friday night dinner. There were many other guests and the food and company were enjoyable. There was plenty of delectable food and it all looked and smelled wonderful. The host family was open and warm to all their guests with young children running amok. There was singing in a strange tongue and the different guests spoke many languages. Moshe was completely overwhelmed with the goings-on and received much enjoyment from the company, but this was his first step. In due course, he would learn to understand what was happening and incorporate it into his act.

Moshe observed the simple surroundings of the Sherman apartment. The living room and dining room were combined and the center of attraction was the large dining room table surrounded by guests. The walls were covered with bookcases that were overstuffed with books and tomes of all sizes most of which were well used. Moshe was amazed, never having seen such an extensive library in his life. There was virtually no other furniture, save a pile of mattresses in one corner, presumably, for the children or guests.

One of the guests at the Sherman *Shabbos* dinner was memorable in his appearance; Moshe would never forget him. Mordechai Samuel was unusually tall, had clear blue eyes and a shock of red hair. He talked with a slight lisp and was well dressed. Moshe was intrigued by this ginger-haired man.

Over the next week, Moshe returned several times and spent some time with Rabbi Sherman and his family. He expressed an interest in his "Jewish heritage." Rabbi Sherman was excited with the interest Moshe was expressing in Judaism and recommended a decent starter *Yeshiva* for Moshe.

The following week, Moshe ended up in a *Yeshiva* for Jewish returnees, learning what he needed in order to mingle comfortably with those he would be infiltrating in order to carry out his nefarious acts of savagery. However, every time he recalled his recent nightmare, he wondered what his mother might have been trying to communicate with him. Whenever he thought about that night, it sent shivers down his spine.

He made sure to follow the rules and go to all of the *Yeshiva* events and functions. He *davened* with the *Yeshiva* thrice daily and attended every class on his roster. He started keeping *Shabbos*. He was used to celebrating his holy day on Friday, but he could change it by one day: it made no difference to him. He liked keeping kosher, as the food in the *Yeshiva* was quite good. The food was better than he was used to in the squalor in which he used to live and in most respects in line with the halal foods he was accustomed to eating.

Over the course of time, he developed feelings for his distant cousins and realized they were good people who treated everyone with respect. These were not the savages he was raised to believe; they were normal and decent people. He often wondered to himself why his people hated Jews so much. He also saw firsthand that Saddam Hussein was correct; none of them had horns on their heads.

In the back of his mind, he was starting to have second thoughts about the attacks they were planning. What else had he been lied to about the Jewish people?


# August 2, 1982
## Jerusalem, Israel

Rivkah Somers took some time to study in Israel and attended a top seminary in Jerusalem, Shlomit Women's Seminary, where she grew in leaps and bounds. Her favorite teacher was Mrs. Weinblatt.

She kept in touch with her good friend Emily Archer about the latest developments in the computer world. No one around her had a computer, but she devoured every letter from her friend.

Rivkah enjoyed going to the Kossel on Fridays; it was an

uplifting experience for her. She would *daven* and then say some Tehillim in preparation for *Shabbos*.

As Rivkah was leaving the Western Wall Plaza one Friday, she noticed a shirtless man being arrested for indecent exposure. The shirtless man was pointing to a retreating *Yeshiva bachur* saying that the young man took his jacket, shirt, and wallet.

She thought it strange and was curious to know what happened to his shirt, but she kept walking. She had much more important things to accomplish; she had to get ready for *Shabbos*.

One of her teachers in Shlomit Women's Seminary lived in Bayit Vegan near Shaare Zedek Hospital in a beautiful area. Rivkah was going to visit Mrs. Weinblatt for *Shabbos* and wanted to buy a cake for the family. Leaving the Old City, she headed north into Meah Shearim to purchase some confections and then caught a bus going west to Bayit Vegan.

She all but forgot the strange occurrence earlier in the day.

# August 2, 1982
## Jerusalem, Israel

Things were going well for Mordechai Samuel: his investments were keeping him busy, and he lived the high life. He knew that his looks helped him in his contrivances and he fully used that to his advantage. He was six-foot-four-inches tall and struck an imposing figure in a fancy suit. Most people were smitten by him and that enabled him to do what he did best.

Despite his lisp, Mordechai also had a glib tongue, which helped convince people to join in his investments. Most of the money he received, he would use to pay off earlier investors; the remainder would be used to pay for his extravagant lifestyle and excursions or trips. Given these circumstances and his wealth, he was able to afford a trip to Israel.

While he was in Jerusalem for a few weeks, he went to visit his friends on Arzay Abira Street and see if he would yet be able to convince them to join in his ploy. The two problems he encountered were they did not discuss business on *Shabbos* and they did not have much in the way of money to invest. Actually, they barely eked out a living and had no money to invest with Mordechai. All their money was invested in their precious *mitzvah* of *hachnasas orchim*, inviting guests.

Mordechai prayed at the Kossel with Rabbi Sherman before

joining him for the Friday night meal. Just before *Kiddush*, in walked a man who could have passed as a light-skinned Arab, who, if he did not know better, Mordechai would not have thought of him as Jewish. However, Rabbi Sherman would not have invited the man if he were not a member of the Tribe. He had to be a recent returnee to the fold. Clearly, by his actions and speech, he did not know even the basics of Judaism.

# August 1982
## US/Mexican border

Adolf Leipzig helped arrange transportation for Ahmed who was itching to start his escapades. He would have to spend a significant amount of time and money on the planning of the infrastructure for his terrorist attacks. For the first time in his life, Ahmed felt excited about his destiny. He had goals and a clear direction for the foreseeable future.

Ahmed entered the United States through the porous Mexican border. For most people entering the United States illegally across the southern border, the trip was perilous and could take several months. Many who attempted the journey, did not survive the trip. The arduous and protracted trip was fraught with people suffering and even succumbing to thirst, hunger, and attacks by wild animals. *Coyotes* charged exorbitant fees and often just robbed the wretched and miserable people leaving them for dead. It was treacherous, dangerous and often ill-fated. Most of the people seeking succor and safety by fleeing to the United States were frightened to take this trip.

Ahmed's *coyote* snuck him across the border into Laredo, Texas. He did not have most of the concerns or fears of the majority of illegal immigrants: he had money and papers. His papers were forged, but they were more than most of his fellow travelers had.

Without much effort, Ahmed found temporary lodging in Laredo. About one-third of the population of Laredo lived in poverty. Bethany House had just been founded to help the poor: there were accommodations and food to be had. He spent a week there where he met another disgruntled and angry Muslim.

Hussein Abdulrashid was living on the street, desolate with nothing to his name. He was dirt poor, dressed in tattered clothing and frowzy. Hussein took after his father who was tall and resembled his extremely thin mother. He was angry and could not understand why he could not find a job. Hussein was an engineer, and engineers were supposed to have good jobs and make decent salaries. He was unable to understand why he could not hold down a job in his chosen profession.

The problem was that calling him an engineer might have been a bit too generous. He was able to throw around engineering terms well. He knew the difference between a radius and a diameter; intensity vs. amount; he knew about interstitial space; reflected ceiling; and a few more things.

However, Hussein was only able to spout off the lexicon; not much more. He was a mediocre mechanical engineer with only a basic education. He always exaggerated his expertise so others thought him more knowledgeable. His problem was that anyone who hired him immediately saw right through his façade.

Hussein was born at Polyclinic Hospital in Harrisburg, Pennsylvania, in 1963. Harrisburg was a thriving town on the Susquehanna River. His parents came to the United States on a tourist visa from Iraq and never left. Since Hussein was born in the United States, he was a citizen by birthright.

Hussein's parents were controlling religious Muslims. They stood over him and everything he did, and nothing was ever good enough. His parents criticized everything he did and were not loathe to deliver rebuke in public. They were not an emotional family.

His father, Mufaddal, was tall at just over six-feet, and overweight. Mufaddal worked at what he considered a lowly job cleaning floors in an office building on banks of the river, south of the Governor's Mansion, overlooking the Susquehanna River. A Jew owned the three-story red brick building and was his employer. Hussein's mother, Hadiya, was thin and short and was not allowed out of their house since, in those days, Muslim women in *hijabs* were not acceptable in public. The family lived on a small street, with the Susquehanna River just a short walk to the west. Hussein was able to ride his bike everywhere he needed to go, including school.

One day in late autumn, Mufaddal caught a cold. Because he could not afford to take time off, he did not get the rest he needed and continued to push himself beyond his abilities. He was unable to recover from the cold, and then weakened by it, developed the flu. After developing the flu, he still did not take care of himself and eventually, the flu turned into pneumonia. At that point, he became bed-ridden and was unable to go to work for over two months. He was in the hospital for several weeks of that time. His employer was understanding but had to let him go. It was not Mufaddal's fault he got sick, but his employer had a business to run. By chance, another

Jew replaced Mufaddal. He was angry and considered it nepotism that a Jew hired another Jew to replace him when he was sick. He did not understand that it was just business and not personal.

Suddenly, Mufaddal hated the thought of even working for a Jew and furthermore it took a long time until he was able to find new employment. Mufaddal conveyed that anger and hate to his son Hussein.

Hussein was not a studious person, but he knew he needed the education to get a decent job. After high school, he went to Harrisburg Area Community College and decided to become an engineer. To help pay for college, he took a job similar to that of his father and became a custodian in the same hospital in which he was born. Every day, he noticed that across the street from the hospital was a large Jewish Orthodox *shul*, Kesher Israel. The gray building of the *shul* stretched across almost half the block. It was an imposing building, but the Rabbi and congregation were welcoming to all who entered its portals. Automatically, almost on instinct, Hussein hated the place as it represented everything he despised. The longer he worked at the hospital, the more vitriol he had for Jews.

On occasion, Hussein saw Rabbi David Silver* who was the Rabbi of the synagogue and the community. He automatically hated the *Rav*, but there was no reason for that enmity. *Rav* Silver was known for his kind words and an open heart for all, Jew and Gentile alike. That was irrelevant to the angry and irreverent young man. Had he given the *Rav* a chance, Hussein would have lived a different life. If Rabbi Silver knew what was in the heart of this young man, he would have humbled himself, approached Hussein, and tried to help him.

After Hussein finished college with barely passing grades, he found an engineering job in San Antonio, Texas. He did not care where the job was located, as long as it was far from the reaches of his father. He could not get far enough, fast enough from his parents, especially his domineering father.

San Antonio was a large town and the job was great. Well, it would have been great for Hussein if he had been completely honest with his abilities and experiences in engineering. He was quickly terminated from his position, as he was woefully unqualified to do the work.

With extreme prejudice, he blamed the Jews. There was no reason for the animadversion of the Jews in this situation, as there were none involved with him losing his job. However, in his acrimony, he did not let facts get in the way of his opinion. The Jews were an easy scapegoat for him. In the recesses of his mind, he thought about somehow taking revenge against his nemesis.

After losing his job, Hussein headed further south to Laredo, Texas. It was a border town and the cost of living was significantly lower. Maybe he would be able to find employment or some other opportunity in that area. At this point, he had no support system, nowhere to turn and no employment prospects.

To get even with all who wronged him, he wanted to do some serious damage to the U.S. infrastructure, especially if it involved Jews. Hussein became obsessed with his vengeful thoughts to the point where it was almost all of which he could think. He was not concerned with collateral murder and damage, as long as his targets were included. However, he did not have the resources to wreak the havoc he had in mind. Hussein was angry and wanted to vent that rage; he remembered even as a child he was quick to anger. He hated dealing with people, which is why he became an engineer. As an engineer, he did not have to engage with others, as did those in other professions. At least that is what he thought.

"I thought engineers were supposed to have good-paying jobs." Hussein was angry, dejected, and venting to his new acquaintance, Ahmed. "I spent so much time studying engineering. It was all for naught."

"You know as well as me that it's the blasted Jew's fault. They steal all the good jobs and leave us with nothing; not even scraps." Ahmed was helping to stoke Hussein's anger, wanting to see how far he was willing to go. "If he takes the bait," Ahmed thought to himself, "I'll add him to my cadre."

"It's their fault. Someone should do something about them."

"I agree. There's got to be something someone can do about them," Ahmed was fueling the fire.

"I would love to kill all the infidels." Hussein was taking the bait. "I just have no way to do anything."

"What if there was a way?"

Hussein was suddenly curious but not the most cautious person in the world. "What do you have in mind?" He was intrigued.

"I have plans, methods, and money. I need someone with your capabilities and education. Want to join me?"

"Yeah! I really want to," he enthused. He was willing to do anything to get out of the straits in which he found himself, and here was someone offering him exactly what he wanted.

"I am the leader of the cell. Can you follow orders?"

"That's not a problem." By nature, Hussein was more of a sycophant than a leader, preferring to follow others. Besides, maybe now he would have a place to live and food to eat. He was intrigued and suddenly aware that his whole life was about to change. He liked the possibility of the new prospects on his immediate horizon and was eager to explore the possibilities of an easy life and future.

After much conversing, they came to the realization they both wanted the same thing. They decided to join forces and help one another to accomplish their goal - the destruction of the beast called The United States, which was the essence of everything evil; apart from the Jews, which were even eviler than The United States. Ahmed had the money and some connections to help him get his plans off the ground while Hussein had the engineering background and the impetus to help Ahmed accomplish the terrorist acts they were contemplating. Hussein also had some explosive knowledge that would come in handy. They were going to attack the belly of the infidel. Ahmed's dreams were beginning to coalesce and he was happily anticipating a ripsnorter adventure of destruction.

After spending a week in Laredo, they had to make their way to New York where they planned to make their first series of strikes. To be cautious, they traveled via different routes to the Big Apple.

Ahmed was able to procure some weapons and small munitions in Laredo. Being close to the Mexican border, illegal arms were not difficult to obtain. His next stop was Chicago, Illinois. He was still concerned about using his fake identification, so instead of taking a plane, he decided to take buses to Chicago.

Ahmed had a specific reason for making the diversion to the Windy City. He knew that Chicago had the strictest gun control laws in the country, and only law-abiding citizens followed the law. Therefore, it was easy to get his hands on several illegal weapons to bring with him to New York.

In the meantime, Hussein stopped over in Baltimore, Maryland where he was able to get his hands on some illegal arms before continuing on his way to New York. It was closer to Harrisburg than he wanted, but he was still about ninety miles from his parents, so he felt safe.


# September 1982
## B'nei Braq, Israel

Rabbi Mishovsky was a humble man and a great *mekubal* who constantly lucubrated and was having thoughts of foreboding, foreseeing a catastrophe and the need for him to be in the United States. "Not my people," the *Rav* thought to himself. "I have to be in a position to protect my people." He asked his *talmid* Yaakov to arrange for him an apartment in Borough Park.

"It's time for me to move to America," The *Rav* said to his student. "Please help me make arrangements."

Applebaum was incredulous. "I would consider it an honor to assist *Rebbi* in this matter. Is there anything, in particular, the *Rav* wants or needs?"

"I prefer somewhere in Borough Park, close to a *shul*."

Yaakov thought a moment. He had an idea that would be beneficial for everyone. "May I suggest a house with a *shul* on the first floor? Would that work for *Rebbi*?"

"That's fine. Nothing fancy."

Rabbi Mishovsky wanted to be able to share his intuition to prevent as many deaths as possible. He had already experienced the worst tragedy in human history and would do everything he could to prevent more suffering. He wanted to be in the right place at the right time. He knew that since HaShem gave him the premonition of some disaster, HaShem would put him in a position to do something about it. He just hoped he would understand what the Master of the universe wanted and that he would be able to act accordingly. He would *daven* for that augury and the wisdom to decipher that message.

He would continue to make it known that his door would be open twenty-four hours a day, seven days a week. It did not matter to him who needed him or for what reason, he would be available. The *Rav* knew he was respected and held in high esteem, but he also knew that everything was a gift from the Merciful One and that He could take it all away in an instant. He also knew it was due to the merits of his ancestors he had foresight others did not.

# September 1982
## Jerusalem, Israel

Jake Benjamin and Yisrael Applebaum were among the most influential on Charles Outterridge. He was so impressed with everything about the two wonderful families that he wanted to be a part of whatever they were. While spending quite a bit of time with them under their tutelage and guidance, he started to explore Judaism. He was intrigued by every bit of new information learned and each new *mitzvah* he started observing. He loved everything about Judaism, and after a while, he converted calling himself Chaim and took a year off to continue his studies in a *Yeshiva* in Israel. He loved studying Torah and especially Gemara, and was excited about the new direction his life was taking. He was fascinated as he found many parallels in the Gemara and *halacha* to his chosen profession of nutrition. He wrote a small epistle comparing and detailing what he learned about nutrition from different Torah sources.

Chaim became a serious student trying to make up for what he considered the lost time before his conversion. He spent as much time as humanly possible studying Torah, continuing to grow in knowledge and observance. It was a great time in his life as he became a different person; a true *ben* Torah.

Being a nutritionist, Chaim was quite popular in the *Yeshiva* with everyone always asking him questions about health. When someone was ill, Chaim was there to give freely of his education and advice. He was happy to share his knowledge even making some nutritional changes to the menu at the *Yeshiva*.

Serendipitously, Moshe/Mohamed was in the same *Yeshiva* and was even in a few classes together with Chaim. Moshe did not ask many questions in the classes he attended. For the most part, Moshe just occupied a seat and did not participate. He had his agenda and was not too interested in what was being taught. Moshe was a loner and did not associate freely with the other students. However, some of the schoolings still rubbed off on him; subconsciously, he picked up some of the ethical value systems of the Torah. In some respects, he became a bit confused: he was in the *Yeshiva* to fulfill his part of the plan; however, he also learned that these distant cousins of his were not as bad as he was raised to believe.

For reasons unknown even to himself, Chaim did not feel comfortable around Moshe. He felt that something was off, but since there was nothing concrete, he did not disclose his sentiments. Chaim just tried to avoid Moshe as much as possible, which was more difficult than it sounded, as it was a small *Yeshiva*. In any interaction between the two men, Chaim was always respectful and courteous. Generally, Moshe was cold and kept to himself and was not interested in developing friendships.

MOSHE WAS SCARED AND RUNNING for his life. He was panting heavily while running down a narrow cobblestoned street; someone was chasing him and yelling something unintelligible from behind. As he was running, he quickly glanced around and although he did not recognize his surroundings, they looked somewhat familiar. Mohamed was lost and did not know where he was or how he got there, but it was almost as if he was on these ancient streets just a couple of months ago.

He was sprinting, short of breath, sweating copiously and was barely able to call out to his pursuer, "What do you want from me?"

His pursuer yelled to him, but, he could not discern anything, but somehow the voice seemed somewhat familiar.

He did not understand what was going on, why he was being chased, where he was or from whom he was running when suddenly he stumbled and fell face down in a puddle in a dark alley. He was now in pain from the scrapes and bruises sustained from the spill. His clothing was torn, he was dirty, wet and bleeding from a large gash on his forearm.

He turned over and suddenly saw an ogre standing over him and taunting him. The pursuer was larger than life and appeared to be a behemoth ready to attack him. Suddenly the apparition changed to a wisp of smoke and then appeared to be his mother. He called out in tears, "*Ema*?" (Mother)

He heard what sounded like someone calling his name, from the distance, "Moshe, Moshe."

The apparition pointed her finger at the frightened man on the ground, opened her mouth to speak, but her mouth grew larger and larger until it engulfed him inside of a box. Suddenly he felt trapped, inside an enclosure from which he could not extricate himself. He started flailing his arms and screaming for his mother while being thrashed around with arms grabbing at him.

Abruptly, with a flash, he sat up and realized that he was in bed in the *Yeshiva*. His roommate was trying to wake him by shaking him and calling his name. It was all a nightmare, a horrible and vivid hallucination that he had before, but this time was a bit different. He was breathing heavily and shaking like a leaf. His pillow and bed sheet were soaked with his sweat. His nightmare unnerved him and again some doubts about the purpose of the mission continued to creep into his mind.

## September 1982
## New York City, New York

Computers and computer technology were proving to be more than just a passing fad. Many people foresaw how computers were going to be the future, and they positioned themselves to be in the forefront. Many anticipated the need for computers in business, while some even predicted that people would want them in their homes. Others scoffed saying that computers were just a passing mania and would not amount to anything.

Started in 1969, the U.S. Defense Department's Advanced Research Projects Agency Network (ARPANET) was still in its infancy. ARPA-funded researchers developed many of the protocols used for Internet communication today. In 1995, this technology would become better known as the Internet.

New York Institute was a fine school and one of the first colleges in the United States to offer computer classes. Because of her fame in the computer industry, Emily Archer was offered a prestigious teaching position on how to use computers and how they would benefit the business world at large.

Emily became a well-paid teacher at New York Institute, for computer sciences. She did not have a degree, but she knew computers and programming better than anyone else. Since she was keeping Rivkah up to date with computer developments when Rivkah returned she would be able to substitute for Emily's classes and maybe even the pair could go into business together.

Emily had a flair for teaching and was easily able to impart her knowledge to her students. Giving her first class was challenging as she also had to write the curriculum for the course. There were no books available for the subject matter, so all she had available was her brilliant mind and her notes. Before the semester started, she ran the curriculum past the dean, who was so impressed that he immediately approved. Her class was successful and the following semesters saw increased enrollment in her class.

# October 1982
## Borough Park, New York

Ahmed was going stir-crazy and needed a comfortable place to live and use as his base of operations. He did not mind the fast pace of New York; it was much better than the dead city from which he hailed. Nothing was ever happening in Al-Awja, but in New York, there was always some adventure, some excitement, something going on and he learned to love and thrive on it. He understood why it was dubbed, "The city that never sleeps." There was always something to do; there was always something for everyone. He enjoyed walking the streets and learning his way around while watching people and their activities.

When he first arrived in New York, Ahmed rented a few rooms in a hotel on Twelfth Avenue in Borough Park; it was almost in the heart of the observant Jewish community. This was too close to the Jews for his comfort, as he hated them and wanted to kill and maim as many as possible. Anytime he passed a Jew in the street, he had to fight the urge to vomit and the vile feeling in his heart to reach out and strangle him. He did not want to live in a hotel for the next several years; besides, a house would afford him the privacy he required to plan and carry out his nefarious machinations.

After spending a week in the hotel, he was able to find a semi-furnished house for rent that would serve his purpose. It was located on Sixty-Fifth Street, just outside of the Jewish community, but close enough where he could keep an eye on his nemesis.

Ahmed decided it was about time he started educating himself for the forthcoming attacks, so he decided to matriculate. "It's paradoxical," he thought to himself. "I'm going to attend college and get an education from the same sub-humans I'm going to kill. I love it! I can almost taste the irony of it." He knew that while the Jews were his primary target, there would be plenty of non-Jews killed in the collateral damage. If he thought of his intended victims as less than human, maybe it would assuage what little guilt he would have over his involvement in their deaths.

While he was swimming in the pleasure of his plans, he was doodling on a piece of paper and perusing college brochures. He was glad he received tutoring in English before leaving Iraq. With his fake identification documents, he was able to apply for and be accepted into college.

Ahmed attended some classes in New York City, at New York Institute, to learn basic computer skills. He did not know that his teacher, Emily Archer, was Jewish. He thought she was too pretty and too smart to be Jewish. She was a tough teacher, but she knew the material well: she should as she wrote the curriculum for the class.

After Ahmed completed the computer class, he went to New York Medical College in Manhattan to learn infectious diseases. The classes he took were quite difficult. In addition to the language barrier, he knew nothing about the new material.

He learned that a microbe is a microorganism, especially an agent such as a bacterium that causes disease. He took classes in biology, chemistry, and mathematics and learned how diseases were spread and how to prevent them. He did not really care how to prevent them, but he felt the knowledge could come in handy at some point.

He was practical, "I guess I should learn about vaccines and prevention for protection for myself and my cadre," he told himself. However, in actuality, he was not concerned about the others, just himself.

Hussein also went to New York Institute to update his engineering knowledge. He struggled in the classes and barely passed. He was disheartened while he strove to pass the courses, but once it was over, he was relieved. He hated studying and taking classes, but it was what he had to do for his newfound benefactor.

Ahmed also wanted, nay needed, to add to his cadre. He required advice so he sent a letter to Saddam Hussein.

> To the honorable and most beloved, he who is the leader and ruler of the Muslim world, soon to be the leader and ruler of the entire world. May all the blessings of Allah be upon his head.
>
> Your Excellency,
>
> Please forgive me for taking his eminence's time, but I need guidance. I would like to add a few of our holy and dedicated Muslim men to our holy cause. However, I am not sure who I can trust.
>
> Can his eminence please suggest a trustworthy place I can turn to find someone to join us in our holy mission?
>
> Thank you for your time and consideration of this matter. I appreciate your dedication to our people.
>
> I humbly await your gracious response.
>
> In utmost deference, I remain;
>
> Ahmed Yousef al Rashim

Saddam Hussein could not deign to respond to the letter. He had his secretary reply that Ahmed should go to a particular Mosque in Brooklyn. The Imam there would help him. He was trustworthy.

# November 1982
## Borough Park, New York

It was a cool and starry November night; one felt one could almost reach up and touch the stars as they twinkled from so far away. He walked down the street like a stalking tiger: in a sense, he was on a prowl. Bert Sobol was not looking for trouble, but trouble often found him, as he was not hiding from it. He was not afraid of the night, as others have become, especially in the big city like New York; he was well trained and proficient in several forms of martial arts and held advanced belts in several disciplines.

He patrolled almost every night: it was a dictate, almost a calling. He tried to make sure he did not break any laws. Well, except for assault, but he was doing that in order to protect others, so in his mind, it was acceptable and legal.

He did not consider himself a vigilante. He thought of himself more like someone who wanted to protect those weaker than himself. He enjoyed helping people, especially the underdogs, so when he saw someone about to become a victim of a crime, he just had to do something.

The first thing he noticed that night was two people starting to fight. Bert Sobol sprinted over, stood between the two adversaries in equipoise, interrupting the fight.

"What in blazes do you want?" one of the men demanded of Bert.

"Stop fighting. There is no reason for violence."

The two strangers looked past Bert at each other in complete shock. "Who the blazes are you to tell us what to do or what not to do? Get lost!" he said.

"I just don't like to see people get hurt. Please, no fighting. Try talking it through."

"You buzzard," one of them screamed and threw a right roundhouse punch toward Bert's left cheek. The fist never made contact.

Bert, always on the alert, saw the aggressive move, sidestepped into a right neutral bow and parried the hand away causing his opponent to spin around halfway. The aggressor was a bit confused and un-centered. Bert firmly placed his hands on the man's back and shoved him forward. The man stumbled but did not fall down.

While the first man was still stumbling, the second man jumped forward with a right kick aimed at Bert's groin. Bert dropped a left block down to deflect the oncoming kick. This caused the man to land his right foot far away from his left.

Not wanting to cause any serious damage or pain, Bert just stepped forward and shoved him back. Because his feet were so far apart, the man lost his balance and fell on his rump. The stranger's ego was hurt more than his body.

The pair realized they were seriously outmatched and ran off in opposite directions. They would probably continue their altercation at a later juncture.

This incident was rewarding as he was defending people and in a strange way, making peace. Bert was glad he was able to break up that fight before anyone was seriously hurt: he felt proud of himself.

ANOTHER TIME, BERT WAS OUT at dusk walking northeast on Thirteenth Avenue. At the end of Avenue, he turned left onto Thirty-Sixth Street heading toward Twelfth Avenue. As he was passing Clara Street, he looked to the right and saw something amiss.

Bert sprinted over just in time to stop a mugging by a scrawny dark-haired man with brown eyes. He shoved the attacker away and helped the victim to his feet. Before the perpetrator could run away, Bert grabbed his arm and demanded, "What's your name?"

"D-Donny, Donny Coombs" he replied frightened for his life. He did not know if this man was a cop or the vigilante about whom he had heard. Donny was a twenty-four-year-old high school dropout, struggling to feed and shelter himself.

In a stentorian voice, Bert told him, "If I ever see you attacking another person, I will put you in the hospital. Now get lost."

Donny realized this was the vigilante and now knew what he looked like. He ran toward Thirteenth Avenue as fast as he could, like a lion chasing a zebra, and then turned right, out of sight and out of breath. Donny was usually homeless and scrounged for food from the dumpsters on Thirteenth Avenue. Often he did odd jobs just to put some food in his empty stomach. He regularly slept in the empty houses he was housesitting at the time. He was living hand-to-mouth and hated his predicament but saw no viable way to change his predicament.

It was because of this association in the Jewish community that he was able to pick up some Hebrew and mannerisms of Jews. Most in the community treated him well, and whenever they hired Donny to do odd jobs, they often gave him something to eat. He was envious of the wealth he imagined seeing in the Jewish community. From the sparkling Shabbos finery, the book-lined walls, the multitude of children and more, he was jealous and wanted some of that affluence for himself.

Tikva Benjamin was one of those who felt compassion for the wretched young man. She often used him to help her carry her bags and she would engage him in conversation. She treated him with respect and he appreciated the warmth of the family. On occasion, Jake paid Donny to run errands for his company and even help on

some construction jobs.
No good deed goes unpunished.

# 1983

## January 1983
## Borough Park, New York

**Bert** Sobol was enjoying his vigilante work and was confident in his abilities, prowess, and *savoir-faire*. He patrolled several nights a week, which led to him finding it difficult to stay awake at work. It was not easy trying to balance his patrolling with his work and it could sometimes be dangerous working under cars or on their engines. Since he was single and not dating anyone, he was not overly concerned about his nocturnal excursions. He did not do it for the accolades, awards or a boon. He often helped people, especially his brethren, and that seemed to be his calling and made him happy, maybe a bit too much.

One cold evening, Bert saw a carjacking in progress on Eighteenth Avenue. The driver was screaming as a criminal was trying to pull her out of the car. Bert took a deep breath of the crisp air, sprinted to the car and yanked the perpetrator to the street. The malefactor got up and brandished a knife.

In the dim light of the street lamps, Bert saw the flash of the steel blade and stepped back into a right neutral bow, minimizing his body as a target. He cocked his hands in a defensive posture ready for an attack.

With the knife in his right hand, the criminal lunged forward toward Bert's chest.

With his left hand, Bert executed a forceful left outward block to the forearm, which blocked his opponent's hand and caused him to drop the knife. At the same moment, he kicked the man in the left knee with the side of his right foot, shattering the kneecap.

Due to the force of the shattered knee, the attacker bent forward. Bert turned to his left while stepping forward with his right leg, checking his opponent. He reached around with his right arm over the man's head and put the attacker in a headlock to restrain him. At the same time, he kicked the knife away. Bert also grabbed his left arm and twisted back to pin the man.

His opponent tried to resist, but Bert held him firmly.

"When you stop resisting, I'll let you go."

"Okay, I give up," the man said breathlessly.

Slowly, Bert released the man but stayed alert. The man was considering making a second attempt.

Bert saw the dilemma in the man's mind. "Don't do it." Bert shook his head while wagging his finger.

The stranger reconsidered and barely limped away in extreme pain and humiliation. He needed to go to the hospital to tend to his shattered kneecap.

The former victim from the carjacking tried to thank Bert, but he was already leaving the scene. "Who was that man? Where did he come from?" the driver asked no one in particular.


# January 1983
## Borough Park, New York

Yaakov Applebaum briefly traveled to America and found a decent house in the center of Borough Park. The house had three stories and a basement; Yaakov liked the house and bought it. He helped Rabbi Mishovsky and his family move to the new house where he set the *Rav* up on the upper two floors, with a *shul* and *bais medrash* on the main floor. He arranged the basement as an apartment to rent to establish both financial and spiritual income for his future. Yaakov paid to have the *shul* remodeled to meet the needs of the new tenants and even set up a small office on the first floor for the *Rav's* use.

In the near future, when Zev finished writing his *Sefer* Torah, Yaakov would bring it to America and put it in the *shul*. In the meantime, they would borrow one from another *shul*. He was excited that his own scroll would soon be completed and then he would make a *simchas hachnasas Sefer* Torah, to honor HaShem. Yaakov could almost taste the excitement but would have to bide his time. He felt that this would be his greatest accomplishment so far in his life.

While in New York, Yaakov spent some quality time with his family, making no mention of his being in the *semicha* program. When he returned to Israel to continue his Torah studies in the *Yeshiva,* he delved into his studies with zeal.

Soon the Rabbi Mishovsky was established in his new American home and made it well known that his door was open twenty-four hours a day, seven days a week for anyone in need. He also held Friday night *tish* for anyone who wanted to come and be inspired.

NOT LONG AFTER THE *RAV* moved into his new abode, a childless couple came to see the *Mekubal.* They had been married for many years and the doctors despaired of them having children, and told them that medically, there was nothing that could be done. Every day they *davened* for help from on High, to no avail; they had nowhere else to turn. They were in so much pain and their bloodshot eyes gave proof to years of tears shed. They pined to hear the pitter-patter of young feet running around the house.

With desperation but hopefully optimistic, the young couple entered the *Rebbi's* humble office where he listened with rapt attention as they poured out their hearts. The *Rebbi* was in tears as his great heart went out with love and compassion to the couple in distress. They were hoping the *Rebbi* would intercede on their behalf in Heaven. After almost seven years of marriage, they were desperate for progeny, without which, they felt so alone and empty.

"We are hoping the *Rebbi* will give us a *beracha* to have children. It's been so long and the Merciful One has not blessed us with offspring," they broke down in grief.

The *Rebbi* closed his eyes and thought for a few minutes while the couple looked at the wall of holy books behind him. It was clear to the petitioners that he was feeling their pain and trying to take some of it on himself. He opened his eyes and in a modulated voice said, "There are seven days to the *Shabbos* Queen which is a day of joy."

The couple looked at each other confused; the husband raised his eyebrows and said, "In seven months we celebrate our seventh year of marriage. Is the *Rebbi* trying to tell us something?"

"There are seven days to the *Shabbos* Queen which is a day of joy," the *Rebbi* repeated cryptically.

The couple looked at each other quizzically; they had no idea what the Rabbi was saying. It was enigmatic. Was he giving a *beracha* or not? Was there another hidden message? What were they to do?

"There are seven days to the *Shabbos* Queen which is a day of joy." The *Rebbi* reiterated, looked warmly at the couple, smiled, and picked up his *sefer* and resumed his studying.

The befuddled husband and wife got up and left. Even though they did not feel they had received a *beracha* from the great man, they did feel comforted and as if their burden was somehow lightened.

Seven months later, on a *Shabbos*, they gave birth to a healthy baby girl. It was at that point they understood the ambiguous *beracha* from the *Rebbi*. She did not know it at the time, but she was already two months pregnant. The *Rebbi* must have known as he had emphasized the *Shabbos* Queen and kept mentioning the number seven.

Seven months after their first meeting, they went back to the *Rebbi* for a *beracha* for their newborn daughter who was born on *Shabbos*. The *Rebbi* immediately recognized them, greeted them with a warm smile, and bestowed another *beracha* and they made a *lechayim*.

Forthwith, word spread about the power of the *beracha* of Rabbi Baruch Mishovsky. It was already known, but now word spread everywhere in the New York Tri-State area and beyond. Petitioners, both Jewish and Gentile, both lay and scholars came to see Rabbi Mishovsky from far and wide. They sought his blessings and advice on a wide range of topics, and he seemed to have unlimited availability and patience for everyone. Many also came to discuss Torah thoughts with him and he always gave freely of his time.

ONE DAY, A WOMAN WHO was confined to a wheelchair, went to see Rabbi Mishovsky. Due to a car accident, Na'amah had been in a wheelchair for several years and was paralyzed from her waist down. Her doctors were unable to help her any further, and she had heard wonders about the power of the rabbi's blessings. She was a young and vibrant woman who was depressed because she was stuck in a wheelchair and therefore saw few prospects of a future marriage.

She went to see Rabbi Mishovsky in order to pour out her woes and maybe receive a *beracha*. Since she was not able to go up the stairs in the front of the building, and there was no handicap accessible ramp, someone brought her message to the *Rav*.

Immediately, the Rav walked outside to greet her, hoping his presence would give her some comfort and hope.

When she saw the *Rav* coming to greet her, she cried and

begged for help. "Forgive me for not standing up to show honor to the *Rav*, but I cannot stand."

His heart rent, "You do not have to stand for me; I am but a simple man. Besides, one who is incapable of standing to honor the Torah is not obligated to do so."

"I am sorry for disturbing the Rav's Torah learning," she said demurely.

"As our holy Torah teaches us, HaShem Himself visited Avraham after his circumcision. This shows us how important the *mitzvah* of visiting and taking care of the sick is to HaShem. Our job is to emulate Him and by me coming out to see you, in a small way I am trying to do just that. What can I do for you, my precious daughter?"

While the *Rav* listened attentively, as if he had all the time in the world, she poured out her heart. She talked about her accident and how she was crippled and the doctors could not do anything for her.

The *Rav* said, "The doctors are not the arbiters of medical outcomes; only HaShem, our merciful Father, has true power and we influence Him by our following His Torah and doing *mitzvahs*. I will give you something." He went inside and returned with a small bottle and gave her a potion he made with the wine from the *Pessach kos shel* Eliyahu, wine from *havdalah* after Yom Kippur and water from the *mayim shelanu* from *shemurah matzah*. Rabbi Mishovsky did not give this potion out easily but made it fresh every year. He used this potion often as it had deep kabalistic power.

He instructed her to rub some of the potion on her legs every night before saying *hamapil*. Then she should say a *passuk* from Isaiah 60:1 "קומי אורי כי בא אורך, וכבוד ה' עליך זרח" - "Arise! Shine! For your light has arrived, and the glory of HaShem shines upon you."

"Every night, say that *passuk* with deep concentration. Contemplate the meaning of every word. Then say *hamapil* and *shema*. With a complete heart, forgive all who wronged you. Do this every night for thirty consecutive nights and then return to me. Every day, *daven* to the One who heals for free; it is in His power to heal you. Put your faith in Him and only Him."

"I will do as *Rebbi* instructed," she said with commitment and confidence. She was hopeful that in a month, she would start to feel better and begin her slow trip to recovery.

A month later, she returned to the *Rav*. "I did as instructed."

Rabbi Mishovsky had her repeat the *passuk* aloud three times, concentrating on each word, while he did the same. After that, the *Rav* said the first word almost in a shout, "Arise!" Then he told her to stand up. She was dubious but did as instructed.

Slowly, hesitantly with caution, she slowly pushed herself up from the wheelchair. Tentatively, she put weight on her legs and let go of the arms of her chair. To the astonishment of those around, she stood completely on her own; she was completely healed. She did not need rehabilitation or physical therapy; she was able to walk and no longer needed any walking aids.

"May HaShem Yisbarach continue to heal you and may you soon find a shidduch. May you be worthy of your namesake Na'amah* who was the wife of Noach* who saved the world."

"Amen," was the resounding response from those around them.


A YOUNG COUPLE WAS GOING out of their minds; they were at wits' end and did not know what to do or where to turn. Their five-week-old baby was sick, and they were scared out of their minds. The infant had projectile vomiting, stomach contractions and was dehydrated. He always wanted to nurse, but was unable to do so and was crying often, without tears. The parents took him to see the pediatrician who sent them to a gastrointestinal surgeon. The doctor determined it was pyloric stenosis and wanted to do surgery immediately to correct the blockage. The young couple was aghast: how could they put their precious baby through a major surgery?

The couple consulted with Charles Outterridge who said, "I am only a nutritionist, if you question the doctor's opinions, get a second opinion. I would also suggest you go see Rabbi Mishovsky. However," he advised, "don't tarry, this is serious."

They decided to seek the advice of the *Mekubal* and ask for a *beracha*. Recognizing the urgency of the matter, they went the same day. As with every petitioner, Rabbi Mishovsky saw them immediately and the couple explained as best they could what the problem was and what the surgeon said. They were anxious and in tears.

"May I hold your precious child?" the *Rav* asked. They could see the love in his eyes and readily handed their son to the rabbi.

"He is a *tzadik* and *im yirtzeh* HaShem will grow up to be a strong and healthy man."

"Amen," they answered. They immediately felt better from hearing the words of the *Rebbi*. However, they were hoping for more.

The *Rebbi* caressed the child's stomach in a clockwise direction, bent down and kissed him on the forehead. The baby immediately expressed a series of loud belches. The parents were embarrassed but the *Rebbi* just smiled. The child stopped crying and started cooing.

"Your baby is fine and doesn't need surgery," he said handing back their child. The child gave indications of wanting to nurse. "See the *Rebbetzin*, she will give you some privacy." The *Rebbi* then continued with his studying.

The couple was astounded and in their mind, they just witnessed an open miracle wrought by Rabbi Mishovsky. They left a large donation on the table, which ended up in the coffers of his *bais medrash*. That *Shabbos*, the couple made a *Kiddush* to thank HaShem for the miracle of saving their child.

LAURA FELD WAS A GREAT server in Glatt Chow Restaurant and was attentive to the guests in her section. Laura loved her job and met all kinds of people, the majority of whom were Jewish and tipped well.

There were several reasons she enjoyed working at Glatt Chow. Laura was not the most religious woman, but keeping *Shabbos* was important to her, and her job never required working on *Shabbos* or Jewish holidays. The owner liked her and made sure it was a safe environment for her and all the employees. Laura lived around the corner, so she was able to walk to work and did not have to concern herself with parking.

One of the most important reasons she appreciated working at Glatt Chow was a particular policy with regard to the police. To show his appreciation, the owner said that any first responders and emergency personnel could eat at Glatt Chow for a fifty-percent discount. As a result, there was often a police presence in the restaurant, further strengthening an air of safety. In light of the gracious discount offered by the restaurant, the first responders always tipped well.

When Bert was there to protect the restaurant from being robbed, he had been sitting in Laura's section. He became a regular there and they developed a friendship of sorts.

Sobol enjoyed the ambiance of Glatt Chow restaurant, while the food was delicious and plentiful. He did not want to take advantage of Mendelssohn's generous offer of free meals, so he did not go every day, but he did go about every other week. Just walking into the restaurant, his olfactory system was inundated with the delicious aromas emanating from the kitchen.

One time after enjoying his meal, after leaving a generous tip on the table, Bert got up to leave. Officer Connors also happened to be enjoying an evening repast in the restaurant and noticed that Bert was about to walk out the door of the restaurant.

"You probably didn't realize, but I believe you forgot to pay for your dinner," Connors said to Bert while impeding his exit from the restaurant. Liam had been keeping an eye on Bert for a while. He suspected Bert as being the vigilante, but as of yet, had no proof.

Bert turned to the manager and said, "Hey, Menashe, you know I ate dinner, right?"

"Yes," the manager replied.

"You know I did not pay."

"Right."

"May I leave?"

"Sure."

Turning to Connors, he asked, "Any questions?"

"No," he said confused but realizing that Bert was in his rights for just walking out of the restaurant without paying for his dinner.

"May I leave?"

Connors just stepped out of his way. He thought to himself, "I don't like this guy. He is arrogant and bombastic, and I'm sure he is the one behind the vigilante attacks."

"By the way, officer, are you following me? I've noticed that recently you happen to be in many of the same places I am."

"No, I'm not following you, just lucky I guess." Connors just turned around and returned to his dinner, which was getting cold.

Bert did not believe the lawman but he moved on. "I have to keep my eyes open for that cop. I am sure he's following me."

Shoshanna Somers was also at the restaurant enjoying a meal with a classmate when she noticed this unusual episode and wondered about it. Sixteen-year-old Shoshanna closely resembled her older sister Rivkah; even their personalities were similar, but Shoshanna preferred nature and being outdoors. She was aware of the restaurant's policy of a deep discount for first responders, but Bert was not such a person. He was a mechanic, "Maybe sometime in the future I will ask him," she thought to herself.

# January 1983
## Brooklyn, New York

After spending a year in a *baal teshuva Yeshiva* in Israel, Mohamed/Moshe decided it was time he joined his conspirators in the United States. Under the circumstances, he thought it would be best if he maintained his cover as an observant Jew. This pleased him, as he liked and appreciated the lifestyle he had assumed for the past year. He moved into the house that Ahmed rented in Brooklyn, NY. He was intrigued by his learning, so he continued to go to *shul* and took a class on Chumash. Ostensibly, he was living as a Jew to maintain the persona of being a Jew; at least that is what he told himself and his friend. He did not want to think about it too deeply as he was afraid of the ramifications and implications.

However, living this duplicitous lifestyle was stressful on him giving him no heartsease. He was nonplussed: on the one hand, he was living as a *baal teshuva* as a religious Jew: he liked the lifestyle and morals. On the other hand, he was raised to hate these heinous infidels and was making plans to kill them. He soliloquized, "This double lifestyle of living is very stressful and is wearing on me. I hope I can maintain my cover over the long run."

Mohamed introduced Ahmed to Hussein while they went for a walk on Coney Island Boardwalk where they eventually found a bench to sit on and converse. There were other people enjoying the outdoors while strolling on the Boardwalk, taking in the sights, smells and sounds of nature. There was someone in shorts jogging while seemingly completely oblivious to the cold. An obviously Jewish, interracial couple was clearly on a *shidduch* date; they seemed nervous but were enjoying each other's company. Another couple with significant tension in their gait and conversation was walking their baby in a stroller: they were clearly not a happy couple. The couple was looking at the would-be terrorists and it made them uncomfortable. They quickly got up from the bench and walked away. As they walked, the three thugs compared notes and renewed their plans for the future.

They had quite a bit to discuss and the outdoors afforded them privacy and got them out of their house. They enjoyed walking on the boardwalk, as the smell of the fresh ocean air was refreshing. Looking south over the chilly blue waters of the Lower Hudson Bay, they were reminded of the cold winter solstice. The trio bundled their coats tightly around them while they walked and talked.

They needed to have freedom of movement, so they decided that Hussein would look for and purchase a car. Although public transportation was quite good in and around New York, having a car would make it much easier for them to carry out their nefarious plans. They did not care what type of vehicle they bought as long as it was reliable. A car would enable them to safely transport their explosive devices and take them out of the city to their future bunker.

BERT SOBOL OWNED A SMALL mechanic shop at the edge of Borough Park, right next to a subway station. He had several bays and was meticulous with his clients, never taking advantage of anyone. He was well aware of the bad reputation auto mechanics engendered and he wanted to be the exception to the rule.

Hussein walked into the mechanic's shop and approached Bert who was behind the counter. He had just finished with a previous client and was happy to turn his attention to the new customer.

"How may I serve you?" Sobol asked solicitously.

"I'm looking for a reliable used car. Do you know of any I could buy?" he asked.

"I have a customer who mentioned to me last week that he has a car for sale. I can put you in touch with him. Please understand, I've never seen the car and know nothing about it. I take no responsibility for its condition," Bert said being scrupulously honest as he was wont to do.

"I understand. I'll give it a test drive before I purchase."

Bert gave Hussein the contact information of Henry Davis who kept the car domiciled in a rented one-car garage in Flatbush.

Henry was a confidence man; or as most would call it, a con man. He dressed well as a young *Yeshiva* man of twenty-one, was tall, clean-shaven and looked sharp. Being lazy, he was always trying to find ways to work the system so he would not have to work or find a job.

After making contact, Hussein met Henry at his rented garage and looked over the vehicle; it looked nice and the body was in great condition. It was a Chevrolet Caprice Classic 1980 with about 27,000 miles on it; 305 V8 engine; dark gray four-door car. Nice, clean and discrete. Henry moved the car from the garage to the street.

"I would like to take it for a test drive. Is that okay with you?" Hussein asked.

"Sure. I would expect nothing less. However, since I don't know you, I go with you," Henry said. "You do have a valid driver's license, right?"

"Not a problem and yes I do."

Hussein walked around the vehicle and kicked the tires. He was not sure why, but he knew he was supposed to do that. He wanted to seem knowledgeable in front of the seller. They both climbed into the car and Hussein started the engine, which purred nicely. They drove around a few blocks and he was satisfied. He paid cash for the vehicle and Henry signed over the title, happy to be rid of the headache, and then terminated the rental of the garage.

Although the vehicle had a good reputation as a solid and reliable car, this particular one had problems. It was a lemon. When it rained, the electrical system would occasionally short out. Soon, the transmission started to grind at higher speeds. When Hussein purchased the car, he did not check the windows for function: besides, who opens the windows in January? One of the rear windows was stuck. Since it was a used car and a private sale, there was no recourse since the sale had the law of "as is."

Hussein repeatedly took the car to Bert's mechanic shop for repairs. It was one thing after another, Hussein was angry, and becoming exasperated as the bills kept adding up. He vowed vengeance against Henry Davis. It did not help that Ahmed was very unhappy with the condition of the vehicle that Hussein purchased and the money that was being spent to fix it.

On several occasions, Hussein had to have the car towed to Bert's garage. He was not happy about it, but Bert said he had some experience with Rafe Bradford and he seemed to be a reliable tow truck operator. On several occasions, Hussein used Rafe and his girlfriend, Alesha Bates to tow their car back to Bert's garage. Rafe seemed a bit shady, but that did not bother Hussein. Rafe was a large and muscular man weighing about 250 pounds, standing at six-foot-three-inches tall. Hussein thought that in the future, having a tow truck and a driver available might come in handy one day. They kept in touch.

After some time and much effort, Bert was able to get the car running properly. He had to replace the transmission and the window motor. Eventually, he was able to find the electrical short and replace the wires in question. It cost a pretty penny, but the car was finally functioning smoothly.

Hussein went back to Henry's rented garage, but he was just a previous renter and the owner of the house had no idea how to find him, or so he professed. Bert also had no further information on Henry, so Hussein laid in wait for him a few times in front of the garage with no sighting. So far, it was a dead end.

Two months after purchasing the lemon, Hussein was still regularly driving up and down streets in the neighborhood of the garage, in his heretofore-fruitless pursuit of Henry. He felt taken advantage of and duped out of a small fortune in repairs. Eventually, he spotted his nemesis walking up the street; gleefully, and with anticipation for sweet revenge, Hussein quickly parked his car and stealthily walked up behind Henry. He realized this would be the first time he killed someone and his hands shook slightly with nervousness. Matching his pace, Hussein took in a deep breath and steadied his hands for the horrible task. He sported a knife and since no one was around, plunged his knife deep into Henry's kidney, and kept on walking. Circling the block, he returned to his car satisfied that he exacted revenge; he took a deep breath, relaxed and relished the feeling.

Someone must have seen Henry on the ground bleeding and called 911. As Hussein was sitting in his car enjoying the pleasure of having killed Henry, he heard the wailing of an ambulance in the distance. He hastily departed the area and returned to the rented house, gratified with a job well done. He realized that having snuffed out a life did not seem to bother him at all, in fact, he felt quite good.

Henry was not mortally wounded in the attack, but he was in critical condition. The surgeons tried valiantly to save Henry's kidney, to no avail. Henry Davis' kidney was dead and he would require dialysis for the rest of his life unless he could obtain a new kidney. He was angry; he had no idea who stabbed him, or why. The police spent a significant amount of time and resources looking for the knife-wielding criminal. Law enforcement did extensive interviews with people in the neighborhood, but no material information was unearthed about the incident, and the police despaired of finding any leads and did not know what to do to extract justice.

# February 11-12, 1983
## East Coast United States

Snow: some people love it while some people hate the white stuff. When it is a blizzard, the whole situation changes; cities shut down, schools and businesses close; public and private transportation comes to a standstill. The only enterprises operating employ snow removal personnel. Children playing in the snow have so much fun they seem oblivious to the cold, that is until they go indoors to melt themselves out by a radiator. As her squealing children run in the door to warm themselves, the wet galoshes and the open front door exasperate mothers. However, the joy of the young excited children quashed the concerns of the agitated parents.

The blizzard of February 1983, delivered a large amount of snow from the Mid-Atlantic States through southern New England in a relatively short amount of time. In New York City alone, there were over eighteen inches of snowfall. Heavy snow fell all day over the New York area but slowed its northward progress during the morning of Friday, February 11, 1983. All morning and through early afternoon, it was a windy, bitterly cold day with a solid gray overcast sky. When the leading edge of the snow did at last resume its northward movement, the first flakes quickly transitioned into a heavy windblown snowfall, beginning between one p.m. and two p.m. and progressing northeasterly during the rest of the afternoon.

The sudden onset of heavy snow before the evening rush hour created chaos on the highways and gave rise to lasting stories of commutes taking over ten hours. As snow quickly piled up around the barely moving traffic, many cars and their occupants became stranded. Scores of motorists were "rescued" via snowmobile and given overnight shelter in local firehouses and hotels, evoking memories of the legendary Blizzard of 1978, a quinquennium earlier. In fact, many more motorists were stranded during this storm because of the timing of the onset of the storm, as well as the relative vagueness of the weather forecasts prior to the event. While a significant snowfall was forecast, there was considerable uncertainty over how severe it would be.

In the end, snowfall totals approached as much as two feet in Long Island over a roughly a fifteen-hour period and the strong winds accompanying the storm produced blizzard conditions.

At times, snowfall rates of several inches per hour fell forcing hundreds of motorists to abandon their vehicles on the different highways and expressways.

# March 1983
## Borough Park, New York

Since Mohamed/Moshe had to maintain his cover of being Jewish and he wanted to try a good restaurant, he decided to go to Glatt Chow. He was interested in the Jewish/American epicurean experience. He had experienced Israeli food and liked it better than the slop he had had back in Iraq.

Dressed in his finest toggery, Moshe walked into the restaurant and was impressed as he looked around at the ambiance; to his perspicacity, it was opulent and he felt underdressed. There was nothing similar to it in Iraq: well, at least nothing he had ever experienced. In short order, he was escorted to his table and presently his server approached.

"Hi, my name is Laura. I'll be your server today." Laura said with a smile as she handed Moshe a menu. "I'll be back in a few minutes to take your order." Before she walked away, she filled his glass with iced water.

"She is very pretty," he thought to himself as he smelled the delicious aromas emanating from the kitchen. He had never been to a sit-down restaurant where there was a server to take his order and bring him food. The new experience excited him.

Moshe had to be careful at the restaurant as there was often law enforcement in Glatt Chow. Officers Calvin Lund, Liam Connors and Peter Jackson often enjoyed a repast at the restaurant.

One of the things that made Laura a good server and endeared her to her clients was that she rarely forgot a face or name. She had a penchant for remembering her regulars and how they liked their food, always taking good care of them. Over time, Moshe became a regular guest of the restaurant and made sure to sit in Laura's section.

"Moshe seems nice," she thought to herself after meeting him a few times at the restaurant. "He treats me with respect and remembers my name. I appreciate that. He wears a *yarmulke* and makes *berachos,* but doesn't seem overly religious." Laura appreciated this, as she herself was not a "fanatic", as she thought of some of the *frum* people she saw in the neighborhood and as guests of the restaurant.

They had great conversations on a variety of subjects where Laura did most of the conversing since she was more worldly than he. When her section was not busy, Laura broke protocol and sat with Moshe while he ate and he appreciated her company.

After a while, a shy Moshe asked Laura out on a date and she agreed. He treated her well and they enjoyed extended walks in Central Park; they went to Battery Park; they took long drives. They laughed, joked, and saw a few movies. They went to a few restaurants to eat and one time they even went to Glatt Chow. Laura had never been there as a patron, and for her, it was a unique experience.

# March 1983
## Borough Park, New York

One cloudy evening, Bert was walking down the Avenue hearing the clacking of a subway train rattling overhead. Most native New Yorkers are so used to it, they do not even notice the prevalent noise or the sparks from the passing trains. Always alert, Bert was acutely aware of every sight and sound in his immediate environs. Passing a small grocery store, he glanced through the plate glass door and noticed two men with revolvers standing by the cashier. He was sure they were not there for peaceful reasons, but he decided to investigate for himself.

Bert entered the shop and decided to use his height to his advantage. He was six-foot-three-inches tall; the perpetrators were each about five-foot-eight-inches tall. Bert picked up each perpetrator by the collar, one in each hand, turned around and proceeded to toss them through the plate glass door, like overgrown bowling balls. In the process of being forcefully evicted from the store, they dropped their guns.

The two would-be burglars, not expecting or prepared for this type of resistance, got up and ran like triathlon runners. Even if they were still in possession of their weapons, they did not think it was worth the effort against such brute physical strength. The pittance they could have pilfered from the store was no longer worth the effort.

"Thank you so much," the proprietor said in complete shock. "How can I ever repay you?" He could barely catch his breath and was deeply appreciative of the Good Samaritan, but he had no idea who this stranger was.

"Don't charge me for the glass door." He smiled while shrugging his shoulders. They both laughed.

"Of course not; what else can I do to thank you?"

"Nothing at all; it's my pleasure to help. If anyone asks, you saw nothing; I was never here."

The owner of the store covered his eyes, they both laughed and Bert quietly left. The owner of the store decided not to call the police.

# May 1983
## Borough Park, New York

On numerous occasions, Bert was able to stop or even prevent burglaries and muggings. Many of these incidents required him to use his martial arts training, while a few episodes did not necessitate his physical prowess. Often times he was able to talk the would-be perpetrator out of committing their malevolent act. He preferred those opportunities where he could use his glib tongue and avoid a more substantial confrontation. His heart swelled with warm feelings whenever he was able to help people; however, he never let it go to his head.

One particularly warm night, while on patrol, from the distance, Bert witnessed a stabbing on the Parkway. He ran as fast as he could, but the perpetrator was long gone by the time he arrived.

He was upset with himself that he was not there in time to prevent the attack. He ran to a payphone and called the police and an ambulance; he then returned to the victim and tried to administer medical assistance. The victim was not mortally wounded but needed urgent medical care.

Liam Connors showed up and took Bert's statement while the paramedics tended to the victim. Bert was unable to give a description of the criminal, but the victim made it clear that he was not the one who stabbed him. "I see you around quite a bit. You're regularly at different crime scenes," Liam said while folding his arms across his muscular chest.

"I do alot of walking. It's good for my health. There's no crime in that." He was a bit concerned as he suspected that the police were keeping an eye on him. Sometimes he felt as if a spotlight was shining on him and he did not like the scrutiny, imagined or real.

"No, there's no crime in walking around. However, I find it interesting that you're often at muggings or burglaries."

"Just lucky I guess," Bert replied cautiously. He was being prudent, not wanting any trouble with the law. "Maybe I shouldn't have stuck around for the police," he thought to himself wishing he were elsewhere.

"Just make sure that it's just walking you are doing. Keep your nose clean."

"I did nothing wrong," Bert reiterated. "Am I free to go?"

Instead of responding, Connors just turned around to continue his investigation.

Bert returned home feeling disgusted with law enforcement officials, at least this one, "They show no respect to the citizens who they are supposed to serve and protect. It's no wonder people can't stand some police," he thought to himself. He decided that he would take a week or two off from his patrol to distance himself from any more unwanted encounters with police. He was sorry to do so since he very much wanted to protect the neighborhood, but he felt it had to be done to protect himself first.

## May 1983
## Borough Park, New York

Moshe and Laura continued to see each other and things seemed to be going well for them. They were enjoying each other's company and they got together as often as they could.

## 1983

Ahmed was angry with Mohamed for dating a Jewish woman and this caused a major schism between the two. Mohamed, who liked Laura, used the excuse that it was part of his cover. Ahmed did not buy the explanation and they argued about it on several occasions. This was an ongoing point of contention between the two. Hussein was on Ahmed's side, although in his mind, he appreciated Mohamed's opinion. After all, on a few occasions, he met Laura and she was attractive and seemed nice.

"How can you date that Jew woman?" Ahmed again demanded of Mohamed.

"I'm just maintaining my cover. I'm pretending to be Jewish: that is what people do. They date." Mohamed responded.

"You need to stop dating that Jew woman! Find someone else, a good Muslim woman or at least someone not Jewish." Ahmed said angrily to Mohamed.

"Why?" he asked obdurately.

"Because you are a Muslim!" He was outraged at his cantankerous friend and could feel the pressure in his temples increasing with his anger.

"So?"

"Jews are pigs. You can't date a pig," he said.

"She's not a pig. She's nice and I like her." He belatedly realized he should not have mentioned his feelings for her. He hated to gainsay his friend, but he wanted his girlfriend in his life more than he wanted to protect his friend's feelings.

This squabble repeated itself so often it was prosaic. One day, their argument became so heated they ended up in a brawl.

"Stop dating that Jew!" Ahmed demanded.

"No."

"That's an order! You stop dating her!"

"Absolutely not! You can't give me orders," Mohamed retorted. He was shocked that his friend thought he could order him around.

"I'm the head of this cell and I give the orders. I am also the elder. You stop dating her or else!" He did not understand why Mohamed insisted on dating a Jew. He was irritated with his friend.

"Or else what? Are you threatening me?"

Ahmed was red with fury and turned his back to Mohamed while clenching his teeth. He could not tolerate insubordination from Mohamed and had to do something to make a stand. Ahmed could not let Hussein see him abiding defiance from Mohamed. It did not look good for his command if he countenanced dereliction of duty, especially from his number two.

Ahmed clenched his fist and turned around hard and fast. His right fist encountered Mohamed's jaw and caused him to spin around and land with his hands on a table, stopping him before he fell to the ground.

Angry, in pain and shock, Mohamed clenched his fists and lunged at his longtime, true-blue friend. Mohamed and Ahmed ended up rolling around on the floor trying to pummel one another with their fists.

Neither of them was a skilled fighter so it was more of a street fight and they did more damage to their clothes than to each other.

They were evenly matched and both just collapsed from exhaustion, neither one the clear winner, both slightly bloody. They resumed their friendship, although it was now a bit strained and neither one completely trusted the other. It would take a while until the animosity would settle down between them; for the time being, they would give each other a wide berth and try to keep their personal issues from the fore.

# June 1983
## Borough Park, New York

Thrice weekly, Bert Sobol was on patrol again and knew that, as of late, one heavily populated street in Borough Park was a hotbed for crime. He was walking down the street and noticed a light moving about in a house. It looked like a flashlight moving back and forth in a house he knew should have been vacant, as the owner was out of town on vacation for another few days. He also knew it was not the night before Pessach where the owner of the house would be searching for *chometz*.

Patiently, Bert waited outside by the front stoop and when the criminals exited the house, he made his presence known. The perpetrator's hands were laden with their booty, so he had an additional advantage.

"Hi there," Bert called to them. "Need help with your packages?" He asked rhetorically.

Startled by the sudden sound of Bert's voice, they dropped their newly "acquired" wares. They looked at Bert who was standing in their way, with his arms folded across his muscular chest. He smiled at them while exuding confidence.

The interlopers decided it was not worth the risk and they dodged Bert and beat a hasty retreat down the street.

Quietly, Bert picked up the almost purloined goods, returned them to the vandalized house, locked the door and then calmly returned to his patrol. He was feeling good about what he just did. He stopped a burglary without any violence and the homeowner did not lose anything in the process. Bert felt confident that the would-be criminals would think twice before attempting their unlawful activities, and maybe even consider licit endeavors in the future.

# June 1983
## Brooklyn, New York

Ahmed was a good Muslim who went to the mosque every Friday, where he became known amongst his fellow parishioners as a devout Muslim. Not wanting to draw attention to himself, he was reticent, rarely associating with anyone else. He prayed five times a day, ate only hallal meats and fasted from sunup to sundown for the entire month of Ramadan. He was a good leader of his small clan, but he wanted one more person to join his terrorist cell: someone to do the grunt work. In pursuit of this, he found another Muslim with the same leanings as himself.

Eric Spence was an American who had recently converted to Islam and changed his name to Nizar El-Amin. Although still a neophyte to the Muslim religion, he was a regular at the same mosque which Ahmed frequented. Over the course of time, they had many conversations during which Ahmed came to the realization that Nizar could be helpful to his cause. He was almost as radical as he was but definitely more so than Mohamed. Nizar had never done anything that would even remotely be considered an act of terrorism, but Ahmed was willing to give him a chance. Nizar did not have any special skills, but he was an American and spoke English perfectly, had a real driver's license, as opposed to his forged one, and knew his way around.

Eighteen-year-old Nizar had recently graduated high school near the bottom of his class. During his junior year, he was exposed to Islam and liked the way women were treated. He did not want to have to treat women as equals so he converted to Islam. Growing up, he was always rejected by the girls in his public school, so he grew to hate women and preferred the company of men. He looked forward to being able to treat women like chattel and order them around to do his bidding.

Nizar never knew his mother as she ran off when he was just

a toddler: this did not help foster a positive image of women. Then there was the way his father treated his own multiple girlfriends which was not a stellar example for the impressionable young man.

Nizar was not studious and did not intend to attend college. He barely made it through high school and saw no reason to subject himself to more torture from obtaining a higher education. He had no direction in life, so he fit in well with Ahmed quickly becoming comrades in arms with the misanthropic group.

# Monday, June 6, 1983
## Borough Park, New York

It was a balmy, sunny, Monday afternoon when Bert was walking up a busy street with few trees to spread their umbra on shoppers and pedestrians. Further up the block, Sobol noticed a man who looked shifty as though he was about to do something criminal, so he stayed alert and paid close attention to the man's ministrations. It seemed to Bert as if the man was following a woman too closely as if he were her shadow. The stranger was even mimicking the woman's gait.

Suddenly, the man lurched forward, grabbed the woman's purse, and sprinted in Bert's direction. The woman started to scream but everyone was too stunned to do anything but stare at the hysterical woman.

Bert stepped to the side so as not to be in the way of the purse-snatcher. As the criminal passed by, Bert braced himself and stuck his arm out in front of him. The perpetrator caught himself just below his neckline on Bert's outstretched arm, causing his body to continue its forward momentum while his head stayed where it was. His body flipped up from the force of motion and he fell down on his back with a loud thud.

There was a rousing round of applause from the onlookers as Bert picked up the purse and returned it to the victim. She was effusive in her appreciation and offered a reward that was politely refused.

Bert just smiled at her, bowed slightly and walked away.

# Monday, June 6, 1983
## Borough Park, New York

Yehoshuah Benjamin was a sweet and precocious child of ten who loved to sing along during *davening* in *shul* and *zemiros* at home. He had a golden treble voice and was careful to use it only for good. When he sang, he was able to project his voice powerfully, and with no effort, to produce the most beautiful vocal timbre, range, and expression. He had over three octaves of range encompassing alto to the soprano. His favorite *mitzvah* was *shemiras halashon*; he only wanted to use his voice for the service of HaShem. Jake and Tikva were proud of their child and considered entering him into an audition with a boy's choir to sing on an upcoming record. He would need some singing lessons to help further his innate musical abilities. He also showed a knack for the piano which also needed to be developed.

One morning Yehoshuah was singing one of his favorite songs while walking to *cheder*. He was looking forward to the test in Chumash class; last night he studied with his father and was ready to ace the exam. He was not feeling as optimistic about the social studies class that afternoon. He was in a world of his own when suddenly Donny Coombs approached him.

"Hey *tzadik*," Donny called out in an affected honeyed voice. "Would you do me a *hessed* and tell me where's the Lelov *shul*? I can't find it."

Donny had practiced his routine and had it down pat: he knew what would entice the child. He also knew that all Jews were rich, that the Benjamins owned a thriving business in Borough Park, and that Mr. Benjamin was an author. "They must be rich," he often thought to himself when he had been in their house doing odd jobs. They did not need his services, but they hired him out of the kindness of their hearts and he was about to repay their kindness with treachery.

Yehoshuah was a respectful and trusting child and gladly responded to the adult who seemed vaguely familiar, that what he was looking for was on the next block, and he pointed the way. While Yehoshuah was pointing, Donny grabbed the lad's arm, cupped his mouth and pulled him into the open side door of the waiting panel van.

Donny had pilfered the van in the middle of the previous night from a commercial parking lot. Uncharacteristically, he had enough foresight to exchange license plates with another vehicle to cover his tracks. He carefully wiped his fingerprints off both plates and anywhere he may have touched the two vehicles.

In fewer than ten seconds, Donny gagged, tied and blindfolded the child. It was so fast, the hapless child had no clue what happened and did not even have time to react; he was shocked and confused with the alacrity of what just happened to him.

Donny quickly jumped into the front seat and drove off to a hideout he had prepared for the occasion. His refuge was on the outskirts of Borough Park, in a basement apartment he rented with cash, under a false name. Donny drove in a circuitous route he had pre-planned, to make sure he was not followed. He drove slowly and changed lanes often and did not detect anyone following him. Yehoshuah was fidgeting, but not fighting: he was tied and gagged well. The scared child was trying to scream, but the gag prevented him from calling out and even though the ordeal was only a few minutes old, he was exhausted.

Tears were streaming down his face as he begged through the restraints for his mother, "Ema," but his voice was completely muffled.

"Shut-up," Donny yelled at the poor child.

Yehoshuah's pleas were unheard and unrequited while his wrists turned red from resisting against his restraints and his crying made it difficult for him to breathe.

On the corner of Fort Hamilton Parkway and Thirty-Seventh Street, he pulled up to another car and double-parked next to a cemetery. Ignoring the blaring horns assaulting his ears from behind, he waited there for a few minutes to determine whether he was being followed. He saw some people milling around whom he suspected were dealing drugs but saw no one who seemed to be following him, so he continued on his way, turning left on Sixty-Fifth Street and drove until he was near his apartment. He parked his van and climbed into the back. In a horse sotto voice, he threatened Yehoshuah, "If you make a sound, it'll be your last. Understand?" he asked threateningly.

The child vigorously nodded his head in the affirmative: he understood the veiled threat. He was scared, had tears streaming down his face that was making it difficult to breathe. He was shaking like a leaf and desperately wanted his parents. "Maybe if I'm good he'll set me free," he hoped, afraid to consider an alternate possibility. "I never really saw his face, although he did seem familiar." He wanted to go home and forget this horrible experience.

Donny was about to open the door to exit the van when he noticed two Middle-Eastern looking men walking past. He waited a couple of minutes until the coast was clear, then Donny opened the door and half dragged, half carried Yehoshuah around the side of the house to the entrance of his basement apartment. He unlocked the door and roughly tossed the frightened child down the few steps into the apartment. The landlord would be away for another month, so it did not matter if they made some noise. Donny tied Yehoshuah to the radiator and went outside to move the van a few blocks away to where he had his own car. He parked the stolen van, wiped it down carefully and drove his own car back to his hideout.

That same morning, Ahmed and Mohamed were outside walking on Sixty-Fifth Street. They were feeling a bit stir crazy and felt a nice morning walk in the summer air would do them some good. While out walking, they saw something that was not out of the ordinary: a white panel van double-parked on the street.

However, there seemed to be too much movement inside the van. Although it was not atypical, it did stick out in their mind, as there were no identifying marks on the van to indicate its purpose.

They just ignored the heavily quivering van and continued their walk.

Donny returned to his hideout to find the frightened child squirming and trying to break free from the restraints. Donny tried unsuccessfully to comfort the child. He was worried that his parents would be scared for his safety.

Donny removed the blindfold and gag from Yehoshuah and a torrent of tears flowed down the boy's face. After a few minutes, Yehoshuah started to calm down and stopped actively crying. He gulped down some air and smelled the putrid stale odor emanating from the apartment. The stench was so bad that he was able to detect it through the congestion from his crying. The smell bothered him as he was used to a clean environment at home, which this was not.

At ten o'clock in the morning, the *cheder* called Mrs. Benjamin wondering if everything was Okay. "Yehoshuah did not come to *cheder* today. Just checking to make sure he's alright."

"What!? What do you mean?" she shrieked into the phone. "He left for *cheder* as usual. He should have been there on time. Oh no, where is he?" She started to pace and her knuckles turned white as she gripped the phone receiver with all her might as she struggled to catch her breath.

"He's not here. Is he with your husband?" The disembodied voice on the phone from the *cheder* remained calm.

"No, my husband is at work. I was about to leave for work myself. Oh no! What should I do?" she asked frantically while desperately pacing the room in a panic. Tikva Benjamin was not given to such a state of frenzy, but this was her precious son who was not where he was supposed to be.

"The first thing you should do is take a deep breath and then call your husband. If he is not aware of anything, walk Yehoshuah's route and see if maybe he just got lost or distracted. If you don't find anything, call the police immediately," the administrator advised the distraught woman. She tried to calm Tikva as best as she could over the phone. "I'm sure he's alright."

"Okay, I will do that immediately," Tikva replied, unsuccessfully trying to get a hold of herself. She was too distraught to breathe properly. She was like a mother bear who wanted to protect her cub from harm.

"I'll call back later to check on him. If there is anything we can do, let me know. In the meantime, I will send our custodian to look for Yehoshuah in the immediate area of the *cheder*."

They hung up and shaking with fright, Tikva immediately called her husband.

Jake dropped everything and rushed home to find his wife crying hysterically and on the verge of a nervous breakdown. She had run back and forth to the school using the route their son usually took but found nothing. Yehoshuah was nowhere to be found, and Tikva was frenzied, she was sweating from the excursion to the school and her *shaitel* was disheveled from the run. Tikva was too emotional to realize that in her haste to find her son, she may have missed something.

With as much composure as he could muster, Jake took control of the situation, "Tikva, you call the police, I'll start searching the streets and talking with anyone I can find. Maybe someone saw something." He needed something to grasp hold of, to give hope to himself and his wife that all would be well. He was beside himself with worry and concern, but he knew he had to maintain the façade of tranquility for the sake of his wife.

"I am sorry, ma'am, unless there is evidence of foul play, we don't take a missing person's report until twenty-four hours have passed." The police officer sounded sympathetic but there were regulations, which he had to follow. "The vast majority of the time, it's just a runaway and the child will return on their own. Maybe he went to a friend's house."

Tikva was hysterical, "My son did not run away and is not at a friend's house, he is missing. He is a good boy and would never do anything to upset his parents." She shrieked into the phone, ineffectually trying to get the police officer to do something. She was shaking her head in exasperation while tears flowed unchecked down her cheeks.

"I'm sure he is fine and will return home shortly." He was trying to be understanding but firm; he wanted her to calm down.

"Please help me find him. He's missing. Something bad has happened to him!" she pleaded into the phone to the unknown and seemingly uncaring officer. Little did she know that the man on the other end of the line actually did care about the situation, but there was nothing he could do.

"Call me tomorrow morning and we will do what we can," he gently hung up the phone.

Tikva sat down, put her head in her hands, and cried uncontrollably. Her home, always full of vim and vigor, seemed so vacant and vapid. She felt ill at ease in her own house that no longer felt like a home, her home. She suddenly felt like a stranger enclosed by these inhospitable walls. In her haze, she did not recognize anyone or anything around her.

Tikva's senses were on high alert when she thought she heard something outside and ran to the window to see her son. Her hopes were dashed as there was nothing outside that would require her attention and definitely not her son. She dropped down into the sofa, completely spent.

# Tuesday, June 7, 1983
## Borough Park, New York

The next morning, police officers of all stripes were crowded into the Jacobs house en masse, asking questions and starting an investigation. All tunnels and bridges out of Brooklyn were closed; every vehicle leaving the city was inspected. An alert was put out to the surrounding boroughs and areas.

As part of their quest for the child, auxiliary police officers canvassed the neighbors on the way to the school. The police vetted every door between their home and the school with no realization of their quest.

During the canvas, someone remembered seeing a white or gray van, but no one recalled any details. No other clues about the whereabouts of the perpetrator or child were discovered.

That evening, Donny called his captive's parents and made his ransom demand. The police and FBI were there in force to assist the family.

Several days before his nefarious act of treachery, Donny

purchased a voice-altering device from an electronics store in Manhattan. Disguising his voice with the machine, he said, "I have your son." The strange, creepy voice came out of a speakerphone the FBI set up in their dining room.

Tikva shrieked; Jake gulped air: their entire world seemed to stop. They had been anticipating this phone call; however, when it came, it shocked them to the core of their beings. It was as if their whole world was collapsing in on them and they had to sit down to prevent themselves from crumbling. They could not speak and felt as if the room was disintegrating on them. It felt as if years had passed since they had last seen their precious Yehoshuah.

After what seemed an interminable amount of time, the strange voice on the phone repeated itself. "I have your son."

"Please don't hurt Yehoshuah." They had been told to use his name as much as possible. It makes it all that more personal and the perpetrator would be less likely to hurt the child. "We will do anything you want. Anything you ask." They were panicking and pleading with the outlandish sounds coming from the speakerphone on their table.

"I have not hurt him, yet," he said in a not so veiled threat. "I want five million dollars in non-sequential, unmarked bills. I will call back tomorrow night with instructions." He was not sure how much time the police needed to trace his call, so he quickly hung up the phone. He had taken the precaution to make the call at some distance from his hideaway.

The couple was beside themselves with worry for their missing child. The police recorded the phone call and took the recording to their lab for analysis. A social worker stayed behind to lend aid and support to the family. They would need counseling for a long time to come, especially after their child would return home: if he returned. They had to be prepared for the worst-case scenario. An FBI agent or police officer was with the family at all times.

"What if we never see Yehoshuah again?" Tikva cried to the social worker.

"Perish the thought," she quickly responded with an arm on Tikva's shoulder. "We will get him back safe and sound." She was trying to comfort the distraught couple, but it was a daunting job, like trying to stem the flow of a massive river with pebbles.

"Where are we going to get that kind of money?" The couple asked no one in particular.

The FBI agent said, "We'll help with that. Don't worry. You have enough on your minds. The kidnapper obviously watches TV." The agent was trying to distract the parents from their immediate crisis.

"What makes you say that?" Jake asked.

"The only way to obtain sequential bills is to get the money directly from the Treasury Department who prints the currency. It's not the Fed who prints money, as is commonly thought.

"Once money goes into circulation, no one sits and puts the money back in sequence by serial numbers. It's just on TV and movies that this is said to add excitement and drama. When money is repacked into bundles and tied with bands, it's in random order.

"Cash money is fungible. It can be spent anywhere, anytime and in any denomination and is never put back in sequence."

"Then clearly the man is not from our clique."

"Why do you say that?" the officer asked.

"Because people in our circles don't watch TV or go to movies."

The officer had never heard of such a thing and was curious, but now was not the time for such questions.

The local LEO's (law enforcement officers) and the FBI went into high gear trying to get more information. Now they had evidence that Yehoshuah had been kidnapped, and they had to work on the assumption the child was still alive.

Jake Benjamin ran as quickly as he could to Rabbi Mishovsky for a *beracha* and advice. He hoped the *Rav* would *daven* that his son would be released immediately and be unharmed. Jake was so desperate he had tears streaming down his face as he practically barged into the *Rav's shul*.

When the *Rav* saw Jake, he immediately noticed the distress written on his features, and he invited the distraught man to sit down while he sent someone, who was studying in the *bais medrash,* upstairs to the *Rebbetzin* to come down with some water and a piece of cake.

The compassionate man invited the aggrieved guest to take a deep breath. "I see that something terrible has happened. Before we talk, we need to take a moment and do a *mitzvah*. In the *zechus* of a *mitzvah*, we will have the *siyata Dishmaya* for guidance from on High."

At that moment, the *Rebbetzin* approached with a small platter of refreshments. Jake turned down the cake as he was in no mood to eat anything. The *Rav* himself made a *beracha* and took a small bite.

Reluctantly, Jake carefully and slowly made the two *berachos,* to which the *Rav* answered *baruch hu uvaruch shemo,* and *amen.* The *Rav* smiled, "Not only did you make the appropriate *berachos* with *kavana,* but you also caused me to answer them and those are additional *zechusim*. You also followed the directives of a rabbi and that is also a meritorious act.

"With these *mitzvahs* in hand, how can I be of service to you my friend?"

The distraught father took a deep breath and tried to speak, but all that came forth from his mouth were sobs. Seeing the pain, the *Rav* also shed tears for the broken heart in front of him. The *Rav* handed Jake a tissue while waiting patiently, and quietly saying Tehillim, begging HaShem for the ability to help the petitioner.

After several minutes, Jake gulped air like a suffocating man and was able to compose himself enough to relate the tragedy that befell his family and brought him to beg for the *Rav*'s help.

While crying openly, Rabbi Mishovsky placed his warm hands on Jake Benjamin to help comfort him. The *Rav* called over the man who had summoned the *Rebbetzin* and asked him to gather everyone and say Tehillim. In the meantime, he closed his eyes and thought in silence. Despite his closed eyes, there were still tears streaming down his sagacious face. The *Rav* was *davening* and hoping for a message from Heaven to help guide the anxious and concerned man sitting before him.

After a few minutes without having moved a muscle, the *Rav* opened his eyes that were red from the tears. Softly, barely above a whisper, he said, "Not my people."

Jake was about to ask what that meant when the *Rav* continued. "סעדני ואושעה, ואשעה בחקיך תמיד." Tehillim 119:117, "Sustain me that I may be saved, and I will always be engrossed in Your statutes."

"What does that mean?" Jake wanted to know. He was desperate for some concrete information about his son. "Please help my family."

"You are always doing *chessed*; your son will be Okay. HaShem put this *passuk* in my mind, the answer you seek is in it: study it well. I will also try to find an answer and clarification. *Daven* constantly to HaShem, everything is in His Hands. Continue to do His will and He will deliver your son safely to you soon."

"Amen!"

The *Rav* also suggested giving *tzedakah*.

When Jake returned home, his wife was anxiously waiting with bated breath for a message from the *Rav*. All Jake had was an enigmatic response of an obscure *passuk* in Tehillim.

Their friend and colleague, Alexander Bently, volunteered to make flyers to post all around Brooklyn and the surrounding areas. The message of the *Rav*, the *passuk*, was also written on the flyer.

Maybe someone would understand its hidden meaning.

"סעדני ואושעה, ואשעה בחקיך תמיד." Tehillim 119:117, "Sustain me that I may be saved, and I will always be engrossed in Your statutes."

# Wednesday, June 8, 1983
## Borough Park, New York

The next evening, law enforcement was with the Benjamins in anticipation of the subsequent phone call. Both Mr. and Mrs. Benjamin were saying Tehillim when the shrill of the phone woke them from their assiduous, and tearful, supplications.

It was just a sales call; they hung up in frustration and looked at each other with desperation. The phone rang again almost immediately.

The unrecognizable but familiar voice on the phone demanded, "Do you have my money?"

"Not yet. That's more money than we can get our hands on. We need more time."

"I will give you another two days. No more."

"Let me speak to my Yehoshuah," he pleaded with the caller. Tikva was crying. The FBI wanted to drag out the call as long as possible to try to trace it. Jake was not without emotions.

"I don't have him with me; he's in a hiding place. He's safe, for now." Another veiled threat.

"I need to hear his voice, I - I mean, Yehoshuah's voice," Tikva pleaded into the speakerphone. "Please. I need to know he's okay."

"I will call in two days and have a recording of his voice."

"Please, can I talk with Yehoshuah? I need to talk with Yehoshuah and hear his voice."

"No! A recording will have to do. I'm not compromising my position. I'll call in two days - Thursday night."

"No!" they screamed as the phone went dead. Tikva's hands flew to her face.

During the phone call, an FBI communications technician was fiddling with dials and buttons trying to better characterize the voice and to trace the call. At the conclusion of the call, he continued trying to work his magic with the electronic device.

After a few minutes, he announced, "All I was able to trace is that he was calling from a payphone somewhere in northern Queens.

That's all I got." No one was happy with the lack of progress, especially the Benjamins.

Another FBI agent, a forensic psychologist on the scene, added, "All I can tell is that he is an American white man with no more than a high school education. He's probably in his early twenties and a loner."

"It's not much to go on," a detective commented dryly, "but every bit of information helps bring us closer to finding the child."

An abandoned stolen white panel van was found, but it had been wiped down; however, most criminals forget the seat adjustment lever. A fingerprint was found on the lever but it was not in the system, so it was a dead end. They found a few hairs in the van that seemed to match those of the missing child, but there was not enough genetic material for analysis.

Mr. and Mrs. Benjamin spared no effort looking for their child, while the police and FBI were helping in every way possible. The *Yeshivas* were continuously *davening* for the safe return of Yehoshuah Benjamin. Jake's employees rallied together by picking up any slack in the work, allowing him to spend every second with his family and looking for his son. The auxiliary police again canvassed the neighborhood and expanded their search radius.

Shoshanna Somers helped with babysitting for the Benjamins during this trying time.

The enigmatic words of the *Rav* were publicized and everyone was trying to discern its meaning. So far, no one had been able to divine its special connotation or significance.

# Thursday, June 9, 1983
## Borough Park, New York

Thursday night arrived finding Mr. and Mrs. Benjamin frazzled and at their wit's end. They could not imagine their son's likeness on the proverbial milk carton, or worse. "Things like this do not happen in our circles, especially not to us," was a common theme in their conversations. They were bemoaning their lot and at the same time, trying to strengthen their faith in the One Above. They realized this was an incredible test of their religious convictions and were determined to pass. They felt so alone, despite having each other, family, and friends with them constantly and supporting them through this impossible time.

The phone rang and despite the fact that they had been

waiting for the call, they both jumped in surprise at the shrill ring. They were both anticipating and dreading the call and were at the end of their nerves and not sure what the future held. Thus far, there had been no clues of any kind and they were hoping something would lend itself to showing them where to find their son, alive and well – the could not allow themselves to contemplate an alternative.

"Do you have my money?" the strange voice demanded.

"Let us speak with Yehoshuah, please," they pleaded into the speakerphone.

"Answer my question. Do you have my money?" He was not letting himself be distracted.

"We have some of it. We're not rich. It's taking time to put it together," they were being honest about that.

"What do you mean you are not rich? You are Jews and all Jews be rich. Besides, you own your own business, you are wealthy!" He insisted.

"I don't know where you got your information from, but we don't have money. Not all Jews are rich, that is just a fallacious stereotype."

"I don't know what that means, and I don't believe you..." he was somewhat confused with the verbiage.

"Let me talk with Yehoshuah," Tikva interrupted with tears running down her face.

"Since you don't have my money yet, I'll only play for you a recording of his voice." That is all he planned for anyway, but this way he felt as if he was in control of the situation and punishing them for their non-compliance with his directives.

They heard their son's weak and soft voice come through the speakerphone. "Ema! Aba! I'm okay, but I'm scared. I'm not hurt. Please help me."

"I will call again Monday night." The line went dead.

Tikva screamed and fainted. One of the detectives was able to catch her before she hit the ground and gently eased her to the floor.

Jake called Hatzalah while a detective radioed for an ambulance. The Hatzalah members showed up first and were quickly able to revive the wretched and pitiable woman. By the time the ambulance arrived, Tikva was doing much better and refused to go to the hospital. She wanted to be available for the rest of her children and for when Yehoshuah would be found and returned home. Tikva was trying to be strong and wanted to be there for her husband and other children.

While the EMT's were tending to Tikva, the benumbed FBI

technician continued to fiddle with the electronic instrument. "He was calling from a payphone in Lower Manhattan. He's being careful. This ain't going to be easy. Clearly, the kidnapper has not left the jurisdiction." Belatedly he realized he should have softened his language in front of the distraught couple.

The authorities were doing everything they could. Yehoshuah's picture was on every TV station, posters were plastered in every neighborhood, and shopkeepers put the flyer in their store windows. Everyone in the five boroughs and beyond was looking for the child. The search was focused on Brooklyn since they assumed the kidnapper had some knowledge or acquaintanceship with the family. All of Jake's neighbors, employees, and stores in close proximity to his office had been vetted with no success.

During the night, the forlorn and inconsolable couple was barely able to sleep. They had nightmares with Yehoshuah calling to them but they were not able to answer his calls. They woke up and were unable to breathe. They had to get hold of themselves to be strong for their other children. Their neighbors and friends stood by their side and took care of the children, carpool, food, errands or anything else that was needed.

Their *Shabbos* was spent low key. More out of habit than anything else, Jake went to *shul*, but sat in the back, *davened* quietly and refused any honors. He purposely showed up just as *shacharis* started and left as soon as the last *kadish* was finished, so he would not have to talk with anyone. There was almost no talking among family members: they were all scared and apprehensive. Much of *Shabbos* was spent saying Tehillim and trying to avoid crying on the holy day. Realizing the difficulty in front of them, they were trying to step up to the lofty goals of what HaShem wanted from them.

Donny tried to get the poor child to eat something. He was not without a heart: at least that is what he thought. He did not consider himself evil, just someone who was taking advantage of those who could afford to share their wealth. Donny capitulated and made sure to have fresh fruits, vegetables and kosher snacks for the boy. He also had some kosher bread and cool water and even bought a kosher pizza for the child. Yehoshuah ate only because he was starved and did not know how long it would be until he would be rescued. At least the food was kosher, albeit not nutritious nor his mother's cooking. That thought reminded him of his parents and he cried with constant worry for them and the predicament in which he found himself. He did not want his family to suffer on his account and he wondered if he would ever see them again. How they must be suffering! Due to this tragedy, he felt himself mature very quickly and he knew he had to be strong to get out of this alive.

Yehoshuah begged his captor to bring him a *siddur* and a *Chumash*. Donny went to a nearby shul on and appropriated the two requested books. At least the lad could *daven* and study some *Chumash*. His normal routine was to sing all of the prayers, especially on *Shabbos*, but reason, he did not feel like doing that and barely read the words. Despite his sudden newfound maturity, he was still too young to understand those sentiments or any of the strange emotions he was feeling: he just wanted to go home to his family.

# Monday, June 13, 1983
## Borough Park, New York

Monday night came with another phone call, "Do you have my money?"

"Yes we do," they lied. The FBI supplied them with only one million dollars of marked bills with die-packs, hoping to trick the kidnapper and lure him out of hiding. The Feds knew he was an amateur with no experience in this type of caper, but he was not stupid. Their main goal was to get the child back safely. All the money was cataloged and scanned in case some of the money turned up in circulation at a future time. "Let us talk with Yehoshuah, please," they begged.

Ignoring their appeal as if it were an inconsequential ant, he said, "In Grand Central Terminal off the main concourse, there are baggage lockers. Place the money in a plain gym bag and put it in locker #C436. Put the key in an envelope and leave it discretely on top of the locker two to the right. Do this tomorrow at noon. When I'm sure it's safe and that no cops are watching, I'll get the bag. Once I have the money and am clear of the area, I'll call with instructions on where to find your son. Do you understand?"

"Yes, but..."

The phone went dead. Everyone jumped. Tikva screamed, "No!" as her hands flew to her face. Stupefied, Jake cried softly as he felt his heart fluttering in his chest. He walked around the living room and dining room like a caged animal.

Jake spoke with Charles who suggested some valerian to help deal with the stress which Jake immediately purchased for himself and his wife.

# Tuesday, June 14, 1983
## Manhattan, New York

The next day at noon, with a federal marshal at his side, Jake went to Grand Central Terminal in search of locker #C436.

Nervously, he opened the locker and put the bag inside. Upon closing the locker, he deposited a quarter and removed the key. He placed the key inside an envelope and hid it on top of the required locker, and then left with his escort. Before leaving the area, he turned wistfully with a heavy heart to look at the lockers, pining for his son. He knew beyond hope that his son would not be there, but he still hoped to see him running into his arms. Jake was completely oblivious to the throngs of people moving about, each with their own direction and task. The cacophony of sounds assaulting his hears had no effect on the man as he was in a world of his own.

Meanwhile, Donny was in a cafe in the Grand Central Concourse nursing a coke and observed the proceedings from afar. He was unable to discern what was in the bag, but he would find out soon enough. He was anxious to get his hands on the money and be rid of the nuisance child, but he had to bide his time. In his mind, he had already spent half of the money that he felt was due him on a new house with a butler and maid, and a new car to replace the one he never had.

He waited impatiently and his fortitude paid off. Shortly after Mr. Benjamin left, a man appearing to be the replacement usher approached the attendant of the baggage locker area. From his perch, Donny noticed the newcomer flash what looked like a badge and conversed briefly with the attendant.

Donny watched as the first man nodded his head and walked away and the second man took his place as the attendant. Donny presumed the second man was a cop or another federal agent. "These feds are so incompetent," he thought to himself. He was shocked at their ineptitude.

Without further ado, Donny got up and left without collecting the ransom. He took the subway back to his car and drove to his hideout. During the entire trip back, he was fuming and once in the privacy of his own car, he fulminated vociferously with many expletives. With his fists, he hit the steering wheel multiple times in anger until his fists were red and tender.

When he returned to his basement apartment, he was still angry and sore. As vengeance, he decided that there would be no communication from him to the Benjamins until Wednesday night. He controlled himself to an extent in the presence of Yehoshuah, he did not get physically violent with the scared child. However, he had some choice invectives that he spewed in the presence of the boy, which scared Yehoshuah even more. The wretched boy, never hearing such words or experiencing such anger, cowered into the corner as if he could make himself vanish, trying to ensconce himself into the radiator to which he was tied. He dared not make a sound lest he bring himself to the attention of his captor and be the victim of physical abuse. He was shaking like a leaf in a windstorm.

The federal marshal waited fruitlessly for someone to approach the designated locker. He did not know that his quarry was long gone. After checking with his advisor several hours later, he collected the bag and left his post.

Jake and Tikva waited by the phone with bated breath for a call that would be long in coming. They did not know an observant Donny and a bumbling federal agent had thwarted their plans. Every sound startled the frazzled couple; every time the phone rang, it gave them new hope that was quickly dashed. Shoshanna Somers was there to help with the children and she gladly cooked dinner for the family who barely tasted anything. The young woman had a great heart and freely gave of herself to help the distraught family.

The Benjamins and the law enforcement agencies were mystified when no one came for the money. The couple was heartbroken and languishing and desperately wanted their son back. There were no tidings from the captor of their son and they began to wonder if he had somehow eluded the authorities and left the vicinity. The situation seemed dire with no end in sight.

# Wednesday, June 15, 1983
## Borough Park, New York

"You betrayed me," Donny flippantly bellowed into the phone on Wednesday night when he finally called from Staten Island; never calling from the same area twice. He had hoped this would be over by now and he was still angry and felt betrayed.

"I don't know what you are talking about," Mr. Benjamin said. "Where is Yehoshuah?"

"Yes you do," he said angrily into the phone. "There were cops waiting for me at Grand Central. I am not that stupid." Donny ignored the question about his captive. He was so upset that he almost forgot to use the voice-altering device.

"We didn't send the cops," he lied. He was desperate and needed something on which to hang his hopes. He did not want to anger the stranger on the phone. He wanted his son; that was his only goal.

"Since you betrayed me and are lying to me, you need to be taught a lesson. Your son is alive and well, but the ransom is now ten million and you will not hear from me again until Monday night." He slammed down the phone to the screams of the desperate couple. Jake and Tikva sat there agape in total shock with their hearts barely beating in their respective chests.

They had barely slept since their son had been abducted, and they did, it was marred with nightmares and tears. The entire family was struggling and their nerves were completely frayed and everyone was on edge. Jake was given to pacing their house while Tikva was constantly crying into her Tehillim. They were bemoaning their plight and situation and wondered why HaShem was doing this to them. Their faith was being taxed to beyond their abilities and they had almost given up all aspiration and faith in everything.

The police and FBI had all but given up hope of finding the boy alive. They re-canvassed the area and expanded their search radius even further. No new developments came to light in the tri-state area or beyond. They wondered why the police and FBI could not find their son and bring him home to them. How much more could they endure? How much longer? What else?

# Monday, June 20, 1983
## Borough Park, New York

It had been almost a fortnight and they were struggling to have *emunah*. It was difficult for them to believe that the abduction of their precious son was for the good. They had gone to Rabbi Mishovsky several times for *berachos*. The Rabbi was constantly *davening* for Yehoshuah, as was everyone else. Every time the Benjamins came to see Rabbi Mishovsky, there were tears streaming down his wise face and he saw them without a moment of delay.

Rabbi Mishovsky always had words of encouragement for Jake and Tikva and told them to call on him any time of the day or night. The *Rav* had barely slept since this whole episode started. He kept repeating the *passuk* from Tehillim and was often heard saying, "Not my people. They should not have to suffer like this." Clearly, there was a message in that *passuk*, but no one understood what it could mean. The most anyone could divine what that somehow the *passuk* was telling them to do more *chesed* and that their child would be alright. However, there had to be more; they needed there to be a deeper message from HaShem.

"סעדני ואושעה, ואשעה בחקיך תמיד." Tehillim 119:117, "Sustain me that I may be saved, and I will always be engrossed in Your statutes."

The Benjamins felt some comfort from the *Rav*, as he was able to ease their burden to a small degree, but what was hidden in the verse? Why was no one divining the meaning and finding their son? They knew he was doing everything he could to help them and even tried to help fortify their faith in HaShem. Why was this happening to them? Why did they, of all people, have to suffer like this?

BERT WAS MAINTAINING A NIGHTLY vigil trying to find clues to the whereabouts of the missing child. He had seen Donny in the neighborhood and because of their previous encounters, suspected that even if he did not have Yehoshuah, then maybe he knew who did. Bert knew that Donny was a troublemaker and someone who could possibly carry out this heinous deed. Somehow, this kidnapper had eluded detection for an unusually long time. Everyone was on high alert for any clues to the whereabouts of the missing boy.

On Monday afternoon, Donny went for supplies and food. Barely able to contain his excitement, he was again counting the hours until he had his newfound, ill-gotten wealth. In his deluded mind, he had already spent half of the money he was going to receive for his caper. He could not believe things were going so well for him and did not even consider the possibility that something could go wrong.

He did not realize how much work a kidnapping was and he would be glad to get rid of this nuisance boy and move on and away. Donny had grandiose plans for living the lifestyle of the rich and famous, that he felt he richly deserved. His chimerical mansion had an Olympic style swimming pool and several acres of finely manicured lawns and gardens. He envisioned a butler and maid to tend to his every need. While he was woolgathering, he was not scrutinizing his surroundings carefully. He should have paid more attention to who might have been following him, rather than to his fanciful dreaming.

Bert spotted Donny, and covertly followed him for a while and found where his hideout was located. He was on Sixty-Fifth Street when he suddenly understood the *passuk* repeated by Rabbi Mishovsky.

Tehillim Chapter 119 goes through the entire alphabet with eight verses for each letter. Verse 117 corresponds to the letter "o" which is the numerical value of sixty. However, the exact verse is the fifth in the sequence. Hence the number sixty-five; they were on Sixty-Fifth Street. Bert was shocked that the *Rav* had been so specific and clear. He also wondered why no one had divined the hidden meaning: however, in hindsight, it was obvious. The *passuk* also talks about being saved, implying that the child would be safe.

Buoyed with this thought, Bert waited until Donny went inside the house before springing into action with alacrity. Stealthily, he came close to the building and tried peeking inside, but the shades were drawn. He heard some muffled noises from the basement, so he ran to the corner store and called 911. In order to try to protect Yehoshuah, Bert wanted to be nearby until the police arrived, so he quickly returned to the house to make sure Donny did not run off. After obtaining an emergency warrant, officers Connors and Jackson broke down the door and entered the apartment in force. They found Donny hiding in his apartment and tried to arrest him, but he resisted and a minor scuffle ensued. In short order, a bruised and sore Donny was subdued and taken into custody.

Yehoshuah was found in good health; he was in shock and a bit dehydrated, but otherwise physically unharmed. He would need a significant amount of counseling to overcome the trauma of the kidnapping. Yehoshuah became severely depressed and angry from his horrible ordeal and refused to talk with anyone about anything. He shut his mouth as tight as a bank vault and refused to open it for anything except to eat and drink.

The Benjamins made a large *kiddush* that Shabbos to thank HaShem for returning to them their precious child. Rabbi Mishovsky was also jubilant over the tidings.

The evidence against Donny Coombs was damning. He was caught with the missing child bound and gagged in his own apartment. Once Donny was in custody, his fingerprints were compared to those found in the van and were a match.

Donny ended up before Judge Richard Archer, pleaded guilty to second-degree kidnapping, and was sentenced to ten years at Fort Dix Federal Corrections Institute in New Jersey. With no possibility of parole, he would be serving his entire sentence and then be on probation for an additional ten years.

Bert Sobol had been instrumental in finding the child and was hailed as a hero. Because of his help with finding the kidnapped child, he was buoyed and feeling good about his vigilante work. He had a renewed confidence in what he was doing. In fact, he was euphoric, stirring him to do more.

# July 1983
## Borough Park, New York

Alexander was happy. He had made the flyers that were used to try to help locate Yehoshuah Benjamin. He felt that in some small way, he was instrumental in aiding with the return of the precious child to his parents. More than anything, he was grateful the child was unhurt.

Although he worked from home, Alexander was busy in the community. He loved the commute, sometimes listening to the traffic reports and laughing. It was his way of dealing with his back problems and pains. From a young age, he had been diagnosed with scoliosis and was unable to get around well.

Idiopathic scoliosis is a sideways curvature of the spine with no known cause. As a child, Alexander wore a brace to help straighten his spine. It helped to an extent, but he still lived in constant pain. Because of his weak back, he had to do muscle-strengthening exercises every day.

He often felt humiliated because he was only thirty-two years old and required a cane and sometimes a walker. It was reminded him of being disabled in high school and often being the butt of teasing and ridicule. Sometimes he felt depressed because of the constant pain. His doctor filled out the application for him to get a handicap parking placard.

One day Alexander went to a mall in downtown Brooklyn and was unable to find an available handicap parking space because someone without a placard parked illegally in a reserved spot. He walked across the parking garage with his cane and struggled to get around the shopping center. He was frustrated that he was unable to park proximate to the mall since someone was so insensitive and probably thought, "I will be just a minute," or some similar lame excuse.

Upon entering the mall, he noticed someone walking with a service dog and asked him about the dog.

"Service dogs are great," the stranger said. "Obviously, for the blind, they help the handler get around. However, they can be used for anyone with a disability."

"Do they need specialized training or certification?" Alexander asked.

"That's a common misnomer; according to the Americans with Disabilities Act, no. There are three requirements for a dog to be a service dog. It has to be well behaved; cannot eliminate in inappropriate places, and be able to perform at least one service for the handler.

"In fact, I can take my service dog anywhere I go; hospital ER, restaurants, government buildings, and more. When I go to a hotel, they cannot restrict my access with my service dog, and cannot charge me extra for him.

"All you need to do is find a dog to your liking and train him. Rescue one from a shelter and give him a good home. Once he is trained to do a few services for you, get him a 'service dog' vest and you are good to go."

They continued to talk about the type of services, dogs and the needs of both the animal and handler. The stranger was helpful, patient and a veritable fountain of knowledge.

"Thanks so much for your time. I'll find out more and I think I will get myself a dog. I could use the help." Alexander was enthused with the idea.

After doing additional research on service dogs, Alexander went to an animal shelter to look for a large dog he could train to be his service animal. He found instruction books in the library about dog training. It is not difficult to train a dog, if you have the right canine for your needs and if you have patience, which he did. There are many types of service dogs and training specific to each type. Alexander needed a dog that could help him open doors, support his weight when needed, and pick things up off the floor for him.

He found a large Labrador mixed breed that was about one hundred pounds. A bit large for Flatbush, but it was what he needed. He named the dog Remmi, short for Rembrandt. Alexander was an artist and thought the name apropos.

Remmi was so happy to be out of the shelter, he would do anything to please his master. Alexander started training Remmi in his own backyard and the dog picked up the training well and was soon able to be a service dog. Alexander bought Remmi a service vest and started to take him everywhere.

One of the things that Alexander learned is that from the animal's perspective, the more time he gets to spend more time with his master, receives extra treats, gets to go places and explore, the happier he is. When a service dog is "working", other people should not interact with the dog, as it distracts the animal from his job, which is to take care of his handler. The dog should be completely ignored.

A service dog for people with disabilities was still a fairly new concept and many people were not used to seeing one. In fact, it is a misdemeanor to tease a service dog and a felony to abuse one.

Alexander took the service dog into stores, the post office, and many other places. Anywhere Alexander went, Remmi went.

One evening, Alexander decided he wanted to go back to Glatt Chow for dinner since it had been a few months since he had last been there.

"Work," he said to Remmi. His service dog loved to go to "work." A service dog is on call for the handler twenty-four hours a day, seven days a week.

They went to Glatt Chow Restaurant which was not crowded, and that suited him well. He walked into the restaurant with Remmi and asked to be seated.

The manager, Menashe, immediately approached Alexander and said, "I'm sorry, pets are not allowed in restaurants."

Alexander patiently replied, "This is not a pet. Remmi is a well-behaved service dog and according to the ADA, he can go anywhere I go. I would like to be seated, please."

"Pets are not allowed in food establishments, and your dog is quite large. Please come back without your dog."

"I would like to be seated and my dog is staying with me. He is a service dog, not a pet," Alexander reiterated patiently.

"Please leave or I will have to call the police." The manager was getting upset and did not want to cause a scene.

Alexander just stood there, Remmi sitting quietly by his left side. "Menashe, I have been here before, this is a service dog, not a pet and I would like to have dinner."

Frustrated, Menashe turned around, picked up the phone and called the police. A few minutes later, officers Connors and Jackson arrived on the scene and introduced themselves.

"What can we do for you?" Jackson asked.

The manager said, "I want this man to leave. He cannot bring his pet in my restaurant. Dogs are not allowed in food establishments. The gentleman is welcome, but not his dog."

The police officers turned to Alexander questioningly. They saw the service vest and asked, "Is that a service dog?"

Alexander knew exactly what three questions were coming and he was prepared. He knew the law, "Yes."

"Are you disabled?"

"Yes."

"Please give me an example of a service the dog performs for you."

Alexander said, "He is able to pick things up off the floor for me."

Connors turned to the manager and said, "This dog is a service dog who is accompanying his handler. According to the law, you are required to allow him and his service animal entrance into your restaurant. You have to treat him as you would any other client. You cannot seat him in the back of the restaurant, but in the same place you would seat any guest. Is that clear?"

"Yes, officer." Abashed, Menashe turned to Alexander and said, "I'm so sorry. I didn't know. Please accept my humble apologies. You and your service dog are welcome here anytime. I will make sure to inform and educate the entire staff. As a way of apology, your entire dinner is on me."

"Thank you. I appreciate your offer and I accept your apology. And thank you, officers."

The police went on their way happy that all was resolved peacefully.

# August 1983
## Flatbush, New York

Esther Weiss, (nee Goldschmidt) was a lonely woman. Despite being married with two beautiful children, she felt completely alone. Hers was a bitter life.

Esther was born in 1963 to a good family; she was intelligent and grew up with love and acceptance from her large family in Queens. She was a top student in her school and seemed to have everything going for her with a bright future. It was not a surprise to anyone when she got married to a young budding *talmid chacham* who was also from a well respected Torah family.

When Esther Goldschmidt was in high school, she was a nerd with glasses, a bit chunky and awkward. Because she was so *klutzy*, she often had bruises on her legs from bumping into things. However, when she turned sixteen, all of that changed. She started wearing contacts, lost some weight, did her hair up nicely and she was no longer a *klutz*. It was as if she became a new person. She grew out of what she considered a previous incarnation and became a woman.

Because Esther knew what it felt like to be an outcast, she became sensitive to others who were in her previous predicament and often got herself into trouble because she had a difficult time saying "no". When she graduated high school, she was a beautiful and soft-spoken young woman who was gentle and had a sensitive soul, although still a nerd. Immediately after high school, Esther went to Israel to study in a woman's seminary. Shlomit Women's Seminary in Jerusalem had a fantastic reputation and Esther had a wonderful experience and grew spiritually. She became close with one of her teachers, Mrs. Weinblatt, and was sad to lose that propinquity when Esther returned to the United States. However, she tried to maintain a correspondence with Mrs. Weinblatt upon her return.

NACHUM WEISS WAS BORN IN 1961 into a good family on Staten Island, New York. He was a bit of a troublemaker, but overall a good and debonair student. There was nothing specifically outstanding about Nachum, except his lineage. His father was a well-known *talmid chacham* from a prestigious family, and his mother also came from illustrious origins. Nachum went to the right *Yeshiva* high school and then a good post-high school *Yeshiva* in Israel. He was not particularly studious, adventurous or even interested in sports. He may have been in class physically, but his mind was never there; he always woolgathered and footled instead.

There was a dirty little secret about Nachum that only his immediate family and closest friends knew: he had a bad temper. Never mind that, he had an explosive rage. Most of the time he was a calm person; however once in a while, he would seriously lose his temper. Woe to the person who was nearby when he would erupt, no one was safe from his venting. He was not averse to cursing someone or throwing things in indignation.

ESTHER AND NACHUM WERE INTRODUCED by a *shadchan,* Mrs. Benjamin. If Tikva had had any idea as to the explosive nature of Nachum, she would never have subjected Esther to him.

Everyone loved Esther and was so happy for her when she became engaged to Nachum Weiss who seemed to be the quintessential *Yeshiva bachur.* He presented himself as a lively, fun and energetic young man who seemed to be well learned and a *mentch.* Maybe marriage would tame him.

They dated for three wonderful months, became engaged and then married three whirlwind months later. Rabbi Ginsburg, Nachum's Rosh HaYeshiva, was so happy for the young couple and gladly performed the wedding as the *mesader kedushin.* However, he was only cautiously optimistic and would keep the couple in his thoughts and prayers. He hoped that Esther would help Nachum turn himself around and become a better person. Over the years, Rabbi Ginsburg had tried to influence Nachum with gentle and firm *mussar;*

maybe some had affected the young man.

At their wedding, everyone was so happy for the newlyweds. Their families and friends danced with exuberance usually reserved for only the best of couples. The excitement and dancing continued all through the week of *sheva berachos* and beyond. Esther and Nachum seemed like the perfect couple and had everything going for them. They rented a two-bedroom apartment in Flatbush, Brooklyn. Their joy and happiness knew no bounds and was compounded when Esther got pregnant right away.

The first year of their marriage was wonderful; until their first child, a son, was born. That was when the trouble started and Nachum could no longer control himself and started to show signs of anger. He had been able to conceal his internal tempest until then. When they talked, he was short with her and his tone was strident. She was not used to being talked to in that manner, "It's not so bad. In time he will get better," she thought to herself. "I can handle it and be a better wife to him."

One evening during dinner, she asked her husband, "Can I use your pen? I want to add to the shopping list."

"Don't bother me while I'm eating," he declared in a stentorian voice and threw his pen across the room. She was shocked at the outburst - it was completely uncalled for and unexpected. She looked at him in utter shock not sure what just happened as she quietly got up to retrieve the pen. The tension in the air was so thick, one could practically see it as if a heavy fog settled between them, and he just continued eating his meal.

A few nights later, dinner was good, but not one-hundred-percent to his liking. "This food is vile!" he exclaimed in disgust tossing his full plate in the sink breaking the plate and ruining the food. He then stormed out the door and went to Glatt Chow to eat.

Esther sat there aghast and cried silently while thinking, "The food is good. Even if the food was not good, that was no way for him to treat me," she thought bitterly. "What did I do wrong?" she wailed to herself with tears in her eyes. She was confused and considered calling her mother, but was too embarrassed. She suffered in silence.

In March 1983, the couple was walking on Coney Island Boardwalk with their son in a stroller. There was tension in their gait and they were barely talking. They observed three Middle-Eastern looking men talking by a bench. Esther was concerned: her woman's intuition told her something was wrong. Nachum just made fun of her.

"Don't judge people by their looks. Look at what's inside. You can't see their personalities from here." Nachum said paraphrasing the Mishneh.

"That is ironic," she thought to herself. "Nachum is a good-looking man, but his *middos* are horrible." Esther immediately regretted thinking bad thoughts about her husband. Esther knew she was far from perfect but was on a mission to improve her middos in the service of HaShem. She had a long way to go, but Nachum seemed to be the antithesis of what she was trying to accomplish.

"It is not their looks that is making me feel uncomfortable. It's just a feeling I have. Call it women's intuition."

"It's hogwash," he said in derision.

She became another statistic: she was the victim of domestic abuse. It was horrible. Esther was concerned that her precious young son would learn from the actions of his father. "Maybe, for my son's sake, I should leave. Maybe if I am nicer to my husband, I'm sure he'll be better. He is not so bad; maybe he'll be nicer in time. It's my fault that he's angry so much," she repeatedly thought. These were some of the thoughts that flittered through her mind on a daily basis. She did not realize that it was not her fault he was treating her like chattel. She was in a quandary as she wanted a normal home for her son, but this behavior of his was not customary nor appropriate.

As time went on, he continued howling at her and then even started cursing her. He got in her face and even humiliated her in public. When he was angry, he would stand mere inches from her face and bark at her at the top of his lungs, like a rabid dog foaming at the mouth. When they were out, if she even glanced in the direction of another person, he would become enraged. "You have to give me your attention. I am your world, no one else. You pay attention to me!" He spat the words out from his vile mouth with such venom that passersby were shocked and disgusted with his behavior. He was becoming more narcissistic by the day, making her every action revolve around him, even to the exclusion and detriment of their son.

She started to walk around with her head lowered in humiliation, and fear in her eyes. He was escalating; she was crying almost constantly and apologizing to him at every turn. Esther started to have a nervous tick in her neck and was always looking at the ground in shame and embarrassment.

One day, for no apparent reason, Nachum was again angry and slapped Esther across her face. She was astounded and her hands instinctively went to her cheeks. She had never experienced or even observed physical violence and she stood there in shock with her mouth agape not knowing what to do. She was petrified and shaking and her face stung and was red from the blow. Nachum was also shaking, but he was quivering in anger, not even sure why he was angry.

Another day, in anger, Nachum, with the open back of his hand, slapped her hard in the stomach. Esther ran into the bedroom, locked the door and called the police. Her hands were shaking and had a difficult time dialing the number, while her voice quivered trying to tell the emergency operator what was the problem.

Nachum banged on the bedroom door, "Open this door!" he demanded vociferously.

"I called the police. You just wait!" she called through the closed door. She was crying bitterly, scared and shaking. She felt so lost and alone, trapped in her small bedroom with the walls closing in on her.

This enraged Nachum even more and he banged fiercely on the door, almost breaking it. Esther was so frightened; she was shaking like a leaf in a windstorm. She had never been so petrified in her life. "I did not know Jewish men could be so violent," she thought to herself woefully. "What am I going to do?" She noticed her son in his crib and he started to cry from all the noise. She ran to him, picked him up and buried her head in his wails. He was also unnerved from all the banging.

When he heard his son crying, Nachum stopped banging on the door. "What's wrong with the baby?" he demanded. He was so enraged that he could not even remember his own son's name.

"You woke him up with your yelling. He is scared from all your banging."

"It's your fault. Open this door, now! You buzzard!" he screamed at the top of his lungs.

It is normal for an abuse victim to believe their abuser is in the right and her in the wrong. While waiting for the police, Esther tried to console her crying and scared child.

Officers Liam Conners and Peter Jackson arrived at the apartment and introduced themselves. Esther complained to the police that her husband assaulted her. He denied the abuse and said that she was probably just suffering from post-partum depression. There were no visible marks on her body except a bit of redness on her cheek, so they did not believe her and instead, advised the couple to get marriage counseling. The police left and Esther was angry and mortified; she was depressed, scared and frustrated. She did not know what to do or where to turn for help to manage the abuse she was getting from her husband.

Goaded from the lack of action by the police, he continued to hit his wife, but carefully avoided her face. He felt his actions were excused, as there had been no repercussions. At first, he only slapped her, then he started to hit her with the back of his hand, then he graduated to punching her.

On more than one occasion, he physically held her down while becoming violent and forceful with her.

ESTHER'S MOTHER, MRS. GOLDSCHMIDT, WAS cleaning up after having some company for *Shabbos*. Her guests had brought some flowers to brighten up the *Shabbos* table. While putting away the Waterford Crystal vase, it slipped from her hands and shattered on the dining room floor.

"Oh, my!" she exclaimed. "It should be for a *kaparah*."

Her husband, hearing the clamor of the shattering glass, came quickly. "Are you okay, sweetheart?" he asked concerned.

"Yeah, I'm fine. I dropped this vase and it shattered, but my intuition is that something is wrong. I don't know what it is. Just a feeling; it's probably nothing."

"I will clean this up. You just relax."

She smiled at her husband who was always trying to make her life easier. However, the bad feeling was not going away; she could not shake it, and it concerned her.

She decided to say some Tehillim; that always helped.

ANOTHER TIME NACHUM WAS IN his usual angry mood and humiliated his wife in public in a restaurant. This was not a peccadillo: he often hurt his wife physically, mentally and emotionally, both in private and even in public.

"Nachum, a bit of the soup is in your beard," she quietly said to him.

"You cow! How dare you tell me how to act," he burst out in anger.

She started to cry and in a loud voice, he insulted her even more. "Awww, look at the poor baby, holding a baby, crying," he said acerbically. His words deeply cut into her psyche and she burst into uncontrollable tears. She felt as small and worthless as a gnat and so humiliated, that she wanted to crawl into a hole in the floor.

Alexander Bently was enjoying a meal at Glatt Chow during this exchange. He was in shock, as he never experienced public humiliation like this. He saw the public degradation and felt bad for the woman, but was unable to get involved. "It is when I see animals like that man I wish I was not disabled and could help her," he thought to himself. Because of his disability, Alexander was unable to intervene if things became physical.

Menashe Mendelssohn, the manager, came over and asked Nachum to lower his voice or leave the restaurant. Quickly, Nachum just shut his mouth and did not say another word throughout dinner, giving her the silent treatment. Esther was crying silently, her tears mingling with her food making it taste salty. Esther no longer had taste for her food mostly moving it around the plate and only eating to avoid angering her husband even more.

Mohamed happened to be at Glatt Chow at the same time and thought to himself, "So Jews treat their wives just like Muslims do."

Over the course of time, Esther called 911 several times, but the police did nothing except to tell her to stop calling for nothing. One time the police just told him to go to the gym and let off steam.

Another time a woman police officer told Esther, "Be a better wife and you won't have any problems."

Even another time, a police officer said to her, "It's not so bad." The police even threatened her that if she did not stop calling 911 for frivolous reasons, they would arrest her. She could not believe what was happening to her and that she was unable to get help from law enforcement. She felt simultaneously abused by both her husband and the system that is supposed to protect her. She was trapped with nowhere to turn for help and nowhere to go.

Nothing was done to Nachum or for Esther and most of the time, the police did not even write a report. All this just emboldened Nachum to abuse his wife even more and he became completely unhinged.

In order to prevent Esther from calling the police again, Nachum unplugged the phone and took it with him when he was not home. He felt great that the police never did anything to him, but he was perturbed by their seemingly constant incursion into his apartment.

Eventually, she got pregnant again and he hit her many times; she almost lost the baby. She thought that maybe his end game was to kill her and her unborn child. She even considered the possibility that he had a huge life insurance policy on her. On several occasions, Esther had to go to the ER from the copious beatings. Liam Connors showed up because the nurse called the police for suspected domestic abuse.

"Mrs. Weiss, the nurse tells me you were assaulted. Is this true?" Connors asked the frightened and shaken Esther.

Recognizing the policeman from previous visits to her home and his lack of any action on her behalf, she decided to not say anything. "No officer, I'm just clumsy and fall a lot. I have been this way since I was a young child." She brought to the fore of her mind her awkward and clumsy childhood.

"Are you sure someone is not hurting you? You are safe here with us. We can protect you."

Petrified of any retribution from her husband, she said, "N - no, everything is fine."

"If someone is hurting you, we will arrest him and you will be protected. Are you sure? Your injuries are indicative of someone beating you. Please tell me who is doing this to you."

"No one is hurting me, officer," she said meekly while lowering her eyes. "I'm just clumsy."

"I seem to recognize you from somewhere. Have we met?" Connors asked. He was not flirting; he was trying to gain her trust to help the victim. He needed her to come forward and admit being the victim of abuse and he could help her.

Now even more frightened, she hurriedly stammered, "Ummm, n-no officer, I don't know you." She quickly shook her head in the negative and turned her head away, lest he scrutinized her more closely and remembered her from somewhere.

Connors did not believe her. "I'll have to check my files for her name," he thought. "Mrs. Weiss, here is my card. Please be safe and call me if you need anything."

The police officer left shaking his head.

Another time the couple was out, Nachum was treating his wife poorly, again. He was not ashamed to treat his wife as trash, even in public. He felt she was little more than chattel and he could do with her as he pleased.

Bert Sobol saw the abuse, intervened, and told Nachum, "Treat your wife better!"

"How dare you?" Nachum responded angrily.

"Very easily. You are a so-called *ben* Torah. Act that way."

"I will act any way I want."

Esther was about to interject when Nachum roughly grabbed her arm and yanked. "Ouch!" she exclaimed, "that hurts!".

Bert grabbed Nachum's hand and twisted back and out, his thumb pressing on the central nerve where the ulna and median nerve trunks meet on the back of the hand. He had total control over the rogue, "Don't abuse your wife."

"You're hurting me. Let go of my hand!" he pleaded, suddenly changing his attitude.

"You've been hurting your wife. If it was up to me, I would give you a taste of your own medicine." He suddenly let go and Nachum fell to the ground, rubbing his sore hand.

"Treat your wife better or I'll be back," Bert said as he walked away.

Nachum cursed Bert to his back. Bert heard the invective, turned and bowed graciously with a smile. He turned back around and continued to walk away. Esther struggled to suppress a smile and secretly was happy that her husband had gotten a bit of his own medicine. She hoped that he would learn a lesson, but it was not to be.

When Esther was at the end of the second trimester of her second pregnancy, Nachum beat her horribly. She could not take it anymore; she had enough and needed to talk with a friend and went to visit Shoshanna Somers. Despite the four-year age gap, they used to be close until Esther's son was born. Esther had been tight-lipped about the abuse she had been enduring. Now, she needed to confide in someone; she needed a friend.

Shoshanna was a sweet young woman in college and had been exposed to some of the harsh realities of the world outside the insular *frum* community. When Shoshanna was in high school, because of a speech impediment, she attended special classes. She stuttered, and when she was nervous, her stuttering became worse. She had taken speech therapy classes, but it did not do her much good. This translated into making her speech class, a required course, a nightmare for her. Every time she had to speak in front of others, she could barely get out a word. The exception to that occurrence was when she was with children. Amazingly, then she was in her element and her stuttering vanished. It was because of this that she was taking classes in early childhood education, and was doing well, as long as she did not have to speak in front of her classmates.

To help her along, she took every opportunity to babysit for anyone who needed her help. She was wonderful with young children, if not their parents.

It was to Shoshanna whom Esther turned. Esther did not mind that Shoshanna stuttered. In high school, some of her classmates made fun of her, but Esther always came to her defense and was her protector.

"T-t-to what d-d-d-do I owe this g-g-g-great honor?" Shoshanna asked her friend when she opened the door. "P-P-P-Please come in, my d-d-d-dear friend. Let me g-g-get some cake and t-t-tea."

"Thanks so much, Shoshanna. I need a friend."

"You l-l-l-look haggard. Your former g-g-glow and the t-t-twinkle in your eyes are m-m-missing. Please d-d-don't be insulted." She could not believe her eyes; Esther looked like a shadow of her former self.

Esther could no longer hold back, she broke down and sobbed. Shoshanna handed Esther some tissues and let her cry to her heart's needs. It was such a catharsis for Esther and after several minutes of crying, Esther gulped a few deep breaths of air.

"Thanks, I needed that."

Shoshanna placed her hand on that of her friend and said, "What's w-w-w-wrong? What c-c-can I do for y-y-you? I am here f-f-f-for you."

"I don't know where to begin," Esther began hesitantly.

"Anywhere you w-w-w-want. Take your t-t-time."

Slowly, between sobs, Esther told Shoshanna her tragic story. Shoshanna could not believe her ears, "How anyone could hurt this precious woman," she thought to herself, "is incomprehensible." She was incredulous and found herself bawling with her friend. She had heard of marital abuse, but never thought it would manifest itself in the Jewish community, let alone, one of her friends.

After conversing for a long time, Esther nervously said, "I've got to get home. I need to be back before Nachum returns. He is going to want dinner as soon as he arrives home." Her reaction of wanting to cater to her husbands' every need and whim to this extent, even before being asked, was normal for an abused woman.

"Esther, p-p-p-please keep in t-t-touch. Call me anytime. M-m-m-m-most importantly, d-d-d-don't let him hit you anymore. M-m-maybe move back home to your p-p-p-parents house."

After she closed the door, Shoshanna felt bad for her friend. Emotionally spent, she fell against the door, broke down and cried for quite a while. "I wish there was something I could do for her," she said aloud to no one in particular. Once she was able to calm down, with tears still streaming down her face, she said Tehillim for her friend.

After leaving, Esther felt much better as if a huge weight was lifted off her shoulders. However, when she came home from visiting with her friend everything changed and went back to normal. Her husband was there waiting for her with his arms folded across his chest in anger. He was fuming mad.

"Where have you been, you buzzard?" he demanded loudly while standing only inches from her face. She could easily see the anger on his face as he screamed at her. He was red with rage and his temples were beating in rhythm with his rising pulse. He was seething and ready to explode like a nuclear explosion.

With a trembling voice, she said, "I just went to visit my friend Shoshanna Somers. You know her; she was at our wedding. I didn't think you would be home yet. I'll make your dinner right away." She was cowering and hoping to avoid him hitting her again. She wanted to avoid another confrontation, especially a physical one.

"I shouldn't have to wait for my food. It should be ready for me when I get home. There is no excuse," he bellowed at her. "From now on, you will not leave the apartment without my permission."

Esther stood there looking dolefully at her husband. "He is a narcissist," she thought to herself. She was so petrified she was shaking like a flower in the wind.

The next day he changed the lock on the door to a deadbolt that needed a key for both ingress and egress. Nachum did not give his wife a key and she became a prisoner in her own domicile. She no longer considered it a home, just a structure in which she was confined as an animal in a cage. He took away her driver's license, credit card, and car keys. He even strictly restricted her food intake: she was being starved. He did not want another child and was doing everything he could to make her body abort the child she was carrying.

Thankfully, their second child, a daughter, was born with no ill effects from the starvation and the beatings her mother endured.

One time Nachum was without his wife at Glatt Chow and did not like his food.

"This food is disgusting! You shouldn't even feed it to a dog! How dare you give it to me!" he yelled furiously at Laura. His outburst shook the other patrons of the restaurant and Laura cringed in fear from his tirade. He was out of control and did not care a wit.

Bert saw the outburst and was in shock. He recognized the man and was almost ready to step in to protect Laura, but she was able to placate the pugnacious man.

"I'm terribly sorry that your meal wasn't to your liking. I'll be happy to get you something else. And to make it right, your dessert is on me," she said in a soothing voice.

He calmed down and ordered another entree. Before bringing Nachum his food, she surreptitiously spat in it. The food was not damaged, but she felt better. She later regretted her actions, but could not undo her feat.

Eventually, Esther got up the courage to run away with her children, to her parents, the Goldschmidt's, in Queens. She had no money or identification, but she was able to find some small change in a drawer in the living room end table. Esther climbed out the window and carefully took her two young children with her. She was able to get the double stroller out to help her transport the babies. She ran to Coney Island Avenue as fast as her frail body could manage and used a payphone to make a phone call.

When Mrs. Goldschmidt answered the phone, Esther broke down and cried. "Ema, I'm in trouble, please help me."

"Esther? What's wrong? Where are you?" her mother asked concerned and shaking.

"I'm on the corner of Coney Island Avenue and Avenue O. I have my babies with me. Please come and get me. I'm scared." Her hot tears were staining her taut face. She was wailing like a child. Several passersby noticed the broken woman, but no one stopped to render aid.

Mrs. Goldschmidt heard the desperation in the voice of her troubled daughter. "We are on our way. Stay there."

After hanging up the phone, Esther noticed her reflection in the plate of the payphone and was appalled at the image staring back at her. She remembered being such a pretty, young woman, but the stress of being an abused woman for years had taken its toll on her. She had lost quite a bit of weight and looked pale and gaunt. Her *shaitel* was not brushed and she did not have on any makeup. She did not recognize the woman staring back at her in the reflection.

An hour later found Esther sitting in her parents' car. They both came to get her and did not recognize the emaciated young woman who got into their car. Her clothes hung on her weary and skeletal body as if on a hanger. On their way to Queens, Esther cried bitterly as she poured out her heart to her parents. They listened in stunned silence to her unbelievable tale and were barely able to contain their anger at their son-in-law. How could he treat their daughter like a punching bag? This was unheard of in their circles: Jewish men do not treat their wives like this. They were outraged at him and the lack of appropriate action by the authorities.

When they arrived at their house in Queens, Esther started to feel safe once again in the protective shelter of her loving parents.

Her father said, "I want Ema to take pictures of you in case this goes to court. I want proof of the hell you have been enduring. I also want you to take this notebook and start writing everything you remember. Write down every detail and nuance. Include as many dates as possible."

"I don't remember the dates, I barely know what today's date is."

"Do the best you can. The more you document, the better off you will be in the end. Also, make note of anyone you told anything to; doctor visits, hospital visits and anything else that would help document the abuse."

Nachum later returned home to an empty apartment. He was furious and started throwing things around the apartment, screaming in enmity for his wife as he tore her clothes to shreds. He raged on for about thirty minutes. When he calmed down from his tirade, he thought about calling the police, but when he looked around the now slovenly apartment with the torn clothes strewn about, broken furniture and other household goods, he reconsidered.

The next day, when his wife had not returned home, he was not sure what to do. If he called the police, he would have to explain the locks on the doors and the destroyed clothing. He decided to contact his in-laws instead.

"Hi, this is Nachum," he decided to play coy and innocent, "have you seen my wife? She left here yesterday without a word. I'm concerned?" He was still so angry that he could not even bring himself to mention her name.

"You've got to be out of your mind!" Mrs. Goldschmidt shouted into the phone. "How dare you! You abuse and beat my precious daughter, the mother of your children, and you have the audacity and unmitigated gall to pretend to be concerned?" She slammed down the phone, she sat down shaking, put her head in her hands and cried.

Esther came over to her mother, sat down on the sofa, and put her thin boney arm on her mother's shoulder and they cried. The temerity of Nachum's phone call surprised them and shook them to their core, "That buzzard!" Esther cringed thinking about the man to whom she was married. She wondered what happened to the man she once loved and married. Was that person only a façade, a figment of her imagination? All the pain and misery over the past several years seemed like decades ago to her.

"Sweetheart, even though he is a nasty and bad person, don't lower yourself to his level. You are better than that and we must turn to HaShem to guard and protect us. Come; let's say some Tehillim and daven to HaShem, if not for His salvation, then for your mental and emotional recovery."

Nachum plotted his revenge. He had to get her back and the only way he knew how to do this was to wreak havoc on her family. It is amazing how delusional a narcissistic person can be, thinking that if he does more harm to someone that it will entice them to return.

His first act of reprisal was to disturb their sleep by calling their house in the middle of the night. As soon as someone answered, he hung up the phone. It got to the point where they just screened all of their incoming calls by letting them go to the answering machine.

He then sent them threatening letters, but did not have the courage to sign them. The Goldschmidts kept a log of every incident and filed the letters for the future.

He stalked them by sitting in his car outside their house and places of work, making sure they saw him, they took pictures. He bought a police band scanner so when the Goldschmidts called the police he quickly drove away. He made up lies about them and reported the prevarications to their places of employment, in an unsuccessful attempt to get them all fired.

He went by their house in the middle of the night and punctured their car tires. No one saw anything, but they took pictures.

One night Nachum cut the brake line of their car. When Mr. Goldschmidt tried to drive to work in the morning, he had no brakes and was in an accident. Thankfully, no one was seriously hurt. The police investigated and although they suspected Nachum, they found no evidence to verify his involvement.

One time, he even mailed them a bullet as an unveiled threat. There were no fingerprints on the projectile so there was no evidence pointing to the sender.

Immediately after moving to her parents' house in Queens, Esther filed for a civil divorce. After a while, Nachum finally signed the papers and the couple was legally divorced. However, he refused to give her a *get,* just another way to harass her and make her life miserable.

The Goldschmidts made sure it became public knowledge that despite the *bais din* requiring him to give a *get* he refused. As a result, he was ostracized from the *shul* and the general Jewish community. He was not given an *aliya*, he was not allowed to lead the services and no one would sit near him. He was never invited to a *kiddush* or other *simcha*. This shunning continued for about a year.

He lost his job because of his abnegation of withholding the *get*. Since no Jew would hire him, the only job he was able to get was as a cab driver for a non-Jewish company. He felt humiliated with what he felt was this low-level job for degenerates. However, his anger kept him steadfast in his dogged determination to inflict as much pain as possible on his ex-wife. He was not going to let his pride get in the way of his retribution for her leaving him. He did not even consider the possibility that it was his own fault for treating her in such a despicable way.

Esther again became another statistic and was now an *agunah*, a woman chained in a marriage that was no marriage at all. She tried to rise above the situation, but it was not easy. She was unable to move on from her dissolved marriage since according to Jewish Law, it was not abrogated until he gave her a *get*. Some friends tried to intervene and influence him but to no avail. Nachum was being stubborn and not willing to relent in any way.

Esther and her two children were living with her parents but felt so alone. She was depressed but was trying not to let it affect her, by plastering a smile on her face. She endeavored to do so especially in front of her parents in order not to bring them more pain. Her parents were mortified that their precious daughter was in such dire straits and there was nothing they could do to extricate her from the horrible situation in which she found herself.

Rabbi Ginsburg had been unaware of anything untoward in Nachum's behavior toward his wife. In August 1983, word reached the Rosh HaYeshiva about what his former *talmid* was doing and he immediately went to talk to him in private. Rabbi Ginsburg was willing to humiliate himself to free a woman from the binds of being an *agunah* and with alacrity, went to the apartment of his former *talmid*. He cried with the recalcitrant husband; he begged and cajoled Nachum to give a *get*.

Nachum was intractable and adamantly refused to give a *get*. Grievously, Rabbi Ginsburg got up to leave. "I would like to remind you of the Mishneh. 'A woman acquires herself in one of two ways; either with the receipt of a *get* or if her husband dies.'"

"Bahh. It is nothing," he said depreciatingly while waving his hand and scoffing his former *rebbi* and the Mishneh. Nachum was exasperated and angry with everyone and did not care anymore.

Shocked at what he heard, and disappointed with his former student, Rabbi Ginsburg just shook his head, and with tears in his eyes, he left. His heart went out to Esther. He thought to himself, "This should not be happening. Not my people." He did not care for his own honor, but that Nachum should scoff the holy Mishneh, that was untenable and a grave mistake.

# September 1983
## Flatbush, New York

Mordechai Samuel looked sharp in his fancy suit; his bearing was striking and memorable. In fact, Mordechai used his appearance to his advantage. He was six-foot-four-inches tall with a shock of red hair and blue eyes. Although he talked with a slight lisp, he spoke well.

Mordechai had what he considered a great investment plan. He had been doing small investments for a few years and had several investors who trusted his word. He was not greedy; he made sure his clients made a small but consistent return on their money. This had worked well for a number of years; particularly well for him.

Because of his success with his first investors, he was able to convince new investors to join him and that is when Mordechai started to get greedy.

Slowly, he lowered the expectations of his investors. He wanted to keep more of the money that was flowing through his hands. The new investors did not receive as many details of the investments as did his first clients.

With some of the investment money, he bought himself a new car. He got away with it and that encouraged him to become bolder and start living the high life. Mordechai started paying returns to the original investors from the new infusion of capital paid by the new investors. He was pocketing some of the money and using it to live well.

He was building a proverbial house of cards that would inevitably collapse. This is a Ponzi scheme and is illegal: nearly everyone loses money, usually significant amounts.

He misappropriated some of the money to rent a nice office in Borough Park. He used the space to look sophisticated and meet with more prospective clients. When the new investors saw his fancy digs, they became excited and he was able to seduce additional investors. When he met with new people, he was jovial, debonair and affable, often taking them to a restaurant; everyone loved Mordechai. He was smart and did not promise unrealistic returns.

He still invested the money in legitimate investments, but he took some of the incoming money for himself. This worked well as he was getting additional clients. He kept doing this repeatedly and he was taking more and more off the top for himself.

Eventually, things started to get complicated and he was running out of money to pay the earlier tier investors. He kept trying to find new investors to pay the original ones, but it was becoming increasingly difficult. The pressure on him was increasing weekly. Things were starting to fall apart and he was concerned. He would stay up all night trying to conceive new ideas to get himself out of the quagmire and during the day, he often appeared disheveled and haggard.

His Ponzi scheme finally collapsed at the end of 1984 and he was arrested. When things came to a head and everything disintegrated, he felt the tremendous pressure lift from his shoulders only to be replaced by the burden of a possible stint in jail.

Mordechai proclaimed his innocence and said it was all just a big mistake. He was scared and did not want to go to prison, so he went to Rabbi Mishovsky and asked for a *beracha*. The Rebbe cryptically said, "May HaShem reveal the truth."

Mordechai ended up in front of Judge Archer and was sentenced to eight years in Fort Dix Federal Prison in New Jersey. He had to pay a large fine, make restitution and was sent to prison at the beginning of 1985.

# September 8, 1983
## Flatbush, New York

Rosh HaShanah has always been a time for introspection and trying to become close to HaShem. Most people use this special time to elevate themselves spiritually and most often are rewarded from on High with reciprocity: HaShem sees His children trying to come close to Him, so He draws nearer to them in turn.

Nachum Weiss knew he was wrong, but was too angry to care and he wanted his revenge. Already he could not remember the exact reason he wanted retribution, it was something he had to have. He knew it was a sin, but his anger and resentment made him not care, despite the fact that his own family did not support his actions. Withholding the *get* from his wife was his only weapon and he was going to lord that over her as long as possible, even though he was also suffering.

He had a vivid memory of the not-so-veiled threat from his former *rebbi*, Rabbi Ginsburg, but was not going to let that stand in his way.

On the first day of Rosh HaShanah Nachum sat alone in a *shul*. Since no one was willing to sit next to him, he took a folding chair and sat in a corner. He knew he would not receive any honors or even greetings from other congregants, so he just sat quietly with everyone else in *shul*, in seclusion. He felt so alone and longed for any human contact, even from the *gabbai* to ask him to open the ark, but it was not to be. No one even looked in his direction and it made him feel even worse; it almost brought a tear to his eyes with remorse.

During *davening*, just as the first few blasts from the *shofar* were sounded, Nachum was suddenly struck with a tremendously sharp pain in his temple. He dropped to the floor, writhing in pain that was so acute he almost passed out. He felt as if someone had driven a screwdriver into his temple. Despite the fact that he was going against the *bais din* and not issuing a *get*, one could not stand by and watch him suffer and possibly die. Someone in *shul* immediately called Hatzalah.

He was rushed to the hospital with massive migraine headaches, photophobia, and dizziness. He mentioned to the ER doctor that he had nausea, lethargy and was feeling weak. Until the hospital staff had run their tests, he was unable to have any pain medication. After a few hours of tests, during which he endured unbearable pain and suffering, they gave Nachum something to take the edge off the pounding in his skull.

After several days and numerous tests, the medical staff finally came up with a diagnosis. He had an idiopathic subdural hematoma.

There was no apparent cause for the bleeding in his brain. More testing was needed to find the cause for a twenty-three-year-old man who was otherwise healthy, having bleeding on the brain with no known trauma.

Nachum was confused and did not understand why he was in so much pain. What could have caused this brain bleed? He just wanted to get on with his life but was too self-centered to think that there may be a correlation between his sudden illness and his recalcitrance in giving a get to his ex-wife.

They did more testing and scans, and finally came to a conclusion, but it was not good. Nachum had stage-three brain cancer. It was hypercellular: and the cells were actively dividing. It was often called anaplastic astrocytoma, was inoperable and he did not have much time left.

On *Erev Yom Kippur* morning, he received the shocking information of his impending demise. He was devastated and could not believe that he was dying at such a young age. He felt his entire world was spinning around him out of control and he was scared. The news shocked him to the core of his being and he was pacing the room like a caged animal.

As quickly as possible, he mustered the courage and ran to Rabbi Ginsburg crying. "Please *daven* for me," he implored his former *rebbi*. "I don't want to die. Not like this. The doctors tell me that it will be a slow and painful death." He felt that there was no one else to whom he could turn; no one who would understand him or his predicament.

"Give your wife a *get*," he said unemotionally.

"Okay. I will, after *Succos*; maybe in a month or two." Nachum responded quickly.

"Not sufficient. Your wife has suffered long enough," Rabbi Ginsburg said sternly.

"When?"

"Now! You have waited too long."

"I can't."

"Get out!" demanded the Rosh HaYeshiva unceremoniously, pointing to the door.

"Please help me," he pleaded. He was scared.

"Give her a *get*, now."

He fell into a chair feeling empty and full of despair. "Fine," he reluctantly agreed submissively. He was defeated and feeling as if his whole world was collapsing in on him. He had no other choice but to comply.

"Don't move," ordered the Rosh HaYeshiva.

Rabbi Ginsburg immediately went to the other room and made a few phone calls. Within fifteen minutes, Rabbi Starr, Esther Weiss and two of Rabbi Ginsburg's students joined the clique. Esther arrived escorted by both of her parents. She could barely contain herself with excitement, anticipating what was about to finally come to fruition.

During the next thirty minutes, a *get* was written and Nachum dropped it into the hands of Esther Weiss, the former *agunah*. She was now a free woman.

Esther sat there crying in her mother's arms, while the Rosh HaYeshiva gave Nachum a heartfelt *beracha* for a speedy recovery.

Everyone had an uplifting *Yom Kippur*, even Nachum. Esther and her family were ecstatic with her newfound freedom crying tears of thanks to HaShem throughout the holy day. Rabbi Ginsburg said that Nachum was welcome and could *daven* in his *Yeshiva* for *Yom Kippur*. Nachum, who felt relief both mentally and spiritually, accepted the offer, where he cried to his Maker for healing from his brain tumor. He was feeling emotionally spent, but strangely contrite and relieved. The Rosh HaYeshiva made it clear that Nachum had done *teshuvah* and was no longer to be ostracized from the community; to publicly demonstrate absolution, he made sure Nachum received an honor.

For some reason, at the conclusion of *Yom Kippur*, Nachum was feeling better on several levels. When the *shofar* was blown at the end of *Yom Kippur*, his headache went away with the blast. To him, it was a miracle and Nachum attributed his good cheer to the uplifting *Yom Kippur* he just experienced. He also accredited his changed disposition to the fact that he had finally given the *get* to Esther. Rabbi Ginsburg suggested to Nachum that he seek out Rabbi Mishovsky for a *beracha*.

The next day, Nachum disclosed to the *Rav* his entire story, concluding with the mention of his brain tumor and asked the *Rav* for a *beracha*.

When Rabbi Mishovsky heard about the brain tumor, he waved his hand deprecatorily and said, "ברוך רופא חולים." (Blessed is the Healer of the sick.)

Nachum was in shock. "Is the *Rav* saying that I am healed? That nothing is wrong with me?"

The Rabbi just smiled and returned to his learning.

As per doctor's orders, two days after *Yom Kippur*, Nachum went back to the hospital for more tests. All the medical professionals were shocked when all the evaluations revealed there was no cancer. There was no trace of the subdural hematoma or any other medical problems. The doctors had no explanation; they had never seen anything like it and concluded that there must have been a mistake with the first scans. Nachum was surprised, but at the same time, he was not too incredulous. He felt enormous relief and was glad he was sitting down when he received the news.

Nachum went back to his Rosh HaYeshiva to tell him the news. Rabbi Ginsburg just smiled. From then on, Nachum became an ardent and staunch follower and supporter of Rabbi Ginsburg. He was a changed man.

Unfortunately for Nachum, Esther and her parents filed charges for assault, unlawful imprisonment, battery and more.

Remorsefully, he plead guilty and was sentenced by Judge Richard Archer to five years in Fort Dix Correctional Institute in New Jersey. When he got out, he would start life over and be the upstanding citizen and Torah man he was meant to be.

Rabbi Ginsburg kept up a correspondence with Nachum while he was in prison, even going to visit him on a few occasions.

# October 1983
## New York City, New York

Ahmed had taken several classes in infectious diseases and planned to use that knowledge for his terrorist plans. Because he also had computer knowledge and training and spoke two languages, he was in demand. He applied for and quickly landed a job as a technician in a virus lab in Manhattan. Although he made decent money, this was not his goal. He did not care if he made a good salary; he just wanted access to the infectious bacteria, pathogens and other chemicals only available in that type of lab. His issue was that it took time away from his planning, and more importantly, his relaxation. He hated having to work, as by nature he was a lazy person.

Nostalgically, he recalled his lazy days and weeks back home in Iraq when for the most part he could live like a sloth. However, he did not miss living in squalor and not being able to rub two pennies together. Nonetheless, he missed being able to get up at the crack of noon. Oftentimes he would just walk around the town, sometimes whiling away the day playing *sheshbesh* (backgammon).

"I wish my friends could see me now," he thought to himself. The problem was that back home, he had no friends.

THE MOST INFECTIOUS BIOCHEMICALS WERE stored in a specialized virus vault in Utah and quite a number were stored in Fort Detrick, Maryland; many states also had local labs. They all worked in conjunction with the Centers for Disease Control and Prevention.

A virus vault is an environmentally controlled and highly secure chemical and pathogen storage facility. Some delicate and sensitive chemicals were also stored in these vaults; many had been weaponized. The antidotes were also stored in the labs for easy access.

When walking into such a building, one has to go through a screening process. After a detailed security screening, everyone has to wear special clothing. Each level has its own air filtration system and negative pressure.

There are five levels of contagion in these types of labs. The first level house the least contagious diseases. On this level, basic precautions are all that are needed: simple disposable gowns, gloves, and cloth facemasks.

The first level is completely below the ground. Each successive level further beneath, contains stronger and worse infections and bacteria.

The fifth level was almost one-hundred feet below ground and contained the most virulent and infectious bacteria. Only someone wearing a complete airtight body suit and breathing apparatus could even enter into the airlock leading into the highly secure lab on this level. Even under such conditions, all work and experiments were conducted in an environmentally sealed box.

On every level of this type of lab, each virus and contagion is stored in individual special air-lock type containers under specific environmental conditions: individually monitored and maintained for its specific contents.

In the worst-case scenario – the release of a deadly pathogen - the entire facility would lockdown and be set to implode upon itself within a few minutes, causing all of the bacteria to be destroyed. The side effect of this is that nothing would survive: including humans and any animals inside.

Ahmed had a good idea of what chemicals he would want and need for what he considered his adventure. Getting his hands on the chemicals and viruses would take time. He could not just walk out with everything he needed as if it were a grocery store.

Over the course of time, and in minute quantities, he was able to surreptitiously sneak different biological and other chemicals he would need, out of the lab. He was cautious with his misappropriations; there was no rush to get these supplies.

Ahmed was part of a team that was working on a modified Marburg virus. The Marburg virus is a hemorrhagic fever virus of the *Filoviridae* family.

The technicians at the lab had been able to make a variant to the virus that was airborne and had an incubation period of only hours instead of five to ten days. They were now looking to create a vaccine, inoculation or cure.

Ahmed was intrigued and had an idea.


# November 1983
## Borough Park, New York

It was an exciting and yet confusing time for Laura while dating her new friend Moshe. After about eight months of dating, Laura realized that although she liked Moshe and he was a nice guy, something was off about him. She could not figure out what was wrong as there was nothing specific upon which she could put her finger.

Laura needed someone to talk with about her beau and went to her friend Emily to get her opinion. "I like this man, but something is wrong. I just can't place it. Something seems to be off. I know he is a *baal teshuvah*, but his affectations are just slightly ...I don't know... He makes me feel uncomfortable, but I don't know why."

Emily was not sure as she did not know the young man, but offered a friendly ear and the willingness to observe him.

At the behest of Laura, Emily went to the restaurant while Moshe had dinner one evening. "He seems Okay, but maybe you should ask Rabbi Mishovsky. He is prescient and may see something to guide you."

"That's an exceptional idea. Thanks for the advice."

Just prior to her going to see Rabbi Mishovsky, she also mentioned her concerns to her friend Bert Sobol who watched Moshe for a few days and realized that he was not who he said he was. Bert noticed that Moshe hung around Muslims, lived outside of the Jewish community and always took off his *yarmulke* before entering his house. He could not figure out exactly who he was or what his end game was, but his actions seemed strange.

"Rabbi, I have been seeing a man for a few months. His name is Moshe. I don't know, but something seems strange. I can't place it, but I'm confused. I need advice."

"נאמנים פצעי אוהב, ונעתרות נשיקות שונא" Mishley (Proverbs) 27:6 "Faithful are the wounds inflicted by a friend, but superfluous are the kisses of an enemy."

It took Laura some time to decipher the cryptic words of the Rabbi, she was not even sure what he meant, however, she took it to mean she should terminate the relationship with Moshe. Before she had the opportunity to do so, she chanced upon Bert.

"I will be honest with you, I can't define it, but something is wrong with him. Given your concern, you should consider breaking up with him." He also told her of his observations and where he saw Moshe hanging around.

"Thanks for your help. I spoke with Rabbi Mishovsky and I will be ending it."

"What did he say?" Bert inquired.

"You know the Rabbi, he just quoted a *passuk*, but I think I know what he meant.

"He said, 'Faithful are the wounds inflicted by a friend, but superfluous are the kisses of an enemy.' I understand this to mean that the wounds of a friend are not a problem, but even the kisses of an enemy are bad. He wants me to break it off with Moshe."

"Good luck to you. Let me know if you need anything."

Laura took a few days to ponder her predicament and exactly how to go about it. She knew she had to break it off with her beau but was not eager to do so.

She knew that she was not resolute, but had to forge forward. "If I do this in person," she thought to herself, "I will capitulate to the pressure I know he will place on me. I'd better not do this in person."

"Moshe, this is Laura," she said into the phone the next night, "I think we need to stop seeing each other." Her voice was shaking since there was part of her that did not want to break off the relationship, but logically, she knew it was the right thing to do. Her heart did not want to stop dating Moshe, but her head was telling her that it was necessary.

"Why? What's wrong?" he asked concerned. He was not expecting this and did not want to lose her, his first girlfriend.

"We need to break up." She was evasive, as she did not want

to give a reason.

"Did I do something wrong?" he asked, a bit more terse than he wanted to be. He was agitated and felt he was losing her, but did not know why.

"No. It's nothing to do with you," she said ambiguously but trying to be resolute. She did have feelings for Moshe and yet was confused at the same time.

"So what is it?" he asked becoming desperate.

"We need to break up," she said quickly, wanting to end the conversation.

"Is it someone else?" he asked suspiciously.

"No, there's no one else," she said defensively feeling insulted by the insinuation.

"So why?"

"We need to break up," she reiterated. "That's my reason. Nothing more."

"That's not a reason," he pleaded with desperation in his voice. He wanted to know why she was ending the relationship, this way maybe it was something he could counter or reason about with her. He did not want to let go of her, "I like you and really want to continue to date you. Please, don't end it."

"That's my reason. It's the only reason I'm giving." She felt she was beginning to waver in her resolution. "I have to end this call or I will recant," she thought.

"Please, let's meet and talk about this in person."

She was about to relent when she suddenly remembered the Rabbi's words to her. "Faithful are the wounds inflicted by a friend, but superfluous are the kisses of an enemy."

"No, I'm sorry," she affirmed. This has to be it. Please don't call me or come to the restaurant..."

"Wait," he interrupted. "Please, I need you in my life. You mean so much to me." In actuality, she was the only woman he had ever dated and was afraid to end it and lose her. He was petrified he would never find anyone else. In some ways, Laura reminded him of his mother Sarah.

"Goodbye," she said firmly, hung up the phone and took a deep breath. Suddenly, she felt a tremendous weight lifted off her shoulders. Forthwith, she felt good about her decision: it felt right. She smiled to herself, and in her mind, she closed the book on that part of her life.

Unfortunately, Moshe did not feel the same way and he wanted her back.

Moshe immediately called her back. "Hello?" she said into the receiver.

"Please don't hang up. I need you in my life."

"I asked you not to call me. Our relationship is over," she said adamantly. "I am hanging up again and this time, do not call me back."

She gently placed the receiver back on its cradle.

Moshe did not get the hint. Well, it was not a hint; it was a definitive call for the termination of the courtship. However, he was not willing to give up on her.

He called back.

She let the phone ring and even unplugged the answering machine. Moshe hung up and called again. She just stood by the phone trying to ignore the blaring tones as a tear came to her eye. She remembered when just recently she would have pined for him to call and when she anticipated hearing his voice. Now she was dreading the sound.

Laura felt as if the walls of her apartment were closing in on her and decided to go for a walk. The cool crisp air felt good and helped her relax and feel better about her decision.

After walking around for about an hour, she felt much more composed. Immediately upon returning to her apartment, the phone started ringing and startled her. Before she even lifted the incessant ringing device, she knew who was calling.

"What?!" she barked into the phone.

"Uh, hello?" a male voice responded: it was not Moshe. The voice was familiar, but she was so nonplussed she could not immediately place it.

"Sorry, I've had a rough day," she said and then immediately regretted revealing something so personal to some unnamed person on the phone. "Who is this?" she asked more cordially, the tension still in her voice.

The disembodied voice said, "This is Bert Sobol. I wanted to make sure you were okay. I know you were planning to break up with your friend and I wanted to make sure things went well for you."

"I'm so sorry for snapping before. I broke it off with him and he is not letting go. He's not getting the message and has been repeatedly calling me. I'm on edge."

"No wonder you answered the phone the way you did. Look, would you like me to talk with him?" he asked sincerely. Laura was a nice woman but not Bert's type. She was too middling for his tastes. However, that would not stop him from trying to assist her.

"That would be appreciated. Thank you."

"Certainly."

After they hung up, her phone rang again. This time she was more cautious when answering. "Hello?"

"Hi." It was Moshe.

She was exasperated and just hung up the phone.

For the next few hours, there was a respite from the incessant ringing of the phone. After taking a shower and eating some dinner, she decided to sleep for the night. She had to work in the morrow.

Laura was in a fitful sleep when the ringing of the phone abruptly awakened her. The sudden ring cut the stillness of the night like a knife and frazzled her nerves. Without even answering the phone, she unplugged it and returned to bed. The blissfulness of sleep evaded her for the rest of the night. She was frustrated and now clearly saw why Moshe was not for her.

Once the morning came, she realized she had actually fallen into a desultory sleep and was not feeling fresh. She took another shower to help her feel more refreshed, but it did not accomplish much.

Laura went to work at Glatt Chow and had a cup of hot coffee to help her wake up. She was not in the mood to work, but persevered and did her job to perfection, as always. Every time the door opened, she jumped a bit thinking it may be Moshe invading her space. Menashe noticed that she was not herself and inquired as to her wellbeing. She was evasive and he just let it drop. She had another cup of coffee.

In the early evening, Moshe showed up at the restaurant. As he was about to enter the restaurant, Bert appeared out of nowhere to prevent his ingress.

"Who are you?" Moshe asked as he was trying to get past the muscular man.

"I am here at the behest of Laura Feld. She does not want to hear from you. Leave her alone."

"Get out of my way!" Moshe demanded.

"Leave here or I'll call the police. You are not wanted here."

"You are not my father or my boss," Moshe said as he reached out with his right hand to shove Bert aside. Big mistake. Bert stepped to his left and slid his left foot forward to check Moshe's right leg. Simultaneously, he executed a right inward and left outward parry to the inside and outside of his outstretched arm, respectively. This forced Moshe to bend forward.

Moshe was completely off balance and was forced to put his left hand on the ground to prevent himself from falling flat on his face.

Bert released Moshe from his iron grip. Moshe stumbled from the sudden discharge of his arm and got to his feet. "Get lost and don't ever bother Laura again."

Moshe walked away in frustration while muttering something unintelligible under his breath. He was humiliated and angry.

Moshe was disquiet and not sure what to do. He thought that if he left Laura alone for a few days, she would miss him, come to her senses and would want him back.

Laura was enjoying the quiet and tranquility of the next several days. She had not heard from Moshe and was hoping he had moved on to someone or something else.

The phone rang. Absentmindedly, Laura put down the book she had been reading and reached for the phone.

"Hello?"

"Hi Laura, this is Moshe. I miss you."

Surprised by his call, she did not hang up the phone, she just sat there, mute.

"Are you there?" he asked.

"No!" she screamed into the phone. "Stop calling me. I don't want to hear from you again." Before he could respond, she slammed down the phone.

This went on for a while. Laura documented every incident in a notebook. She called the police to get a temporary restraining order (TRO). Because she had documented the harassment, a judge ordered a TRO that was put into place for two weeks. After the two-week period, there would be a hearing to determine if a more permanent restraining order was needed. Once the police delivered the TRO to Moshe, everything stopped; he no longer harassed her.

A few days after the court order was implemented, Laura was in a store on Thirteenth Avenue near Forty-Eighth Street. While there, she noticed Moshe and immediately approached the proprietor.

"Sir, I'm sorry to bother you, please call the police." Laura frantically begged the owner while her heart pounded heavily. "There is a restraining order on that man to keep one-hundred yards away from me."

"I will call immediately and then restrain him. Don't worry; I will protect you if it comes to that. Stay next to me."

"Thank you." She immediately felt better knowing that this man was looking out for her.

The police arrived a few minutes later. Liam Connors conducted a brief investigation.

Connors turned to Laura, "Ma'am, I completely understand what is going on here." He was trying to be compassionate. "I was the officer who delivered the TRO to Moshe. However, he has not violated the court order..."

"What do you mean?" she frantically interrupted Connors. "He is within one-hundred yards of me! How can he not be in violation of the TRO?" she asked incredulously with tears in her eyes.

"It's very simple," he replied patiently. "Although I understand your feelings, according to witnesses, he was in the store before you entered. He did not come within one-hundred yards of you. You came into space he was already occupying. I cannot arrest him as it was not his fault."

"Oh," was all she could muster to say as she lowered her head and looked at the floor.

"Ma'am, I will stay with you until you get back to your home. You are discombobulated and I want to make sure you feel safe." Connors was being gracious and professional.

"Thank you officer; I would like to go home now."

When she appeared before the judge at the hearing for the permanent restraining order, he did not see a cause for the continuance of the order. Much to Laura's consternation, the TRO was terminated. However, the judge did strongly suggest to Moshe that he leave Laura alone.

# December 1983
## Yerushalayim, Israel to Borough Park, New York

It was time and he was so excited he could barely contain himself; everyone was happy for the *simcha*. He had never done anything similar to this and no one he knew personally had done so either. *Rav* Horowitz spoke eloquently about the importance of this forgotten *mitzvah*. He spoke about making sure to write every letter and word as transmitted from HaShem to Moshe *Rabaynu*, carefully and accurately. The Rosh HaYeshiva spoke briefly about the different types of scripts that have been used over the millennia. The Ancient Hebrew script has not been used in over 3,000 years, but it is still part of our history. It is similar to the Phoenician alphabet, but not the same.

The Rosh HaYeshiva extolled the *middos* of his *talmid* who was blushing at the sound of his name. At this auspicious occasion, he encouraged others to follow Yaakov's example.

Zev had taken a little longer than the two years he originally planned on to write the *Sefer* Torah for Yaakov. Applebaum was not concerned at all, often checking on the progress of the writing, but was excited to be doing this great *mitzvah*. On every occasion that

Yaakov went to check on the writing, he would first go to the *mikvah*. Zev showed Yaakov how to hold the feather quill and use the ink and Yaakov even wrote some of the letters of his own *Sefer* Torah. He was so excited and happy.

At the concluding ceremony of the writing of the Torah, Yaakov made a small celebration. However, the dancing and celebration at the *Yeshiva* went beyond this and continued for several hours. About fifty people wrote the last few *pesukim*. Of course, the Rosh HaYeshiva, his sons and sons-in-law, Yaakov, his *chavrusah* and many others, wrote a letter.

There was a beautiful procession with singing and dancing that left from the *Yeshiva*. Yaakov went with his new Torah to Ben Gurion International Airport. He would personally be taking it to America to its new home.

Once in America, at JFK airport, the celebration continued. A large procession picked Yaakov up from the airport and took him to Borough Park. The police had cordoned off the entire street in front of Rabbi Mishovskys *shul*. The celebration started at one end of the street with live music and dancing. The *Rav* danced excitedly in front of the new Torah. He grabbed his *talmid*, the owner of the *Sefer* Torah and his benefactor, and danced unabashedly together to honor HaShem and His Torah. It was a remarkable sight.

The celebration continued unabated inside the *shul* where wonderful words of Torah from the *Rav* and other rabbis were said repeatedly. The *Rav* spoke about the holy emanations that were brought down with every letter that was written in holiness.

He also explained, "To name something is to describe and define it and put it into the realm of our reality. HaShem, who is infinite and indefinable, cannot truly be named. Thus, God has no name, only names which are descriptions of the various behavior patterns that can be ascribed to His influence on our lives and His creations.

"HaShem said to Moshe Rabaynu, 'Tell the Children of Israel, that My name is *Eh-he-yeh*.' Where was I all these years and where can I be found? With you. I am being, I am existence, I am reality.

"In the words of the Medrash, 'God said to Moshe: you want to know My name? I am called by My deeds. I might be called *E-l Sha-dai*, or *Tzevakot*, or *Elokim*, or *Ha-Va-Ya-H*. When I judge My creatures, I am called *Elokim*. When I wage war on the wicked, I am called *Tzevakot*. When I tolerate the sins of man, I am called *E-l Sha-dai*. When I have compassion on My world, I am called *Ha-Va-Ya-H*...' (Shemos Rabbah 3:6)

"If we want to understand how to direct our prayers to Heaven through the correct channels, it helps to understand the Holy Names of HaShem. One should be aware that all the Names revealed in the Torah are the keys to anything a person needs in the world. When we contemplate these Names, we will understand that all of the Torah and Commandments are dependent upon them. At the point when we know the purpose of every Name, we will realize the greatness of 'He who spoke and thus the world came into being.' We will be fearful before Him and we will desire to cleave to Him through His blessed Names. Then we will be near to HaShem and our petitions will be accepted, as it is written: 'I will keep him safe, for he knows My Name. When he calls on Me I will answer him.' The *passuk* does not promise safety by merely mentioning His Name but by **knowing** His Name. It is the knowing that is the most significant. Only after the knowledge does the passage present the petition, '... when he calls on Me I will answer.'

"This means that when the time arrives we should know the Name that is intrinsically tied to what we need; then when we call, 'I will answer'. An example of this is when Jacob in time of trouble calls out *to E-L Sha-day* saying, 'And may *E-L Sha-day* dispose the man to mercy toward you.' (Bereishis 43:15).

"'Then will you understand the fear of *YKVK* and attain knowledge of HaShem.' (Tehillim 2:5) It is a shame that people who are beginning scholars of *Kabbalah* abuse these names, writing and saying them freely with no true fear of HaShem. 'Before His fury, who can stand, who will rise when He is angry?' (Nachum 1:6)[1]

Before the spellbound crowd, the *Rav* continued to expound on a few of the Holy Names of HaShem and their meanings.

Finally, Yaakov had a few words prepared for the occasion. In part, he said, "On two separate important occasions in our history, our entire nation has been elevated with our souls and spirits in such a way to be called the children of Avraham, Yitzchak, and Yaakov.

"The first major event was when we left Egypt. When Moshe *Rabaynu* announced to the Jewish people the redemption, it was a perfect opportunity for the people to ask him pertinent and relative questions. For example, how we would get out, the direction of travel, sustenance for three-million people and animals, and many other questions. However, the desire for the Redemption and more importantly, their faith, overcame their need for the knowledge and information. They had blind faith in the Word of HaShem through

---

[1] The forementioned *devar* Torah is from Introduction to Sha'are Orah, Chassidus Kabbalah and Meditation, page 94. By Reb Moshe Steinerman

Moshe. That is the meaning of Exodus 4:31 'ויאמן העם, וישמעו כי פקד ה' את בני ישראל וכי ראה את ענים ויקדו וישתחוו.' 'And the people believed, and they heard that HaShem had remembered the Children of Israel and that He saw their affliction, and they bowed their heads and prostrated themselves.' As the prophet says, Jeremiah 2:4 'זכרתי לך חסד נעוריך אהבת כלולותיך לכתך אחרי במדבר בארץ לא זרועה' 'I recall for you the kindness of your youth, the love of your nuptials, your following Me into the Wilderness, into a barren land.' This showed the maturity of the People of Israel. This showed the faith they had in our Maker, in the Big Boss.

"The second episode was at the time we received the holy Torah. In the first instance, when we followed HaShem out of Egypt, one could say it was due to the oppression and slavery that we were willing to endure. That could have been the reason we did not ask any questions of our pending exodus from Egypt. We did not ask questions because we were desperate to get out of the slave labor.

"However, when Moshe *Rabaynu* brought to us the Word of HaShem, we also could have asked questions. We could have asked, what was written in the Torah? Is it good for us? What will it do for us? And much more.

"We again rose to the occasion. Our faith overcame our desire for questioning. We knew and understood that anything HaShem offers us is for our benefit. That is why we said, 'We will do and we will listen.' That is the difference between them and us. The non-Jew first asks questions and wants details. We first turn to our faith and everything else will fall into place.

"We have to have faith and believe that everything the Big Boss does is for His people. This is the Torah. This is what He wants from us. This is why we celebrate the writing of a *Sefer* Torah that is transmitted letter by letter as it was given to us by HaShem through our great teacher Moshe.

"May we all be *zocheh* to follow in the great footsteps of our antecedents."

There was a resounding "Amen" from everyone present. It was an awe-inspiring experience for all involved that would be remembered for a long time to come.

It was a beautiful *seudas mitzvah*. Mr. and Mrs. Applebaum were proud of their son and were proud to help sponsor the festivities.

# 1984

## 1984
## Queens, New York

**Atarah**  Justin owned a nice house in Queens, New York left to her by her late husband. She was comfortable, although lonely without her husband. Her son, Tuvya, lived with her, but he was rarely home preferring to do odd jobs for people and gallivant around sowing his wild oats. After her husband died, Atarah's own health started to deteriorate and Tuvya became depressed, not wanting to get out of bed or go to work. He was upset that he lost his father and was afraid of losing his mother soon as well and being completely alone.

Atarah had been teaching piano for close to thirty years, and some of her students went on to perform music with different symphony orchestras around the country. One of her students became a pianist with the New York Philharmonic Orchestra; that student was her pride and joy. Atarah was an excellent pianist and teacher and enjoyed a great reputation.

Atarah started teaching Yaakov Applebaum piano when he was in junior high school. Yaakov was not planning to be a professional piano player; he just wanted to play the piano and learn more about music. He played well and had good tempo and fingering: he had innate musical talent.

One day in April 1981, after a piano lesson, Yaakov was

leaving Atarah's home studio to return to his parent's home. As he opened the door, Rivkah Somers was about to enter for her lesson. Yaakov held the door for her and said, "Hello."

Bashfully, Rivkah replied, "Hello." She thought to herself, "He is a nice-looking young man."

Yaakov thought to himself, "She has a *chayn* about her." Little did they know, this would not be the last time they would meet.

Since her husband died a few years ago, Atarah became concerned, almost to the point of being obsessed, about being without food and other essentials. She vividly remembered the New York City blackout on July 13 and 14, 1977. She also recalled the nor'easter - caused snowstorms of 1978 and February 1983. She and her son became preppers and started stocking food and water in their basement. As their stock built up, they bought some shelving units to keep their emergency supplies organized. They kept an accurate inventory of their stock and made sure to rotate their stores so nothing would become stale.

They came across a book called <u>Doomsday Bunker Book</u> and started to use it as a guide to building a safe-room. They decided to build a safe-room into the interior of the house to protect from a possible catastrophic and devastating situation that might arise in the future. The book was replete with information about what and how to stock, and how to fortify their house. There was also information on what to do in case of a nuclear explosion.

They redesigned their living room and den to make them a bit smaller and have a safe-room situated between them. They did not tell anyone they were building a safe-room, as there was a stigma against preppers with some people calling them crazy. The safe-room would also give them more privacy in case of a catastrophe. They would not have to be concerned about marauders if no one knew about their safe-room. It was their secret hideaway and a perfect bunker.

Tuvya was a skilled handyman and he remodeled their home to build the hidden safe-room. The safe-room was six feet wide and sixteen feet long, almost one hundred square feet. He lowered the floor about six-inches and made an additional raised floor to create a one-foot space in the floor for additional storage. He also constructed a loft to provide additional space for their cache. Their safe-room was tight and cramped, but habitable and safe.

Water and electricity were supplied via the main structure, and a toilet and sink emptied into the plumbing of the main house. The entrance to the safe-room was by means of a hidden panel in the hallway.

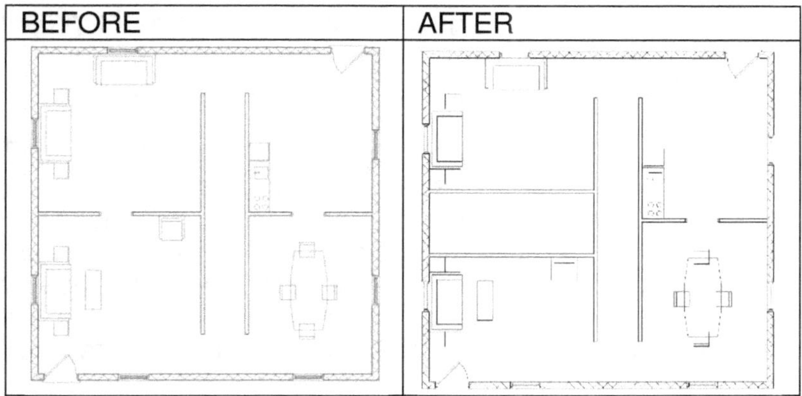



# January 1984
## Borough Park, New York

While in college, Ahmed again came across the publication, <u>Doomsday Bunker Book</u>. It had been a few years since he first saw the book in Saddam Hussein's office and seeing it brought back memories of his encounter with the dictator. He was now reminded that he wanted to use this book to help him design his own underground bunker to protect his cadre. Ahmed went to a local bookstore and bought it and read it cover to cover devouring it as a parched man in a desert would drink water. Because of the details in the book, he was able to get a good idea of how he wanted his own bunker designed. He had the funds available and thought it would be a good idea to protect himself and his conspirators. Ahmed was able to track down the author of the book, Jake Benjamin, who had an office on Thirteenth Avenue in Borough Park.

Ahmed contacted Jake and made an appointment to discuss his architectural needs for his future bunker. Based on the name of the author, he assumed the author was Jewish and therefore was loath to contract out to him. However, since Saddam Hussein himself had this man's book on his desk, Ahmed was willing to overlook that shortcoming; as long as circumstances suited his needs.

Ahmed had a few days to mull over the curious situation into which he was about to enter. He, a devout Muslim, was about to hire a Jew to design a bunker to protect himself and colleagues from the long-term terrorist attacks he was about to unleash on the Jews and other infidels who, in his opinion, were responsible for the ruination of the world. The irony of it all made him smile.

Ahmed saw a small sign on a door announcing the presence of the upstairs office for the architect, Jake Benjamin. As Ahmed opened the door to ascend the steps, he noticed a large *mezuzah* on the right doorpost.

"Oh no," he thought wryly, forcing a smile on his face. "This man is an orthodox Jew. This is even more ironic than I initially thought." He sucked in his breath and went up the stairs to the meeting. In the end, Ahmed did not care who designed his bunker, as long as it worked and was safe. It was more enjoyable since it was going to be an orthodox Jew who was going to be doing the design work that would protect him from his machinations to destroy the Jews.

"I've read your book and love it," he said with a heavy Middle-Eastern accent.

"Thank you very much," Jake responded with a modest smile.

"I'm concerned for some horrible tragedy that may befall us." Ahmed had his plan worked out in his mind. He would pretend to be a prepper and use that cover when conversing with Mr. Benjamin. "I want to build an underground bunker. It doesn't have to be anything fancy or large, just functional. I like the design in your book." He also noticed a large black *yarmulke* perched on Jake's head and stifled a smile along with a desire to strangle the infidel sitting across from him.

Jake Benjamin thought it fascinating that he had received several inquiries about designing bunkers. His book was selling quite well and it was leading to others wanting him to design a doomsday style bunker. It was clearly worth the massive effort to write and publish the book.

"I will be purchasing a property soon and when I have, I will give you the specs of the property so we can make sure there are no conflicts."

"You will need a surveyor for the property. I do some work with Abstract Surveyors. When you are ready, contact them. They do work in the Tri-State area." Jake gave Ahmed their contact information. For the next hour, they continued to discuss Ahmed's desires for the bunker. At the conclusion of the meeting, Jake had a good grasp of what Ahmed wanted.

After he left Jake's office, Ahmed walked a few blocks up Thirteenth Avenue to Forty-Fifth Street to an electronics store. He bought a Canon A-1 camera with a few lenses. He wanted a normal 50mm lens and a zoom. For the zoom, he went with the Vivitar 28 to 200 f/2.8 zoom. Ahmed purchased the Canon Speedlite 199A for the flash. He also bought a brick of 35mm, 200 ASA film with 36 exposures. He wanted to be able to take pictures as needed of his targets and of the construction of his bunker, and also to be able to reminisce and enjoy the fruits of his labor in the future. Ahmed was learning to be practical and thorough in his planning.

## January 1984
## Catskills, New York

Ahmed set up an appointment to meet with a real estate agent in the Catskills, New York. He wanted a piece of property that was close enough to New York to make it convenient enough to carry out his plans, but far enough to be safe and secluded.

Ahmed and Mohamed wended their way up the New York State Thruway toward the Catskills to White Lake, New York. About one-hundred miles north of Manhattan, they met with the realtor who showed them several properties. It was a beautiful and serene area along the largest natural lake in the region. They decided on a property that was just over ten acres of land that would be perfect for their needs. The property was mostly wooded and was a bucolic setting.

It had been an exhausting day driving around looking at various properties. However, it had been productive. They went back to the realtor's office to sign the papers and place a deposit. After they signed the papers for the purchase, they went to a local restaurant for something to eat. After dinner, since it was late, they rented a room in one of the hotels for the night. They were satisfied with a fruitful day; they would ratify the contract and then settle in a month.

## February 1984
## New York

It was a chilly day in February and Ahmed was wearing a heavy sweater. He still was not used to these cold winters in New York and preferred the relatively warm winters in Iraq. Here in New York, the outdoor temperature was hovering around thirty degrees. He remembered with a shutter a year ago on February 11 and 12, 1983, there was a major snowstorm called the Megalopolitan Snowstorm, an El Niño caused the storm that deposited about eighteen inches of snow in the New York metropolitan area. He shivered with the memories as he walked over to the thermostat and raised the heat two degrees.

"It is high time we get started," Ahmed thought to himself. "We have spent enough time with preparations; it is now time to start unleashing our wrath.

"I want to make a colossal fire in Manhattan in Grand Central Station. I want to kill as many infidels as possible. I want to start with something big. Any suggestions?" Ahmed asked his clique while pacing the floor, the chill in the air contrasted with the heat of hate in his heart.

Hussein said, "I can make a firebomb with potassium permanganate and sugar."

"Explain," Ahmed said, hopeful that the conflagration would match the fire he felt in his eyes.

"Potassium permanganate can be gotten from movie houses or prop houses. It's a salt made from manganese dioxide used to age props. Potassium permanganate acts as an oxidizer and added sugar, which is highly flammable, acts as a fuel source. When you mix the two together it makes a powerful fire. It can be the perfect incendiary device." He was proud of himself that he knew his chemistry and that his knowledge and skills were about to come in handy. Maybe he finally found his niche in life and a direction for his future.

Ahmed said, "That's great. Can you get, ummm, the chemical?" He did not want to embarrass himself by trying to pronounce the chemical's name.

"Yeah, I can get it; won't be a problem."

"How do we get it to Grand Central Station without being caught?"

"I have a few ideas," Hussein said. "There are underground tunnels in Manhattan that I can use to get it there. The mixture is highly volatile, so I'll have to be very careful. However, I know of a chemical mixture that I can apply to my body and clothes to protect myself. I will basically be fire retardant."

"You can do all this?"

"It will take some time and effort, but yes. I can do this. I'll carry the chemicals separately and make the mixture on location."

"Get to work," Ahmed ordered.

"I will give you a list of chemicals I will need. Some you can get from your lab, others from chemical supply houses. These are for the fire retardant to protect me."

"Okay. Give me the list and I will see what I can do," he said morosely.

Hussein sat down to make a list of the chemicals he would need and gave it to Ahmed.

> One ounce of sapphire
> One cup of aqua vapor from nicotine
> Two ounces of mercury
> Two ounces of liquid borax
> Half a cup of Myrrh
> Four ounces of ground hematite
> Some ground red-stone flakes

"You expect me to get all these?"

"If you want me to make a fire at Grand Central Station, then yeah; I don't want to burn to death."

Ahmed thought to himself, "Where's a good suicide bomber when I need one. I don't care if he dies or not. He's expendable, but I had better get those chemicals for him or he won't do the job."

Nizar went to get the potassium permanganate from a prop house in Manhattan. There was no difficulty obtaining the chemical, as it was widely available and not restricted or regulated. On his way back to the house, he also picked up some sugar. While in the city, he went to Grand Central Station to take some pictures to help in the planning of their attack.

NEW YORK HAD TWENTY-SIX subway lines and four hundred and sixty-eight subway stations. It was an efficient transportation system and would take him where he needed to go. He had already done research in the public library and had a good idea of what he needed.

Mohamed wanted to head toward Manhattan so he got onto the Fifty-Ninth Street Station in Brooklyn and got on the N train heading toward Ditmars Boulevard - Astoria. Twenty-six minutes later, he got off at the Fourteenth Street - Union Square (Uptown) Station. Ten minutes later, he boarded the six-train toward Pelham Bay Park and disembarked seven minutes later at the Fifty-First Street Station. It took him forty-three minutes. Not that he was in a rush, but he wanted to know as part of his planning.

Mohamed walked south to Grand Central Terminal and saw the impressive, majestic building. The main hall with a large American flag hanging from the vaulted ceiling was beautiful. The plethora of shops, signs, and people overwhelmed him. The cacophony of noise and the varied aromas assaulted him as he walked around and observed the organized mayhem. He was aghast and not ready for his senses to be stimulated by the sights, smells, and sounds of Grand Central Terminal.

Despite the fact that Nizar had already taken some pictures, Mohamed took some more in the Terminal and then went down to the Station below to do the same. He was pretending to be a tourist, which was not far from actuality. He took pictures of the different platforms and stairwells to help decide where to place the bomb.

After taking about a roll and a half of pictures, Mohamed then went back outside and walked five blocks north to the Waldorf Astoria.

He walked into the hotel and his jaw nearly dropped to the floor: he had never seen or imagined anything like it. The place was beautiful beyond anything he could have imagined, and the opulence scared him. In his mind, he thought, "This must be how kings live." He took some pictures of the outside and the inside of the building. He wanted to remember what this place looked like: it was palatial.

The hotel had such a glow it was as if the place was exuding warmth, even in February, and it looked as if all the walls were gold. There were mosaics on the floor, paintings on the walls, extravagant chandeliers, and wall sconces. He wondered if anyone played the highly polished grand piano in the lobby. There were small palm trees placed strategically around the lobby. It appeared that everything was chosen to match the coordination of charm and elegance around the hotel. He took a deep breath and felt refreshed from the clean air and pleasant fragrances in the hotel.

Mohamed entered Peacock Alley. It was a 300-foot glamorous corridor of marble and cherry wood. There was a world-famous five-star restaurant and bar with recessed lighting whose aromas aroused his olfactory senses. On the other side of the Alley, were the elevators. He went around the elevator bank to the Main Lobby of the hotel and rode the elevator down as far as it went to the lower basement level and he then exited the elevator. He looked around and saw no one, so he turned and headed north and found a discrete door labeled "Stairs E". The door was locked. He checked around and was glad that he was alone. He then drove a screwdriver into the old lock and easily broke it, opened the door and disappeared inside. He headed down a long flight of stairs with several landings. He estimated that it was about two flights or so. "The air down here is very still and heavy," he said out loud and the echoes off the walls startled him.

After exiting the stairwell, he turned south, flicked on a light switch and continued down a dimly lit corridor that looked as if it had not been accessed in years. In actuality, this sub-basement had not been in use since President Franklin Delano Roosevelt used it on October 21, 1944, when he addressed the Foreign Policy Association.

He found a locked entrance to a secret station that was down a stairway, concealed behind a brass door marked "101-121 49th Street", below a sign that read "Metro-North Fire Exit". No one ever came down here and he easily broke open the ancient lock. He entered a yellow stairwell and flicked a switch that turned on a single incandescent light bulb. He proceeded down the stairs an additional two stories. By his estimation, when he got to the bottom, he was about six or seven stories below ground level.

This was the secret "Track 61." He quickly took some pictures of the dimly lit cavern and expeditiously withdrew. He already had part of his plan worked out and his pictures taken.

He promptly made his way back to Brooklyn and dropped off the four rolls of film at a one-hour photo developer on Thirteenth Avenue.

The next day he picked up the pictures and made his way to the house to sketch out his plans.

Once Hussein had all of the chemicals he needed, he started to prepare for his attack. First, he reviewed the pictures and decided on the exact location for the fire and then he made plans of how he would get to the target zone. He would use the tunnels under Manhattan. Hussein also made the fireproofing chemical to apply to his body and clothing.

"We need more time to plan something in Grand Central Station: we're not ready. In the meantime, we can do something in the World Trade Center." Since taking the lead as the head of the cell, Ahmed became methodical and deliberate. He wanted additional time to make sure everything was in place.

Hussein was concerned he was being edged out of the attack. "Does that mean we are scrapping the fire?"

"No, you will still make the fire, but instead, just do it in the World Trade Center. It will take less planning to do it there. We will do something else at Grand Central Station at a later date."

"Okay, that's fine. I don't care where it happens." He liked the idea of a fire, especially since it was his idea. In actuality, he liked the smell of fire, he liked the way flames danced and the sounds of the cracking of the burning wood.

The next day, Hussein went to Manhattan with a backpack and supplies. He walked around the financial district enjoying the multitude of people. He walked along Wall Street. This was named for the wall built by the Dutch in the Seventeenth Century to protect themselves against attacks from the British, pirates, and various Native American tribes. Wall Street took the path of that wall. On April 30, 1787, on Wall Street is where President George Washington took the oath of office.

Slowly Hussein made his way to the North Tower of the World Trade Center.

Once inside the North Tower, he found the second-floor restrooms and entered a stall. He proceeded to liberally coat his body and clothes with the chemical mixture he prepared as a fire-retardant. It smelled horrible, but if it would protect him, he did not care. He mixed the sugar and potassium permanganate in a paper bag crushed it against the floor to cause friction. Immediately the mixture started to increase in temperature and started to smoke. He ran out of the bathroom to throw the smoking paper bag over the rail to the open concourse below. It was too late. While still in his hand it combusted and the next thing Hussein knew was that he was engulfed in flames. A few other people were minorly injured from the embers, only Hussein fared worse. The flame retardant mixture was completely ineffective and he screamed in horrible agony while burning to death and leaving a horrible stench in the air.

When Ahmed heard on the news about the failure of the terrorist act, he was furious at Hussein's incompetence. He was unmoved with the painful death of his cohort.

Ahmed called WABC news talk radio and said, "The Palestine Liberation Group claims responsibility for the fire in the World Trade Center." He immediately hung up the phone.

There was a big tumult as no one had ever heard of the Palestine Liberation Group. Immediately the news agency contacted the FBI with the tape of the admittance of responsibility. The FBI took it seriously, but there was no information about the Palestine Liberation Group in any of their computers and none of their contacts had ever heard of this new terrorist organization. They did not know if it was local, homegrown or international or even if it should really be taken seriously or not since the attack was a complete failure.

# February 1984
## Flatbush, New York

Yona Glick was desperate. He was still living in pain and had nothing to help ease the misery. He tried acupuncture, massage, and chiropractic treatments. He even went to a hypnotherapist for help. These modalities helped to a small degree but nothing took away the torment he lived with all day, every day. He could not live like this anymore. It was untenable and he was at wits' end with no one to turn to.

Yona lost his job and could not hold down another, so he was living in a homeless shelter and begging for food. He was completely out of control and had nowhere to go. He was struck by the dichotomy of the two different times of his recent life. Before his accident, he was living a comfortable life, had a good family and a nice house. After the collision, he was in penury and his life had fallen apart, his wife left him and he was living on the street.

He was hoping for compassion and again went to see Irwin for drugs; something for the pain, anything for the pain. He was despondent and went to see his supplier by the cemetery on Fort Hamilton Parkway and Thirty-Seventh Street. He did not have money for any drugs, so he begged and pleaded. He physically threw himself at Irwin, trying to get at any drugs he had on his person. Irwin never had anything on him to reduce his chances of being arrested with the incriminating evidence. Irwin just sidestepped the desperate lunging man who fell to the ground scraping his hands and knees on the concrete pavement. Clumsily Yona got up, stumbled and again fell on Irwin. However, this time, Irwin was ready with his knife. As Yona fell on him, he impaled himself on the protruding knife. Irwin jerked the knife upward, further into the chest of his attacker and let go of the knife. Yona stumbled backward with the knife still in his chest. Instinctively his hands went to the wound and his mouth flew open in shock. Irwin bolted up Thirty-Seventh Street to get as far away as possible.

Since it was February and cold, Irwin had worn gloves so he was not concerned with any fingerprints. When he was several blocks from the scene of the crime, he disposed of his coat and gloves and kept on walking.

A passerby noticed Yona on the ground with a knife protruding from his torso and called 911. He was bleeding profusely and was rushed to the hospital in critical condition with significant damage to some of his vital organs. He was malnourished and due to the drugs he had been taking, he was far from healthy and was also dehydrated. There was nothing that could be done for him.

His ex-wife Devorah was called and she rushed to the hospital with her two children. They came and were able to say goodbye to Yona before he died the next day.

The police investigated but no one saw anything, and if

perchance someone did see something, they were not talking. There were no fingerprints found and Yona could not offer any clues since he was dead. The case went cold.

Before the accident, he was a good husband and father, and Devorah encouraged her children to say *kadish* for their father. The *shivah* period was difficult for them, especially since they all had been hoping to eventually reunite and salvage the family. Now it would be impossible and the young children would have to grow up without their father.

# March 1984
## Borough Park, New York

Ahmed was excited when he went to Jake Benjamin's office to receive the completed blueprints for his bunker. He had already started the clearing and excavation of the land. He knew he would have to excavate down at least fifty feet, and about forty feet in diameter. He also had the construction crew on standby since he did not want any delays.

He had his bunker designed similarly to what was in the book. The bunker was going to be thirty-one feet in diameter and have both of its levels underground. The main floor was going to be the main living level and include the entrance. The upstairs was to be set up as the bedrooms and storage. The plans for the food, water, air, and electricity were going to come directly from the book.

"Here are the blueprints for your bunker," Jake Benjamin said to Ahmed. "I hope you like them."

Ahmed was excited as they perused the five "E"- sized documents. Jake pointed out a few distinct points on the drawings. He showed Ahmed the monolithic dome, the slope of the ramps, the electrical system, plumbing controls and more.

"They look perfect. Exactly what I want," Ahmed enthused.

Jake was happy that his client was satisfied. If he knew the purpose of the bunker, he would not have been elated, but extremely angry and distressed.

"Would you mind autographing your book for me?"

"No, not at all," Jake said as he took the proffered book and signed it.

Ahmed would be using Jake's book as his guide for living in the bunker. There was quite a bit of information in the book specifically for Jews, but Ahmed was unperturbed. They were clearly delineated in the book and he would just ignore those sections.

The book discussed raising goats, hens, and bees for food, but this did not interest him. He was going to purchase what he needed and store supplies in the storage areas of the bunker.

There was also the issue of water and air and he liked what it said in the book, so he was going to follow the advice therein.

As far as electricity was concerned, he did not think he would need as much electricity as was called for in _Doomsday Bunker Book_, but it would not hurt to have more than he needed. After all, a bunker completely underground needs some way to have light, power the air and water filtration systems, refrigeration for food and more.

Ahmed and Mohamed made a few trips to their property in White Lake to check on the bunker site and the status of the construction. Everything was going fine and they took copious pictures of the bunker while it was under construction.


THE DAY BATSHEVA SCHNEIDER SAID yes to Chaim (Charles) Outterridge was an exciting and happy day for the two of them. Chaim was a _ger tzedek_ of three years and a budding _talmid chacham._ He had just entered the _shidduch_ scene and was surprised to find someone so quickly. It was so fast that everyone, including the _shadchan_, Mrs. Benjamin, was surprised. However, everyone was happy for the couple.

When Chaim first went to see Mrs. Benjamin, he was nervous. It was his first time going to a _shadchan_ and he was not sure what to expect. She quickly put him at ease with some hot aromatic tea and homemade sugar cookies. After the basic introductions, the _shadchan_ asked him the requisite questions and the image of Batsheva popped into her head. Normally, she was deliberate when it came to making a _shidduch_, but something about these two just seemed to click in her mind. It was more than the fact that they were both tall with Chaim being a six-foot-three-inch black man and Batsheva was big-boned and tall for a woman. There was something in the personalities Mrs. Benjamin thought would make them a perfect match.

Uncharacteristically, she immediately told Chaim about Batsheva. In the past, Mrs. Benjamin had set her up with other men, and something in each of those cases just did not seem to be suitable. However, Mrs. Benjamin was optimistic that this time it would be different. It was. They started dating and it was great for both of them.

On one date in March of 1983, Chaim and Batsheva were walking on the Coney Island boardwalk and saw three men walking in the other direction. The three men looked like Muslims and were talking in quiet but animated voices; both Batsheva and Chaim were uncomfortable. They were not sure what specifically made them uncomfortable, but they trusted their instincts. They kept walking to get away from those men as quickly as possible.

They also noticed a young *frum* married couple pushing a stroller who seemed upset.

Batsheva and Chaim were so happy and quickly became engaged and started preparing for their upcoming wedding. Chaim wanted his Rosh HaYeshiva, Rabbi Ginsburg to perform the wedding and Batsheva was amenable. He was a wonderful man and it would mean so much to them. Rabbi Ginsburg was happy for his *talmid* and his fiancé.

The couple made an appointment to see his Rosh HaYeshiva. Before performing any wedding, as would any *Rav*, Rabbi Ginsburg met with the couple to discuss some things with them in private. Of course, one of the things discussed was their lineage.

The Rosh HaYeshiva greeted them warmly in his simple office in the *Yeshiva*. Batsheva was demure, as she had never met as great a *talmid chacham* as Rabbi Ginsburg, herself coming from a non-observant family. They had met briefly when they were dating, but this was a more formal meeting to discuss their upcoming nuptials.

The Rosh HaYeshiva had a warm and gentle way about him and was quickly able to put the young couple at ease. Since he knew Chaim, he just asked to see his conversion papers again. He had seen them when Chaim first entered the *Yeshiva*, but he needed some of the information for the *ketubah*.

"That's good." The Rosh HaYeshiva responded with a smile after perusing his papers and returning them to Chaim. He turned to the young woman and asked about her family. "Is everyone Jewish? Any divorces?"

Nervously, she responded that she was a product of her mother's second marriage. "However, my mother got a divorce from her first husband. I have seen it. Everyone in her family is Jewish, although most are not observant."

The Rosh HaYeshiva thought a moment and then gently asked, "What about a *get*? Did your mother receive a *get* from her first husband?"

She hesitated, "I-I don't know. I never thought to ask her about it. I just assumed she did get one. I guess I should have asked her about it."

"When a couple gets divorced, the *bais din* gives both the

man and woman a receipt for the *get*." Rabbi Ginsburg patiently explained, "I will need to see the original receipt from the *bais din*."

"I'm sure that won't be a problem. I will talk with my mother right away. When would be a good time to return to the Rosh HaYeshiva?" She asked hopefully.

"When you have the receipt, just call me and I will be happy to make time for you," Rabbi Ginsburg said with a smile.

Batsheva asked, "Will the Rosh HaYeshiva also want to see the *ketubah* from my mom's second wedding?"

"It can't hurt to see it. It may shed some light on some of the details."

The young couple got up and Chaim backed out of the Rosh HaYeshiva's office and Batsheva mimicked his actions. They did not turn their backs to the Rosh HaYeshiva, as a sign of respect.

"Why did we walk backward out of his office?"

"It is a sign of respect for the Torah that he teaches and embodies. Just like when a Torah is brought out or returned to the holy ark, we stand and face it, so too with any *talmid chacham,* Rosh HaYeshiva or older person, we do not turn our backs on him, as a sign of respect."

Batsheva said, "He is so nice, but I am scared that something is not right." She was not normally a pessimistic woman, but somehow her intuition told her that something was amiss.

"I'm here for you, no matter what. I'm sure things will work out," Chaim responded sincerely.

She looked at her fiancé fondly and appreciated his warmth and gesture. She knew she had chosen well.

Quickly, they made their way over to Madelyn Schneider's house who told her, "I never received a *get* from my first husband…"

Batsheva gasped as her hands flew to her face almost as if she was trying to cover her shame. She understood the possible ramifications.

"I'm sorry, sweetheart," she said. "I don't even know what happened to him. After we took care of the legal issues for the divorce, I never heard from him again. It is as if he just disappeared off the face of the earth.

"Before the divorce, I was never too *frum*. After the divorce, I stopped being *frum* altogether. When I married your father, we did not concern ourselves with what we considered trivialities. Although your father is Jewish, we did not have a rabbi marry us. It just wasn't important to us. We went to a Justice of the Peace.

"Once you started to become observant a few years ago, Dad and I didn't even think about it. That was a lifetime ago. I am so sorry," she had tears in her eyes.

Knowing what this meant, Batsheva was devastated and felt as if the carpet had been pulled out from under her and she was falling down. She had been to Shlomit Women's Seminary in Israel and knew enough Torah to understand the consequences of what her mother just revealed. She sat down on the sofa, put her head in her hands and cried. Madelyn sat down next to her and put her arm around her shoulders. She felt bad for the pain she was inadvertently causing her daughter; mother and daughter burst into tears.

Chaim was in shock and did not know what to say or do. This was beyond him and he did not know how to deal with the situation. His mind was racing and he was not sure how to be there for his fiancée. He understood that if his fiancé was a product of her mother's second marriage and her mother never received a *get* from her first husband, Batsheva was a *mamzeret*. He could not marry her; no one could marry her. He was scared for himself and for the woman with whom he wanted to spend the rest of his life.

Chaim tried to be strong and went to sit near his bride to be there for emotional support. He was not ignorant, but his Talmudic training did not cover anything like this. However, his *mussar* training did teach him how to be a *mentch*. After a minute, he got up and brought his intended a glass of water and some tissues. She gratefully accepted both. His heart went out to her and she looked up at him and tried vainly to smile. They both wished they could go back to the peace and tranquility they had yesterday, even a few hours ago. Alas, that was not to be as time only moves forward.

Batsheva looked up at Chaim. She was scared, but felt the warmth from him and greatly appreciated his efforts and that he did not disappear. "I imagine most men would just run as far away and as quickly as possible," she thought to herself.

The only thing he could think of doing was to run back to his Rosh HaYeshiva and cry on his broad shoulders. Chaim needed *daas* Torah and guidance and Rabbi Ginsburg would know what to do. They would go together, as a couple.

Chaim picked up the phone at what he thought was going to be his future mother-in-law's house and called the Rosh HaYeshiva. Serendipitously, the Rosh HaYeshiva was in his office and answered on the first ring. "This is Chaim Outterridge," he said crying. "We have a problem and need the Rosh HaYeshiva. Can we come back over? Please?" He knew he was begging, but he felt desperate and wanted to make his woman happy but did not know what to do. Chaim also understood that the sooner this was resolved, the better Batsheva would feel.

In the back of his mind, Chaim was wondering why, as a new Jew, HaShem was doing this to him? He had given up so much to be where he was today, and today was turning out to be a horrible experience that was testing him to his limits.

Hearing the urgency in Chaim's voice and understanding there must be an urgent need, Rabbi Ginsburg said, "Come over right away. With guidance from HaShem, I will do whatever I can to help. *Hatzlacha.*" The Rosh HaYeshiva hung up the phone and learned for the *zechus* and *siyata dishmaya* to be able to help his *talmid*. Instinctively, he felt this was going to be a challenge and he *davened* that he would be able to help in some small way.

Chaim turned to Batsheva and told her that they could go right now to Rabbi Ginsburg. "The Rosh HaYeshiva is waiting for us right now if you are willing. He will know what to do."

Batsheva was not sure what to do. On the one hand, she wanted to get the comfort she desperately needed from her mother. On the other hand, she wanted to be with her man and see Rabbi Ginsburg who might have some answers for her. She just wanted to curl up in her room and have a good cleansing cry, but she knew it would not accomplish anything. Her heart was racing.

Batsheva hugged her mother; her mind was made up. She said softly, "I'll be back soon."

Her mother said, "I love you. I'm so sorry; I never meant to hurt you." She had tears in her eyes and wished she could go back in time and fix this.

On the drive over to the *Yeshiva*, the young couple talked about the possible ramifications. They were both scared and needed each other's strength. They both knew this could mean she was a *mamzeret*, but neither of them wanted to say the word. It was as if just saying the word would make it more real than it already was.

When they arrived at the *Yeshiva*, the Rosh HaYeshiva was still in a meeting. They were too apprehensive to sit in the waiting chairs, so they just paced in nervous agitation. They did not say anything, as there was nothing more for them to say but they stayed close to each other for a shared strength.

After just a few minutes, that to the nervous couple seemed an eternity, the Rosh HaYeshiva was available to meet with them.

With heads held low and heavy hearts, they walked into Rabbi Ginsburg's office. Although only a few hours had transpired, for Chaim and Batsheva it seemed as if it was last year. So much had happened in a short amount of time, they felt as if they had walked the entire diameter of the Earth.

The Rosh HaYeshiva knew from the phone call and

immediately saw from their countenances that things were not good. Rabbi Ginsburg knew there must be a problem with the *get*, but he also knew that he should wait for them to say what was needed. If they were able to voice their feelings, it would be the beginning of a catharsis for them.

Chaim and Batsheva sat down and they both took a deep breath, almost as one. Rabbi Ginsburg patiently waited for them to begin. In his mind, he was reviewing a *halacha* as his mind never left the world of Torah. However, his heart was with his young *talmid* and his fiancée who were going through a difficult time. Rabbi Ginsburg wanted to be there for this young couple.

Batsheva opened her mouth to start talking, but all that came out of her mouth was sobs. The Rosh HaYeshiva handed her a box of tissues, which she gratefully accepted.

Chaim looked at his *kallah*. His heart went out to her and he wanted to take away her pain. "With the Rosh HaYeshiva's permission and if my *kallah* doesn't mind," he tearfully began, "may I bring the Rosh HaYeshiva up to speed with what happened?"

Batsheva smiled gratefully at her *chassan* knowing that if things worked out, she would be getting a gem of a man. She would be forever grateful to Chaim and always treat him as if he were a king. He deserved as much because of the way he was acting and treating her in her time of trouble. A person can be defined by how he acts when things are difficult. This situation was beyond being difficult and Chaim was showing himself to be outstanding.

"We went to Batsheva's mother, Madelyn Schneider, and she said that she never received a *get* from her first husband. In fact, after the divorce, her ex-husband disappeared and has never been heard from again. We don't know what to do. We are scared."

Chaim had good *middos,* and Rabbi Ginsburg was impressed with how Chaim was trying to be there for his bride and how he was showing her respect. The *Rav* was duly concerned for the immediacy and seriousness of the situation.

Immediately, Rosh HaYeshiva got down to business. He leaned forward onto the desk, "First of all, I want to say how impressed I am with the two of you. The way you are handling this situation is commendable. Secondly, I need to see your mother's *ketubah*. I would also like to speak with her. Can she come here tomorrow?"

Batsheva responded immediately, "We will be here! Thank you."

"Please have her bring any paperwork she can find. If she has the civil marriage license, divorce papers, *ketubah* and anything else."

Batsheva said, "Okay." She had a glimmer of hope that things would work out and be all right. A smile almost broke through her sad eyes.

As the couple left, they decided to go for a walk to talk and help them relax. While on their walk, they met Yaakov Applebaum.

Chaim introduced his fiancé to Yaakov. "I have done some work with Yaakov's father who is a chemist."

"*Mazal tov*! I am so happy for you." Yaakov enthused with a huge smile on his face.

In unison, they responded in a quiet, "Thank you."

"What's wrong?" Yaakov asked concerned. He noticed the sadness on their faces and the lack of enthusiasm in their voices.

Chaim turned to his *kallah* and she shrugged her shoulders and nodded. The three of them walked down the street as Chaim poured out their woes to his friend. Yaakov listened quietly, noticing how Batsheva was in quiet tears. As he was listening, Yaakov was also on the verge of tears never having heard of such a tragedy in the Jewish community.

Yaakov was in shock. "I am so sorry," he said when Chaim finished. "I wish there was something I could do for you. I don't have tissues for you."

"Thanks, but I have some," she reached into her purse for one.

"Tomorrow, we are going to see my Rosh HaYeshiva. We will see what he says. I hope that he will find something. He is a big *talmid chacham*."

Yaakov nodded his head in agreement. "Your Rosh HaYeshiva is a great *talmid chacham*; however, if he can't help, consider going to Rabbi Mishovsky. I am close to the *Mekubal* and will be happy to give you an introduction. Maybe he can come up with an idea."

Chaim said, "Thank you so much. I appreciate your help. If it comes to that, we will take you up on your offer. Thanks for your friendship."

Batsheva gave a faint smile and whispered, "Thank you."

Batsheva then asked, "Are you related to Mrs. Elana Applebaum?"

"She is my mother, why do you ask?"

"I work with her. I'm also a teacher. She is a wonderful woman and a fantastic instructor."

Yaakov blushed. "Thank you. Call me any time. I am here for you."

CHAIM, BATSHEVA, AND MADELYN ARRIVED at the Rosh HaYeshiva's office the next day as scheduled. The Rosh HaYeshiva was anticipating their return and was hopeful he would be able to find something to help this young woman and avoid her from becoming a *mamzeret*. He felt this would not be easy.

After the appropriate introductions were made, the Rosh HaYeshiva got right down to business.

The Rosh HaYeshiva carefully scrutinized the *ketubah* but could not find any problems. He asked Mrs. Schneider about the *mesader kedushin* and the witnesses and everything seemed kosher. He looked at the other documents she brought and was in a quandary, as he did not see any loophole to invalidate the first wedding; that was the key. Rabbi Ginsburg sat quietly cogitating for a few minutes, which to his guests seemed like an eternity. They could hear the give and take of the learning of Gemara coming from the *bais medrash* and Chaim longed to be there too, but he knew his responsibility was in this room. They knew the Rosh HaYeshiva was thinking and trying to come up with some idea. Some obscure *halacha* that would permit them to marry. They were hopeful. They were about to be disappointed.

The Rosh HaYeshiva addressed his guests, "I must refer you to someone greater than myself; someone who may be able to help you more than I can. Someone I'm hopeful can find a *heter*.

"I will set up an appointment for you to see Rabbi Shimshon Horowitz who is a world-renowned *posek* and is in America right now. He has been able to find *heterim* where others were not." The Rosh HaYeshiva understood the urgency of the matter, as there were human hearts in play. He quickly picked up the phone and dialed the number he knew well. He spoke with Lev Baumgarten, the *shamash* and made an appointment for the next day for his precious *talmid*, his *kallah,* and her mother.

They were grateful for his sensitivity but were curious to know what the Rosh HaYeshiva was thinking. However, Rabbi Ginsburg kept his thoughts close to his own heart, as he did not want to cause them more stress or pain.

The following day found three nervous and scared people waiting for Rabbi Horowitz in his office. Batsheva's future lay in the wisdom of Rabbi Horowitz and his ability to find a *heter*. Madelyn was concerned for the pain she was causing to her daughter due to her inaction many years ago. Chaim was lost not knowing what, if anything, he should be doing beyond what he already was. On their way in, they noticed Yaakov in the *Yeshiva*. They nodded to Yaakov but no one said anything, as there was nothing to be said. Lev made them as comfortable as possible and then left. The Rosh HaYeshiva walked into the room and all three guests stood up out of respect. The Rosh HaYeshiva immediately bade them sit, but they waited until Rabbi Horowitz took his seat.

"What can I do for you?" the *Rav* asked solicitously.

Chaim made the introductions. "I am Chaim Outterridge, a *ger* and I learn in Rabbi Meir Ginsburg's *Yeshiva*. This is my *kallah* Batsheva Schneider and her mother Madelyn Schneider." Chaim looked to his *kallah* and she nodded her head. He took a deep breath and continued, "My *kallah* was born from her mother's second marriage. The problem is there was no *get* from the first husband. We brought the *ketubah* and anything else we thought the Rosh HaYeshiva would want to see." He reached into his folder and placed the appropriate documents on the table in front of Rabbi Horowitz. Chaim also mentioned having been referred by his Rosh HaYeshiva yesterday.

No matter how many times the Rosh HaYeshiva had been presented with cases such as this, it never failed to tear at his heart. He looked across his desk at the three people whose possible future hung on his ability to untangle this mess. It was never an easy situation. His priority must be the *halacha*, but he must be delicate with the hearts of the petitioners.

"With the help of HaShem *Yisbarach*, we will find something," the Rosh HaYeshiva said hopefully. He slowly picked up the documents and carefully perused each document individually.

Rabbi Horowitz asked of Madelyn, "Please confirm for me the date of your first wedding."

She did. It matched the *ketubah*.

"Who was the *mesader kedushin*?" he asked.

She mentioned the name. The Rosh HaYeshiva recognized the name as a reliable *Rav*.

"Tell me about the witnesses."

"One was a friend of mine; one was a friend of my ex-husband. No one was related, both were Sabbath observant." Madelyn was clearly distressed over the situation and what it was doing to her precious daughter as she was about to embark on what was supposed to be the happiest time of her life.

Rabbi Horowitz again picked up the *ketubah* and went over the details; the names, spelling, name of the town, the date and more. He could not find any problems and realized that this was going to be a challenge. The Rosh HaYeshiva asked Madelyn some more questions, but every question led to the same answer. The marriage was *halachically* kosher and there was nothing he could find to invalidate the wedding or the *ketubah.* So far, it seemed to him that Batsheva was a *mamzeret* but he did not want to say the word. He felt for the couple and what it would do to them and her mother.

Batsheva was scared and visibly shaking while she was practically holding her breath. She knew that her status was uncertain and was concerned her mother would blame herself for her daughter's troubles.

Chaim perceived that things were not going well for them. He saw the Rosh HaYeshiva's brows were knit and he sensed the quandary going on in his mind. He decided to try something, "Forgive my intruding on the Rosh HaYeshiva's thoughts, I have an idea."

The *Rav* looked up with red eyes as if he was holding back tears. He nodded, "Please." His voice was barely above a whisper.

"Yesterday, when we left my Rosh HaYeshiva, we met Yaakov Applebaum. He noticed our stress and we told him what was going on. He suggested that maybe we should go to Rabbi Baruch Mishovsky and ask his opinion."

The Rosh HaYeshiva practically jumped on the idea. "I think that is an excellent idea. I'm not trying to pass this on to someone else, but so far, I can't find anything. Rabbi Mishovsky is a *gadol beTorah,* one of the leading *gedolim* of our time and sometimes he can see things that others cannot see even though it is right in front of them.

"The holy Vilna Gaon* comments on the prayer, 'and His servants (the angels) all stand at the heights of the world, and announce with fear and a loud voice the words of the living God and King of the Universe.' The Gaon explains that at the start of each day, the angels announce God's plan for Creation and the events that are destined to occur on that day. Knowing Rabbi Mishovsky, I believe, like a finely tuned radio, he is able to hear those daily announcements.

"Please ask him and let me know what he says. In the meantime, I will continue to do research in case I can come up with something. I will also *daven* for you." The Rosh HaYeshiva gave them a heartfelt *beracha* that everything should work out.

Although there was no answer, the three of them left with a warm and hopeful feeling from Rabbi Horowitz. They were hoping for a straw onto which they could grab hold. As they were leaving, the young couple looked at each other when they again met Yaakov.

"I'm so concerned, I was waiting for you. Was the Rosh HaYeshiva able to help you?" Yaakov asked with genuine affection and concern.

Chaim introduced who he hoped would be his future mother-in-law. "The Rosh HaYeshiva agreed with your suggestion that we go see Rabbi Mishovsky; maybe he can help. This doesn't look hopeful," he said morosely. "Can I impose on our friendship for an introduction?"

Yaakov glanced at his watch and said, "It wouldn't be any imposition; it would be my honor. My car is up the block, let's go right now." Yaakov understood the hearts of these people and wanted to help. He knew he could not *pasken* on the issue, but he could facilitate their meeting with someone who may be able to help.

They grabbed onto the hope Yaakov was extending, as a drowning man would grab onto a life ring buoy. Yaakov took this on as if it were himself who was going through this difficult time. It did not matter that he barely knew this couple. He saw a fellow Jew in distress and it was his nature to help in whatever way he could.

An hour later, the foursome was entering the humble apartment of Rabbi Mishovsky. Yaakov introduced his friend, his friend's fiancée and her mother to the *Rav*. Then, Yaakov quietly left as it was not his place to remain. He adjourned to the *bais medrash* to say Tehillim and learn while waiting.

The *Mekubal* raised his eyes to his petitioners and thought a heartfelt *tefilah* that he should be able to assist them. He saw the pain in their eyes and it almost brought him to tears, and he had not yet even heard what they had to say. They were Jews in distress and it did not matter why they came. They needed his help and he would do everything he could to help them.

Rabbi Mishovsky asked, "With HaShem *Yisbarach's* help, what can I do for you?"

Tearfully, Chaim again repeated his story. To him, it seemed so long ago that they had embarked on this difficult drama when in reality, it was only a few days. He wondered if he would get past this without completely breaking down. After he finished telling the story to Rabbi Mishovsky, he handed the folder with the documents to the angelic-looking man sitting across from him. It was at that moment he noticed the *Rav* had tears running down his face.

Quietly, Rabbi Mishovsky took the folder and placed it on his desk. Without opening it, he lifted his left hand, which still had his *tefillin*, and placed it on the folder. The sensitive heart closed his eyes, still with tears staining his cheeks, and sat that way for several minutes without moving or saying anything. If not for the active tears, the petitioners would have thought he had fallen asleep. However, the *Rav* was anything but asleep.

Suddenly, Rabbi Mishovsky opened his eyes. "I have one

question for Mrs. Schneider. Whatever happened to your first husband? Where is he now?"

She looked confused. "I-I don't know," she stammered. "After the divorce, which was acrimonious, I never heard from him again."

"Please look into his whereabouts and get back to me." He picked up his *sefer* and returned to learning.

They thanked the angel and left with a glimmer of hope that things would work out for them. For some reason, just being in the presence of the *mekubal*, made them feel better. Things did not look as bleak as they did a few minutes ago when they entered the presence of the *Rav*. He did not give them an answer and did not even look at the *ketubah* or any of the documents. He did not ask many questions; in fact, he asked the one simple question they did not have an answer for, and yet they felt relieved. He asked the one question no one else thought of asking. It was as if Rabbi Mishovsky had taken some of their pain onto himself.

When they left, Yaakov offered them a ride to anywhere they wanted to go. Yaakov was curious as to what happened inside to make their faces appear less stressed, but his *mussar* training taught him to keep quiet.

"That man is a *tzadik*." Chaim declared. "He asked only one question. The one question no one else asked; the most obvious question." He was practically in tears but smiling at the same time. His emotions were running high and they confused him.

Since Chaim opened the door, Yaakov inquired, "May I ask what that one question was?"

"He wanted to know whatever happened to my future mother-in-law's first husband. We don't know. We have to do some research."

"That's a brilliant question. I'm surprised no one else asked that. It's so obvious. That's why he is such a *gadol hador*. I wish you much *hatzlacha*," Yaakov responded. "Let me know if I can be of more service to you. Don't hesitate to call me."

"You're a *tzadik*. Thanks so much for pointing us to Rabbi Mishovsky." Batsheva said quietly but with hope.

"I'm glad to do a small part in helping bring peace of mind to a fellow Jew. It was nothing."

It took quite a bit of research to find any information. On their own, they did not have the resources to find any clues to his whereabouts and it was frustrating for the young couple. They decided to hire a private investigator to help them along and find more information.

A tense few weeks later, the private investigator came

forward with some new intelligence. He gave them a certified copy of Mrs. Schneider's ex-husband's death certificate. When the young couple saw the death certificate, they practically jumped for joy! They were so elated they were barely able to contain their excitement; mother and daughter hugged and danced in jubilation. They took the precious document, as if it were solid gold, and rushed to Rabbi Mishovskys apartment.

They showed the official death certificate to the *Rav*. He looked at it and said, "According to this, the first husband died the day before your mother remarried. I am happy to say that everything is kosher and you can get married."

Rabbi Mishovsky continued with a broad smile on his face, "Let's make a *lechayim* to thank HaShem for this wonderful *chessed.*"

Batsheva said, "Would the *Rav* honor us by coming to our wedding? It would complete the circle and mean so much to us."

"It would be my honor as HaShem allowed me to be involved in a small way in your miracle. Please let me know when it will be, *besha'ah tovah umutzlachas.*"

When they went to Rabbi Ginsburg's office, he had the same reaction. To the inquiry, the Rosh HaYeshiva said, "I will be happy and honored to be the *mesader kedushin* for this miracle *chasunah.*" He was jubilant.

On behalf of Chaim, Yaakov told Rabbi Horowitz what had happened. The Rosh HaYeshiva was so happy but berated himself for not thinking of that question. To compensate, he decided to review all pertinent *halachos* and write a paper on the subject in order to help others.

When the Rosh HaYeshiva saw how dedicated Yaakov was to helping others, he decided it was time for him to start *shimush*. Yaakov was getting closer to achieving his goal of receiving *semicha*.

"You have excelled in your learning and I am pleased. In addition to the now increased learning I expect, I want you to report to my son to start *shimush*. You need to learn how to *pasken*. It's not enough to have the book knowledge; you need to understand the process without compromising the Torah or *halacha*. You also need to understand people."

"I'll report immediately." This was unexpected, but not without merit.

"You will continue to learn and take *bechinas*, so don't let your learning lapse."

# April 1984
## Brooklyn, New York

In order to be more secure with their illegal acquisitions, Ahmed and Mohamed decided to rent a warehouse in Brooklyn. The building was part of a block of warehouses between the Brooklyn and Manhattan Bridges. This was one of the northernmost points of the borough, two blocks south of the river. It was not a fancy neighborhood, but they did not care since they would not have to worry about nosy neighbors.

One of their long-term plans was to destroy the financial system of the United States. Throwing a bunch of ersatz money into the banking and financial system would lower the value of the dollar. The complete process of counterfeiting money was classified and took a significant amount of investigation. They had to go to different libraries to garner information.

After reviewing the entire process to counterfeit money, they gave up on the idea for the time being. It would take too much time and cost too much money to make it worth the efforts, but maybe for the future.

# July 20, 1984
## Catskills, New York

"It's time to go again and check on the status of the construction. I want to go tomorrow morning," Ahmed said. It was exciting to watch the ongoing construction of their bunker so they tried to go every few weeks. On every excursion, they made sure to photograph the different stages.

"I'll pack lunch and dinner. I want to be back the same day. I have so much to do." Mohamed responded. Although he enjoyed going to restaurants and staying at hotels, right now he could ill afford that luxury.

"What could you possibly have to do? Date that Jew again?" he asked sardonically.

Ignoring the caustic remark, Mohamed said, "I have studying and homework to do." He did not like Ahmed attacking him for having dated Laura.

# July 21, 1984
## Catskills, New York

The next day they were driving up the New York State Thruway, "Wow, that car is going pretty fast," Ahmed said to Mohamed as a car passed them going at a high rate of speed.

Mohamed said, "Yeah, probably about twenty miles over the speed limit."

A few minutes later, they passed the same car sitting on the side of the road with a police cruiser behind it with lights flashing.

"Had to expect that," Mohamed said.

When they arrived at the bunker site, they met with the indefatigable foreman, Stewart Osborne, who had been in construction his entire adult life. Since his work ethic was impeccable, a few years ago he was promoted to project foreman. However, his ethics in other areas were questionable. Over the years, being careful, he had pilfered some of the construction equipment from the different work sites.

Together, they went over the blueprints, notes and the status of the construction. They had several questions, which were easily addressed, and everything was proceeding as planned. The foreman gave them a tour of the site showing them that the foundation was already in place as were some of the walls and the basement floor. The access ramps were completed but did not have the ceilings in place. The shed was on site, but not in place until the bunker itself was complete. Their personal dirt driveway would be the last thing to be completed.

The terrorists were excited and they took many pictures.

HENRY DAVIS WAS DRIVING UP the New York State Thruway, a bit faster than he should have been. He was enjoying the exhilaration of speeding about twenty miles an hour over the speed limit. He knew he was charismatic and had a glib tongue, and felt confident he could talk his way out of any ticket. He was a legend in his own mind: he was important, it is just the world did not know it yet. He was going to be the next *gadol hador*, just like *Rav* Moshe Feinstein, ZT'L*. He knew it; he just had to convince the public. He knew he was important and a truepenny; it was not his fault that not many other people knew it yet. Well, to be honest, no one knew it.

It did not matter to him that he was still quite young and not well learned. That was just incidental. Henry would get there soon enough.

He had one major hitch in his plans that took much time away from his learning. It was his kidney. Since his mugging in January of 1983, he was in need of a new one. He hated the dead time he had to spend thrice weekly on dialysis. It was such a waste of time, especially for the next *gadol hador*. Henry did not even consider that he could have used that downtime for learning and studying. He was frustrated and upset, and as a result, became passive-aggressive and refused to study while he was on dialysis. Henry was a mountebank, and would rather just sleep, read the newspaper, or a novel instead of trying to advance himself.

Most people can live with just one functioning kidney, but Henry liked to drink. It would have been great if his choice of drink was water, but that was not the case. He did not think he was an alcoholic as he could stop drinking any time he wanted. Henry did not drink in excess and he rarely got drunk, but with only one working kidney as a filter, he should have completely abstained from intoxicants. He could not do that; he did not want to do that. He liked how he felt when he drank, but was careful never to drive after having imbibed. Because of his drinking, his one good kidney was working too hard and was unable to do its job properly, and needed to be replaced. He did not tell his physicians about his habit.

Kidneys are amazing organs. They are one of the major filters of the circulatory system helping to regulate the blood pressure, electrolyte balance and red blood cell production.

Because one of his kidneys was dead and the other was working overtime, he had to be on dialysis to clear out the build-up of waste products in his body. If he did not go to the clinic for dialysis every Monday, Wednesday and Friday, Henry would get sick. The dialysis process was critical for Henry to prevent potassium from building up in his bloodstream; without it, he could get abnormal heart rhythms and sudden death. Kidney disease is irreversible and if left untreated, would be fatal.

When he came to the clinic, a nurse gave him a checkup and he then settled into one of the recliners encircling the room. A technician came by and slipped two needles into his arm. One of the needles near his wrist was to extricate the blood via a plastic tube to the dialysis machine. The other needle was to return the cleaned blood from the machine sitting next to the recliner.

He was connected to the machine to remove the waste and extra fluid from his blood for about three hours each time. On occasion, his blood pressure would drop and he would feel woozy, but it never lasted long.

Because Henry was a stabbing victim, he was placed on the

UNOS (United Network Organ Sharing) list. Since only about fifty-percent of people who need a kidney receive one through UNOS, he was also trying to find one on his own.

These were the thoughts going through his mind as he was speeding up the New York State Thruway and inevitably he was pulled over for speeding.

Officer Calvin Lund was sitting in his favorite spot on the Thruway to apprehend speeders. He was well concealed just beyond an overpass support structure. When a car sped past him at about twenty miles an hour over the speed limit, he had his mark and he quickly turned on his engine and lights and pulled into traffic.

Out of the corner of his eye, as he passed the overpass, Henry saw the hidden police car, but it was too late; he knew he was caught. His heart started racing and he was hoping, beyond hope, that the cop was actually after someone else. However, when the police car quickly pulled up behind him, with lights flashing and siren blaring, his hopes were dashed. He quickly put on his turn signal to indicate to the police that he was cooperating and pulled over immediately. The police officer parked behind Henry and started checking for wants and warrants on the car. Nothing popped, so he exited his cruiser.

Henry rolled down his window, had his ID on his lap and put his hands on the steering wheel. He wanted to make the police officer at ease and this was the best way to do so.

When Officer Lund approached the driver's side window, he immediately noticed the open window and the position of the driver's hands. This relaxed him as he realized the driver was no threat to him.

Technically speaking, when a police officer pulls someone over, they are under arrest, but most often, the driver is released on their own recognizance with a ticket. Was this going to be the case? Since the driver was clearly not a threat, that would be more likely.

"Hello, my name is Officer Calvin Lund. Do you know why I pulled you over?"

Henry knew this was a ruse to extract a confession. You should never answer this question, as you have the Constitutional right against self-incrimination. However, Henry knew he was a smooth talker and decided to take a chance. "Yes officer, I know I was going a bit fast."

"You were going twenty-three miles-an-hour over the speed limit. I hope you have a good reason."

"Well, in actuality, I'm a rabbi and I am on my way to perform a wedding. I am running very late. You know how rabbis are."

Lund looked confused for a moment and then nodded his head and gave a knowing smile. "During the Three Weeks? I don't think so. You are definitely getting a ticket and I should run you in just for lying to a law enforcement officer."

Sheepishly, Henry handed the officer his documentation and did not say another word.


# November 1984
## New York City, New York

Lev Baumgarten liked Henry, who he thought was a big *talmid chacham* and he was going to be the next *gadol hador*. Lev was convinced of that. Born in 1964, Lev was nondescript and intelligent, but also naïve. He was average height and weight and the type of person who turned no heads and drew no attention to himself.

To Baumgarten, Henry seemed to be the quintessential *talmid chacham* and the paradigm of humility. When Lev tried to address Henry as Rabbi Davis, he was often steered to address him by just his first name. Henry did not have *semicha*, but that did not stop him from allowing some to call him by that appellation. It did not seem to bother Lev that Henry did not use his Jewish name, but instead preferred his secular name.

In public, especially when people he knew were in attendance, Henry was stringent with *halacha*. He always had a *d'var* Torah on his lips, but they were simplistic with no depth. He was minimalistic in his food intake; at least in the presence of other people.

Lev was devoted to Henry and would do anything to assist him in becoming known as the next *gadol*. Henry had an overweening opinion of himself, and often complained to Lev about his bad kidney and that he needed a new one. Henry lamented over the waste of time he spent on dialysis. "It takes time away from learning Torah," he remonstrated.

Over time, Henry convinced Lev to give him one of his kidneys. Lev wanted to make sure the next *gadol hador*, Henry, would be around and be able to learn as much Torah as possible.

Lev lived up to his name. He had a good heart and with Henry's cajoling, gave Henry one of his kidneys.

Thankfully, the surgery and recovery went well for both donor and recipient.

Lev was feeling good that he was able to help the man who

he thought would be the next *gadol hador.*

After the surgery and recovery, Henry avoided Lev since he did not want to have to answer to, or thank, his benefactor. He had the new kidney and was happy to continue with his life without being tied down to a dialysis machine and was going to enjoy his newfound freedom to its fullest.

Lev needed to walk daily to maintain his health and strength after the surgery and one day was walking down Kings Highway. He used the time well to cogitate and review *musar* teachings, and window shop. Sometimes he would listen to a Torah tape or *daf yomi* on a Walkman. He wanted to grow and be like Henry.

While these thoughts were passing through his mind, he received a major shock. The last thing he expected to see was his good friend and mentor, the next *gadol hador*, Henry, sitting in a non-kosher restaurant eating dinner.

He became furious and raging mad at what he saw. Without even thinking, he walked into the restaurant and confronted his former friend.

"What are you doing?!" he demanded with the air of someone who understood not to confront someone who should have known better.

Henry stammered and turned crimson. He was caught red-handed and there was nothing he could say or do. All he did was meekly say, "I'm sorry."

Lev was so angry; he wanted to push Henry into the plate of non-kosher food he was relishing. He got control of his emotions; without saying another word, he walked out of the restaurant, went back to his apartment and cried.

Lev went into a severe depression. He did not know what he was going to do. He felt completely lost and alone.

Lev did not want to get out of his bed, but he needed to regularly go for his walks to recuperate from his surgery. Every day he went for his constitutional but did not care where he went. God always directs the paths of man and one day his excursions took him to Fourteenth Avenue and Avenue P. He ended up in Rabbi Ginsburg's *Yeshiva.*

Lev walked into the *bais medrash* and sat down on the back bench. It felt good to be sitting in a *Yeshiva* where he felt at home, despite him not feeling comfortable with who he was at that moment. He picked up a Tehillim and started saying the comforting words and tears started welling up in his eyes. The eternal words of King David have a way of doing that to a broken heart.

The Rosh HaYeshiva saw the distressed Jew and went over

to offer his heart to the man.

"Welcome to my *Yeshiva*," Rabbi Ginsburg said to the distraught man. "I am Meir Ginsburg. Is there anything I can do for you?"

Lev started to stand up in front of the Rosh HaYeshiva but was told to sit down. "Thank you for your kind words. My name is Lev Baumgarten. I'm not sure what to do; where to go. I'm lost and feeling so alone."

"Please come to my office where we can talk privately."

"Thank you," he said with a tear in his eye and appreciation in his heart.

They went to the Rabbi's office. The Rosh HaYeshiva brought some tea, which was gratefully accepted.

"Take your time and feel free to tell me anything you need."

Lev told Rabbi Ginsburg about his trials and tribulations with Henry. He went over the details of the surgery and how he was duped into giving up his kidney. He concluded by mentioning seeing his beneficiary eating in a non-kosher restaurant.

The Rosh HaYeshiva gave him comfort and suggested he consider going to Israel to *Yeshiva*. He would be able to start fresh. Lev liked the idea.

"I would like to add an additional suggestion." He placed his hand on Lev's and said, "Go see Rabbi Mishovsky for a *beracha* before you leave."

"I'll do that. Thanks for everything."

"In the meantime, you are welcome to spend as much time as you want here. I will be happy to give you a recommendation to both Rabbi Mishovsky and a *Yeshiva*."

Lev was touched by the warmth and caring of this stranger who he had just met. "I am a *shamash* to Rabbi Horowitz and I will go with him to his *Yeshiva* in Israel."

He was feeling much better and immediately started to arrange for a trip to Israel. He spent the next several weeks learning in Rabbi Horowitz's *Yeshiva* as a student and not as a *shamash*. The Rosh HaYeshiva understood his change in demeanor and took it in stride as Lev prepared to join him in Israel.

Before his departure, Lev went to see Rabbi Mishovsky. He was not nearly the same angry and depressed person he was a few weeks ago when he related his story with equanimity to the *Rav*.

The great *mekubal* was shocked at the depravity of another jew and predicted that Henry would soon end up in prison for his misdeeds. Rabbi Mishovsky gave Lev a *beracha* that he should live a long and healthy life.

BECAUSE HENRY WAS CAUGHT IN his deceit, he forsook his plan of being a *gadol hador* and he went on to his next scheme.

Henry set himself up as a booking agent for a few small local hotels. He would find guests, book them into specific rooms and take a small commission from the hotels. He arranged car-service rides in limousines; he booked tours as needed for his clients. His business model was sound, at first.

Since Henry was Jewish, he catered mostly to his brethren. However, he was happy to take anyone's money.

At first, he made sure to treat his clients royally and was not concerned with making too much money, as long as he could use his first clients as referrals for new ones. Things were going well and his enterprise was growing as he was getting new clients and his previous clients were returning.

However, as the idiom goes, "A leopard cannot change its spots." Soon enough, Henry was back at his old games as a caterpillar.

At first, he started booking hotel rooms at a higher price than could be had directly at the hotel. He set himself up as a vendor with a credit card company so he was able to charge what he wanted. He started out small and slowly increased the amount he charged, claiming that the higher prices were for his customer service and personal attention to the client.

Once he had the client's credit card information, he could not help himself; he would purchase some things over the phone and have it shipped to a neighbor's house. He would then collect the item before the neighbor returned home. Among other items, he bought himself a nice camera on someone else's credit card. He was not concerned for the victims of his crimes since they would not be held responsible for the theft; Henry did not consider the repercussions for the credit card companies, as they had big money.

After his initial successes in this deception, Henry became emboldened to do more and reach deeper into other people's pockets. He would sometimes book a hotel room on the eighth floor of a hotel that only had six floors. He even went so far as to book clients into hotels that did not even exist. Henry started charging double what his vendors were charging and often would not forward the money he owed. Sometimes, he would even double book a client for the same tour or car service.

He did not always return calls, but as long as he had the credit card information, he thought he was set. On occasion, he would have to refund some money, but he was able to use the money until then and he thought he was doing well for himself.

Henry had his office in his home but used a post office box for all of his correspondence so his clients and vendors did not know where he lived.

After a number of reports to law enforcement, the police started to investigate and they set up a sting. Several undercover agents booked rooms through him and were defrauded. The agents staked out his mailbox and subpoenaed his phone records and they were finally able to apprehend him.

There were multiple states involved, so the case was placed before the FBI and Henry went before a federal Judge. Judge Archer sentenced him to ten years at Fort Dix Federal Corrections Institute in New Jersey. He also had to pay significant fines, make restitution and do 300 hours of community service at the conclusion of his prison term.

AFTER HAVING DONATED HIS KIDNEY under false pretenses, Lev Baumgarten was concerned about his health. However, after some time, he noticed that he never got sick; not even a sniffle. He seemed to always be in perfect health. Later, he recalled the *beracha* he received from Rabbi Mishovsky and attributed his good health to that *beracha*.

# November 1984
## Brooklyn, New York

Tuvya Justin had a less than illustrious and stellar past. The police had interviewed him on a number of occasions but never pressed any charges.

Earlier this year, in February, the police came in force to his apartment on Fifty-Ninth Street in Borough Park. They came to question and arrest Tuvya for the murder of Yona Glick who was stabbed to death in a fight over drugs. Officers Connors and Jackson came with a warrant for Tuvya's arrest but did not want to show it at first. They preferred to question him about the murder of Yona and extract a confession. Henry was not confessing, as he was innocent of the crime: in actuality, Irwin Thatcher murdered Yona.

Officer Connors asked Tuvya, "Do you know Yona Glick?"

"No. Why? Should I?" he asked with a blithe attitude.

"We think you may have had some dealings with him."

"That's nice. Why are you here? What do you want from me?"

Tuvya was beginning to get a little nervous.

"He was found murdered and we think you had something to do with it."

"Ha!" Tuvya laughed.

"What's so funny? We both know you are guilty."

"I had nothing to do with it."

Officer Jackson interjected, "We all know you stabbed him. We want you to fess up and give us the knife that you used."

"I didn't have nothing to do with anything and I don't have no knife that was used in no murder."

"We're going to search your apartment and we will find the evidence."

"Not without a search warrant," Tuvya said.

Upon getting some resistance to his questions, Connors decided it was time to play his trump card. Connors took the arrest warrant out of his pocket, showed it to Tuvya and started to take out his handcuffs. "You have the right to remain silent. Anything you say can be used against you in a court of law. You have the right to an attorney. If you cannot afford an attorney, one will be provided for you at no cost. Are you willing to talk with me?"

Before Tuvya could even respond, Jackson asked him, "Where were you two days ago at around 2 p.m.?"

Tuvya thought a moment and then laughed heartily, "You won't believe me if I told you."

Dubiously, Connors said, "Probably not, but try me anyway."

"I have an alibi that even **you** will have to accept as ironclad."

Disbelieving, Jackson asked, "Now what would that be? Your rabbi? Or better yet, you were in jail?" He asked, dubious that Tuvya could come up with a solid alibi. The officers laughed at the thought that Tuvya may have been in jail.

"No, someone even better," he smirked.

"Who?" demanded Connors.

"Judge Richard Archer. I was at his house all day. Call him, or if you would like, I'll call him right now. I suspect even the police will believe a judge." He was feeling sure of himself and did not care if the police believed him or not. He knew he was innocent and had a rock-solid alibi. "You can't get a better alibi than a federal judge," he thought to himself.

Sheepishly, they left without Tuvya and had the Federal Assistant District Attorney contact the Judge about his alleged alibi.

The next day, the FADA went to see Judge Richard Archer in his chambers. "Your Honor, I'm sorry to disturb you. Are you familiar with a man by the name of Tuvya Justin?"

"Yes, why do you ask?"

"He said he was with your Honor three days ago."

"He has been at my house all day for several days doing some remodeling. I'm having the second story of my garage converted into an apartment. Yes, he was there three days ago. My daughter and I were there with him. Why?"

"The police went to arrest him for a crime that was committed three days ago, but if he was at your Honor's house, he has an alibi."

"That he does. I assume my word, as an officer of the court, is good enough."

"Of course, your Honor. He is clearly no longer a suspect. Thank you for your time."

That was then; this was now: this time, things were different. Connors and Jackson were on his trail for drug trafficking. They knew he was doing drugs and had evidence he was in possession of a large quantity and would now be facing trafficking charges. They had a warrant for his arrest and this time the judge would not be able to help him.

He had been spotted purchasing a large number of drugs from Thatcher on Fort Hamilton Parkway. Thatcher was already in police custody for drug trafficking and had turned State's evidence in exchange for a lighter sentence. He had turned on several of his customers and even his supplier, most of whom were already in police custody. One thing he had going for him was that he had a reputation of never selling drugs to children. Because of this discretion and his turning State's evidence, he was given a lighter sentence of only ten years with no time off for good behavior.

Many people were talking about the huge drug bust on Fort Hamilton Parkway. Many people were under arrest or about to be taken into custody and Tuvya knew he was in trouble and expected to be apprehended by the police at any moment. He went on the lam.

Connors and Jackson went to Tuvya's apartment on Fifty-Ninth Street with a warrant, but he was not there. They went to his mother's house in Queens to interview her. They executed a search warrant of her house but found nothing: no drugs, no Tuvya Justin. They staked out Atarah's house for several weeks and even tapped her phone, all with no results. Law enforcement watched public transportation for his egress from the city but it was as if he just disappeared into thin air.

It was not much later when Atarah passed away. She had been sick and died in January of 1985, and Tuvya was devastated because he was unable to attend his mother's funeral. He was sure the police would be waiting there for him: they were, he was not. The case looking for Tuvya went cold as it was not a high priority and the department was unwilling to put more time and money in searching for a low-level criminal.

# December 22, 1984
## New York City, New York

Various New Sources:

Bernhard Hugo Goetz* was born on November 7, 1947, in Kew Gardens, Queens, New York. On December 22, 1984, he was taking the subway to work, as he did every day. Mr. Goetz alleged that while transporting electronic equipment in 1981, he was attacked in the Canal Street subway station by three youths in an attempted robbery. They smashed him into a plate-glass door and threw him to the ground, permanently injuring his chest and knee. Goetz assisted an off-duty officer in arresting one of them; the other two attackers escaped. Goetz was angry when the attacker spent less than half the time in the police station than Goetz himself spent, and he was angered further when his attacker was charged only with criminal mischief, for ripping Goetz's jacket. Goetz subsequently applied for a permit to carry a handgun, based on routinely carrying valuable equipment and large sums of cash, but his application was denied for insufficient need. He bought a five-shot .38-caliber Smith and Wesson Model 38 Airweight revolver during a trip to Florida.

In the early afternoon of Saturday, December 22, 1984, four young African American men from the Bronx - Barry Allen*, Troy Canty*, Darrell Cabey* (all nineteen) and James Ramseur* (eighteen) - boarded a downtown #2 train (Broadway-Seventh Avenue Line express) carrying screwdrivers, apparently on a mission to steal money from video arcade machines in Manhattan.

At the Fourteenth Street station, Goetz entered the car through the rearmost door, crossed the aisle and took a seat on the long bench across from the door. Canty was across the aisle from him, lying on the long bench just to the right of the door. Allen was seated to Canty's left, on the short seat on the other side of the door. Ramseur and Cabey were seated across from the door and to Goetz's right, on the short seat by the empty conductor's cab.

Approximately ten seconds after Goetz sat down and the train started moving, Canty asked him, "How are you?"

Monosyllabically, Goetz responded, "Fine."

The four men gave signals to each other, and shortly thereafter

Canty and Allen rose from their seats and moved over to the left of Goetz, blocking him from the other passengers in the car.

Phillip Rush was on the same train and was a witness to what was about to happen. He wanted to get involved, but he could not since there were four of them and only one of him. He wanted to help and felt bad, as he knew what could happen. His fears came to fruition, except that Goetz was armed and defended himself from his attackers. Phillip was also concerned about going to the police. He knew that he himself was skirting the law and did not want to invite scrutiny.

After the four men surrounded Goetz, Canty said, "Give me five bucks."

Bernhard Goetz, fearing for his life, pulled out his gun and shot the four young black men when they tried to mug him. He fired five shots, seriously wounding all four men.

When the guns came out, the other passengers ran to the far end of the car. Phillip was amongst them and was glad the stranger was able to protect himself.

Goetz was dubbed "The subway vigilante." Nine days later, he surrendered to police and was eventually charged with attempted murder, assault, reckless endangerment, and several firearms offenses. A jury found him not guilty of all charges except for one count of carrying an unlicensed firearm, for which he served eight months of a one-year sentence.

# 1985

## 1985
## Queens, New York

**They** were living high and well in a nice house in Queens, New York and planning to move to Long Island in the near future. They had nice, fancy furniture throughout, and their house was adorned with plush carpet with a thick pile. There were expensive Oriental rugs hanging on the walls; an elaborate chandelier hung in the dining room over an elegant table with a fancy china closet on the side. Every year the family all leased new cars and took expensive vacations. Theirs was a great life.

The entire family was into real estate in one form or another - that is how they made their money. At least that is what they wanted everyone to think, the only problem was it was all a carefully constructed façade involving the entire family.

Matthew Greene was a real estate developer and his wife Batyah was a real estate developer and appraiser. Their son, Avinoam was a mortgage broker and real estate developer. They were grifters and claimed to own properties in Brooklyn, Manhattan, and Queens. This was fine except for one small problem - many of these only existed in verisimilitude.

For about ten years starting around 1974, they used different names and fraudulently obtained mortgages and other types of loans from different banks. They obtained these by providing false information to lenders about their employment, income, bank accounts and properties they owned. They were able to obtain more than thirty million dollars in loan proceeds in connection with more than twenty fraudulent loans. The preponderance of the loans went into default and the majority of the proceeds were never repaid.

As part of the scheme to defraud, they used the fraudulent proceeds to personally enrich themselves and their families.

Fraudulently obtained loan proceeds were used for, paying credit card debts amassed for their fancy wardrobes and lifestyle, paying their personal mortgage loans, purchasing other real estate and personal property.

They routinely falsely claimed the purposes of the loans were to purchase or refinance their primary residence, when, in fact, the property was not their primary residence, and the loan proceeds were later distributed to others.

Some of the properties were either non-existent, owned by others not involved in the fraud or owned by themselves using fake names. They were able to show ownership by false and forged documents. Since these fake names were not real people, the banks could not collect funds. They used these fraudulent properties as security for other purchases and loans. Batyah appraised the properties at a value much higher than what they were worth. Several properties allegedly had swimming pools that were nowhere to be found.

In order to hide some of their crimes and protect themselves, they created several shell corporations. These non-existent corporations owned many of the properties. A shell corporation would take out a loan, buy a property at an inflated price, sell it at a loss to the Greene's and then default on the loan and the corporation would declare bankruptcy.

Following default on a fraudulently obtained loan, coordinated efforts to deceive the lender into granting a satisfaction of the debt at a significant loss, were put in place. These efforts included ideas such as proposing short sales of properties that, unbeknownst to the lender, were not arms-length transactions.

Matthew was the organizer of the fraudulent scheme. He personally participated in many of the fraudulent loans, in various roles, including the borrower, borrower's power of attorney, mortgage broker, distributor of fraudulent loan proceeds and arranger of short sales.

All three of the Greenes were borrowers who fraudulently obtained loans from banks upon false representations, documents, and pretenses.

At the same time that they were falsely representing to banks that they had substantial income and assets, they were also representing to state and local agencies that they had little or no income or assets and were entitled to receive various forms of public assistance, including Medicaid, Food Stamps, and Home Energy Assistance Program ("HEAP") benefits.

They claimed that their income was under $200 per month each. On the other hand, in order to receive loans, they claimed an income of $15,000 to $20,000 per month in rental income.

Eventually, their house of cards fell apart. The forensic accountants at the banks and the FBI, along with the IRS figured out what was going on, froze all of their assets and pressed charges. They were indicted by the Grand Jury and warrants were issued for their arrest and their forfeited assets were to be used to pay back those who were defrauded.

Federal Marshals showed up at their house to arrest the trio, but only Avinoam was home. When he saw four large black emergency vehicles converge on his house, he quickly called his father.

"The feds are here, I'm sure they're about to arrest me." He was scared as he again glanced out the window.

"What? Are you sure?" Matthew was shocked.

"Yeah, I am pretty sure. Four black fed cars are outside and it looks like they are converging on the house."

"Can you run?" Matthew asked, concerned for his son. His mind was racing trying to come up with ideas to protect his family.

"No, but you, and Ema can. Please run!" Avinoam begged. "There may be an opportunity to help me later."

"Okay." The call was terminated.

As soon as Avinoam returned the phone to its cradle, there was banging on the door.

"Federal Marshalls! Open up! We have a warrant," someone called from the other side of the door.

Petrified, Avinoam called out, "I'm coming." With shaking hands and a quick look around the living room, he opened the door and there were twelve law enforcement agents standing there with their weapons drawn. Another four marshals had gone around back to prevent anyone from escaping from the back door. Avinoam was more scared than he had ever been feeling as if his life was coming to an end and he had no idea if his parents would be able to flee and eventually rescue him.

One of the marshals stepped forward and introduced himself. Then said, "Avinoam Greene, I have a warrant for your arrest. Please turn around and put your hands on the wall."

Avinoam immediately complied, "Yes sir."

"Do you have any weapons or sharp objects on you?" the Marshal asked.

"Just a pen in my shirt pocket," Avinoam said still shaking.

As he was being frisked and handcuffed, some of the neighbors gathered outside to watch the goings-on. No one could fathom what Avinoam could have done to peak the ire of the feds. He was such a quiet and gentle young man.

"Is there anyone else home?"

"No, I'm alone," Avinoam declared honestly. Marshals were already inside thoroughly searching the house.

"Where are your parents?" someone asked.

"I - I don't know."

"If you are lying, it's a felony of obstruction of justice and lying to law enforcement officers."

"I don't know where they are," he hoped they were already on the lam and as far away as possible. Everything was happening so quickly that Avinoam was discombobulated and desperately wanted things to slow down. That is a tactic of law enforcement: they act and talk so quickly to disorient a suspect in order to get them to confess, oftentimes to things they did not commit. Although it is against the law for a citizen to lie to a law enforcement officer during an investigation, it is accepted practice for them to lie to a suspect.

When it was discovered that Batyah and Matthew were not home, the feds put out an APB (all-points-bulletin) for them.

"THAT WAS AVINOAM," MATTHEW SAID to Batyah when he hung up the phone. "The feds are at the house, he thinks he is about to get arrested." He was nervous and not sure what he should do.

"What?!" Batyah screeched.

"We have to run. Now!" he declared grabbing his coat and car keys.

"What about Avinoam? We can't abandon our son," she pleaded. Her maternal instincts were running high and she wanted to protect him. "We have to go back for him!"

"There's nothing we can do for him right now. We have to go. Now! Once we are safe, we will see what we can do for him."

Resigned to her sudden change in fate, she acquiesced knowing that her husband was correct. Quickly, they went to an ATM and withdrew as much cash as they could, only a few hundred dollars each from various accounts. They quickly got into their car and drove off. They were not sure where they were going, but they had to leave immediately.

Withdrawing money from the ATM was a catastrophic mistake. The feds had flagged their accounts for any activity and now the feds knew where to begin their search.

They drove as quickly as possible to Fort Hamilton Parkway and turned left. They thought the best place for them to disappear, was Lakewood, New Jersey. Few people knew them there and they would at least have a *Torah* community in which they could live. They quickly got onto the Gowanus Expressway and headed to Staten Island. As they approached the Verrazano Narrows Bridge, they were concerned that they would be apprehended. They were sure the authorities had their photos or at the very least their description and that of their car.

They decided to use the toll machine to avoid contact with any human and easily breezed through the toll booth.

As they drove through Staten Island, they did not talk as they were both lost in their own thoughts, fretting about the future and their son.

They were sure the feds were after them and they were panicking trying to get out of New York as quickly as possible. Batyah and Matthew were worried about their son, but right now, they had to protect themselves. Later they would do what they could to help their son, but right now, they were on the lam and could be of no service to him.

Matthew was also concerned about what he would do for income in the future. How would he take care of his wife and son? They would have to make plans to get their son out of prison, maybe somehow even contact the Mafia for help. The likelihood of getting their son out of prison was a pipedream, but it was something onto which the distraught couple could grab. For the immediate future, they would have to live underground on the run from law enforcement.

They did not have much cash with them and they figured their credit cards were flagged or canceled. Belatedly, they realized they should have hidden cash in case they needed to flee. They had no worthwhile identification or supplies, and Matthew did not even have his *talis* and *tefillin*.

"We need to switch vehicles," Matthew said to Batyah. He was trying to formulate a plan and needed her input on what to do and where to go. He did not relish the idea of giving up his late-model sedan but realized it was the logical and safe thing to do.

"We don't have another car with us. Where are we going to get another car?" She thought he had lost his mind and that she was not far behind. She looked over at him driving the car: his knuckles were white from grabbing the steering wheel so tightly from the tension. She could see perspiration beading on his forehead while he was not moving his head looking at anything but straight ahead. Up until now, they had lived a good life of luxury, but that was all gone and they had nothing. She wondered if they got out of this without going to prison, what their life would be?

"We'll get onto the Garden State Parkway South and stop at the first rest stop. We'll steal a car and swap the plates. That will buy us some time." He was trying to concentrate on the steps he had to do in order to get hold of his life that was careening out of control with no end in sight. He knew that his previous life of leisure was over and all he could do was hope that his term in prison would be relatively short.

"That's a good idea. If we wipe down this car from our fingerprints, it should give us even more time to disappear." She wanted to help in any way she could and coming up with a few easy ideas and being supportive was all she was able to do at this point.

They exited at the first rest stop and pulled off to the far corner. Batyah quickly went to the bathroom and emerged with a handful of paper towels. She started wiping down every inch of the car. While sweating profusely, Matthew removed their license plates and went in search of another vehicle. He was grateful that he always kept a few simple tools in the trunk of his car.

He found a small unpretentious car also off to the side that looked as if it had not been touched in days and would probably be another few days until it was discovered stolen. Instead of putting his old plates on the new vehicle, he took some black electrical tape and made a few modifications to give the impression it was a different license plate. He stowed his old plates in the trunk of the new car.

He broke the steering wheel lock, tripped the ignition wires, started the car and quickly drove off and continued south. They had to get off the main roads as quickly as possible. Matthew drove as fast as he dared, trying to be careful not to arouse the interest of the police.

An observant and perceptive police officer saw them driving and his instincts were aroused. Something was wrong. He noticed the couple seemed to be very nervous and he was concerned that not everything was as it should be. He pulled behind them at a distance and ran their plates for wants and warrants.

"There's a cop behind us," Matthew nervously said to Batyah.

"Are you speeding?"

"No, my driving is fine," he said a bit more caustically than he should have. He was petrified and was unsure of what to do.

"Don't snap at me!" she demanded angrily.

"I'm sorry, Batyah. We're both scared and nervous. What should I do?"

"Right now, nothing; hopefully, he will find someone else to harass and just leave us alone. Just drive and obey the traffic laws," she said wisely.

"If he runs the plates, we're in trouble. They don't match this car. Modifying the plates was a bad idea."

"There's nothing we can do about that now," she said.

Matthew put on his turn signal to change lanes. The state trooper did the same. He knew he was behind a stolen vehicle or at the very least, a vehicle with mismatched license plates.

"He's on to us," Matthew cried out in desperation while gripping the steering wheel even tighter.

"We are only two miles or so from the exit to Lakewood. I think we should make a run for it. What do you think?" you could almost smell the tension in the air between the couple.

Without responding, he floored the accelerator. The car leaped forward following the directives of the frantic driver.

Immediately, the trooper turned on his lights and siren and took up the pursuit. He picked up his radio and called for assistance and backup.

Matthew was in the far left lane driving about eighty miles an hour.

"You are going to miss the exit!"

"I want to try to lose the cop." At the last moment, he swerved to the right, cutting off three cars. The other vehicles blared their horns in frustration and barely avoided a serious multi-car accident. With screeching tires, he drove over the gravel of the exit ramp barely missing the guardrail.

"You are going to get us killed. Be careful," Batyah screamed in fear while watching her life pass in front of her eyes.

The police car missed the exit. He quickly pulled over, backed up his cruiser and cut the exit. He radioed ahead his position and situation. Other state troopers were quickly dispatched to Route 195.

The Greenes got off the highway and almost missed the turn they needed, but with screeching tires, they made the right turn and drove like a lunatic trying to flee the police. Batyah wailed as they drove through the residential area, and she was terrified.

State troopers and Federal Marshals gave chase while Matthew was driving like a maniac trying to outrun the authorities. That was a futile mistake: it is nearly impossible to elude law enforcement in a car chase.

They drove at speeds in excess of sixty miles-an-hour through residential streets and the houses and cars whizzed by at a dizzying speed. They were not relenting. Matthew was weaving all over the road trying to avoid hitting other vehicles, running red lights and stop signs narrowly missing other vehicles. He realized there was no way out of the situation; he knew he was going to go to prison and his reckless driving was only adding additional charges against him.

The Greenes were risking their own lives and the lives of innocent people and the marshals wanted to end this chase before someone was seriously hurt. They understood that the Greenes were trying to get to Lakewood and disappear in the Jewish enclave and had to be stopped before they got to Lakewood and put more lives at risk in the densely populated town. In order to prepare to disable the car the Greenes were driving, law enforcement cleared the street and put puncture strips across the roadway.

One of the marshals was going to do the "pit maneuver" on Greene's car. A pit maneuver is a precision immobilization technique that is a difficult, dangerous and precise driving operation.

The marshal came up hard and fast to the back left corner of the fleeing vehicle. The other marshals had created a buffer zone to prevent any other vehicles from being affected by the pit maneuver.

They were about a mile before the puncture strips, when the marshal nudged the back left-side corner of the fleeing car with the front right corner of his bumper. This caused the Greene's vehicle to go into a counter-clockwise spin. As the car was rotating, the marshal pushed on and hit the car broadside with the front of his cruiser. He had total control of the other vehicle and was able to maneuver it to the side with no injuries.

Batyah was screaming at the top of her lungs in fear with her arms and legs splayed to protect her from any impact. Matthew was holding onto the steering wheel for dear life while watching the street from a ninety-degree perspective.

Without further incident, they were taken into custody. The couple was taken to the hospital in Hamilton, New Jersey, to make sure they were not injured, and then to Federal detention.

All three were sentenced to ten years each in federal prisons. All of their assets were sold to repay money that was stolen in their criminal enterprises, and collectively, they had to pay a fine of five million dollars. They would be paying those fines for the rest of their lives.

Avinoam was sentenced to ten years in Fort Dix Correctional

Institute.

# February 1985
## Jerusalem, Israel

The couple had gotten married in Chicago, IL and made the unusual move and relocated to Jerusalem in the late 1970s. This was a difficult time in Israel but they immediately loved the country and were willing to live frugally so they could reside in the Holy Land. The Weinblatts were pioneers and understood things would be difficult for their new family. They were mentally and emotionally prepared for the challenges and were willing to live shabbily to fulfill their dreams.

Poverty in Israel had been rampant until the 1970s when it was only marginally improving. More and more people were purchasing refrigerators, agriculture improved and fresh fruits and vegetables were becoming plentiful. Meats were all but impossible to procure, and chicken was widely available but at a high price. Most people only had a small piece of chicken for *Shabbos* and holidays. Almost everyone had a gas range and televisions were in almost every secular home while washing machines were only available in about seventy-five percent of homes. Laundry was often done by hand and few people had dryers as most just hung their clothes on clotheslines to dry.

Only one-third of families even had a car, while families with two cars were unheard of. There were only 3.5 million people living in Israel. Medical advances were not nearly on par with the United States.

In 1985, Zev and Miriam Weinblatt were frightened and at wit's end. They had five beautiful and wonderful children and so much for which to be thankful but, they were despondent and felt as if they could not go on anymore. Their youngest son was sick and the doctors had all but despaired of any hope of his recovery.

When Miriam was pregnant with their youngest, she developed preeclampsia.

Preeclampsia occurs when a pregnant woman develops high blood pressure and protein in the urine after the twentieth week (late second or during the third trimester) of pregnancy.

Preeclampsia affects the arteries carrying blood to the placenta. If the placenta does not get enough blood, the baby receives less oxygen and fewer nutrients. This will lead to slow growth, low birth weight or preterm birth. Premature birth can lead to breathing problems and other difficulties for the baby.

When Tzvi Weinblatt was born, there was a knot in his umbilical cord which exacerbated his problems. Although it was not one-hundred-percent certain, the doctors believed this caused the stroke the baby had soon after birth. The stroke affected the entire right hemisphere of his brain and there was no way to know the extent of the damage; only time would tell. When the doctors did an ultrasound of his brain to see the damage of the swelling, they found an aneurysm called the Vein of Galen in the middle of his brain. This aneurysm caused his heart to work extra hard. While looking at his heart to see how much it was overworking, they found two holes. The physicians were hoping that over time, these would fix themselves; once again, time would tell. As far as the surgery went, the neurosurgeons and cardiac surgeons were going to determine the safest time for him to have surgery. At his young age, an operation was difficult and rarely successful. His heart was stable for now and that gave hope he would be alright until he was at a safe age for the surgeons to operate. This would be at approximately one year of age or older. He was small and not growing well while his cognitive level seemed well below where it should have been.

It was decided to add another name to the child. He was to be called Rafael Tzvi Weinblatt.

Zev was learning in Rabbi Horowitz's *kollel* in Israel and was busy with *safrus*. Yaakov had commissioned Zev to write a *Sefer Torah* on his behalf, they became close and Yaakov suggested they go to the United States for more testing and research for Rafael Tzvi. He was upset when they refused to go, not wanting to leave the holiness of Israel.

After significant pressure, Yaakov dragged Zev to see the Rosh HaYeshiva for advice. He was hoping the Rosh HaYeshiva would also pressure Zev to take his son to America.

Yaakov started the conversation. "As the Rosh HaYeshiva knows, Reb Zev has a sick child and the medical professionals here in Israel have not been able to offer any help. I suggested to Reb Zev that he goes to America for testing and treatment."

The Rosh HaYeshiva said, "Rabbi Applebaum has a good point. What do you have to say, Zev?"

Yaakov was a bit taken aback by what the Rosh HaYeshiva called him and interjected, "Begging the Rosh HaYeshiva's pardon, I am not a rabbi."

Ignoring Yaakov's comment, the Rosh HaYeshiva turned to look at Zev waiting for an answer.

"I don't know. It's a major undertaking. My wife and I are

unsure, there are great medical facilities here and HaShem can help us in Israel. As the famous joke goes, from here it is a local call."

"I agree that HaShem can help you anywhere, but you have to do your *hishtadlus*. It's a major trip and expensive but your child is worth it." The Rosh HaYeshiva's heart went out to Zev.

Zev said, "I have no idea how I am going to pay for this, plus accommodations and more. What about my other children?"

"I have *maaser* money already set aside for this and I will help you find an apartment," Yaakov volunteered.

"Zev, Rabbi Applebaum has addressed your points. I think you should go as soon as possible." Rabbi Horowitz smiled at his *talmidim*.

"Begging the Rosh HaYeshiva's pardon again, but I don't have *semicha*. I am not a rabbi." Yaakov was wondering what was going on as clearly the Rosh HaYeshiva knew better than anyone else did that he did not have *semicha*. Zev was also wondering what was going on with the Rosh HaYeshiva calling Yaakov a rabbi, and Yaakov saying he was not a rabbi. Was there some drama playing out in front of him of which he was not aware?

The Rosh HaYeshiva again ignored Yaakov and addressed Zev, "I know that you don't want to take money from someone, but Rabbi Applebaum said that it is *maaser* money already designated, so it's not really his anyway. Talk to your wife and make travel arrangements as soon as feasible."

In exasperation, Yaakov said, "Since the Rosh HaYeshiva insists on calling me rabbi, maybe he wants to give that to me in writing?"

Smiling, the Rosh HaYeshiva took a piece of paper and wrote up the ordination making it official. Yaakov was now to be known as Rabbi Yaakov Applebaum among the Jewish people. Yaakov was in shock and his jaw dropped open. "Maybe that was the final test, to see if I was humble enough for the Rosh HaYeshiva's aspirations for me," he was thinking as he watched the Rosh HaYeshiva write the coveted certificate. Yaakov was so happy and shaking from the excitement, but trying to control his emotions. All these years of diligent study had finally come down to this moment. It was exhilarating for Yaakov. It was somewhat of a catharsis of his emotions.

The Rosh HaYeshiva was smiling inside; divining what was in the heart of his newly ordained student. "*Mazal tov*, Rabbi Yaakov Applebaum," the Rosh HaYeshiva said emphasizing the newly bestowed title.

Zev was standing there watching the proceedings. He was

genuinely happy for Yaakov and wished him a hearty "*Mazal tov*" as he proffered his hand for a warm handshake. Yaakov ignored the hand, grabbed his friend, and pulled him close for a hug. Yaakov was practically jumping out of his skin and wanted to call his parents with the news, but he had important things to take care of with his friend.

"Thanks so much, my friend. I am totally shocked." Turning to the Rosh HaYeshiva, he said, "And thank you to the Rosh HaYeshiva. I was not expecting this."

"You earned it and I am proud of you my son." Rabbi Horowitz said warmly. "Now let's get onto more important issues."

"Okay, I will talk with my wife and we will leave as soon as possible."

The Rosh HaYeshiva cried. He was moved that his *talmid*, Rabbi Applebaum, was willing to go to such efforts for a friend. The Rosh HaYeshiva suggested to Zev that he take his entire family and move to New York where he could get better medical care for his son. He could also continue his learning in the *kollel*. If he wanted, later, the family could move back home to Israel. He also advised that Zev keep their *dirah* and rent it out for some financial assistance while he was living in America.

The Rosh HaYeshiva turned to Yaakov, "Rabbi Applebaum, your *chessed* for Zev goes way beyond anything I have ever seen. Your actions and humility have touched my heart. Just as you have shown extraordinary *rachamim* here, may the One Above extend to you *rachamim* and show you your *zivug* soon. It is time for you to start looking for your life partner."

"Amen," exclaimed Yaakov and Zev in unison.

Zev was convinced and went home to discuss the whole situation with his wife; she tearfully agreed. "If the Rosh HaYeshiva says we should go, then with the advice of *daas* Torah, we go," she said decidedly.

The decision made, they started to pack and make arrangements. They would do everything to leave as soon as humanly possible.

*Shabbos* after the fateful and emotional meeting with the Rosh HaYeshiva, before they headed to the United States, the Weinblatts invited Yaakov for *Shabbos* lunch. This was going to be the penultimate *Shabbos* during which he was going to be in Israel for a while. He also had to travel abroad.

There were other guests at lunch and Yaakov noticed one particular young woman with sparkling blue eyes and long brown hair who seemed to have a special *chayn* about her. She identified herself as Rivkah Somers. She seemed intelligent and also looked familiar to Yaakov as if he had seen her somewhere else under different circumstances. Yaakov was introduced as the "Newly ordained Rabbi Yaakov Applebaum." Everyone wished him a *mazal tov*. Rivkah was impressed.

"This will be the last time we get together in Israel for *Shabbos*," the Weinblatts said to Yaakov.

"When you get set up in America, we will have to get together and continue this 'tradition'. I have to stop in England for a few weeks, and then I will be there. I am at your service."

Zev and his family were grateful to Yaakov and wondered if they would ever be able to repay him. On the other hand, Yaakov considered himself beholden to Zev for the opportunity to be able to assist his family.

Rivkah took note of Yaakov, "He seems so genuine and sincere. He said a beautiful *d'var* Torah and sang the *zemiros* nicely. He seems like such a *baal chessed*. He just received *semicha* from Rabbi Horowitz, so he must be a *talmid chacham*."


# February 1985
## Borough Park, New York

Ahmed and Mohamed just heard that Adolf Leipzig had died a few months ago. They again speculated as to his identity.

"I really think it may have been Adolf Hitler," Ahmed hypothesized. "It sure looked like Hitler. Remember the portrait of Hitler on the wall behind Leipzig's desk?"

"I remember and the resemblance is uncanny. But it couldn't have been him. Hitler killed himself in a bunker in Berlin in 1945."

"Maybe he got out somehow. Maybe it wasn't his body they found. Maybe it was a double in the bunker."

"Surely he would have been found out by now. I just can't believe it was the Fuhrer."

"Well if you don't think it was him, then who was it?"

"Maybe his son?"

"This man was too old to be his son."

"Maybe another close relative or brother," Mohamed suggested.

"I don't think he had a brother, but he did have a sister Paula. I guess we'll never know."

"We have to carry out Saddam Hussein's order. He wants us to do some major damage at Three Mile Island. In Leipzig's memory, we are going to carry out a major attack and blow up Three Mile Island. Destruction of the nuclear power plant would cause a lot of death, destruction, and suffering."

Nizar El-Amin (formerly Eric Spence) had been volunteered by Ahmed and Mohamed to do the malevolent deed. He was to drive a car with the bomb into the reactor and thereby cause a nuclear disaster. Nizar was going to be a suicide bomber.

Nizar rented a car for the occasion and had everything planned: the route, the bomb, the schedule, even a stop for lunch. He had a few empty gas cans in the trunk. He was ready.

The bomb was fifty pounds of military-grade C4 in the trunk designed with a trigger to explode on impact. There was a sensor in the front of the vehicle, under the hood, that would send an electric impulse to the C4, upon a collision. The full gas tank and gas cans would add fuel to the incendiary device wreaking more damage. The resulting explosion would cause the destruction of the cooling system in the nuclear reactor and therefore a nuclear disaster of catastrophic proportions.

# February 7, 1985
## Dauphin County, Pennsylvania

On February 7, 1985, Nizar left New York for the three-hour drive to Harrisburg.

He got onto the New Jersey Turnpike South and then the Pennsylvania Turnpike going west. It was a peaceful and relaxing ride that gave him time to cogitate. He was not in any rush to die, so he stopped at one of the rest stops on the Turnpike for a few minutes.

He was going to be a martyr. Nizar was excited and scared at the same time and was anticipating the ethereal reward awaiting him, but was also afraid of the unknown. He did not like pain and was hoping that his death would be instantaneous. He was not courageous; he was a bit of a coward and not looking forward to fulfilling his mission.

His itinerary included a stop in Harrisburg for a bite to eat and then to continue on to Three Mile Island. While in Harrisburg, he topped off the gas tank and filled the gas cans to add fuel to the explosion. The smell from the gasoline nauseated him, but it was necessary as part of his plan.

Nizar drove his rental car down River Road, Route 441, across the bridge on the north side of Three Mile Island. He barreled past a checkpoint at the entrance to the nuclear plant. Staying to the right at the fork, he was driving frantically at forty-seven miles per hour and almost lost control of the vehicle. He stormed past the guards, hitting and injuring one of them while he sped on and broke through an entry gate. He eventually crashed the car headlong into a secure door of one of the buildings on the west side of the island.

He was dazed by the impact when his head hit the windshield and he realized the bomb did not go off. He had a deep gash on his forehead, which was bleeding heavily, and his neck was strained from whiplash. The impact of the car with the building should have caused the bomb to explode. It did not. He was nervous, confused and disoriented and did not know what to do. He should have been dead. He had no time to ponder why the bomb did not explode. Frenetically, he tried to restart his car; it was no use, the car was dead, he hit the steering wheel in frustration.

Corybantic, he jumped out of his car, abandoning it and the bomb as he limped away from the car, realizing he was in a significant amount of pain. He had no weapon, not even a pocketknife. Had the plan worked, he would not have needed one but he had no backup plan in case of failure, as misadventure was not an option they even considered.

He was lost and not sure where to go or turn, he ran past the first two buildings and entered a building that happened to be the Unit 1 reactor turbine building. He was lost and confused and not sure what to do or where to go. Nizar was running as fast as he could with the pain while pure adrenaline coursed through his system.

"Why didn't the blasted bomb go off?" he mused to himself knowing he failed his mission. Even worse, he failed Saddam Hussein. He could never return to Ahmed, he would kill him or worse, torture him. He was not going to be a martyr; he was going to prison. All of these thoughts were rushing through his head so fast the first one had barely been comprehended before the second was already formed.

Not encountering any resistance Nizar ran like a wild man into the reactor building. There were few individuals in sight and he was able to hide in the building. He considered jumping into the Susquehanna River and swimming away. The only problem with that plan was that he was not a strong swimmer. During the next four hours of negotiations with Nizar, authorities determined that he was unarmed, rushed the terrorist and arrested him without incident.

After he was apprehended, the government claimed it was just a man with a history of mental illness and there was no mention of terrorism or the bomb in the car. It was all hushed up quickly.

Saddam Hussein was foiled again.

Nizar ended up before Judge Archer and was sent to Fort Dix Correctional Institute. Because it was a terrorist attack on U.S. soil and the danger to a nuclear reactor, the trial was closed to the public with no mention at all in the media.

Palestine Liberation Group tried to claim responsibility via WABC talk radio. The authorities hushed it all and it was relegated to the annals of history.

"I guess it is just you and me again. The other two were completely incompetent," complained Ahmed.

"Uh-huh. Do you think we should try to get others to join us?" Mohamed asked. Although they had a job to do, he was having second thoughts. "These Jews are not so bad," he again thought to himself.

"We shall see. I have to think." He thought to himself, "I don't trust that Jew-lover. His heart is too soft. I've got to find a way to get rid of him."

AUTHORS NOTE: An actual historic event similar to this took place on February 7, 1993. There was no evidence that the actual event was due to terrorism or that there was a bomb involved.

# February 1985
## Borough Park, New York

Even though he had suspicions the police were watching him, after a brief hiatus, Bert continued patrolling, as usual, being more careful than in the past. He had his calling to protect people and nothing would stop him. As an aside, he found it thrilling to help others. He was confident in his abilities and he knew he would not go too far.

He patrolled exclusively in Borough Park and varied his route regularly. One evening he was walking up Forty-Fifth Street above Thirteenth Avenue. He saw a mugging in progress: he saw someone being badly beaten and he knew he had to intercede.

He sprinted the short distance to the attacker in order to intervene. The mugger drew back his arm to drop another fist into the face of his victim. Bert grabbed the arm and twisted it back. The mugger was stunned as he was not expecting anyone and was caught off balance. As his arm was twisted back, he ended up on the ground while Bert took up a position between the victim and the mugger.

The mugger was not completely ignorant of martial arts, he stood up and came at Bert. He stood up and smiled. "This is going to be fun," he said. He aimed a right roundhouse punch toward Bert's face, but Bert ducked and parried his arm, causing his opponent to twist around like a spinning top.

When the attacker regained his balance, he came at Bert again, this time more cautiously. He took a traditional horse stance and threw a diversionary punch to the chest while throwing a forward kick to his knee. Bert was adroit, avoided the fake punch, and realized the kick was coming. He caught the kick with a backhanded parry and pushed it out to his left. As he did so, the mugger came around with a left hook to Bert's face, which barely missed its target.

Bert threw a right punch toward the muggers' face. It never made contact as he sidestepped the punch to his left while blocking the punch. He turned his back into the chest of Bert and continued turning to land a left elbow to the back of Bert's head. Bert staggered forward, fell to the ground and rolled, but quickly tried to get up. His hands and arms were scratched from concrete; his clothes were torn.

While he was getting up, the mugger sent a kick to Bert's stomach lifting Bert off the ground a few inches. Bert was hurting and had to get control of the situation. He quickly rolled away and jumped up. As he was getting up, the attacker threw an uppercut to Bert's chest. It hurt and he lost his balance throwing him backward to the ground. Bert was not used to any resistance, let alone someone who could give him a run for his money with any skill. While on the ground, Bert swept his feet around and tripped his opponent who went down quickly. Bert was finally able to get up while his attacker rolled a few feet away and jumped upright. Bert needed to end this fight immediately before anyone got seriously hurt.

Bert took a deep breath, calmed down and focused his concentration and energy. He assumed a left horse-stance, pulled back his right arm to his hip, twisted his body forward and directed a straight hammer-fist punch full force to the center of the mugger's chest. He had his entire body behind the punch. The man flew backward a few yards and went down clutching his chest. The man was dead before he hit the ground, but Bert did not know it. Bert turned around, helped the victim, and then walked away.

Bert was completely spent after that difficult fight, so he went home with satisfaction knowing he protected another person. Bert took a shower and realized he had some bruising on his torso and minor scrapes on his hands and arms.

"Oh well," he thought to himself, "no big deal, I will heal soon enough." Then he went to bed in a fitful sleep. Something was bothering him about the fight, but he did not know what. Something was wrong and he replayed the fight in his mind. Suddenly he sat up in bed. "Did I hit that man too hard? Did I do more damage to him than necessary?" he asked aloud; he was alone and not expecting a response. Suddenly, Bert was sweating and he was concerned for the mugger. He was always so careful to control his strikes, but this time, he was distressed that he may not have been as cautious as in the past. He would need to rethink what he was doing and how he was doing it. He loved helping people, but not if it meant seriously hurting someone. He would see about calling local area hospitals in the morning.

He immediately got out of bed and splashed some cold water on his face while relishing the complete silence in his apartment. He said some Tehillim for the other man, hoping he was not seriously hurt. Still feeling ill at ease, but a bit better, he washed his face with some warm water. While drying his face, he noticed his reflection in the mirror and was not happy about having hurt the other man so much. He shook his head in disgust and then went back to his bed. He closed his eyes and fell into a sporadic sleep. He needed to get some sleep so he could go to work in the morning.

A few hours after he had returned to his apartment and was just drifting off to sleep, suddenly there was a banging on his door.

Startled awake from his brief slumber, Bert quickly sat up in bed. He was angry and confused at the sudden disturbance to his already disturbed and broken sleep in the stillness of the night. He looked at the clock on his nightstand and it was 3:12 a.m. Someone banging on his door at this hour of the morning could only mean trouble.

"Open up! It's the police. We have a warrant." He heard an authoritative voice calling from the other side of his door.

"I'm coming; just getting a robe." He did not want his neighbors disturbed by the banging and did not want them asking what the police were doing at his door at that hour of the morning. He was nervous and scared. He heard the police say they had a warrant and suspected it was because of the mugger.

"Hurry up!" he heard someone calling from the other side of the door.

After his altercation earlier in the evening, someone saw the body on the ground and called 911.

The police came and investigated. The mugger had been found beaten to death and it was being ruled a homicide. He had a few broken ribs. One of the broken ribs had penetrated his heart, killing him instantly.

Law enforcement interviewed witnesses and one person gave a description that matched Bert - over six feet tall, well built about 225 pounds, dirty blond hair.

Officer Connors recognized the description of Bert and immediately contacted the Assistant District Attorney for an arrest warrant which a judge immediately signed.

They read him his rights, "We have a warrant for your arrest. Would you like to answer some questions?"

"I am asserting my right to remain silent and I want an attorney." Bert was scared and protecting himself and being prudent by not speaking with the police without an attorney.

"Get dressed, quickly."

Once dressed, they placed him in handcuffs, and he kept his head lowered in shame. He was aghast and felt like an animal being led to the slaughter. He still assumed his victim was alive and pressing charges for assault, little did he know, this was far from the reality of the situation.

They took him down to the police station, "Are you sure you want an attorney or would you like to answer some questions?" Connors asked hoping to elicit a confession.

Bert responded with one judicious word, "Attorney."

It was at this point that Bert received the shock of his life when he found out that he killed the man. He was aghast at the enormity of what he had done. He had actually caused the death of another human being and wanted to break down and cry but knew that he must not do so in these circumstances. He was appalled at his actions and shaking with fright.

Bert was patted down and his pockets were turned out to make sure he was not carrying anything. Then they released his hands and took his fingerprints. The warrant included the ability to take pictures of his body for scrapes and bruises. He was placed in a holding cell and the police ran his prints for wants and warrants; he was clean.

In the morning, he met with his state-appointed public-defender. He went before the Judge Archer and was released on fifty-thousand-dollars bail.

Unfortunately for Bert, the case against him was solid as they had a witness and physical evidence, plus the cuts and bruises on his own body. Bert, under the advice of his attorney, took a plea deal instead of going for a trial.

Bert killed someone while protecting another, so technically he should not have been indicted. However, since he was out looking to be a vigilante, he was prosecuted. He had been out most nights and others came forward saying he had also beaten them. The police and prosecutor went after him vigorously.

Because he had been instrumental in finding Yehoshuah Benjamin who had been kidnapped, the Judge was willing to give him a lighter sentence.

He was convicted of manslaughter in the first degree and was sentenced to six years in federal prison. He would have to pay a hefty fine and when he got out of prison, he would have to do 300 hours of community service.

All told, he was getting off with a light sentence. He was scared but grateful it was not worse. He was remorseful and deeply troubled that he had been responsible for the death of another human being.

The judge gave him two months to put his business affairs in order. He was able to find someone to run his business while he would be in prison. Then he would self-surrender to Fort Dix Federal Corrections Institute in New Jersey.

# March 1985
## Catskills, New York

The call was not unexpected. Their bunker was complete and they were agog with the news. The lease on the house they were renting was about to expire, so they just packed up their few belongings and hit the road. They were going to move into the bunker and keep the warehouse as a base of operations.

Only Ahmed and Mohamed were still alive; Nizar was in prison and oblivious of the bunker and they were not going to tell any future conspirators about the bunker. Any other Muslim extremists or other iniquitous individuals who would join them would only know about the warehouse.

The first time they approached their completed bunker was an exciting day for both Ahmed and Mohamed. This was the culmination of one of their dreams. This was their bunker; they designed and built it. They met the construction foreman at the main road by the dirt path that led onto their ten-acre lot.

"Welcome to your property and bunker. I'm sure you will enjoy it," Stewart Osborne said. "Let me give you the grand tour."

They entered the innocuous narrow driveway. After about twenty yards, the driveway started to curve into a serpentine switch-back dirt eight-foot-wide path. There were large boulders and drainage ditches about a foot deep on either side of the driveway.

The driveway ended at a clearing that was about half an acre in size surrounded by a six-foot-tall fence topped with barbed wire. Along one side of the cleared area was a manmade pond about fifteen feet wide and one-hundred feet long.

Near the center of the clearing was a shed that was fourteen feet by twenty-four feet. There were solar panels for electricity on the roof and the gutters collected water that was diverted into the bunker.

They entered the shed: it was nondescript with a small kitchenette, a bed and a small table near the far end. The table was nailed down, or so it seemed. By releasing a hidden latch in the wall, the table was able to be tilted up onto two of its legs revealing a hidden door in the floor.

Lifting the hidden door, there was a blast door thirty-two inches by thirty-eight inches, requiring a key and a combination to open. This enabled them to enter a concrete tunnel that angled down at about thirty degrees. This tunnel was three-and-a-half feet wide and seven feet tall and continued for about one-hundred feet. There were three - four-inch PVC pipes running along with the ceiling of the tunnel for water, air, and electricity. There was a steel door at the end of the tunnel. The entire structure was fabricated from four-inch concrete.

The door opened into a decontamination room that was thirteen feet tall, ten feet wide and thirteen feet long. The decontamination room was at a ninety-degree angle to the actual bunker from the ramp.

At the other end of the decontamination room was another steel door that opened into the main level of the bunker itself. The bunker was round at thirty-one feet in diameter. The main level was for the living areas. Off the back of the bunker were the bathroom facilities, plumbing, and electric circuits. There were also stairs to go up to the bedrooms and the storage room.

Also off the back room was an emergency exit ramp that led to the surface outside the fence.

Over the course of time, they would add more security measures.

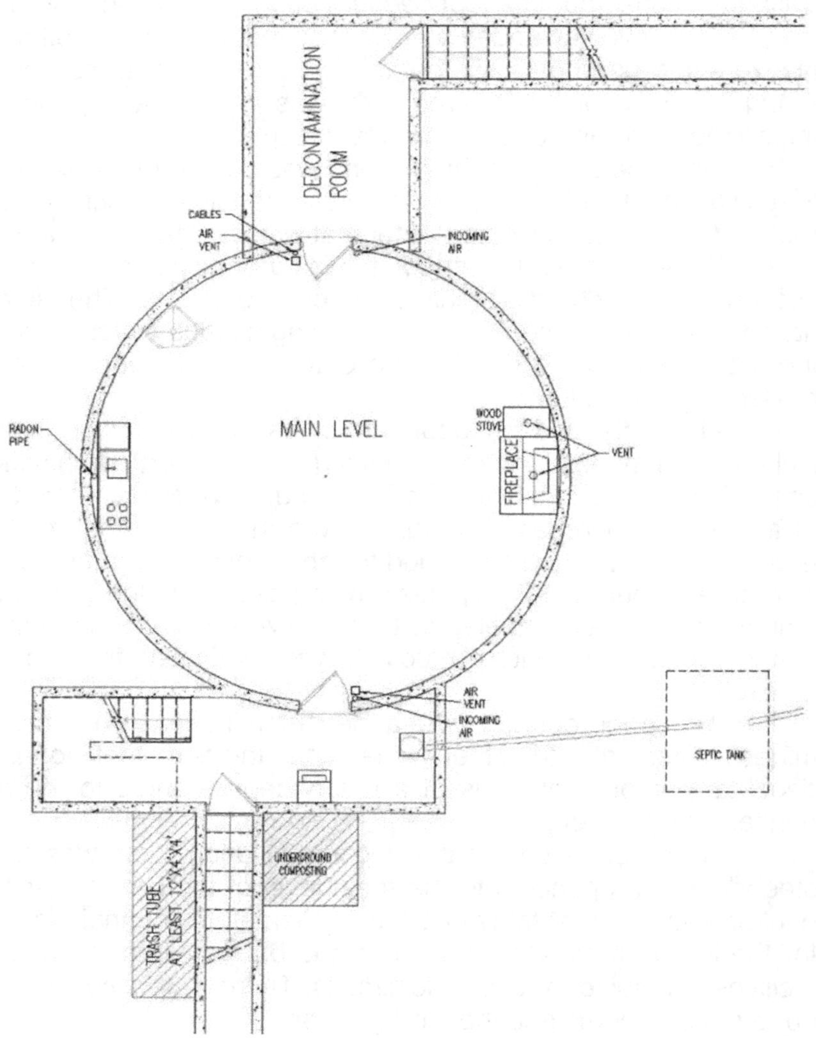



# April 1985
## Manhattan, New York

Various new sources
    On April 1, 1985, the mayor of the City of New York received an anonymous letter. The letter writer threatened to contaminate the New York City water supply with plutonium unless all criminal charges

against Mr. Bernhard Goetz were dismissed by April 11, 1985. Mr. Goetz was the suspect in a dramatic subway-shooting incident on December 22, 1984.

The Mayor immediately contacted local and federal authorities to evaluate the credibility of the threat and to institute a "round the clock" monitoring program by New York City personnel. Although some thought it an April Fool's joke, the FBI took the threat seriously.

Authorities first deemed the threat a hoax but were not taking any chances. Lives could be at risk.

At the time of the threat, due to drought conditions, water levels in the reservoirs were at half the normal volume.

The Environmental Protection Commissioner said that after having conducted tests every four hours, officials detected plutonium.

The Environmental Measurements Laboratory, EML, was requested by New York City officials to analyze a composite, large volume (approximately forty-six gallons), of drinking water sampled by city personnel on April 16, 1985. The composite had been collected from various locations in the city. The concentration measured was twenty-one fCi/l (femtocurie per liter). This was one-hundred times greater than previously observed. The mass isotopic content of the plutonium was unusual and corresponded with the threat. Additional samples were collected one to three months later at various distribution points in the water supply system. The plutonium concentrations were much lower and comparable to EML's earlier data. Mass isotopic analysis of these samples provided more reasonable compositions but with high uncertainties due to low plutonium concentration.

Levels of plutonium trichloride were forty-two times normal levels.

In September 1985, measurements of large volume samples were taken, approximately 265 gallons, from the New York City and New Jersey water supplies which showed identical plutonium concentrations of 0.05 fCi/l. Mass isotopic analyses indicated similar 240Pu/239Pu ratios which were slightly lower than global fallout estimates.

The terrorist letter writer was never caught.

This incident gave Ahmed the idea to poison the water in New York City. He knew he would not be able to get hold of plutonium, but he did have access to other chemicals. Since the news outlets did not disclose the locations of the reservoirs, he would have to do his own research. He had no compunctions about killing and maiming as many people as possible. They would soon have their bunker finished, so in case things went completely awry, they would be safe.

Besides, they would have plenty of water at their hideaway to carry them over for the duration.


# April 1985
## London, England

Yaakov went to London for several reasons. He had some business to conduct and to attend the wedding of a friend. Of course, he made time to learn Torah for several hours every day.

Yaakov spent *Shabbos* with some friends and for *Shabbos* lunch, his host invited some other friends of theirs. Yaakov noticed that one of the women guests was someone he already met. He met the same Rivkah a few weeks ago in Israel at the Weinblatts *Shabbos* lunch.

"I know I met her somewhere else even before that *Shabbos*, I just can't place it," he thought to himself. Their eyes met briefly but they both looked away quickly.

Rivkah also recognized Yaakov from a few weeks ago in Israel and continued to be impressed by him.

The following day, Sunday, Yaakov was happy to dance at a friend's wedding. He was always happy in the *semachos* of his friends and considered it an honor to participate in their weddings. At the wedding of his friend, Yaakov played the keyboard for a few songs during the dancing.

Serendipitously, Rivkah was a guest at the same wedding and noticed that Yaakov was performing with the band for a few songs. She was impressed. "He's talented and plays well."

Suddenly it dawned on her, "I think I remember seeing him years ago at my piano teacher Atarah's house. I wonder if that is him," she thought to herself.

A few days later, Rivkah went back to the United States. Gleefully, she and Emily got together: they had so much on which to catch up and discuss. Emily started to teach her friend everything she could about the latest developments in computers and programming.

Rivkah became a substitute teacher for her friend Emily. Rivkah loved computers and everything about them and planned to open a computer store at some time in the future. She had hopes that her friend would join her in the venture, but time would tell. Emily seemed more interested in teaching and she was an excellent teacher. That was her forte.

# May 1985
# Borough Park, New York

The Weinblatts moved to New York to obtain better medical treatment for their son. Yaakov offered them to live with his family; however, they refused so as not to inconvenience the Applebaums. Yaakov found an apartment for them with reasonable rent, but unbeknownst to the Weinblatts, it was in a house Yaakov owned in Flatbush.

Their young son Rafael Tzvi was deathly ill and they immediately went to Maimonides Medical Center for help. They also consulted Charles Outterridge, who was not able to suggest anything to help the young child.

Yaakov took the Weinblatts to Rabbi Mishovsky for a *beracha* for their son. They were fraught with fear and concern for their child and what would be.

As always, Rabbi Mishovsky was learning Torah when Mr. and Mrs. Weinblatt walked in with their son. The moment the compassionate *Rav* saw them before a word was even spoken, the great heart of the Rabbi broke and he burst into tears. He stood up and approached his guests with tears streaming down his face. Rabbi Mishovsky bade them sit down and he brought them some water and cake.

Yaakov humbly stood in the corner to be able to be of service to anyone if needed. He did not feel as if he was intruding, as he was well aware of the entire story.

After Mr. and Mrs. Weinblatt made the appropriate *berachos*, they painstakingly explained to the *Rav* what had brought them there. They acknowledged the great *chessed* Yaakov was doing for them and even mentioned the *semicha* Yaakov had received a few weeks prior. That brought a smile to the sage's face and made Yaakov's face turn red.

With great despair to the couple, the rabbi did not give them a *beracha*. He cried with them and gave them encouragement. However, there was no *beracha* forthcoming for a healing for their son.

The Rabbi quoted a *passuk* of encouragement from Isaiah 41:10 "אל תירא כי עמך אני אל תשתע כי אני אלקיך, אמצתיך אף עזרתיך אף תמכתיך בימין צדקי." "Fear not for I am with you, be not dismayed, for I am your God. I have strengthened you, even helped you, and even sustained you with My righteous right hand."

The couple was confused and disappointed that Rabbi Mishovsky was not giving them a *beracha* for their child. They looked at each other and did not understand why he withheld a *beracha*, although the *Rav* did say that his door was open for them any time of day or night. They felt the love of the *Rav* as if he was trying to take some of their pain on his shoulders, but when they left, they were disheartened.

Mr. and Mrs. Weinblatt sat by their son's hospital bed in shifts both day and night. Most often, one of the parents were with their son while the other was taking care of the rest of their family. The community banded together to help the distraught family: neighbors helped with preparing meals and driving carpool for them. Shoshanna Somers babysat for their children when the parents were in the hospital with their dying son.

They went to Rabbi Mishovsky on several occasions longing for a *beracha* for their son. However, the *Rav* was circumspect about giving them the requested *beracha*. Every time they came, the Rabbi greeted them warmly and cried with them. He was effusive with his encouragement but would not give them the petitioned *beracha*.

One of the times Shoshanna was needed to babysit for the Weinblatts, Yaakov drove her both ways and he again met Rivkah. They greeted each other, now having recognized one another from previous encounters. However, the rules of modesty prevented them from conversing more.

# May 1985
## New York

They were enjoying the seclusion and safety of living in their bunker, feeling secure that they would be protected come what may. Few people knew about the existence of their hideout. The architect knew about the bunker but did not know its location while the realtor who sold them the property had no knowledge of the bunker. The construction crew was aware of it, but they were a small local firm so Ahmed and Mohamed were not concerned with them.

They had another reason to be secure in their bunker and that was all of the security they set in place. The pair was stocking up with enough food and water to last them a year or more. They had batteries, solar systems, food, water, first aid supplies and more.

They started planning for their next terrorist attack of

poisoning the New York City water supply. New York City water has the purest and most bountiful supply of drinking water in the United States. It utilizes three separate systems of reservoirs, which obtain water from about 2,000 square miles of watershed in upstate New York. They were going to contaminate the water in New York with a large dose of sarin. Ahmed had been able to procure sarin from the bio-chemical vault where he worked. Sarin is a colorless, odorless liquid and is highly potent as a nerve agent. It can be lethal even at low concentrations causing lung muscle paralysis. Sarin is twenty-six times more lethal than cyanide. Initial symptoms following exposure to sarin are a runny nose, tightness in the chest and constriction of the pupils. Soon after, the victim develops difficulty breathing and experiences nausea and drooling. The victim continues to lose control of all bodily functions, plus the victim vomits out of control. This phase is followed by twitching and jerking.

Ultimately, the victim becomes comatose and suffocates in a series of convulsive spasms.

Ahmed also got hold of the antidote of atropine for the two of them. If administered fast enough, atropine is an effective antidote.

Under the cover of darkness, they went to the Catskill Aqueduct in Ulster County, cut through the fence and poisoned the water. They quickly returned to their bunker where they already had close to a year's worth of stored water.

By the next day, people were starting to show symptoms and contamination and get sick.

People started showing up to hospitals and clinics in droves. Thousands got sick and it caused widespread panic.

Because the dose was so dilute, there were just a few deaths, mostly those who were already infirm and weak. Most people just got sick with tightness in the chest, runny nose and constricted pupils. Some people thought it was just the flu, however since so many people were affected at the same time, those presumptions were quickly dispelled. The Centers for Disease Control and Prevention was quickly called and it was found to be much more serious than just the flu. Atropine was expeditiously dispensed and most people made a complete recovery.

Palestine Liberation Group claimed responsibility via WABC radio.

The FBI was called in to investigate and spent an enormous effort trying to find the culprits of the poisoning attempt. Eventually, the authorities found the breach in the fence at the Catskill Aqueduct. They were able to determine that a generic cutter was used but there were no tire impressions they could use, no fingerprints, no evidence.

This terrorist group seemed to be professionals, they were not going to be easy to track and bring to justice.

People were scared of this new terrorist group and were upset with the authorities for not finding them and putting them out of commission. Who were these people? Where did they come from? Who was financing them? Where were they holed up? How could they be caught and brought to justice? When would they be caught?

Ahmed was upset that so few people had died, but was mollified that so many had suffered from his actions. Mohamed kept his ill feelings to himself.

# September 3, 1985
## Borough Park, New York

Mohamed was beginning to feel worse about some of the acts they had already perpetrated and were still planning for the near future. He did not mind as much causing quick death to infidels; he was mostly against causing suffering. In some respects, he was not bothered that they were planning to kill Jews, but there was no reason to maim or kill the general population. He could not stomach the slow and painful suffering of others. However, he had dated a Jewess and he liked her; he wanted her back and that was making him feel abashed. He felt his feelings were duplicitous and felt that he was a hypocrite.

Mohamed was feeling vagarious and addled, not sure what to do. On the one hand, he wanted and needed to continue his escapades with his erstwhile friend. On the other hand, he was sickened and felt antipathy toward their plans of terrorism. He wanted to defenestrate everything and live a normal quiet life, maybe even get back in Laura's good graces. He was so confused and it was taking its toll on him and he did not know where to turn or what to do.

Mohamed decided he would make a compromise and apprise someone to be on guard for their conspiracies. He did not want to tell his ex-girlfriend, as he was concerned she would turn him in to the authorities. Besides, he was also hoping eventually to win her back. In the past, he observed Laura and her good friend Rivkah talking in Glatt Chow. Rivkah seemed smart and would know what to do with the information. It would make him feel better to tell someone and in his mind, he was doing something and that gave him a clearer conscience.

Mohamed wrote a note that he kept in a Ziploc bag in his

wallet for when he felt it could be of use. One day, he saw Rivkah walking down the Avenue and he saw his opportunity. He followed her into a store and was unobtrusively able to slip the note into her purse. He quickly exited the store and went on his way happy with his effort, minimal as it was.

> To Ms. Somers,
>
> For reasons beyond my control, I cannot tell the appropriate authorities. The horrible acts of terrorism that have occurred, are just the beginning, there are more to come. Plans include poisoning people and a bomb in the future. Please use this information appropriately.
>
> Anonymous

After he delivered the note, he regretted clueing her in and wished he had not done so. "Maybe I acted too rashly. I shouldn't have done that. At least I didn't give too much information. She may not figure it out." He was not going to tell Ahmed what he had done. An element of distrust had already developed between the two men and telling him would only make matters worse.

Ahmed felt that Mohamed was too soft and in addition, he had dated a Jewish woman and therefore could not be trusted. "There has to be a way to dispose of Mohamed and start over with a new cadre of 'true' Muslims," he thought to himself. In the back of his mind, he was already planning another assignment for Mohamed that would be a suicide mission. It did not matter to him that Mohamed had been like a brother to him his entire life. The mission must come first: it was *jihad*. He was vacillating between wanting to get rid of Mohamed, killing him or just cutting him out of his plans. But he also understood his feelings of affinity for his longtime friend and had bad feelings whenever he thought about losing him or worse, having a hand in his demise.

Mohamed did not see what was so bad about the Jews and felt that Ahmed was relishing in the suffering of other people. He was having second thoughts, "Maybe I should just get out of this cell before it's too late. Maybe if I tell Laura she will help me reform myself and I will get out of this in one piece," he was thinking. "But she may turn me in to the authorities. I'm so confused and I have nowhere to turn. What do I do?" He was perplexed and distraught. "Notwithstanding," he mused to himself, "Ahmed has been like a brother to me since we were young children. How can I abandon him?" His varied thoughts were racing through his mind so fast that he was unable to contain them or make complete sense of them.

# September 12, 1985
## Borough Park, New York

Yaakov was considering the purchase of a company located in Brooklyn. He had an appointment on Thursday, September 19, 1985, to talk with the lawyer whose office was in the World Trade Center. If he went through with this deal, it would be his largest to date and Yaakov was apprehensive: it was quite a bit of money and could be a big risk. He would have to take out a second mortgage on several of his properties and be deeply leveraged. He was not sure if it was a good idea.

Abstract Surveyors was a busy land surveying company in Brooklyn that was for sale. The owner was getting up in age and wanted to retire and he was glad that a *frum* man was interested in purchasing his company.

Abstract Surveyors did mostly land surveys, but they also did boundary, topography, Alta surveys and more. There were several draftsmen who worked in the office full-time and a few subcontractors who worked from their own homes or offices. The company was positioned to upgrade to the new AutoCAD program by Autodesk, which would enable them to do drafting on the computer. It was an exciting time for them and they were poised to grow with the upcoming technology.

Jake Benjamin was one of the subcontractors who did work for Abstract Surveyors and they did some work for him. He had only good things to say about Abstract Surveyors. The late Yona Glick had done some engineering work for Abstract Surveyors in the past.

Before any major deal, Yaakov always went to Rabbi Mishovsky for advice and a *beracha*. The week before the appointment, on Thursday, September 12, 1985, Yaakov went to Rabbi Mishovsky to discuss the investment and how he should proceed. It was going to be a complicated and risky deal and Yaakov would feel much more confident after having discussed it with the *Rav*.

As Yaakov was about to walk into Rabbi Mishovsky's *bais medrash*, he had a sinking feeling in his stomach but did not know why. He had been to see the *Rav* many times in the past and did not get a queasy feeling, but somehow, he felt this time things might be different. The *Rebbi* always had astute advice and was seemingly prescient in what he said. It was uncanny that the *Rav* would always know what to say and how to say it. However, the *Rebbi* usually talked in cryptic messages and rarely said yes or no. He would usually just quote a *passuk* and not say another word. Was this time going to be different?

As always, Rabbi Mishovsky greeted Yaakov like royalty and welcomed him into his office. "*Shalom alaychem* Rabbi Applebaum," the *Rebbi* enthused, emphasizing the appellation "Rabbi".

Timidly, Yaakov responded, "*Alaychem shalom, Rebbi.* Does *Rebbi* have a few minutes? I have something I would like to discuss with *Rebbi.*"

"Of course."

They went upstairs to the *Rav's* humble apartment for more privacy and sat down at the dining room table, which was piled high with *sefarim* of all sorts. The *Rebbetzin* brought in a piece of cake and some water. Yaakov knew he would not be able to ask his questions until he made the two requisite *berachos.* Yaakov took the piece of cake, nodded at the *Rav* and made the *beracha* with devotion, to which Rabbi Mishovsky responded, "*baruch hu uvorach shemo*" and "amen". They smile at each other and the process repeats itself for the drink of water.

From years studying in *Yeshiva* and learning *Gemara,* Yaakov had an organized mind and a clear head. Carefully, skillfully, and meticulously he laid out the minutiae of the business he was considering purchasing. He explained the business plan; he went over the particulars of the company and why it was for sale.

Yaakov reviewed why he thought it would be a good fit. "I am not going to purchase it next week, but I want to get some more paperwork and information. The main purpose of this meeting is a sit down with the lawyer to get more information and their tax returns for the past few years.

"However, before I go all the way to Manhattan next week, I wanted to ask *Rebbi's* opinion and for a *beracha.* To me, it seems like a good business opportunity, but I am not sure. I am concerned that it might put me at financial risk, as I will be completely leveraged. I was hoping for *daas* Torah."

Rabbi Mishovsky sat quietly with closed eyes in deep contemplation. After a minute or two, he turned to Yaakov and asked, "When and where is this meeting supposed to take place?"

"Next Thursday, September 19, at 10:00 a.m. in the North Tower of the World Trade Center."

Rabbi Mishovsky was again reticent for a few minutes, and Yaakov was not sure that the *Rav* was even going to respond. He could hear the clock ticking from the shelf, making its inevitable way forward, and the *Rebbetzin* must be cooking something as delicious aromas were wafting in from the kitchen.

After a few minutes, uncharacteristically, Rabbi Mishovsky quickly opened his eyes looked directly at Yaakov and gave a resounding, "No! Don't go! Proverbs 1:15 בני אל תלך בדרך אתם, מנע' רגלך מנתיבתם' 'My child, do not walk on the way with them; withhold your feet from their pathways.' "

Yaakov was in shock. He never heard of the *Mekubal* giving such a clear and definitive answer. Yaakov knew he would not go, under any circumstances but he was curious for more details. "I accept the advice. I will not go. However, may I ask *Rebbi* why?"

The *Rav* just smiled and picked up a *sefer* from in front of him and continued learning as if he had never been interrupted.

Yaakov took the hint and said the *beracha acharona*, to which the *Rav* responded, without even looking up from his *sefer*. Yaakov then got up from his chair and walked out without turning his back on the Rabbi.

After Yaakov returned to his office, he immediately called and canceled the appointment. He said he would call back later to reschedule.

# September 16, 1985
## Eastern Seaboard United States

Gloria hit the Northeastern United States with a vengeance. Gloria was a category four hurricane, with winds clocked at up to eighty-five miles an hour, with gusts up to one-hundred and fifteen miles per hour. Gloria devastated the northeast coast until October 2. Hundreds of thousands of people in New York were left without power for over a week; the damage there alone was several hundred million dollars.

Overall, the cost of the storm damage to the United States was estimated at $900 million. Massive trees were uprooted and carried to new locations; complete houses were transported to different neighborhoods in whole or in pieces. Thankfully, only eight people lost their lives in the massive storm.

Yaakov was grateful he had gone to Rabbi Mishovsky and was advised not to go to Manhattan. As a way of thanks to the *Rebbi*, Yaakov sat down and learned for an hour for the *zechus* of the *Rav*. That was the best way he could thank him for saving his life.

September 16 and 17 (Monday and Tuesday), 1985 was Rosh HaShanah. It was an awesome *Yom Tov*, not just because it was the beginning of the Days of Awe. There were not many people who were able to make it to *minyan* because of Hurricane Gloria. Yaakov went to *daven* with Rabbi Mishovsky for an inspirational and moving Rosh HaShanah where, as always, the *Rav* stood for the entirety of the *davening*. Yaakov sang along and harmonized with the *shaliach tzibur*.

Rabbi Mishovsky felt something was wrong and was *davening* to help avert as much of an upcoming tragedy as possible. He knew something was coming and was davening with all his might to forestall as much death as possible.

Rivkah was also there wanting to be close to her cousin, Rabbi Mishovsky. She wanted inspiration and she found it.

After *davening*, Yaakov approached the Rabbi, "Is something wrong?" he asked.

"2 Chronicles 7:1 'והאש ירדה מהשמים ותאכל העולה והזבחים' The fire came down from below and killed the holy ones.' " The Rabbi said cryptically, purposely translating a few words slightly differently than traditionally done. When mentioning the *passuk*, the *Rav* emphasized the final word of "והזבחים".

(AUTHORS NOTE: Actual translation: "The fire came down from Heaven and consumed the burnt-offering and the feast-offering." There are four parts to the *passuk*. The first and fourth parts are not quoted herein, however, it is important to note the number four.)

Yaakov was concerned that something bad was going to happen. He understood that the *Rav* was purposely mistranslating the *passuk* and must have a good reason for doing so. All he could figure was that somehow, a fire would come from below somewhere and people would die. Yaakov also wondered why the *Rav* was emphasizing the last word. He would keep his ears open for any major news event on the radio or the newspaper. He would review the appropriate *passuk* and corresponding commentaries. Maybe HaShem would give someone a way to prevent the death that the *Rav* foresaw.

Trying to emulate the ways of the *Rav*, Yaakov would learn and *daven* for the *zechus* of the unknown people. If even one person's life could be saved, it would be well worth the endeavor. Either way, it would not hurt. Even if the answer from on High were, "No," HaShem would use the merits for something else.

# September 25, 1985
## Brooklyn, New York

On Yom Kippur, they also barely had a *minyan* as Hurricane Gloria was hitting the East Coast hard. Many people stayed home, even on this most auspicious day. Nevertheless, those who did come could not help but be inspired by hearing the supplications Rabbi Mishovsky laid before his Maker.

On Yom Kippur, the *Rav* would not say anything except words of davening and *Torah*. Again, he also stood the entire day; there was no chair by the *Rav's* *stender*.

The *Rav* repeated the *passuk* he mentioned ten days prior. "2 Chronicles 7:1 'והאש ירדה מהשמים ותאכל העולה והזבחים' 'The fire came down from below and killed the holy ones.'". When mentioning the *passuk*, the *Rav* once more emphasized the final word of "והזבחים". However, every time he mentioned the *passuk*, he was visibly crying. Yaakov was concerned by what he observed in the *Rav's* behavior. The way the *Rav* was translating the *passuk* and emphasizing the final word was strange and had to have some hidden meaning. Yaakov was also intrigued why the *Rav* neglected to mention the first and fourth sections of the *passuk*. He wondered if there was a reason for the omission and what was the significance?

THAT SAME DAY, AHMED AND Mohamed sat down and finalized their plans for their next terrorist attack on New York. The two conspirators conferred and reviewed the photos Mohamed took in February 1984, of Grand Central and the Waldorf Astoria. They were surprised that it was already a year and a half since those pictures were taken. Together they mapped out their route to and from their planned attack point under Grand Central Terminal. They reviewed the handling of the bombs and their coordination. They chose a random date of October 8.

They also went over some plans for creating more terrorism in New York and how they would use the different chemicals. Ahmed was gleeful as he was already counting those who would die and suffer.

Ahmed was still wary about completely trusting Mohamed. He had not dated Laura for a while, but he was still too soft for Ahmed's liking. He would not be surprised if Mohamed found another Jew to date.

# October 8, 1985
## New York City, New York

*Simchas Torah* has always been a special celebration for the Jewish people. The Jews lived and unfortunately often died for the holy Torah. Most often, Jews were not even aware of the salvation and deliverance afforded them by the Merciful One. *Simchas Torah* is when, with their minuscule ability, they try to thank HaShem for giving them His precious endowment of the Torah. Maybe it is because of their celebrating the completion and commencement of the Torah that HaShem loves and favors them.

It was barely a week after Hurricane Gloria left the area and headed out the Atlantic Ocean and New Yorkers were still recovering from the devastation.

This was the day Ahmed and Mohamed had ordained to carry out their next plan of destruction. They were both excited and cautious. They had planned everything meticulously and were expecting to kill many people, especially Jews.

Lately, there had been a few terrorist attacks in New York and authorities were on high alert especially after having a tip recently delivered into their hands.

"I just found this note in my pocketbook," Rivkah had said to her friend.

"Let's take this to my father," Emily responded. "He will know what to do." They immediately went to the Federal Courthouse and met with Judge Archer in his chambers.

"I don't know if this is legitimate or not," said the Judge. "However, we can't take a chance." He was concerned, especially after recent events by a group calling themselves the Palestine Liberation Group.

"What should we do?" asked a concerned Rivkah.

"You do nothing. I will get this to the appropriate authorities. Since so many people have touched it, there are not likely to be any usable fingerprints. However, someone is trying to reach out to you. Are you sure you don't know who put this in your purse or when?"

Rivkah thought again. "Unfortunately, I have no idea. Obviously, it had to be recently, within the past week or so. I only returned to the States in May, and I only have just one purse." She did not like the idea that someone had used her as a mule for his or her note, despite that it seemed to be a call for help. She liked the implications of the note and how it may have gotten into her purse even less. This meant that someone who knew her was either a terrorist or connected to a terrorist cell. When she returned home, she would review all of her contacts to see if someone stuck out in her mind. However, she did not know many people outside of her insular community especially someone who would have first-hand knowledge of terrorism or terrorists.

"The FBI may have some more questions for you. You did the right thing by bringing this to my attention." Archer was concerned. He was aware of some of the recent terrorist activities being perpetrated lately by a new group of radical extremists.

People were anxious. Although there had been a handful of acts of terrorism, few had died so far, but several were injured, and people were concerned and did not feel safe. There was the fire in the World Trade Center. More recently, there was the attack at Three Mile Island and then the poisoning of the water in New York City. People were fearful that more was to come.

Ahmed and Mohamed had everything ready. They had the perfect plan to kill as many infidels as possible, especially Jews and nothing was going to stop them today. They packed their backpacks with their supplies. They had water, flashlights, rope, gloves, ski masks, lighters, and incendiary devices. They also packed a few candy bars for snacks. They synchronized their watches and left separately. An hour later, at eleven a.m., they met inside the Waldorf Astoria by the elevator bank. Once they stepped inside the elevator, they donned their masks.

Twenty minutes later, they were standing at the platform of Track 61. This platform was part of the original design of the Waldorf Astoria and was initially built for freight and as a loading platform for a powerhouse that sat above it. It was a highly classified track - few people knew of its existence. While in the library doing research for this attack in Grand Central Station, Ahmed came across a New York Times article from 1929 mentioning the hidden track. He also found out that General John J. Pershing first used it in 1938. After that, it was just a matter of finding the blueprints of the hotel and the track locations. Once he realized there was no track 62, it became easy to find its location and entrance.

This track was abandoned and not used since 1944 when President Franklyn Delano Roosevelt employed it. However, it was kept up and maintained for when a POTUS (President of the United States) visits the city, in case he needed a means of emergency egress from the hotel or immediate area.

When the pair stepped onto the platform, they looked around and were shocked at what they saw. Despite its abandoned condition, lights were still on and there were two sets of tracks still in operational condition. On the far track was one car of a train that was deep blue and heavily armored. There were rivets every few inches for the reinforcement and steel plates covered the wheels. The number on the train car was #MNCX002. The "X" indicated that it was a government vehicle and not owned by the railroad.

There was heavy machinery strewn about the area that looked as if it had been used for digging or could be used for presidential protection and there was an elevator shaft that led to the surface.

The two collaborators took out their flashlights and started walking down the tracks heading south toward Grand Central Station. After walking a few hundred feet, they started to see other tracks that were spreading out in many directions. They kept walking and were amazed by the incredible labyrinth of steel tracks.

They found a spot behind some support "I" beams and a concrete pillar to spread out their accouterments and make ready their destruction. This was going to be their great escapade and they wondered how they would top this. Their hearts were beating so quickly that they thought the other one could hear. The area was dimly illuminated lending an eerie and gloomy feeling; adding to the atmosphere were the squeals and clackity sounds of the subway cars on the tracks.

The comrades split up looking for their respective targets while cognizant of the dangers around them. They had to be careful as there were trains moving about on the tracks taking passengers from one stop to the next. They wanted to remain in the shadows as much as possible so as not to be seen by the conductors.

In the shadows, Ahmed combined one-hundred and eight grams of aluminum powder and three-hundred and twenty grams of iron oxide powder into a large container. He had these premeasured in separate Ziploc bags. This was homemade thermite. Thermite is a highly pyrotechnic composition. (Do not try this at home.) and when ignited by heat, thermite undergoes an exothermic reduction-oxidation reaction. This incendiary device will burn at about 1,850 degrees Fahrenheit, or about 1,300 degrees Kelvin.

Ahmed gently folded the ingredients together. He then took four terracotta flowerpots from his backpack and covered the holes in the bottoms with paper. He divided the mixture between the four flowerpots and in the center of each pot put a magnesium strip protruding above the chemicals a few inches.

In his earlier preparations, he made a black-powder fuse for each pot to use as wicks. Ahmed had purchased a one-pound container of gunpowder from a gun shop in Lower Manhattan. He had soaked a thick cotton string in water mixed with potassium nitrate and then coated the string with the gunpowder. Then he let it dry for a couple of days. Ahmed then cut the fuse to four even lengths of nine-feet each. Each fuse would burn for three minutes giving them plenty of time to escape unharmed, or so he hoped.

Before getting started, they paused to have a snack, each one downing a candy bar and some water to refresh themselves. Despite it being October, they were both sweating in the warm underground subway tunnels. They were also nervous and had adrenaline soaring through their bodies.

Their repast only took three minutes. They each took two pots and placed them on tracks for the 4, 5, 7 and S-trains. They wanted to leave the 6 train clear so they could return to Brooklyn. Ahmed attached the nine-foot fuses to each of the magnesium strips in each pot. He laid out the fuses to the north, in the direction of their egress.

They packed their belongings and made ready to flee. Ahmed lit two fuses while Mohamed lit the other two, after which they ran toward the Waldorf Astoria. They had three minutes of fuse until the magnesium strips would ignite the thermite.

They were almost to the hotel when the thermite ignited causing a huge fire underground, which melted the tracks at four different spots for four different trains. As they were rushing up onto the platform back at the hotel, they heard a tremendous series of crashing sounds.

The first train derailed within minutes of the igniting of their devices. The thermite had burned through about ten inches of the S track and sent its train to derailment. It turned on its side and rolled several hundred yards taking down several "I" beam supports. Twenty-nine people were killed and dozens more were injured.

Within minutes, the entire subway system was shut down, but not before several additional trains were involved in the calamity. After the first train derailed, another two on parallel tracks 4 and 5 collided and caused serious damage. Another forty-six people were killed and hundreds more injured.

The 7 train was just exiting the station and was still ramping up its speed when the conductor saw the pileup ahead. He slammed on the brakes and avoided a collision. However, many of his passengers were injured with the sudden cessation of the forward momentum of the train. Only three people were killed.

In the confusion that followed as people made a mad rush to exit the station and terminal, many more people were trampled and a few lost their lives. It was total bedlam with people screaming, crashing sounds from the trains and support pillars, people panicking, fire, and smoke.

The pair were unable to take the 6 train as they had planned as the whole subway system was shut down. When the conspirators returned to their warehouse hideout via taxi, they turned on the news and were ecstatic when they heard of all the damage, carnage and panic they caused. A total of seventy-eight people were killed. The terrorists celebrated while New York mourned and tried to put together the pieces. Tens of thousands were inconvenienced for the next several days while the city went about repairing the damage.

Mohamed suddenly realized that he did not see any orthodox Jews the whole day. Somehow it slipped his mind that it was *Simchas Torah*. Ahmed was disappointed that more Jews were not affected, but they were busy celebrating in *shuls*.

"We will get more of them next time." He was angry, but this time, he had no one to blame but himself. He should have checked the calendar. "Who would have thought that killing Jews would be such a challenge? I wonder if Mohamed knew it was their holiday and purposely didn't say anything about it."

Palestine Liberation Group claimed responsibility via WABC radio.

After *yom tov* Yaakov was astounded and saddened when heard about the terrible tragedy on the news. He made some interesting observations. There are a total of four parts to the *passuk*, there were four trains affected. There were seventy-eight passengers who were killed, which is the numeric value of the word "והזבחים". Terrorists went down and started the fire in the subway system, which meant that it came down from below. Often times a person who is killed in a terrorist attack is called a holy person.


# October 1985
## Borough Park, New York

Something was bothering Yaakov and he decided to discuss it with his *chavrusah*, "I have to tell you something interesting. You won't believe it." Maybe he was a bit more confused than bothered by some recent events.

"Do tell. I love unbelievable stories. They are so, well, unbelievable." His *chavrusah* loved to tease Yaakov. He was wondering if Yaakov would finally tell him about his financial situation. He was sure the man came from wealth, but he never spoke about it. He was about to be disappointed.

"When I was in Israel in February, I had a small part in helping someone. The Rosh HaYeshiva gave me a *beracha* that I should soon find my *zivug*.

"That *Shabbos*, I was by a friend and there were other guests. I noticed a young lady who seemed familiar to me. It's like I may have met her in the past, or something. A few weeks later, in April, I was in London and saw her again at another *Shabbos* dinner.

"A few weeks ago, I gave someone a ride and saw her again. I have seen her several times and even the first time I met her in Israel, I got the impression I had met her before."

His friend looked at him with a blank stare for a full minute. Then he said, "What? Do you want an engraved invitation to your own wedding? Go out with her." He just shook his head wondering how such a brilliant man could be so naive. It was as if he was walking around with blinders.

# November 1985
## Brooklyn, New York

The temperature was hovering right around the freezing mark but the cold did not deter diehard health enthusiasts from their daily jogs. Some would bundle up; some would wear special jogging suits. Asher Siskin was somewhere in between, and today's inclement weather would not deter him from his self-imposed mission.

Asher recently started dating Laura Feld and liked her, but she was not as observant as he was and this concerned him. He wanted to discuss this with the *Rav*. He never got the chance.

Asher went to visit with Rabbi Mishovsky planning to discuss his apprehensions and disquietude with the Rav. When the *Rav* saw him, he immediately had the *Rebbetzin* call 911 and Asher was rushed to the ER. Everything happened so quickly, that it was as if a hurricane had landed on top of the hapless man.

Asher was kept waiting in the ER for an inordinate amount of time when he noticed and then pointed out his new rash to the triage nurse. When she saw the red angry pustules and the bleeding from his eyes, she immediately raised the alarm. Asher was placed in isolation where his condition quickly deteriorated.

Rabbi Mishovsky had foreseen something that was imperceptible to everyone else at the time and had everyone in the *bais medrash* saying Tehillim for Asher. The *Rav* sent someone to find Asher's brother Danny and alert him to the situation and contact their parents.

Asher had some form of hemorrhagic fever. There was blood oozing from his eyes, nose, mouth, and ears. He knew he was dying and had already struggled to say *vidduy* and *shema*. He was in tremendous pain and his body and mind had already begun to shut down. Asher said he felt as if a bus had hit him. It seemed to him as if everything had stopped; he was barely able to perceive anything either visually or audibly.

The Public Health Department and the Centers for Disease Control and Prevention were on the scene to be of assistance. Any of the medical staff who had been in direct contact with him were wearing full-body environmental suits with specialized breathing equipment.

Many of the people who were also in the ER with Asher were showing signs of the pathogen: clearly, the virus was airborne. Since the virus was spreading, the CDC now had enough information available to make an affirmative diagnosis.

The doctor from the CDC felt it was time to educate the medical staff and those in the waiting room. "Viral hemorrhagic fevers (VHF's) are a group of illnesses caused by four families of viruses. These include the Ebola and Marburg, Lassa fever, and Yellow fever viruses. VHF's have common features: they affect many organs, they damage the blood vessels, and they affect the body's ability to regulate itself.

"After testing, we have concluded that this particular strain seems to be Marburg. However, normally, Marburg has an incubation of between five and ten days, not hours. The only conclusion is that this is a Marburg variant that may have been deliberately manufactured."

Much of this information went over the heads of those waiting for assistance in the ER. However, the staff understood the seriousness and deadliness of the situation and would do everything they could to prevent the inevitable panic that would ensue.

The CDC started to put together a timeline to try and figure out where and how this got started. This could be a catastrophe of major proportions as it was highly contagious being airborne and spreading within an hour. This could be the beginning of a pandemic and had to be stopped immediately.

Asher's body could not take anymore, his heart stopped and he went into asystole. Someone called out, "Code-blue!" and several emergency staff descended en mass on Asher's lifeless body. CPR was started, and epinephrine was administered directly into his heart.

It was not helping so the doctor called for the paddles. 200

joules of electricity was sent through Asher's body, trying to shock it back into rhythm. His body arched up off the bed and collapsed back down with a thud. No change.

250 joules - nothing.

300 joules. The doctors and nurses were getting nervous and had adrenaline coursing through their own bodies while trying to save the dying man. Or more accurately, trying to revive the already dead man.

350 joules. Once, twice, three times. The body did not even budge. It was all over. They respectfully covered his body with a sheet.

In stunned silence, they walked away realizing there was nothing more they could do for him. He was gone. As they were walking down the hall in the ER, the triage nurse who had originally seen Asher, collapsed, going into convulsions on the floor and bleeding from her eyes and ears. She had caught the virus.

Police and the FBI had to find patient zero. Finding out where the virus started was imperative to tracing everyone who may have become infected and also to finding a cure. There was a serious concern that it may have been the Palestine Liberation Group.

The authorities had to build a timeline of the infection. As more people came to the ER with the same symptoms, they were able to get more details and their timeline was developing.

AHMED AND MOHAMED HAD BEEN at the Mosque and had met another radical Muslim. The Imam told Daud Albaf that Ahmed and Mohamed could be trusted. Daud was a short and stout religious Muslim, who was absentminded and kept losing his *kufis* hat used for prayer. As an indirect result, Daud had a specific desire for revenge against a particular Jew. He was angry at Siskin for spurning his needs for a hat. Asher Siskin owned a haberdashery store in Borough Park, Brooklyn that dealt mostly with hats and that catered to a Jewish clientele.

Daud entered his shop and requested a *kufis* hat. Asher said that he only dealt with Jewish style hats and was not interested in dealing with Muslim clothing. He had his clientele and was not interested in expanding into the Muslim or any other community. Asher was happy to sell him one of the many stylish hats that were on his shelves but Daud was not interested. He walked out in a huff, vowing revenge.

Danny, who was in the store at the time, looked quizzically at his older brother and they quickly put the incident out of his mind.

DAUD MET WITH AHMED AND convinced his new friend to get him some chemical poison, any chemical, for a price: a high price. After all, Ahmed was taking all the risks.

Ahmed was able to get one precious drop of the altered Marburg virus his lab had been developing, into a tiny sealed dark flask. He specifically went after this virus, as it was what the lab was working on at the time. It took him some time to accomplish this small feat, but it took him even longer to get it out of the lab. The flask was non-descript that any lab around the country had in stock at any time.

"Whatever you do, don't open this flask. Just toss it in his store when he is there. Then run as fast as you can." Ahmed instructed Daud cautiously. "This is highly contagious and very deadly."

"This flask is so tiny. Is there even anything inside?" Daud wondered aloud.

"There's a deadly virus inside. Be very careful."

Daud was doubtful. He could not see anything in the tiny dark vial and thought he was being cheated. He was paying a small fortune for this vial and wondered if he was being ripped off. He even considered giving it back and demanding a refund, then going to the store on a shooting spree. However, Daud had no weapons and did not know how to use a gun.

He returned to his apartment with his procurement and doubt in his mind. He turned over the vial repeatedly, looking for a clue that something was inside. To him, it looked as if it was empty. After much deliberation and thought, Daud decided to open the vial, but he would be cautious, holding his breath and placing a wet washcloth over his mouth and nose.

He opened the container and when he observed the tiniest speck of moisture inside, he was satisfied. He closed the container and headed to Asher's store. By the time Daud arrived at the hat store, he already had a headache.

"Do you remember me?" Daud asked Asher as he was turning off the lights and getting ready to lock up his store.

"Yes, you were here a few weeks ago looking for a Muslim prayer type of hat. Again, I'm sorry, but that's not something I handle." Asher was sincere, but there was nothing to be done for the prospective patron.

"Good; I'm glad you remember me. I vowed vengeance for your disrespect. Here it is." Daud tossed the vial into the store and ran back to his apartment. His headache was bad and getting worse and he just wanted to lie down in bed. He pressed the heels of his hands against his temples in a vain attempt to stave off the massive ache in his head. He noticed his hands were moist and when he looked at them, he was shocked to see blood. The room was spinning and he felt as if he were about to vomit.

Seeing the broken glass in his store, Asher did not know what the problem was. A bit of broken glass; who cared. He cleaned it up and proceeded on his original plans to see Rabbi Mishovsky.

Wearing environmental suits, the FBI broke into Asher's apartment and business. At his store, the feds found the broken glass in the trash and quickly determined it was a vial that contained the virus. The agents interviewed the neighbors and someone remembered seeing a car driving away quickly from in front of the store.

With a description of the car and the man who fled the store, the FBI was able to trace the whereabouts of Daud Albaf. As there was no answer to their knocks, they broke into Daud's apartment.

Daud had a good reason for not answering the door: he was dead from the Marburg virus. He was patient zero. The federal agents interviewed Daud's neighbors, co-workers and even people from his mosque. There was no information forthcoming, and it seemed to be a dead end.

There was no connection to Ahmed. There was nothing reported missing from the local labs. However, there was only one lab working with this particular variant of the virus. They were contacted for an antidote, which of course they immediately supplied. Unfortunately, it was too late for many of the victims who had passing contact with Daud and Asher.

The FBI interviewed all of the people working in the lab. No one was exempt from the scrutiny. There were some questions about Ahmed and his background, but nothing solid.

The feds decided to keep Ahmed on their radar. There was insufficient evidence to obtain a warrant for surveillance, but they would keep their eyes open just in case. Ahmed felt the added pressure and presence of the FBI and knew he had to be careful.

Palestine Freedom Group took credit for the outbreak of the virus.

Ahmed realized that Daud was dead. "That dullard; I warned him not to open that vial. That is probably exactly what happened," he said to Mohamed. He was shaking his head. "How stupid and irresponsible can people be?"

"Well, he paid for his stupidity and naiveté with his life. He was daft."

"At least he already paid me, so I don't have to worry about that."

Ahmed liked the idea of using a weaponized biological chemical as it clearly worked and had devastating results. If he went that route in the future, he would have to be assiduously mindful of the potential hazards to himself.


# December 1985
## New York City, New York

Spurred by their previous partial successes, they decided to continue on to their next objective: cut underground communications cables.

Beneath the surface of the city lies what could be described as another city. Below the Manhattan streets and buildings are found tunnels, vaults, power plants, caves, sewers, paths and much more. There is still a cow path underground on the West Side and numerous abandoned subway stations throughout the city. There is even a two-story underground research library under Bryant Park, near the main public library, and the library itself has underground vaults stretching for several blocks.

There are thousands of underground electric and communications vaults throughout Manhattan. In these vaults are electric, video and phone cables. Surprisingly, there are also steam pipes for heat distribution throughout the city. In addition, there are pipes for natural gas distribution and are even millions of abandoned and severed pipes and cables.

Pipes and conduits were color-coded for easy identification: red for electrical wire, yellow represents gas and orange indicates communication lines.

There are mini vaults that are only about ten feet tall and six feet in diameter. The mini vaults are mostly junctions and are accessed by manhole covers in the street.

The regular vaults are fifteen feet tall, forty feet wide and about one-hundred and fifty feet long. The top of these vaults are at least fifteen feet below the street and are accessed by secure areas in the subway system. Most often, these vaults have concrete or brick walls dividing them into sections. There are pipes of various sizes running along the walls and ceilings of these vaults. There are millions of cables running through the vaults that are not in pipes.

There are pipes from both size vaults that run along the walls and ceilings of the subway system and stations. These pipes lead to different buildings for their communications and electrical needs.

The terrorists had several options for cutting the

communications lines. For this operation, they knew what they wanted to do, but they would improvise and make final decisions on the fly when they were in the subway system.

After the incident with the Marburg virus, Ahmed suspected the authorities were still watching him, so he was trying to be extra judicious. He snuck out of the warehouse while Mohamed went out of the front door. Neither observed anyone tailing them.

They took the now-familiar route to the Waldorf Astoria. They went to Track 61 and again, headed south into the tunnels. They avoided the area where they had perpetrated their previous terrorist attack on the subway system. Once they walked past some of the track junctions, they turned east, then north.

They walked around being careful to avoid incoming and outgoing trains and the third rail that carries the electricity for the trains. On their treck away from the tracks, Mohamed tripped over a piece of nondescript metal that appeared to be very old. He picked it up and scrutinized it with his flashlight and saw what appeared to be a large "G" with a compass above it and a mechanics square below it etched into the metal. Not understanding the significance of his find, he just tossed it to the side and continued on his hike.

In short order, they came to a junction vault that was about a mile north of the Waldorf Astoria. Using a crowbar, they easily broke into the communications vault, but were surprised to find such disarray of wires, conduits, and pipes; it all seemed completely haphazard. They were expecting it to be more organized and clean. Despite the dirt and spider webs covering everything due to neglect, they were easily able to discern the different color pipes. With tools in hand, they opened several of the orange-colored pipes, being careful not to disrupt anything. The two men were working at two different areas about thirty yards apart. They had no way of knowing which wires contained active communication lines or which ones were defunct. To compensate, they each opened a dozen pipes, giving them access to tens of thousands of wires in the dim light of their flashlights.

With commercial-grade wire cutters, they started cutting wires as quickly as possible. Ahmed and Mohamed were not concerned about being caught, as it would take a while until the cuts were traced and found.

Once they completed severing the wires, they hastily made their way back to the Waldorf Astoria. When they arrived in the lobby, they noticed people unsuccessfully trying to use the phones. They casually strolled out of the hotel and headed back to their warehouse satisfied with a job well done with plans to jubilate with a nice dinner.

Although no one died or was maimed with this escapade, they were happy and excited, although Ahmed would have preferred to have done worse.

Once the news reports announced the citywide problems with phones and other forms of communications, it was time to take credit.

Mohamed went to a payphone in Queens, called WABC radio, and announced that the Palestine Liberation Group claimed responsibility.

Tens of thousands were affected by the break in communications. It took technicians several days to find the cuts in the wires and then another couple of days to make repairs. Except for them taking credit, there were no clues found to direct authorities to this terrorist group. This attack was not as bad as previous ones as no one was killed or maimed. However, people were apprehensively waiting for the next attack and wondering why the authorities seemed to be so inept in finding the perpetrators. The talk stations were abuzz with callers vilifying the authorities and their inability to protect them. People were scared: that is exactly what terrorism attempts to accomplish.

Ahmed was listening to the radio and ecstatic with his accomplishments. Mohamed was apathetic.

# FORT DIX, NEW JERSEY

**There** are over one-hundred federal prisons around the United States with different levels of security for different classifications of offenders. In fact, most of the prisons have several security levels. In every prison, there is another even more secure and secluded ward inside the prison called the Special Housing Unit, or SHU; some places call it AdSeg, or Administrative Segregation. In prison, if someone violates the rules, gets into a fight, or even in fear for his safety, depending on what the warden says he is placed in the SHU for a few weeks to a few months. At a prison, the warden is the highest authority and his word is the law; only the governor can override a warden.

If someone is in PC (Protective Custody) at his own behest, he can return to the general population at any time. However, if he is in PC because of being in a fight or threats to his life, only the warden can return him to the general population.

> The highest level of security is a Super-Max prison
> The next is the Maximum-security prison
> High-security
> Medium-security
> Low-security
> Minimum-security

Fort Dix Federal Corrections Institute (Prison) is located on part of the Fort Dix Military Base in New Jersey. In fact, the housing units of the prison used to be military barracks. It is the largest and most densely populated federal prison in the United States. Fort Dix Federal Prison has two campuses, the East and West campuses having almost identical layouts, each housing over 4,000 inmates. On each campus, there are two mess halls, seven housing units, and one intake-housing unit. There is also a gym, chapel and medical building.

Fort Dix Federal Corrections Prison has two levels of security: low-security (at both campuses) and minimum-security. The minimum-security is facetiously called, "The camp" and is the third campus.

Three sets of eight-foot-tall fencing topped with barbed wire surround the low-security areas. There is also fencing with barbed wire to section off areas and control the movements of the inmates. It feels more like a medium-security prison than a low-security prison.

The minimum-security has no fences and is completely open, affording the inmates more freedom of movement. There is a lower ratio of corrections officers to inmates than in the low-security prison. Technically speaking, in the minimum-security, an inmate could just walk off the prison campus. What keeps the inmates in-line is the knowledge that if they are caught off-campus, they will automatically be sent to the low-security prison (or higher) and it will add at least five years to their sentence. In some cases, inmates are allowed off-site for specific reasons. For example, on occasion, they are sent to drive someone to town or even further. Everyone in the minimum-security section is on "short time" which means they will be leaving prison soon to go home.

In prison, the schedule and movement are tightly monitored and controlled.

One of the CO's (Corrections Officers) jobs is to count the inmates five times every day. They would go from cell to cell and count every inmate; occasionally the count did not tally, the CO's would count a second and a third time if necessary. If after three counts, the numbers did not clear, the captain was called to do the count. The captain was never happy when this happened, and on rare occasions, the fault was the inmates causing trouble. One or more of the cons would sneak from one room into another thereby throwing off the count.

All prisons have good and bad CO's. Most are good at what they do; they are competent and professional. However, there are a few corrupt ones in every prison. A corrections officer receives about nine weeks of training, which includes defensive training and inmate control.

If the average person knew in advance what prison is like, they probably would not have committed the crime that landed them in prison. For some young people, spending a few days in prison would probably scare them straight.

# January 1984

All inmates hold special rancor for criminals who hurt women and children. Everyone in a prison is a criminal, but these types of crimes are considered the most heinous, even among other criminals. Most often, these criminals will wisely conceal the reason for their incarceration. Sometimes they will invent a rationale for their previous felonious behavior. More often, they will invent a fallacious reason for their confinement in prison.

Donny Coombs was not the most intelligent man around and did not conceal the true reason he was at Fort Dix. He was there because he kidnapped a child, Yehoshuah Benjamin, and he quickly became the recipient of the antagonism and animosity of the other inmates. He had no one to watch his back and he had an arduous life in prison.

To make his life more difficult, the inmates did some mean and nasty things to him. At least once a week, someone would short his sheets and occasionally, he would find human excrement in his bed. While walking in the halls, several inmates tried to scare him by making loud noises behind him. There were numerous incidents of his being mugged by other inmates who would smack Donny on the back of his head, and he was prevented from using the main bathroom.

A number of weapons can be manufactured in prison. For example, a club can be manufactured in prison quite easily by taking a newspaper or magazine, rolling it tightly, and soaking it in saltwater. When dried, it is a solid and formidable club. A few times, Donny was hit with a club and ended up in the infirmary for this and other punishments meted out to him.

On multiple occasions, he had his commissary stolen. While in the mess hall, other inmates would take food off his food tray while he was still trying to eat. Donny would return to his cell to find his locker completely empty.

Most often, inmates in this situation ask to be segregated in the Special Housing Unit for their own protection. They spend their entire prison sentence confined to their six by nine-foot cell, twenty-three hours a day. It was an untenable situation, but the alternative was much worse.

After a few months of the harassment, Donny gave up and asked to be put in the SHU. Life was difficult enough being in prison, but it was far worse living in a situation where he was the brunt of aggression by the other inmates. At least in Protective Custody, he would be shielded from physical violence.

In segregation, the inmate is supposed to be alone in his cell for twenty-three hours a day. However, Fort Dix is so densely populated; there are often two or even three inmates housed in a cell designed for one. At least Donny would not be completely alone in the claustrophobic confines of his cell. It was a compromise. He thought that after a few years he would ask to be released into the general population. Maybe he could start anew with inmates who did not remember why he was in prison. Unfortunately, that scenario was unlikely: inmates do not easily forget the most abhorrent of criminals amongst them.

# February 1984

One of the inmates at Fort Dix, Avinoam Greene, was feeling bad and depressed because of his circumstances, but more so because of what landed him in prison. It was his own fault he was incarcerated as he was caught masterminding a huge real estate scheme with his family and caused many families severe financial hardship. Avinoam was responsible for wiping out their entire savings and forcing them into significant debt. One particular family, the Berkowitz's, caused him significant angst as they lost everything, including their house, savings, retirement, car, and his business. They were desolate and had to move into Section 8 housing into a small apartment.

Elazar Berkowitz became so depressed he went up to the roof of the building in which, due to his losses he was now living, to think and be alone. He had been up there a number of times reminiscing about what was and realizing that he would probably have to build his *succah* on this roof. He remembered fondly the large *succah* he had in his backyard with numerous guests, but now it would have to be a small one on the roof of this crowded apartment building.

Mr. Berkowitz was sitting on the edge of the building with his legs dangling realizing that he was unable to support his family and had nothing left. He could not see any hope for the future and became despondent and felt lost and alone with no one and nowhere to turn for help. Elazar had declared bankruptcy and felt bad about not being able to pay his creditors. He felt completely alone, was angry at the world, and just gave up on life. Elazar had not eaten in several days and was sick to his stomach.

Sitting on the ledge, watching people milling about on the street, eight stories below, he was angry, "How can these people just go on with their lives? Don't they know what happened to me? Why don't they help me?" He did not even feel the hot tears running down his face. He took off his glasses, as he no longer wanted to see the people some eighty feet below who did not care what he was going through. That was when he realized he was crying. He gave up and pushed himself forward.

Avinoam found out about the suicide of Elazar after his indictment. When he became aware of the tragedy, he was in shock and felt an enormous sense of remorse and pity for the wretched family. Every time he thought about what had happened to them due to his involvement, he wanted to vomit, especially when he realized that there were other families whom he ruined for his own selfish wants and desires. He became depressed to the point where he did not care what happened to him.

Avinoam felt responsible for Elazar's death and blamed himself for the new widow and orphans. When he found out the repercussions of his actions, he deeply regretted his selfish crime of trying to enrich himself and his family to the detriment of others. He did not realize how badly others would be affected by his fraud and theft, he had not considered his victims. He knew that when his prison time would be finished, he would be paying fines and restitution for many years, but that did not bother him as much as the realization of what he had done to other families.

Because of his crimes, he was to spend the next ten years as a guest at Fort Dix Federal Prison. He had no family or friends to visit or write to him while he was incarcerated. His parents were in other prisons for the same crimes. He had hurt so many people due to his frauds that he had no friends left, as all his former friends shunned him and wanted nothing to do with him. He was not allowed to have contact with his parents, as contact with inmates in other prisons was strictly proscribed. He was completely alone and spiraling down out of control.

All this contributed to his feeling depressed and despondent to the extent that he just wanted to end it all. He felt he could not live with himself and what he did, especially to the Berkowitz family.

Avinoam often wondered how many other families he ruined and he could not bear the weight of his iniquities. He waited until lunchtime when his cell was empty when he fastened his two bedsheets together and tied them around a pipe running along with the ceiling.

One of his cellmates walked in while Avinoam was hanging by his bedsheets and raised the alarm while trying to get him down. Another inmate happened to know CPR and was able to save his life - barely.

Avinoam was taken to the infirmary and put on suicide watch for three weeks, during which time, he also received counseling. Psychological counseling, as well as all medical services, in prison, leaves quite a bit to be desired. During suicide watch, Avinoam sat alone in a completely bare cell being monitored round the clock by another inmate who had demonstrated good behavior for a significant period. Greene was never alone, but he was so much alone.

The cellblock was put on lockdown for a few hours while the authorities investigated to make sure no one else was involved or responsible for the attempted suicide.

# March 1985

In prison, Muslims are considered a privileged class: if they want prayer rugs or special clothing for their prayers, it is never a problem. Every day, they have a civilian Imam come into the prison to conduct their prayer services. There is no such thing as Hallal meats in prison, so they just use the same kosher TV dinners the Jews eat. The Muslim prayer room is quite large and comfortable.

Nizar was in prison after his utter failure at bombing Three Mile Island (February 7, 1985). He was frustrated, but at least he was alive and had other Muslims with whom he could associate. He was not remorseful for committing his crime; however, Nizar was not happy that he was in prison. He would make the best of his situation and at least he was safe from Ahmed and his vengeance.

In prison, one only associated with his own; be it by race, religion or gang affiliation. All Jews stood up for one another, as do all Muslims stand by other Muslims.

There was rarely any cross-association. Cellmates also stick together but the bond is not as tight as with race or religion.

Nizar associated with other Muslims and because of the reasons for his sojourn in prison, he was touted as a hero. The others held him in high regard for his escapades on the outside, which he greatly embellished.

He made it known among the Muslim prison community that he was responsible for an attempt on Three Mile Island. However, he significantly exaggerated his role and the results. He did not mention his panic and running around in abject fear and utter failure.

The story he told to the other inmates, was that he was severely outnumbered by the large military presence guarding the nuclear facility. It was not his fault that the intelligence was flawed. Nizar said that if it were not for the incompetence of the head of his cell, he would have had a successful *jihad* and be with his eternal rewards and Allah.

Among his co-religionists, he was considered a hero; if he needed anything, it was supplied. Because of his tall-tales, he was living better in prison than when he was on the outside. He felt he could get used to living in this fashion with the adoration of his newfound friends.

ONE EARLY MORNING THE FOG was so thick one could not see more than a few feet. Because the CO's who watch the perimeter of the prison could not see well, the prison was locked down for a few hours until the fog lifted. Another inconvenience, but at least this one was short-lived and only happened a few times a year, however, there had been a number of attempted escapes during periods of fog.

Rainy weather was never a problem as it was easy to surveil the perimeter of the compound. Inmates were able to easily move about in the rain. Sometimes, during heavy snow, there could be a lockdown, however, that was not too common as tracks are easy to see in the snow.

There were a few free movements of ten minutes each where inmates were free to go to another building. For example, if someone wanted to go to the gym or chapel, they had ten minutes and then they would have to stay at their new location for several hours until a new movement was called.

If a con was between buildings when a movement was permitted, they could continue to their destination. However, if they were still outside at the end of the movement, they were stuck outside.

No amount of cajoling would entice a CO to open the door to the housing unit. It did not matter to the CO if it was raining or snowing; it was too bad for the inmate. After all, the inmates are just wards of the federal prison system so why should a CO care if they were stuck out in the freezing cold for a few hours? However, there were some CO's who did care.

THE FOOD IN PRISON WAS palatable and nutritious, but far from gourmet. The prisoners usually had access to some food they were able to purchase at the commissary, assuming the inmate had money in their account. At mess, the inmates also had the ability to socialize more than any other time. There could be hundreds of inmates in the mess hall at one time, which can be a time of stress for the prisoners and the guards.

As often happens, people under stress can become rowdy and disruptive; especially when large groups of individuals are in confined spaces; even more so when the people are criminals in prison.

No one knew what instigated the altercation, but there was another melee in the mess hall. Pushing became shoving. Shoving became pushing. Before anyone could intervene, there was an all-out brawl among the inmates. Food and fists were flying all over the mess hall. Food trays were used as weapons. Before the CO's were able to restore order, many of the inmates were hurt, some worse than others. Most of the inmates scampered to the side of the mess hall to be out of harm's way and many tried to exit the building: most did not want to be involved in the altercation. There was cheering and screaming There was such a cacophony of noise that brought the attention of the CO's from all over the prison campus.

Suddenly, a shiv appeared. A shiv is a makeshift weapon made by sharpening something by hand. For example, the handle of a toothbrush can be made into a weapon by rubbing it repeatedly, over time, on concrete. Many of the inmates involved in the brawl were cut and one inmate was killed.

After the fighting was broken up and the mess hall returned to its previous state of cleanliness, the warden declared a lockdown for a week. There was a major investigation to determine who was responsible for the violence. Everyone was questioned but no one admitted to starting the fight or knowing who did. Being a snitch is a serious crime and affront to other inmates. Most often fights did not end with death.

# April 1985

At forty-nine years old, Phillip Rush became another guest of Fort Dix. Well, the term guest may be a bit too generous. He was incarcerated at Fort Dix Correctional Institute with many others who had committed crimes. He jokingly said that the reviews of the place said the swimming pool was not good. Never mind that there was no pool.

Before entering Fort Dix, Phillip had some concerns about his health and how they would be addressed in prison. Phillip was on medicine to control his high blood pressure and high cholesterol. He was told by the authorities that he would receive all of his needed medication without any problems: he was not so sure.

Phillip was not wealthy, but he had been doing well for himself with several real estate holdings in different boroughs. Unfortunately, like many others, he became a bit too greedy.

Phillip was a smart man and understood people's nature, especially when they are excited. Most people were not careful when they read contracts, especially when it came to the emotional purchase of a house. He was counting on people's naiveté and their disregarding some of the small print in the contract.

Choosing carefully, Phillip bought a house in Brooklyn in 1978. The house he procured had been on the market for a while since no one wanted to purchase a house in such poor condition. However, he wanted a house that when fixed up, he would be able to sell on emotion.

Phillip hired Tuvya Justin to fix up the house and put it in a saleable condition. The remodeling took several months, but it was good work and the house looked great: he was even considering living there himself. But that would not fill his needs.

Phillip put the house on the market and it sold quickly. However, he had written an unusual contract with the purchaser.

Phillip had taken a standard real estate contract and retyped it himself with a few extra paragraphs worded carefully. Those extra clauses were hidden in the middle of the agreement so as not to be obvious to the purchaser.

In the fine print, it said that if the purchaser missed even one payment, thirty days later, the possession of the house reverted to the seller and all payments made to-date converted to rent. The purchaser did not take ownership of the house until the final payment of the mortgage was made. The purchaser retained no equity in the house; it all belonged to the seller.

If the purchaser missed even one payment, Phillip, who was still the owner, could sell the house to someone else and the first purchaser had no recourse.

If the second purchaser defaulted, Phillip took possession and flipped it again. The problem with this strategy is that it is a fraud.

From 1978 to 1985, he did this multiple times with several properties. He was caught in January 1985 and was sentenced in April 1985.

While in prison, he had difficulties with his medication. Phillip had been on his medication for a number of years and had worked closely with his doctor who monitored his blood work and pressure. Together they decided on a course of action and he was doing well with the prescribed medication and dosage.

The prison physician felt he knew better than his own doctor of many years. This doctor decided that Phillip did not need such high doses of the medications. He came to this conclusion without any blood work or tests.

Phillip was furious: they were playing with his health and life. He immediately sent a letter to his lawyer.

While waiting for a response from his lawyer, fluctuations with his medication, resulted in him passing out in his cell. One of his cellmates ran to the CO who called the medic from the infirmary. He was revived and placed under observation in the infirmary.

The prison doctor continued to play with the doses of medication going as far as saying that maybe Philip had tried to commit suicide. Phillip's lawyer came to the prison to discuss the situation with Phillip about what could be done under the circumstances. While in the visitation room, the lawyer noticed that Phillip was a bit flushed and slurring his words.

Phillip's attorney made an immediate appointment to see the judge who was appalled to hear about his medical treatment. He immediately ordered an injunction ordering the prison doctor to follow the dictates of Rush's doctors.

Phillip had no more problems with the medical staff changing his medication or dosages. They were not happy with the judge interfering in their domain, but now they had no choice. A judge's word is law.


# May 1985

Most inmates were not happy living in prison with every aspect of their lives controlled and monitored. A few inmates actually enjoyed prison; however, there was no other option and they had to make the best of their situation. They were wards of the federal government sent to prison to serve out their sentences to pay society for the crimes they committed. There were a few inmates who did not care if they were living in prison or on the streets as they were ne'er do wells. Some even enjoyed being in prison since they actually had a place to sleep and three nutritious meals a day that they did not have to work for.

Stewart had been a construction foreman prior to his incarceration when he was caught stealing tools and equipment from his employer that he was using for his personal needs as he was slowly renovating his own house. He was a little too greedy and pilfered too much, his boss caught on and videotaped him embezzling. With the evidence staring him in the face, he copped a plea to get a lesser sentence.

Some inmates were particularly motivated to change their living situation and Stewart Osborne was one. He wanted to get out of the confines of the triple barbed wire fencing surrounding the prison. Once on the outside, however, he was not sure what he would do or where he would go, but he knew he had to escape.

He started to dream and plan in his mind what he could do and where he could go when he would abscond from prison. He was strong and rugged due to his having worked in construction his entire adult life. "When I escape, I can get my hands on some camping gear and live in the wild for a few years. We are not that far from the Appalachian Mountains where I can easily move around and no one would be the wiser."

While at prison work detail, he pocketed a wirecutter and snuck it out of the shop. His plan was to slowly cut the chain-link fences and run away from prison. Over time, he was able to cut a few links at a time on the innermost of the three fences, while leaving the tool near the fence so he would not be caught with it.

Every few days found Stewart at the same fence cutting just a bit more stepping ever closer to his goal of being on the other side of the fences.

After two weeks, he was through the first of the three fences. He was excited by his progress and his vision of living on the mountain range was within his grasp. The second fence was about ten feet further and as he was working on it, he was spotted by the routine patrol who gave chase. He had nowhere to run and was quickly apprehended in no man's land between the two fences. He was disappointed as he watched all his plans disappear in a wisp of smoke. He had no one to blame except himself and would have to suffer the consequences of his attempted self-liberation from Fort Dix.

This was serious and the warden immediately put the entire prison into lockdown for two weeks. The extended lockdown was to prevent other inmates from considering a similar plan of action. It also gave the prison system time to repair the fences and to investigate in case anyone else was involved. Osborne was thrown into the SHU for two months before being transferred to a maximum-security prison. An additional five years was added to his prison term and now there was no hope for him to be able to escape. Because of his attempted breakout, he would never qualify for the camp. He would now be doing hard time.

# October 1985

Bert Sobol was brought to the prison by his family to self-surrender to the authorities where he was to be incarcerated in Fort Dix Federal Correctional Institute in New Jersey. He was feeling depressed and scared but would try to make the best of the next several years. He was resigned to his fate, as there was nothing he could do to change it. He was told to leave his *tefillin* and *siddur* home; he was only allowed to bring a picture and any prescription medicine with him. He was also allowed to bring money to be put into his commissary account. At the security gate of Fort Dix Military Base, he was thoroughly patted down and then brought to the intake building. He was patted down again and then went through a metal detector, stripped-down, cavity searched and given prison clothes.

When the Corrections Officer talked sternly and addressed him gruffly, only by his last name, "Move it, Sobol," that was when reality hit him - he was a felon going to spend the next five years in prison. It was a scary thought and his heart palpated; he felt short of breath. After a moment, he regained his composure, remembering that in prison, he must not show any weakness to anyone.

He had another realization of the commencement of his incarceration as he was walking, in prison garb, from the intake building to his cellblock. Just looking around at the tall fences and barbed wire was intimidating and it was daunting to think he would have no freedom or privacy for the next five years.

He was brought through the intake building and assigned a temporary bunk on the third floor of the temporary housing unit and was given the prison manual. This told the inmate what was expected of him and what times he was supposed to be at different types of activities. This included chow, mail call, work detail, laundry and more. It also discussed the counts, roll calls, commissary, and the dress code. Religious observances and medical issues were also mentioned.

The first evening at chow was when Bert met some of the other Jews in prison. It was a bittersweet moment; on the one hand, there were other Jews with him, on the other hand, there were other Jews in prison.

He had to argue with the head clergy to get kosher food, but the other religious Jewish inmates had the same challenge. He had to prove he was *Shabbos* observant and mindful of the kosher laws. It turned out that religious Muslims did not have any problem with the clergy; they got their meals, prayer rugs and Korans without any problems. It was just the Jews and some of the Christians who had difficulties getting what they needed for their religious observances. Whether it was for *tefillin*, *tzitzit*, *yarmulkes* or any other religious paraphernalia, it was a major fight for each item needed.

The next morning Bert went to *shacharis* where he met more Jews. The Jewish chapel was the smallest of the chapels: it was functional, although difficult to fit everyone in the small room.

Within a week, he was moved to his cell in one of the main cellblocks. Each cell was twenty-five-feet by twenty-five-feet and had six military style bunk beds to sleep twelve men. There were radiators in each cell, but no air conditioning.

All the buildings were made entirely of cinder block and concrete. As such, noise carried: a locker closed harshly would reverberate throughout the hall; loud commotion would be exacerbated and amplified off the walls. Each building was an echo chamber. There was never complete silence, even in the middle of the night.

Conducting business via phone or letters was strictly verboten and considered a major infraction. As all calls were monitored, the possibility of receiving a disciplinary infraction for "conducting business" was a great source of anxiety. When an inmate used the phone and discussed family activities, sometimes it revolved around business, which could lead to a shot by the guards.

All phone calls and mail were monitored, and some inmates were given more scrutiny than others. It depended on many factors, including the length of incarceration, criminal offense and prison record. If an inmate was a high-profile prisoner, he was under stricter surveillance and had to be even more cautious with his behavior and conduct.

THE SIRENS AGAIN, IT WAS horrible to live in this manner all the time. The sirens were disturbing when they sounded, especially while they were in the middle of *shacharis*. It was disconcerting to hear that blaring alarm, which usually signaled a lockdown. How can one concentrate during prayers with the knowledge that they were going to have to stay in place for an indeterminate period of time? It was another reminder that the inmates were behind bars and had no control over anything in their lives. During a lockdown, all inmates must stay where they are in order to be counted and surveilled, and sometimes more. Frequently, there are body searches, pat-downs, or cell searches. Lockdowns enabled the CO's to control, locate and identify every single inmate in every corner of the prison.

"Hey boss, why were we locked down earlier?" Bert asked Corrections Officer Stanley Meyers, using one of the common appellations inmates used for a CO.

The CO just walked away ignoring the question and the questioner.

Another inmate, Mordechai Samuel, heard the question and responded, "The rumor is that two inmates in the SHU (Special Housing Unit) were released into their free-time cage at the same time. The problem was that these two inmates were members of rival gangs. They got into a knock-down bloody fight and by the time the CO's were able to stop them, one was dead and the other was seriously injured."

"That's terrible. How could that happen?"

"It doesn't happen often, but it does happen. There are supposed to be safeguards in place to prevent things like that from happening, but there are so many inmates here, that mistakes are bound to happen.

"Last year there was a young Jewish guy who was playing one gang against the other and he was beaten to within an inch of his life. He had multiple broken bones, internal bleeding, ruptured spleen and more. Everyone thought he was going to die."

"What happened to him?" Bert asked concerned.

"He was rushed to the hospital, rushed being a subjective word around here. He was in the hospital for a few days and then in the infirmary for about two months. Eventually, he was shipped off to another prison."

"Is that what I have to look forward to?"

"Just stick with your own and be careful. Don't insult or start up with anyone. Always watch other inmate's hands."

"Thanks for the tips. I appreciate it."

"Watch your back and don't trust anyone here. No one is your friend. Be polite and respectful, but keep to yourself."

Bert shuddered at the thought. Prison is not the place for a nice Jewish man. "Maybe I need to sleep with one eye open," he thought to himself.

After the fight and murder in the SHU, the entire prison was in lockdown for two days while the incident was investigated. There was so much tension among the staff and inmates it could practically be cut with a knife.

Lockdowns usually made it easier on the CO's as the inmates were all confined; most CO's did not appreciate having to be extra tough on the convicts. They understood it was difficult enough for the prisoners, why make it worse?

CO Ralph Atkins was the exception. He was corrupt, drunk and a nihilist who lived to control the inmates. Atkins took bribes to look the other way; he would sneak in contraband - documents, cigarettes, drugs and more. For the right price, he was willing to let an inmate use his unmonitored office phone. Atkins was angry and mean, especially to Jews who he hated above all. When he saw a Jew having a difficult time, he could not help but smile.

His mother and stepfather raised Ralph and he never knew his biological father; his mother never talked about him. His stepfather was mean to him and beat him regularly. Every weekend, his stepfather would drink away half of his paycheck at a local bar, come home drunk and take out his anger on Ralph.

After his mother kicked his stepfather to the curb, Ralph found out that the man was Jewish. He grew to hate Jews and to think they were evil and vile people. Like his stepfather, Ralph imbibed often, mostly to forget the past, became a drunk and often showed up to work inebriated and irate. He also had a difficult time keeping a relationship going. He tried to start a relationship with his coworker Alice Cooperman, but she nixed that before it even got started. Alice, along with everyone else, despised Ralph.

Ralph was a broad man, six feet tall and over two hundred pounds. As with most CO's, he worked out regularly and was muscular. One time Atkins showed up to work with a black eye and a long laceration on his upper arm; no one dared to ask him the cause. Of course, many of the inmates speculated: some thought it was from a bar fight. Others imagined it was his wife if anyone would even marry him. Even others offered the supposition he had been mugged.

Whenever he was angry at something, anything, he would declare a surprise inspection. If he had a problem at home, he took it out on the convicts; if he got up on the wrong side of the bed, he dished it out on the inmates. He was aggressive about it; especially to the Jews or anyone else he did not like or reminded him of his stepfather.

One of the jobs CO's had to do was to count the inmates five times a day. Two of the counts were called "stand-up" counts, which meant all of the inmates had to be standing by their assigned bunks. During any stand-up count, Atkins made everyone stand at attention at his bunk and doff their hats. It was not a requirement of the prison, just Atkins' rule to show power and control over the inmates. He did not like it that Jews did not have to remove their *yarmulkes.*

Henry did not like this added humiliation so when he checked the prison manual and saw nothing about removing hats during counts, he reported it to the warden. Nothing outward happened, but Atkins was not as scrupulous anymore about the inmates removing their hats.

Most of the other corrections' officers were aware of Atkins' penchant for bringing in contraband and other less than lawful activities. No one liked him since their job was to preserve the peace and law in the prison and here was someone who was supposed to do the same but was perverting and obfuscating those laws and rules. He was venal while the vast majority of corrections officers were ethical and professional. Atkins could not count himself among them, although he did not feel as if he was doing anything wrong since the inmates were just wards of the state and were criminals.

If an inmate wanted to keep something from the ever-present ears of the authorities, they had to find another way to communicate with the outside world. The options were limited since phones were monitored; outgoing, and especially incoming mail was closely audited and there was no privacy during visitation. Some inmates got themselves into trouble trying to write in cipher to people on the outside.

Fortunately for the rare inmate who needed this service, Atkins was happy, for a price, to provide access to a private phone. There was a phone in the CO's office and Atkins would rent it out to inmates. Atkins did not realize that his phone was also monitored by those in charge of the prison. He would have done things differently if he had any inkling that his phone was also constantly monitored.

Atkins would also bring in contraband for inmates. If someone needed drugs or a pack of cigarettes, Atkins was their source.

# December 1985

While returning from commissary one cold evening, Avinoam Greene had just entered his housing unit. He had to carry his large bag of purchases to his cell on the third floor. Walking alone up the cold and bare stairwell was not the safest place to be, and that particular evening was not good for Avinoam who was weighed down with his package. When he was between the second and third floors, three other inmates, who wanted his purchases for themselves, mugged him from behind. One of the muggers grabbed his bag from behind while the other two shoved him forward. Before he knew what hit him, he was splayed on the concrete stairs with sprained wrists and a banged knee. By the time he turned over to look at his assailants, they were long gone. He jumped up and ran out of the stairwell, but there was no one around and no sign of his entire commissary bag.

He decided not to report it to the CO's, as there were no witnesses and even if there were, no one would come forward. There was nothing he could do but keep his eyes open in the future.

However, he did have some scrapes and bruises from the mugging that had to be reported to the CO. If there were to be a mugging in the unit and he had bruises and cuts, it would be assumed he was involved and he would be put in the SHU during an investigation, which could last a month or two. However, if the injuries had been documented before an incident occurred, he would be in the clear with substantiated evidence that he was not involved in an altercation.

"Hey boss," Avinoam said to the CO.

"What?" Alice Cooperman asked.

"I just fell down in the stairwell and my hands are cut and I am developing a bruise. The inmate manual says that I have to report all such injuries to the CO." Avinoam liked Ms. Cooperman as she was nice to the inmates and was easy on the eyes. She was the consummate professional officer while at the same time being polite and respectful to the inmates.

"I hope you're not hurt badly," she said.

"Well, no."

"Good. I have to ask, was anyone else involved? Did someone hurt you?"

"No."

Cooperman did not believe him, but she understood the mentality of the inmates not wanting to snitch on one another. "Okay," she said, "I have to document the injuries and the details of what happened. This is for your own protection."

"I understand," Avinoam said a bit humiliated by the whole ordeal. He was thankful it was Ms. Cooperman and not that scoundrel Atkins.

She took some pictures of his injuries and took his statement.

She went with him to look at the stairs to see if there was anything amiss and wrote everything down. "Are you sure no one else was involved? We can protect you."

"Thank you, but it was just me being clumsy."

They both played the game, but there was nothing else to be done.

The next day at *shacharis*, Avinoam was able to find a sympathetic ear in Bert. He poured out his woes, "I think I need a bodyguard. Do you know anyone who may be interested? Not sure what I can afford if anything."

"I will try to be your bodyguard. We will need to stick together as much as possible." Bert continued, "Whenever you see other cons around you, the first thing you should do is look at their hands. Notice if they are clenched or if they have something that can be used as a weapon. That will be your best protection. As far as paying me, whatever you can send my way will be fine. I'm not indigent. Maybe a soda or some stamps once in a while."

"I can do that, thanks for your help, much appreciated."

"You're welcome, but let's keep this to ourselves," Bert said. "We both will be safer that way." He did not want to disclose his expertise in martial arts.

"Just remember, we go everywhere together. This is just between us. You will also watch my back."

"Will do. Thanks again."


# January 1986

Ramon Gonzalez had a beef to settle with Judge Archer. Archer was responsible for putting him and many others in prison, some of whom were with Ramon in Fort Dix.

"It's not my fault that I'm in prison," he mused to himself. "Just 'cause I put my girlfriend in the hospital, don't mean I should be in prison, she deserved what she got coming to her. It's the judge's fault I'm here and I want revenge."

He was going to bide his time until he got out and then take his revenge. He had plenty of time to come up with ideas and make plans.

Ramon had a difficult upbringing: his childhood was not easy. He never knew his father, and his mother was both an alcoholic and a drug addict and so he was born with a mild case of Fetal Alcohol Syndrome. Due to her addictions and compulsions, his mother was unable to raise him so Ramon ended up in a foster home. For most of his life through his teen years, he was shuttled from one foster family to another. In most, he was abused; in the rest, he was ignored. He felt he did not belong anywhere and grew to resent everyone and everything, especially those in authority. By the time he aged-out of the system, he was already a drunk and a drug addict, just like his mother used to be. He had a long juvenile record that was sealed, but for him, that was his initiation into the world in which he wanted to live. He was angry and proud of it, resenting those who were successful and because of the trouble he had been in, he hated law enforcement. He never finished high school and was not even that street smart, but he did not care and was nonchalant about his future.

At a young age, he joined Mexican Mafia, La Eme, which gave him a purpose and a direction in life. Okay, it was heading down a path of destruction, but he did not care since his only plan was to eventually move up in the mafia and be a boss.

Ramon was domineering and had to have everything his way everywhen. When things did not go how he wanted, he would explode in a fury of anger, not caring who or what was hurt in the process of his tirades. He was given to throw things in rage, often breaking what he had hurled and not caring about any collateral damage.

Additionally, Ramon was a gambler, often playing poker, but he was not averse to betting on the horses or major sporting events. What else was a miscreant supposed to do? He had no real skills, so he resorted to other forms and games of chance, often wagering large monies that he did not have, forcing him into debt.

Poker was his favorite as he had some control over the game. He was good at reading people, and the way to win in poker is to play the opponent before the cards.

One evening, Ramon came home late after losing big. He was in a foul mood, even worse than usual. When his girlfriend did not have dinner on the table, he became even more enraged.

He started yelling and cursing her taking his anger out physically. After a few minutes of his animus and bile, she just folded her arms and gave him the silent treatment while glaring at him with hate-filled eyes.

"I have to leave and get away from him before I get hurt worse," she thought to herself. "He's completely out of control. I'll leave the first chance I get, maybe in the morning."

When she stopped responding to his contemptible behavior, he became even more antagonistic and started throwing things destroying the apartment and everything in it. His girlfriend started yelling at him to stop, but he just escalated getting worse and started hitting her. He repeatedly belted her so hard in the face he broke her orbit bone and one of his fingers. She tried to flee, but he barred her egress.

A neighbor heard the raucous and called the police. By the time they arrived, the girlfriend was unconscious having been beaten so badly her face was permanently disfigured. She had multiple fractures, a black eye, and several severe lacerations. Her right arm was bent at a grotesque angle at the point where it was broken. She would never be the same physically or emotionally.

Officers Connors and Jackson came in response to the 911 call to investigate the reports of a domestic disturbance. Ramon refused to answer the door and his girlfriend was in no condition to do anything as she had passed out and was bleeding on the floor. Jackson heard a noise from within and realized that Ramon was absconding out the back, probably down a fire-escape. They forced the door with their shoulders and were stunned by what they saw. It only took about a quarter of a second for them to notice someone escaping out the window onto the fire-escape. Ramon was heading up to the roof so Connors gave chase out the window onto the fire-escape while Jackson took the stairs and headed to the roof. On his way, Jackson radioed for backup and an ambulance.

Once on the roof, Ramon was barred by the door to the stairwell leading back down and blocked from the fire-escape by a COP on his ascent. Ramon had nowhere to run and was not going down without a fight. When he realized he was trapped, he swung at Connors who was closer to him. Connors took the blow to his face which caused him to spin around into the wall of the stairwell. Jackson pounced on Ramon from behind while Connors regained his balance.

Running on adrenaline, Ramon randomly and frantically punched and kicked at the law enforcement officers. However, he was no match for the trained officers who were able to subdue him; however, they had to forcefully twist his arms behind his back so far they almost dislocated his shoulder. One of the arresting officers had to shove his knee into the back of the perp to keep him down. He had to be placed in handcuffs and shackles. He spat at and cursed the officers so they put a facemask on him.

Their backup finally arrived followed moments later by an ambulance. The girlfriend was rushed to the hospital in critical condition.

In addition to the assault on his girlfriend, he was now facing resisting arrest and assault of a police officer. Due to the extent of the beating he gave her, the prosecutor also proposed the charge of attempted murder.

In 1980, Ramon went before Judge Archer and because of his history and the violence of his most recent crimes; he was sentenced to fifteen years in federal prison. Now he was in Fort Dix and had only nine years left on his stint.

Ramon knew Nizar also wanted revenge against Judge Archer and had conspirators on the outside: maybe they would help in the nefarious deed. Ramon and Nizar talked about different forms of reprisal against the jurist and what they could do to him. They had no way to clandestinely get information out of the prison, so they had to come up with a plan. They made sure to have their conversations outside in the field so they would not be overheard.

Ramon had an idea. "I'll tell ya', Atkins can be a source for help in certain tings. For the right price, he'll get a message to the right people."

"Sounds like a plan," Nizar said.

"I'll talk wit him. I've known him longer. Maybe he's got an idea."

"Does the judge have any family we can get to?" Nizar asked hopefully.

"I don't know, but that be a good idea. We may be able to get at a kid if he's got one."

Later that day, Ramon met with Atkins in the CO's office and they were talking about taking retribution. Ramon wanted Atkins to make arrangements on the outside to find out if the judge had a vulnerable family.

"We've gotda do sometin with Archer," Ramon said.

"Yeah, he's a real buzzard," responded Atkins. "The judge is well protected with security and cops. It'll be difficult, if not impossible, to get at him."

"Does he got any kids?"

"I know he has a daughter, but I don't know anything beyond that," Atkins mentioned.

"I've got someone on the outside if you can get a message to him, he can get to his daughter," he said conspiratorially.

"Give me his name and number," Atkins said as he slid a piece of paper and a pencil to Ramon. "I'll get him the message."

Ramon wrote down the information and said, "He can off her. He's done other jobs for me."

"I'll take care of it."

There was no mention of Nizar or his involvement.

Serendipitously, Bert happened to be outside the CO's office and overheard enough of the conversation to understand there was a conspiracy planned against Judge Archer. It was no easy feat to overhear the conversation as the hallway outside of the CO's office was always busy and noisy. Bert was there to check the roster for the morrow to see if he was needed somewhere or had a specific appointment. It was something every inmate had to do on a daily basis and was why that hallway was always crowded.

Stunned by what he overheard, Bert quickly turned around to look at the clipboard with the roster that was hanging on the opposite wall. Just as he reached the clipboard, Ramon came out of the CO's office in a good mood. Because of all the noise in the hall, he did not think it was possible for anyone to have overheard the plot, so he just went upstairs to his cell.

However, Bert did overhear the plot and immediately called his lawyer and said he needed to meet, urgently. This was something he was not going to mention over the phone system that he knew was monitored.

Two days later Bert met with his lawyer in the visitation room and told him what he knew of the plot. The lawyer was in shock.

"Please do something with this information."

"I will," the lawyer said. "I will contact the judge and also make sure he knows where I got this information. Too bad we don't have any proof, but that may yet be forthcoming."

"Thanks." Bert was glad he was able to help someone, even from prison. He was not expecting any favors in return.

# February 1986

EVERY INMATE IN FORT DIX, as with most prisons, must have a job. The jobs can be anything from keeping one tier of a housing unit clean, snow removal, trash duty, bathroom cleanup, cooking in or cleaning up the mess hall. There was also UNICOR, which was prison work-duty to produce goods or services specifically for government agencies. Most often, UNICOR was used to make uniforms for inmates. If an inmate refused to work, their sentence was increased.

The food the inmates received in chow was cooked every day in the prison kitchen by the cons. Part of the work detail was that many of the inmates had to work in the mess: some did prep work, some cooking, some dishwashing, some serving, some bussing, some clean-up, and some mopping. Those jobs had their advantages and disadvantages. The disadvantages were that it was long hours and the inmate had to get up early. The advantages were that it was sometimes possible to sneak food out of the mess hall and in the winter, it was easy to stay warm in the kitchen.

Ramon worked in the kitchen and was able to sneak some fruit and sugar out of the mess hall. With the fruit and sugar he pilfered, he started to make hooch.

Hooch is prison-made alcohol. It is not difficult to make, but it does exude a strong odor as it ferments. It has to ferment for several weeks and the longer it sits the stronger the alcohol content. A CO could easily find this and the responsible party would get into serious trouble. Hooch was considered major contraband and the punishment for making it or being caught with it was spending a serious amount of time in the SHU and additional time added to the sentence.

Ramon needed a diversion and decided that he would take the risk and try to make hooch for himself and his cellmates. He put all the ingredients into a large trash bag inside another trash bag and hid the double bags in a hall utility room. This way, if it were found, the bag would not lead to him and the only consequences he would suffer would be the loss of the fruit and sugar.

In about a week, the fermenting fruit caused a distinct odor that started to disseminate throughout the floor. During one of the infrequent visits of a CO to the floor, the smell was detected; the bag was found and confiscated. Because it was not in anyone's cell, there was no direct link to any particular inmate. No one got into trouble, but no one had any hooch either, at least for the time being.

Many cons often tried to sneak foodstuffs out of the mess hall to have a snack later. Sometimes it was to facilitate them being able to make another food, for example, sneaking milk out of the mess hall for dry cereal or to make yogurt.

If an inmate was caught, the food was confiscated, and the con got a shot. With enough shots, he went to the SHU.

MONEY WAS ALWAYS TIGHT IN prison; well, actually, money was not existent in prison; cash is contraband and its possession could lead to severe consequences. In lieu of cash, inmates used macks as one form of prison currency between themselves. A mack is a vacuum-packed package of mackerel that cost one dollar at the commissary. However, macks were difficult to come by if the inmate did not have any money on their commissary account.

Many inmates tried to do something to earn something in

place of money or macks. As in life outside a correctional institute, bartering is common in prison: if an inmate has some special knowledge or a skill others wanted, he had an in. Some people could draw and make cards from simple paper, some had legal knowledge and some had medical knowledge. A few had fighting skills and would be a bodyguard for the weaker or more vulnerable inmates.

Most inmates did not have a learned skill or knowledge from the outside that translated into a usable commodity on the inside.

There are few diversions inmates have available; exercise is one of the most common diversions as is walking and reading. There was a small library with a decent selection of books; basketball and handball courts were available; some of the inmates played games and cards. Inmates who wanted to gamble would do so in a small cell after "lights out," as poker and gambling were not allowed. What do you expect from a bunch of criminals?

Peccable in nature, Ramon was the dealer of a poker game he ran almost nightly. Atkins knew about the game but he looked the other way as long as he got his cut. The nocturnal game took place in an empty small bare cell at the end of one of the halls.

Ramon was a man of average build, but a bit pudgy. He liked to think of himself as in good shape with a bit of loose muscle that slipped to his waist. Due to his history outside of the confines of the prison, his presence instilled fear in all he met on the inside. He had numerous tattoos on his body and for those knowledgeable, his tattoos read like a personal diary that was open for all to see and read. Some of his tattoos told the story of his gang affiliation; of those he had allegedly killed, and for his rank in the gang and the mafia. He was not someone with whom to trifle, as he was tough on the inside and out.

Mark Franklin was part of the nightly game and did not care if he was caught in the act of gambling. In prison, he had food and a place to sleep; he was comfortable and that was all that mattered to him.

Despite his lack of skill in the game, Nachum Weiss also joined the poker game as often as possible. Instead of cash, they used macks and other commissary items for their wagers and the other players were more than willing to take Nachum's belongings. Nachum did not like losing at the game, so after the first few nights, he bought his own deck at the commissary and alone on his bunk, practiced both the game and how to shuffle. To the surprise of the other players and unbeknownst to them, he was able to use legerdemain to palm an ace and win a few games. It was difficult to hide the ace, but he had good and dexterous hands and always wore long sleeves. He knew that if he were caught, it would be bad news for him as the others who had been cheated would beat him to a pulp, so he had to be extremely careful.

He felt that it would be safer for him to come up with a better plan and he discretely marked his own deck. When no one was looking and with great difficulty, he was able to swap his deck for Ramon's. This way, if it were to be found out and someone realized the deck was marked, it would be blamed on Ramon.

Nachum thought he was being smart by making sure not to win every hand and not even every night as long as in the long run, he was ahead of his losses. Over time, he started to become a bit overconfident and presumptuous by winning more often.

Over the course of several weeks, Mark became suspicious and watched Nachum's machinations carefully. When he was sure that Nachum was cheating, he discussed it with Ramon.

Ramon thought Mark was being paranoid, but they decided to use a new deck just in case his conjecture was correct.

When Nachum received his cards and did not see the marks on them, he was stupefied and became very nervous. With his heart pounding fiercely in his chest, he turned his cards over to check for his marks which were not to be found. Both Mark and Ramon saw it and knew what his actions meant.

Simultaneously, Mark and Ramon jumped up at the swindler to confront him, "You were cheating," Ramon yelled. He was furious and could barely control himself.

"No way!" he declared fearing for his life and wishing his heart would calm down. He was not sure how he was found out or who switched the deck. He knew his caper was over and in retrospect, he realized he should never have taken the chance, and was ruing the day he started playing poker with these men. There was nowhere for him to run and he knew that he was about to be beaten badly if not killed or both.

Not wanting to be part of the inevitable melee and brawl, the other gamblers quickly and quietly exited the room. It was long past curfew and they did not want to get into trouble. The raised voices were likely to bring a CO.

Nachum was trapped and fearful that his life was going to be cut short. Mark and Ramon knew he had been cheating and now had proof. Not that their proof would stand up in court, but it was good enough proof for them to take appropriate action.

Ramon stood in front of the door to the cell to prevent Nachum from escaping his punishment.

Menacingly, Mark cornered Nachum and punched him hard

in the stomach. Nachum doubled over in pain unable to breathe. Mark grabbed his shoulders, stood him up, and shoved him into the corner. Mark then roughly slammed the palms of his hands against Nachum's ears.

The pain in Nachum's ears was so bad that he fell to the floor unconscious. Just for good measure, Mark kicked Nachum repeatedly.

Mark and Ramon quickly left and returned to their respective cells.

Several hours later, Nachum woke up and was able to limp back to his own cell before the next count, he did not mention the incident to the authorities. Word spread about Nachum's cheating at poker and he was a marked man. When no one was in Nachum's room, Ramon went in and emptied his locker leaving Nachum with nothing except what he was wearing. The rest of his stay at Fort Dix he expected to be difficult and he decided that from that moment on, he would only associate with Jews. It was his best chance to remain alive and unmolested by others. It helped to an extent.

CORRECTIONS OFFICER ALICE COOPERMAN WAS walking between the mess hall and the housing unit for the new prisoners. It was already well into the afternoon, and she was looking forward to a quiet evening at home. She had a few more hours left to her shift and then she could get away from these low-life criminals. She liked working as a corrections officer at Fort Dix Federal Prison. Working there gave her a feeling of power that she did not get while growing up. However, she did not let that power go to her head. Part of her job was to keep these men in line and for the most part, the convicts she had to supervise were well behaved. However, there were some who did not care if they ended up in isolation or even if they had more time added to their sentences.

Alice knew the only women convicts saw were family who came to visit or if some of the corrections officers were women. She knew she was one of the best-looking CO's there, but she also knew to keep her distance from the prisoners and to keep it strictly professional. She was a gentle and sensitive woman but also knew how to be tough when needed. All of the prisoners in Fort Dix had fewer than ten years left on their sentence and for a convict that was not a long time. Most were looking forward to going home to their families in a few years.

Her father did not like her working in a prison, let alone a federal prison, but she felt completely safe. Alice remembered a conversation she had with her father before she became a corrections officer. He was afraid for the safety of his precious daughter working in a prison. He had seen many TV shows and movies depicting violent riots in prisons. Fort Dix was not one of those prisons as it was for inmates with "short time" left on their sentences.

A sudden catcall whistle woke Alice from her reverie. She was startled and looked around, her senses on high alert. She did not see anyone in particular who would have whistled at her as there was not a single inmate around her. She turned to her left and saw there was no one in the vicinity of the mess hall. She pivoted to her right and looked carefully over the housing unit but did not see anything amiss. No one looking out from any of the windows; however, there was no one else around from where the whistle could have come.

She felt humiliated and disgusted. She continued to look at the housing unit scanning all the windows carefully looking for something out of place. She was hoping someone would stick their head out a window. Try as she might, she could not find anyone who would have disrespected her like that. She turned and quickly walked, in a huff, toward the officers building. Just before she rounded the corner of the housing unit, she quickly turned her head to look again at the building. She thought she might have seen someone at one of the windows, but could not be sure. She ran to the officer's building, found her supervisor, and reported the incident to the captain. She was indignant. She felt abashed. She wanted to know who whistled at her.

Her supervisor commiserated with her about the incident and to show her his support, told her to immediately lock down the building. She thanked her supervisor, returned to the housing unit in question, and announced a lockdown to Stanley Meyers, the CO in charge. The convicts were not allowed out of the building except for chow and work detail. They could not even go out to the library, visitation or commissary.

The CO's made it clear they wanted to know who was responsible for the catcall that humiliated Alice. The lockdown and restrictions would continue until then.

None of the inmates was going to snitch on the convict responsible for the catcall. They were complacent to deal with the inconvenience of a lockdown for a few days. No big deal, after all, they were in prison, what is the loss of a few more privileges for a few days.

After three days without any results, the Sergeant decided to take it to the next level. He wanted answers and Alice was egging him to do something about it. She wanted payback.

No microwave, no computers, no phones. Those were the

new restrictions put in place to help encourage someone in the housing unit to come forward. Three additional days passed and still nothing: if anyone had any knowledge of the offending act, no one was willing to disclose any information. There were rumors of some pressure being brought to bear from other inmates: they were getting restless and snippy and wanted things back to the way they were.

The final straw was the withholding of mail: no incoming or outgoing mail. The inmates were showing signs of tension and many arguments, as well as some fights between the inmates, ensued; they were going stir-crazy. Some started to apply pressure for someone, anyone, to come forward to admit to the so-called crime of whistling at a CO. Ms. Cooperman was angry and wished this whole episode would be resolved already, she was even considering dropping the whole investigation.

Overhearing some whispers and innuendos of who the perpetrator was, Henry had more than enough of the loss of the few privileges he had in prison. It had already been over a week he had not been able to go to *shacharis* with other Jews and he was not built for this as he needed the camaraderie of his brethren and was fighting his own internal struggle of being in prison. He waited until there was some quiet time on the main floor of the housing unit before making his move. With a bit of trepidation, Henry knocked on the CO's office door.

"What?" a disembodied voice called gruffly from inside the office. Atkins was inside enjoying the solitude of his sixty-four square foot workspace and hated the idea of an inmate intruding on him.

Henry hesitantly opened the door and peeked inside. He was not happy to see that it was Atkins on duty at the time he wanted to come forward. Remembering some of the stories he heard about Atkins, Henry tried to withdraw.

Henry sheepishly said, "It's nothing, boss. Sorry to bother you." He tried to close the door without entering.

"Clearly, this perp doesn't want to talk with me specifically, so I'll force his hand," he thought to himself. Atkins called out, "Get in here, con! What do you want?" He liked controlling the inmates, making them do what they did not want. It made him feel even more powerful.

Henry opened the door slowly and quickly tried to think of something else to say. His mind went blank as he was startled and could not come up with another idea or plan of what to say. He was nervous and no longer noticed the lack of talking in the hallway.

He felt trapped. "I would like to tell you something in confidence but I don't want it getting out that I told. Most of us can't stand the loss of privileges anymore. I know who did the catcall." He was talking in a whisper almost as if the softer he talked, the less likely this whole episode was actually happening.

"Who?" he demanded.

He was still unsure if he should actually come forward with the information, especially to Atkins, but now he was in a bind. He closed his eyes for a moment and realized that he had no choice. He took a deep breath and said, "It was Mark Franklin. At least that's what everyone is saying." He was trying to diminish his own involvement.

"Okay. Get out!" He barked.

Atkins had an almost sinister look on his face as he contemplated his options with this new information. He was not sure if he should come forward with this information or use it to his own advantage. He thought to himself, "I could blackmail Franklin to keep quiet. Alternatively, I could make myself look good by going to my captain. I can make Franklin's life difficult. I don't like him anyway. Wow, so many choices." He was relishing the potential power he could wield in this situation as he ticked off the list on his fingers.

No one liked Franklin, but no one bothered him as he was a large black man with a reputation for being able to hold his own in a fight. He was not social but he did not care if he had friends or not. He was in prison and would get out eventually and then he would continue his life of crime. He would take revenge on those responsible for his incarceration.

When Franklin arrived in Fort Dix, he had already served six years in a federal prison in Cumberland, Western Maryland. He was transferred to Fort Dix due to overcrowding in Cumberland, Maryland, and only had nine years left on his sentence. He was in prison for the brutal assault on Mr. and Mrs. Singer in 1980 that left them permanently maimed and the loss of their unborn child. However, he exaggerated the events of that fateful night to his fellow inmates and claimed he murdered the hapless couple when they refused to give him money. He said he was only caught because of a bunch of Jews pounced on him from all directions.

Atkins sat in his office for quite a while trying to decide what to do with this volatile and incriminating information. It was a small office with peeling paint on the concrete walls, but it was a place he could relax for a few minutes throughout the day. There were no windows in the small office and the air was still, but it was his office. After a while, he got up from his rickety chair, walked around his desk and opened the office door and a sudden cacophony of noise assailed him from the many inmates standing around frustrated at the ongoing lockdown. He had made his decision.

Atkins decided it was time to make his rounds. Several times during his shift, he was supposed to walk the halls to make sure the "animals", as he thought of them, were kept in line. Usually, he did not make his rounds at all. He hated his job, but he made the best of it by maintaining a solid control over his charges. At least the job paid well. He had his own lieutenants, inmates he controlled by blackmail. He also knew that if he were not careful, he would get himself into major trouble as the inmates could easily turn on him and his whole castle would collapse in on itself and take him with it. He was considering asking for a transfer to another prison where he could start clean and fresh.

In the guise of doing his rounds, he searched out Mark Franklin. He was going to feel him out and find out where he stood in this whole episode. He knew that Mark was not the most popular inmate so Atkins was aware that this might just be Henry being vindictive for some slight, imagined or real. This was a common scenario among convicts and it could be a volatile atmosphere at any given moment. Atkins had seen his share of violence in Fort Dix.

In one of the cells on the third floor, Mark was playing a game of hearts with three other inmates. It was a fast-moving hand when Atkins interrupted and said, "Franklin, my office in fifteen minutes," without waiting for a response, he turned on his heels and walked out. As Atkins exited the cell and closed the door, he heard murmurs of speculation as to why Mark was being called out to the office. Anytime a convict was called to the office was foreboding and a foretelling of calamity for the inmate or several inmates. Atkins enjoyed the power, mystery, and intrigue.

Concentration lost, Mark quickly lost the game. Defeated, he got up and slowly started the trek downstairs to the CO's office. "This ain't going to be pleasant, especially since I've just lost the game of hearts." He bemused ruefully, "I wonder what he wants from me. Does he know I gave the catcall? Does he want more from me for the poker games?" He was concerned he would end up in the SHU. He had been there before and did not like it.

After Mark left the cell, the other men in the cell continued speculating as to the nature of the summons. Several even surmised it was because of the catcall and that he had been discovered.

"It's come to my attention that it was you who was responsible for the catcall at Officer Cooperman," Atkins said as soon as the door was closed. As there were no chairs for him to sit, Franklin just stood there with his mouth agape.

"No. It wasn't me. I didn't do it." Mark interrupted. He was scared. "Somehow, someone found me out and turned me in, I will have to find out who and get my revenge," he angrily thought to himself.

"Don't interrupt me!" Atkins barked. "I have it from a reliable source that it was you." He thought to himself, "This is funny and ironic. A con who is snitching on another con is a reliable source. That is laughable," it almost brought a smile to his face.

"So the question is what should I do with you? Do I turn you in, or do I look the other way?"

"Look the other way."

"What's it worth to you? What do I get out of it?" Atkins wanted to know, always looking out for himself, his *raison d'être*.

Mark looked down at the floor and thought for a moment. "I'm all strapped out right now. Will you take an IOU?" he asked sheepishly, already knowing the answer.

"Heck no, you buzzard! If you don't have cash for me, I'll just throw you in the SHU while we investigate," he snapped. "The investigation should only last a couple of months and then there will probably be time added to your sentence and maybe even loss of some privileges."

Mark gulped and shuddered, as he did not relish the idea of going back to the SHU. "Unfortunately, I got nothing to offer you," he said glumly. He was shaking. He also knew that anything he had in his locker was forfeit and would be raided by the other inmates as soon as his status was disclosed.

"Turn around and grab the wall," demanded Atkins.

"Please don't." He started to perspire.

"Are you resisting?" asked Ralph hopefully. He was pining to rough up Franklin.

Mark turned around and put his hands on the wall. Disappointed with no resistance, Atkins radioed for assistance. Cooperman heard the broadcast for support and rushed to the scene, hopeful. When she arrived in the housing unit and entered the CO's office, she was gratified that someone was being detained and was in flex-cuffs.

"Is he the one?" Alice asked.

"Yep. Do you want the honors of escorting him to the SHU?"

"I would love to," she responded smiling broadly. To herself, she thought, "I just wish it wasn't Ralph who brought him in. Now I'll feel indebted to him. Worse, he will be full of himself and think I owe him something, maybe even a date," she shuddered to herself at the thought.

Mark was feeling defeated and there was nothing he could do

or say to extricate himself from the situation. Cooperman took him to the SHU and made out a report to her commanding officer. Atkins did the same.

With the lockdown terminated and the privileges restored, the restlessness and anxiety of the inmates completely dissipated in a short amount of time. The inmates and the CO's breathed easier.

A few days later, Atkins called Ramon into his office, "You need to take care of something for us both."

"Who and why?" Ramon asked. He already knew that it was a person and not a thing that needed his special kind of attention.

"I need you to take care of Henry Davis. He's a loose cannon. He's the one responsible for turning in Mark Franklin."

"So that's who was responsible. I'm glad that episode is over. It was a pain not having our freedom," he was thinking. Of course, the term freedom is a relative one to a prisoner. "What exactly do you want me to do?" he asked aloud.

"Take care of him. Now, get out of my office."

Ramon just laughed to himself, "There is only one thing to do with a snitch." He was thinking about enlisting Bert. Since having been incarcerated, Ramon did not like to get his hands dirty and preferred to have others do his dirty work. He always wanted to have an alibi or excuse.

Later that day, Ramon found Bert exercising in the gym, "Bert, I want to talk with you privately."

They walked into the center of the field to have a private conversation where no one was within earshot and only the birds could hear them.

"You have a reputation as being able to handle yourself. You have the build of someone who knows his way around a fight. I have a problem with Henry Davis. I need you to take him out."

"You've got to be kidding! I'm not a fighter; I don't do things like that. I definitely will not hurt another person, let alone a Jew."

"The rumor has it that you are here for killing someone. So you are going to do this for me."

"No, I will not," he said ignoring the mention of his crime.

"Yes you will, or I'll make life very difficult for you," Ramon said in a threatening tone.

Bert just walked away being careful not to turn his back on Ramon. He was not going to have anything to do with hurting another person. That was the reason he was in prison in the first place and he was not going to exacerbate the situation. "I must let Henry know there is a price on his head," he thought to himself.

Ramon reported to Atkins. Atkins said, "Don't worry. I'll make his life more difficult."

Atkins singled Bert out for extra work detail and counts. Atkins went out of his way to badger and persecute Bert: surprise inspections of his locker; his bed was not made well enough; his work detail was not completed to Atkins' liking. Bert took it with equanimity and stoicism. Other inmates wondered what he did to earn the extra attention and ire from Atkins.

Surreptitiously, Bert let Henry know that he should watch his back. After that, Henry was cautious about his surroundings and kept a low profile and tried to keep his eye out for Bert.

# March 1986

Officers Connors and Jackson came to the prison to meet with the warden prior to fulfilling their mission. Because they knew the Federal Judge in the case, they had been deputized as temporary federal marshals specifically for this errand. They had a piece of paper to deliver and protocol dictated that their first stop was with the warden. He had suspected there was a problem in his prison, but until recently, there had been no proof; now there was.

There was not much to be said. Connors handed the document to the warden who briefly perused the paper, returned it to Connors and nodded his head.

"The man you want is in building four. He does not know you are expected," the warden said.

"Good. Let's keep it that way," Connors said with finality. The two federal marshals left the warden's office and headed to building four. Seeing law enforcement officers on the prison campus was not unusual, so they did not stand out.

They walked into building four and headed to the CO's office. Without knocking, they opened the door and found Atkins sitting comfortably behind his desk with his feet up on the desk and his hands behind his head.

Atkins was surprised by the intrusion into his domain and was about to say something as he clumsily tried to stand up and get control of the situation.

"Mr. Ralph Atkins," they addressed him formally, "Please stand and keep your hands where I can see them." Connors had his hand on his holstered weapon and with his other hand, was reaching for his standard-issue handcuffs, he did not want to use flex-cuffs. Jackson had his right hand on his Glock 9 mm gun.

FORT DIX, NEW JERSEY

"What's going on?!" he demanded. He was concerned and did not like two cops barging into his office making demands of him. "You are under arrest, now stand up," ordered Jackson.

# 1986

## January 3, 1986
## Catskills, New York

**Belatedly,** Mohamed regretted giving a cautionary note to Rivkah delineating their terrorist plans, but he did not want to get into trouble or alienate his inveterate friend. More importantly, he did not want to go to prison. He still did not see what was so evil about his distant cousins; everyone he met was nice and considerate. At this point, there was nothing he could do about the note.

Most of the time, the two friends spent their days and nights inside their underground bunker. However, sometimes they spent time on the surface, outside of the bunker on their beautiful and bucolic piece of property. On occasion, they enjoyed eating dinner by a campfire reveling in the heat and listening to the crackling sounds of the burning wood. Often they would see deer frolicking a hundred yards away eating berries from bushes that grew wild. It was serene and wonderful beyond anything they had ever experienced and they felt that despite their differences and their mission, they would be happy to live out the rest of their lives breathing the fresh country air on their property.

Due to the cold winter evening of Friday, January 3, the comrades had dinner in the bunker, where Mohamed took a deep breath and cautiously said, "I have a confession. Please don't be angry with me, or worse." It was now he realized to what extent he was genuinely petrified of Ahmed.

Ahmed was expressionless, but was thinking, "I knew I could not trust the buzzard." He was not going to show his emotions, "Now what did you do?" he demanded.

Mohamed could see the anger forming at the corners of Ahmed's eyes and mouth. "You know that my former friend Laura is close friends with Rivkah Somers." He did not want to admit that Laura was his ex-girlfriend; that would only have exacerbated matters. Realizing if he admitted giving the note to Rivkah, Ahmed would kill him, he quickly changed his story, "I briefly met Rivkah Somers through Laura and I get the feeling that Rivkah may be on to us."

Barely able to control himself, he asked, "What makes you say that?" The tension barely concealed behind his words, his teeth clenched tightly.

Mohamed had to think quickly, "It's just a feeling I get from talking with an acquaintance Asher Siskin. He's dating Laura Feld and he mentioned something to me in passing." Mohamed was feeling hot under the collar and was squirming in his seat; he wanted to take back the entire conversation.

Ahmed saw the nervousness in the mannerisms of Mohamed, "He's lying. There's more to his story than he's telling me."

Mohamed swallowed hard and continued nervously, "He mentioned to me that she thinks the Muslim extremists who have been perpetrating the acts of terrorism are local and living in the area. She seems to think she may have an idea how to find them. I'm concerned she may go to the authorities."

"We both know they live in the area, I wonder why she thinks that. We've got to get rid of her, and soon," Ahmed said morosely. He had to come up with a plan to find her and then dispose of the young lady.

Mohamed shuddered inwardly and wanted to run away and hide at the far end of their property, but there was no shelter or anything there. He was feeling trapped realizing that this was not what he wanted. He was not even sure what he wanted to accomplish by bringing this up to Ahmed, but it was already done. He was not thinking clearly and making rash decisions and did not know why. He felt uncomfortable in his own skin and was not sure to what to attribute it.

Ahmed thought to himself, "I've also got to get rid of Mohamed. He's dangerous to the mission and I can't trust him anymore. The *jihad* must continue."

"I want to sleep on it. I need to think of a plan to get rid of her since she could jeopardize all my efforts. I'm just glad no one knows of the existence of this bunker."

Ahmed had quite a bit on his mind and had a restless sleep that night mulling over his decision. He thought to himself, "I have to kill Mohamed. He is becoming a danger to my plan and I cannot tolerate him anymore." he thought to himself. Mohamed had become his nemesis; it was a difficult decision, but it had to be done and soon.

The next morning, Ahmed brought Mohamed his coffee spiked with a bit of sarin. Since sarin was colorless, tasteless and odorless, he was not concerned with Mohamed perceiving the contagion until it was too late. Even before Mohamed took his first sip of the brew, Ahmed was having remorseful feelings since they had been friends since childhood. He was conflicted as last night he wanted to get rid of this man and now he was having second thoughts about what he was doing. He stood fast in his conviction as the *jihad* had to come first, before his feelings.

Mohamed enjoyed the taste and smell of his coffee; since he was in Israel it was his morning ritual without which he could not live. He drank a cup of the bitter brew every morning while reading something to help him with his English. Before moving into the bunker, he would read the morning paper; after moving into the bunker, he would read a book. Mohamed liked thriller novels while Ahmed disdained the fiction books as he felt they were a complete waste of time.

Within a few minutes of ingesting the sarin-spiked coffee, Mohamed started to feel ill. Almost immediately, he had a runny nose, watery eyes and even pain in the eyes. He recognized the symptoms from previous conversations of what they were planning to do in the train station under the World Trade Center; he knew what Ahmed had done.

"What did you do to me?" gasped Mohamed while clutching the table.

"What are you talking about?"Ahmed responded trying to sound innocent.

"You poisoned me with sarin. I recognize the symptoms. Why did you do this?" he castigated Ahmed and wondered what he could do to remedy the situation.

Realizing he had already been found out, he confessed. "Yeah, I put a few drops of sarin in your coffee. I can't trust you anymore. You've become an infidel, a Jew lover. You're too soft. The *jihad* must go on!"

"You're wrong!" Mohamed asserted firmly. "I'm as dedicated

and devoted to the *jihad* as you. I'm completely here and with you and always have been. I am not dating that woman anymore. You and I have been best friends since we were kids. How can you do this to me? Give me the antidote or Allah will take vengeance," he pleaded forcefully as he wiped his runny nose. "I will come back to haunt you," he threatened.

Ahmed was vacillating and considered capitulating and giving him the antidote of atropine. Mohamed quickly got up and ran upstairs to the medical supplies they were stocking. He quickly found the atropine and took a dose with relief.

Mohamed was furious with Ahmed and knew he had to watch his back, he could not trust Ahmed anymore. In frustration, Mohamed walked out of the bunker and went to the surface where it was cold, but the air was fresh and crisp. He could not stand to be in the same room or even building as Ahmed. Since they lived on ten acres of land, he went for a long walk to calm down and consider his options. The absolute quiet calmed him while he sat on a large boulder looking out onto the expanse of his property while listening to the wind softly blow and watching the leaves as they waved in the breeze. He noticed prints in the snow and wondered what animal had left them, and that is when he noticed a deer in the distance and assumed the hoof prints were made from the deer. He observed the animal and was enthralled by its beauty and gracefull movements and it brought to mind that he missed his mother.

Mohamed felt very much alone with no one could turn to for help or advice or even friendship. He was no longer dating Laura and missed her and thought that she would probably like the property. He was thousands of miles from his family, although that did not bother him too much, but he missed his mother and was disconcerted by what he perceived of her in his dreams. However, the worst part was now he was alienated from his lifelong friend and he was feeling depressed and confused. It was several hours before he built up enough courage to quietly return to the bunker.

MOHAMED WAS SCARED AND RUNNING for his life while trying to wipe his runny nose. He was panting heavily while running down a dark alley; someone was chasing him and yelling something unintelligible from behind. As he was running through some underbrush, he quickly glanced around and did not recognize his wooded surroundings. Mohamed was lost and did not know where he was or how he got into this forest. He was not used to this much exertion and was perspiring profusely and his head was pounding from a bad headache.

He was running at full tilt and was short of breath. He was barely able to call out to his pursuer, "What do you want from me?"

His nemesis shrieked to him, but again, he could not discern the balderdash being spewed in his direction, but somehow it seemed a bit softer than before.

He did not understand what was going on, why he was being chased, where he was or from whom he was running. He stumbled over a fallen tree and found himself sprawled face down in a puddle in an alley. He looked around and realized the nightmare was in a different location and he was now in pain from the scrapes and bruises sustained from the spill. His clothing was torn, he was dirty, wet and bleeding. He did not understand how he was bleeding so much with so few abrasions.

He rolled over and suddenly saw an ogre standing over him and taunting him while pointing menacingly at him. The pursuer was larger than life and appeared to be a behemoth ready to attack him. Suddenly the apparition changed to a wisp of smoke and then appeared to be his mother. He called out in tears, "*Ema*?" (Mother)

The ethereal voice demanded, "How dare you?!"

From the distance, he heard what sounded like someone calling his name, but it was not his name, or was it? "Moshe, Moshe." Mohamed was startled and confused.

The apparition pointed her finger accusingly at the frightened man on the ground, opened her mouth as if to speak, but her mouth grew larger and larger until it engulfed him inside of a box. Suddenly he felt trapped, immured inside an enclosure from which he could not find an exit. He started flailing his arms and screaming for his mother.

Suddenly, there was a pounding coming from far away. From the back recesses of his mind, he heard someone calling and did not understand what was happening or where he was or who was chasing him. While he was thrashing around, his arm encountered something and he heard a loud crash.

Abruptly, with a flash, he sat up and realized that he was in bed in his bunker and a novel he was reading had fallen on the floor. It was all a nightmare, a horrible and vivid hallucination that was repeatedly haunting him. He was breathing heavily and shaking like a leaf in a hurricane. His pillow and bed sheet were soaked with his sweat. His nightmare unnerved him and some doubts about who he was and why he was there, continued to creep into his mind.

THE TWO FRIENDS DID NOT talk to each other for several days and avoided being in the same room as one another as much as possible which was difficult in a bunker with open architecture.

Ahmed was not convinced that Mohamed was sincere with his fealty to the cause. "He's not being forthright. I'll have to find another way to do away with Mohamed that is more discrete," he thought to himself. "I don't want to have my hands directly on his death. In fact, I don't want him dead, just out of the *jihad*."

# January 20, 1986
## Borough Park, New York

Because Ahmed worked in a bio-chemical lab, he was able to get his hands on thallium-201.

Thallium-201 is a highly toxic radioactive compound. In a small dose, it is completely safe and used in many medical and other applications. Among the distinctive effects of thallium poisoning are loss of hair and damage to peripheral nerves (victims may experience a sensation of walking on hot coals). Loss of hair generally only occurs in low doses; in high doses, thallium kills before this can even occur. Thallium was once an effective murder weapon before its effects were understood. Thallium poisoning has been called the "poisoner's poison" since thallium is colorless, odorless and tasteless; it is slow-acting, painful, and wide-ranging symptoms were often suggestive of a host of other illnesses and conditions.

Rivkah Somers had to be stopped before she ruined everything. Ahmed was angry and personally wanted to administer the thallium to her. He did not trust Mohamed to actually follow through and poison her and this was a job he wanted to do himself.

If you wait long enough on Thirteenth Avenue, you will probably see every New Yorker you know on the crowded and busy sidewalks. He was determined to find his mark and soon enough his patience paid off. Eventually, he saw his prey coming out of a store near the corner of Forty-Ninth Street. He followed her until he was able to get close enough to touch her. This was quite easy on Thirteenth Avenue as it was always filled with pedestrians going about their own business.

While walking in pace behind his mark, he donned latex gloves and then removed cloth gloves that were saturated with thallium-201, from a Ziploc bag he had prepared. He trailed Rivkah as she walked up Thirteenth Avenue. Ahmed walked up to her and was about to pass her when he pretended to stumble and grabbed her wrist with his gloved hands – poison delivered. Being a sensitive soul, Rivkah made sure the stranger was okay before proceeding.

"I'm fine, just lost my balance for a moment. Thanks for your help and concern," Ahmed said sardonically.

"Not a problem. Glad you're not hurt," she said with genuine concern.

Unbeknownst to her, Rivkah Somers was already poisoned so she continued to go about her daily routine.

Ahmed quickly disposed of the gloves, returned to the warehouse, and took a long hot shower to wash off any residual thallium and cleanse himself from the contact with the Jew.


# January 21, 1986
## Borough Park, New York

The next day, Tuesday, Rivkah, still not realizing she had been poisoned, was feeling a bit under the weather with some nausea and minor diarrhea. It did not deter her from wanting to do a *mitzvah* that was dear to her. It had been a while since she had seen her distant cousin so she went to see Rabbi Mishovsky. She went upstairs to the Mishovskys apartment and was warmly welcomed by the *Rebbetzin,* after which she went to see the *Rav.* The moment Rivkah walked into his room, she saw him crying with tears staining his lined sagacious face. The great Rabbi had a Tehillim in his hands and was murmuring the holy words between sobs.

"Why is Rabbi Mishovsky crying? Is something happening?" she asked. He looked like an angel with eyes shining, wearing his *tefillin* and with tears running down his face.

Without looking up, he said, "כלם יחמו כתנור ואכלו את שפטיהם, כל מלכיהם נפלו אין קרא בהם אלי. - Hosea 7:7 'They have all become heated like an oven and they have devoured all their judges. All their kings have fallen, yet no one among them calls out to Me.' In seven days, there will be a tragedy of seven. Important people will burn; people will look to the sky." He was cryptic and it seemed to make no sense but clearly, he was concerned for some major event that would happen in a week.

Rivkah had no idea what that meant, but she would keep her ears open during the next week for something in the news with the number seven.

At that exact moment, the *Rav* looked up from his *sefer* and looked into her eyes. Rivkah shuddered, as it seemed to Rivkah as if the *Rav* was peering directly into her soul. As soon as he saw her, without preamble, he jumped up and emphatically said, "Go right now to the emergency room! Your life depends on it." He was pointing toward the door.

There was no mistaking his order and she started shaking. She had never seen Rabbi Mishovsky act this way and could not imagine what could be amiss. Now she was concerned that maybe her not feeling well was something more serious than she originally thought.

Knowing who he was, and recognizing the immediacy of his words, she quickly turned around, picked up the phone and called 911, then she went outside to await an ambulance. Satisfied that she was following his orders, the *Rav* sat down and continued to say Tehillim. There was nothing more in the physical realm he could do about the situation while he strained to hear the wailing of the ambulance.

Sitting on the steps waiting for the paramedics, Rivkah was trying to remain calm and figure out what the *Rav* saw. She was too preoccupied with her own situation that she put out of her mind what the *Rav* had said about the number seven and did not even hear the ambulance approaching until it was on the block. When the emergency medical technicians arrived, she was not even sure what to say. "My cousin is a great rabbi who lives here and he told me to go to the emergency room and that my life depends on it. I am feeling a bit under the weather, but nothing serious."

The paramedic glanced around and said, "I assume you mean Rabbi Mishovsky. This is where he lives."

"Yes," she said concerned.

"I know the *Rav* and if he said you need the ER, we are going. You do look a little flushed. I will take your vitals on the way to the hospital."

Once they were on their way to the hospital, one of the paramedics mentioned to her, "Two months ago, we were called here for a man who looked completely healthy. He had no real symptoms, just a headache.

"Nevertheless, we took him to the hospital. It turns out that he had a hemorrhagic fever. Somehow, the Rabbi knew."

When she was brought into the ER, she just mentioned that Rabbi Mishovsky's sent her and it opened doors for her and she was quickly whisked into the inner exam rooms.

While on the gurney being hooked up to monitors by the nurse, Rivkah repeated her story to the doctor while the bright exam lights were shining on her.

"Normally, I would think it is just the flu, but since Rabbi Mishovsky, who has sent other messages and patients here, sent you, we are going to do more tests. Clearly, he is a man of God and has a special connection Upstairs."

Rivkah smiled, as she was proud to be related to the *Rav*. She knew she was in good hands, both physically and spiritually.

Because of the early detection and the warning of the *Rav*, they were able to recognize the poison. She was quickly put into isolation to prevent anyone else from coming in contact with it. Her clothes were removed and burned and she was washed down to remove any thallium from her skin. She was also given a gastric lavage to prevent any further absorption.

Due to the poisoning, the police were called and immediately came to the hospital to question her.

"Can you tell us anything about the person who did this to you?"

"Unfortunately, I don't know when this happened."

"Do you know anyone who would want to hurt you?" the officer asked her.

"No."

"Do you remember anything that could be of any help to find this person?"

"Yesterday afternoon, someone tripped and grabbed me for support," Rivkah mentioned.

"Can you describe this person?"

"He may have had a dark complexion, but I cannot even be sure of that. He had an accent, but I didn't take any note of it."

The investigation also centered at Rabbi Mishovskys house but there was no information to be gleaned. The *Rav* was never a suspect, but the authorities thought he might know something; he did not.

There were trace amounts of thallium on her coat, but not enough to enable a trail to how it got on her clothing. Unfortunately, the investigation died there as there was nothing else on which to continue the investigation.

Rivkah was disappointed: some unknown vile person tried to kill her, or at least make her sick, with poison. She was upset and angry and she could not discern a reason anyone would want to hurt her.

While Rivkah was recovering, her sister Shoshanna was always there to help her. They were close and spent quite a bit of time learning Torah as that was the most important thing in the world to both of them. Rivkah also introduced her sister to the computer world who liked what she saw and enjoyed learning the new material. Shoshanna was highly intelligent and despite her speech impediment was able to pick up the information quickly.

Shoshanna figured that maybe, instead of teaching, she would be able to work with her sister part-time. She even thought that in the future computer gaming would be lucrative.

Try as she may, Rivkah could not recall any details about the man who stumbled into her. Rivkah walked up and down Thirteenth Avenue where the incident occurred, hoping that something would remind her of some more details. She was not expecting to see the man who tried to poison her, but it did not hurt to canvas the area.

Nothing. She was even more disconcerted than before. It was frustrating.


# January 28, 1986
## Cape Canaveral, Florida

Space research and exploration thrilled and excited people, especially during the genesis of the space program. People would be glued to their televisions and radios during space launches. It was an exhilarating time as NASA was sending people into space for shuttle missions, experiments and walks on the moon. Zero gravity was something about which many people were curious, while numerous children dreamt of becoming astronauts and going into space.

The computers needed for the space programs and rockets were gigantic and ran hot. The computers were underground in special air-conditioned large rooms with the access points (terminals) in the command center above ground.

Most people considered these astronauts and mission specialists as heroes who risked their lives to better the lives of the rest of humanity. Technology also grew in leaps and bounds while billions of taxpayer dollars were spent.

On a chilly Monday morning, January 28, 1986, there was a nationwide broadcast from Cape Canaveral, Florida. There was a shuttle launched at 11:38 a.m. and many people were excited about it.

The purpose of the shuttle was to do numerous experiments in space and to bring additional parts to what would later become the International Space Station.

It was a historic event for several reasons.

It was unusually cold that morning at thirty-one degrees; much colder than any previous launch at fifty-three degrees or above and NASA had considered delaying it. Despite the reservations due to the cold, the countdown continued unabated and the launch went off without a hitch.

One of the two payload specialists was a schoolteacher from Concord, New Hampshire, Christa McAuliffe.

Rivkah was one of the millions who was excitedly listening to the radio during this historic and thrilling event. Approximately seventeen percent of Americans watched in horror as the Challenger shuttle exploded seventy-three seconds into the flight. There was nothing that could be done for the seven unfortunate astronauts at 48,000 feet. Tragically, all seven crew members were killed.

Rivkah could not help but shed a tear for the seven souls lost when suddenly she recalled, with a shudder, what *Rav* Mishovsky had said only seven days prior.


# January 1986
## Flatbush, New York

Before he was found out, Ralph Atkins contacted a hitman for a particular job that needed to be done. Many people wanted to take reprisal against Judge Archer; however, he was well protected by law enforcement. There was no way to get to the judge; however, his daughter was possibly accessible enough for someone to do her violence.

When the judge was in the courthouse, there was always security and police within his view. When he was not at the courthouse, his home was a fortress to protect him from miscreants and anyone who would want to do him harm.

The judge's family was not as well protected. He had an ex-wife living on Staten Island with their son who was living a life that was less than stellar, so neither was of any interest for an attack. His daughter was considered a high-value target and was always around. She would be a fairly easy quarry.

Through his attorney, Bert had been able to get word of caution to the judge about a conspiracy to hurt his family, or worse.

"The unmitigated gall of this scum bag purporting to be an officer of the court, to want to hurt my precious daughter. I want him!" The judge wanted to put the CO in chains and throw him into the deepest of dungeons. Of course, that was not an option since the judge was an officer of the court and would let the justice system mete out proper punishment.

Judge Archer wanted to get his daughter out of town for her

own protection.

"I don't want to run and hide, I'm not a coward. How would that help? When would we know when it was safe for me to return home? Who do I hide from?" She had a number of good questions.

"We will put a detail on you twenty-four hours a day until we clean this up," suggested the Chief of Detectives. "You'll be protected."

"That's fine with me," said Emily.

The judge resigned himself to the situation and capitulated to his daughter's wishes. "Please be careful with my precious daughter. She's my favorite daughter."

"Dad, I am your only daughter."

"Exactly."

"We will safeguard her and assure her safety."

The authorities were on high alert. There was always a vigilant undercover officer near her to be able to thwart any attempt on her life.

It finally happened. An attempt was made on Emily's life.

While she was out running some errands, a hitman broke into her apartment above the garage on her father's property. The intruder broke in and almost tripped over her rabbit. At first, he did not even know what it was.

Ignoring the rabbit, he went about setting up his trap, barely noticing how neat and clean the apartment was. He turned on the gas to the oven and stove and extinguished the pilot lights. The apartment started to fill with the unmistakable odor of gas.

To the bottom inside of the front door, he attached several strike-anywhere wooden matches. When the door would be opened, the matches would light and ignite the gas and the resulting explosion would kill his intended victim. Holding his breath from the sulfur smell of the gas, he then quickly made his getaway.

About an hour later, Emily returned home with her security entourage. Before they entered the stairs on the outside of the garage that led up to her apartment, they noticed something amiss. Prior to leaving on errands, her detail left a thread on the doorknob to indicate an incursion into her apartment. The telltale thread was missing.

Suddenly they realized they were smelling natural gas that seemed to be emanating from the apartment above and they quickly backed away from the garage and called 911.

The police, fire department and bomb squad were on the scene in minutes. The judge was also called out of a conference and immediately left the courthouse. Mr. Archer was given a police escort home. The gas was turned off to the garage and the bomb squad attempted entry while Emily and her security guard waited at a safe distance.

On the outside of the apartment door, nothing seemed untoward, so in full-protective gear, with Emily's key, the bomb squad opened the door.

The resulting explosion was quite large and there was nothing left of the building except the concrete foundation. Since the bomb squad men were fully protected in their gear, they survived. When the gas ignited, the shock wave threw the men down the stairs, almost killing them. They would be in the hospital for several days with broken bones and concussions.

The judge and his daughter were safe but enraged that someone would make an attempt on her life. Even a judge's family was not sacrosanct. They felt their own private space had been violated. Emily was devastated to have lost her rabbit.

Now there was proof of malfeasance and a real threat, not just the word of a convict. Officers Connors and Jackson were deputized and immediately dispatched to arrest Ralph Atkins at Fort Dix Federal Prison. Ramon was also arrested.

# February 1, 1986
## Borough Park, New York

After that harrowing experience, Emily Archer decided to take an apartment in Borough Park, far from where the recent bad memories took place that could have ended her life. Her apartment at her father's house was completely decimated and it would be quite a while until it could be rebuilt from the ground up. However, she was not sure if she wanted to move back there. She liked the idea of living completely on her own and was not positive she even wanted to move back to her father's house.

Since the perpetrators of the contract for the explosion were all caught, her life was no longer in jeopardy. Atkins turned on the arsonist in order to get a lighter sentence and the man was promptly arrested. Attempted murder of a federal judge was a serious crime, they were going away for a long time. Since it was the judge's home, the government decided to go after the perpetrators for capital crimes. The government had a strong case against the arsonist and Atkins.

Ramon Gonzalez and Ralph Atkins were both sentenced to

life without the possibility of parole in a super-max prison. They would likely never see the proverbial light of day again.

Emily was feeling good about what she considered the miracle of her being saved from death. Her life was spared and she was most grateful to HaShem, and the people involved.

In order to celebrate her survival and her new apartment, Emily invited Yaakov Applebaum, Rivkah Somers, and some other friends over for a *Shabbos* lunch to her new apartment. Rivkah was feeling great despite her recent encounter with being poisoned a few weeks prior. She seemed completely recovered.

At *Shabbos* lunch, Yaakov and Rivkah again noticed each other with surprise. It seemed uncanny they should meet so many times in so many locations across the globe. They were both thinking it must mean something, however, they were both too shy to explore it any further on their own.

They all had a pleasant lunch with *zemiros* and *divrei* Torah abounding. Yaakov and Rivkah kept stealing glances at each other throughout the afternoon, both impressed with each other.

# February 3, 1986
## Borough Park, New York

A few days later, on Monday, Rivkah went to Rabbi Mishovsky to ask his opinion about the strange meetings with Yaakov.

"I'm glad to see you're feeling better," the *Rav* mentioned.

"Thanks to *Rebbi*," she said.

He waved it off as if it were nothing.

"I want to get *Rebbi*'s opinion on something. I have met and seen this young man several times over the past several years on three different continents. He seems genuine and like a nice *Yeshiva bachur*. I was wondering what *Rebbi*'s thoughts are."

"Where did you meet him?" he asked.

"I think the first time was in Israel at someone's house for *Shabbos* lunch. He sang beautiful *zemiros* and said a nice *devar* Torah. However, I had the distinct feeling I had seen him before that. In fact, he had just received *semicha*. I then saw him in London, over someone else's house for *Shabbos* lunch. Then at a wedding, he was playing the keyboard. Since then I have seen him twice in Brooklyn. Once we passed while helping someone and the second time was also at a *Shabbos* lunch." She was wondering why she had waited so long to ask the *Rav* about him. Now that she had told the story, she realized her naiveté.

"What is his name?" he asked almost immediately.

"Yaakov Applebaum," she said.

Rabbi Mishovsky saw a twinkle in her eye. Clearly, she was excited about the prospects of this young man.

The *Rav* thought for a minute, then looked up, smiled and said, "ותשא רבקה את עיניה" (Bereishis 24:64 And Rivkah lifted up her eyes). He then returned to his learning. Rivkah was not sure what this meant, but backed away in deference and went to spend time with the *Rebbetzin*.

She followed the wonderful smells wafting in from the kitchen where the Rebbetzin was cooking with one of her daughters and mentioned to the *Rebbetzin* what was going on with her. Rivkah patted the child on her head and excitedly, mentioned how she had met Yaakov on several occasions. Rivkah asked the *Rebbetzin* if she had any idea what the *Rav* meant by the *passuk* he quoted.

The *Rebbetzin* advised her to look up the *passuk* and pertinent commentary, "But I think you know exactly what he was talking about." In the back of her mind, the *Rebbetzin* recognized the name of the young man who had done so much for them and thought there might be more news forthcoming about the couple.

Rivkah smiled shyly, but knew her cousin and realized there was nothing more he was going to say. She had to look up the *passuk* and see what it meant for her. She recognized it and knew exactly where to look and was beginning to realize that maybe she did not need to look up the *passuk*. As she was leaving the house she was again feeling excited about Yaakov and maybe a bit foolish for waiting so long to explore a possible *shidduch* with him.

"Why did I wait so long? Clearly, we were meant to meet. Clearly, HaShem's hand is showing and I have just been too blind to see it." She looked Heavenward with a smile and said, "Thank you HaShem for everything."

# February 4, 1986
## Borough Park, New York

Yaakov went to Rabbi Mishovsky on Tuesday to ask his opinion about his having met this young woman several times. He would have gone earlier, but he was busy with many things including assisting people to recover after Hurricane Gloria.

Yaakov mentioned meeting this woman three times lately. He

told over the now familiar story, not realizing that Rabbi Mishovsky had heard it just the day before.

"What's her name," the *Rav* asked, uncharacteristically.

"Rivkah Somers."

Rabbi Mishovsky laughed and said, "ויצא יצחק לשוח בשדה" (Bereishis 24:63 And Yitzchak went out to supplicate in the fields). Yaakov not catching the double entendre behind the laugh.

Yaakov was not sure what the *Rebbi* was hinting about, but when he went to the *bais medrash*, he would check out the *passuk*. "I wonder what was so funny," he thought to himself.

After reviewing the *passuk* mentioned by Rabbi Mishovsky, he decided to ask Emily Archer to set them up on a *shidduch*.

# February 19, 1986
# Borough Park, New York

Yaakov was excited about the new suit he recently purchased. He had a *shidduch* to go on soon and wanted a new suit for the occasion as it would be the first young lady with whom he had gone on a date. It had been a while since he bought himself a new suit and this was the perfect excuse. Because of the unusual circumstances and occurrences, he was optimistic about this *shidduch*.

The suit was stylish, but not ostentatious, which was exactly what he liked. In the store, he tried it on and it was quite comfortable. However, beyond that, he was not able to wear it until he followed the will of the Big Boss and made sure there was nothing preventing him from wearing this nice suit.

Yaakov would always do two things when he purchased something nice for himself, which was a rare occurrence since he did not want to spend his money, preferring to save it and let it keep building up. He would immediately donate the value of his purchase to the poor, and then he would take his new garment to Rabbi Daniel Starr to have it checked for *shaatnez*. Rabbi Starr was an expert in *shaatnez* checking and was certified by the International Association of Professional Shaatnez Laboratories.

ONE DAY A WOMAN BROUGHT a long dress-coat to Rabbi Starr to be checked for *shaatnez*. It was a nice, tan, expensive, wool dress-coat. The Rabbi was not home at the time, so the woman left it for him to check and she would call later to find out if she could pick it up.

She was a high-strung woman and was nervous that the dress-coat should be *shaatnez* free as it was quite expensive. She came back the next day to pick up her dress.

Rabbi Starr said, "It's fine, no *shaatnez*, but I wouldn't wear it."

"Why not?" She demanded nervously. "What's the problem? What's wrong? Why won't you wear it?"

"Oh, nothing is wrong with the dress. I just don't wear women's clothing."

She did not appreciate his humor, but gladly accepted back the dress, happy it was not *shaatnez*.

A few days later, another woman called the Rabbi to have him check one of her garments. She said, "Rabbi, I've already heard about your interesting sense of humor."

The rabbi laughed.

ANOTHER TIME, RABBI STARR WAS a guest at a wedding where the band was having trouble with their sound system: their new speaker was making a strange static noise. The band members were unable to determine the cause of the bad acoustics and were concerned that they should be able to perform music at this wedding.

Rabbi Starr came over and said, "On the *passuk* of Vayikra 19:19 'ובגד כלאים שעטנז, לא יעלה עליך' - and a garment of shaatnez shall not come upon you, the Netziv says that it is a known thing that *shaatnez* causes problems in this world.

"If you remove the cover of the speaker, which contains *shaatnez*, the problem will go away." Because of his expert ability in fiber identification, he was clearly able to identify the forbidden mixture.

The bandleader was incredulous, "How can *shaatnez* cause this noise? However, I'll try it. What have I got to lose?"

At the exact moment when the cover was removed, the strange noise stopped. Rabbi Starr gave a knowing smile as he walked away. The troupe leader was stupefied.

CARRYING HIS NEW SUIT IN a suit bag, Yaakov walked to the Rabbi's house and knocked on the door. He never liked ringing doorbells in case someone was sleeping. Rabbi Starr opened the door and when he saw who it was, a smile instantly appeared on his face. The Rabbi proffered his hand to Yaakov and extended a hearty, "Shalom *Aleichem*, my friend. How are you doing?"

"I am fantastic, *Rebbi*, but I'll get better soon; thanks to the Big Boss. Thank you so much for asking. How is *Rebbi* doing?"

"*Baruch* HaShem, everything is good. Please come in. I see you have something for me?"

"I bought a new suit and *Rebbi* knows I have to do two things before I can wear it."

Rabbi Starr smiled as they entered the dining room knowing exactly what this young man meant.

Rabbi Starr proceeded to inspect the new suit. He sat down at his desk and turned on his special daylight-corrected light. The Rabbi first looked at all of the labels and felt the material. He then examined all parts of the jacket, pants, and tie.

A few minutes later, Yaakov wrote a check for the value of the suit and handed the check to the rabbi to distribute to the poor.

While at Rabbi Starr's house, Yaakov noticed a woman who had a smile on her face, but it was clear the woman behind the smile was not happy. She had sad eyes. Yaakov heard rumors that Yehudis Anderson was an *agunah*. She was civilly divorced, but her ex-husband refused to give her a *get*.

Yaakov was curious about the situation so he approached her for clarification. "Forgive me for being so forward. I hope you don't mind, however, I heard a rumor that you are an *agunah*. Is that true?"

"Unfortunately, yes. I've been divorced for over three years and my ex refuses to give me a *get*," she answered with a frown.

Yaakov continued, "I am so sorry to hear that. Do you mind me asking, what happened? Why is he not giving you a *get*?"

Yehudis answered, "That would be *lashon harah*. I would rather not discuss it."

Humbled, Yaakov said, "You're right. I'm sorry. If there is anything I can do for you, anything you need please let Rabbi Starr know. I wish you much *hatzlacha*." He extended to her his business card.

"Thank you so much," she said demurely as she accepted the proffered card.

Yaakov hated hearing about *agunahs* and wished there was something he could do about it.

# February 23, 1986
## Borough Park, New York

Their first date was on Sunday at Glatt Chow where Laura, who knew both of them, was their server. When she saw them, she could not help but notice the spark in each of their eyes that matched their attitude. She was barely about to contain her excitement seeing the couple on a date, and she made sure to take extra good care of them. Although the food was delicious and aromatic as usual, due to their excitement, the pair barely even noticed.

Although this was the first time they were meeting officially, in a sense, they both felt as though they had known each other for a long time. They laughed at the situation and started to count the number of times they had met. It took them a while, but they concluded that their first encounter was back when they were in high school when they had both taken piano lessons with Atarah Justin in Queens. If things worked out, they would have to call her. She would enjoy hearing about it.

They were astounded at the serendipity of all their rendezvous over the years.

She again wished him a *mazal tov* on having received *semicha* and wanted to know the details. He told her the amazing story but left out the part of his financially helping the Weinblatts at the time. She was duly impressed and effusive with her compliments.

On their second date later that week, they went to sit in the lobby of the Waldorf Astoria in Manhattan. Of the many things they talked about, was their common acquaintanceship with Rabbi Mishovsky; him being a *talmid* and fan and her being related. Yaakov mentioned to his companion, of the *Rav* laughing upon his asking about Rivkah and was pondering the meaning behind the laugh.

They compared *pesukim* and came to the realization that Rivkah had been there the previous day asking about him.

They were quickly becoming fond of each other and both were feeling that this was going to be developing into something more and special. They were both excited and hopeful.

They talked about the latest news about the new terrorist group and the effects they were having on the city and people.

"I hope they are caught soon before anyone else is hurt or worse."

"Yes. Nothing good can come from their terrorism," she responded in kind.

"I'm so sorry to hear about your having been poisoned. Are you okay?" He was genuinely concerned about her as a person and any health ramifications it may have on her that affected her in the long run.

"I am fine," she said. "No lasting effects from the poison. *Baruch HaShem.*"

"I am so glad to hear that. Thanks to the Big Boss. They never caught the man?"

"No, there was nothing to go on. By the way, I like it that you refer to HaShem as the Big Boss."

"Thanks. I figure that if Rabbi Yaakov Yosef Herman*, ZT'L can call Him the Boss, I can use the term Big Boss."

They both smiled. "Have you read the book about Rabbi Herman?"

"My Rosh HaYeshiva had spent time with Rav Herman, quotes him often, and tries to emulate him, so I thought it a good idea to learn what I could about the *tzadik.*"

On all of their dates, their conversations flowed smoothly and they also talked in Torah. They were both quite knowledgeable in *Torah* and *halacha*. Although Yaakov was not looking for a *chavrusah* in a spouse, it was nice to be able to talk Torah with one's wife. Over time, they talked about their goals and aspirations in life and they seemed to be compatible in all areas. They both were interested in doing *chessed* and always having their door open to guests and people in need.

Yaakov did not tell Rivkah about his financial situation. That revelation would come later.

# February 1986
## New York City, New York

Times Square is one of the busiest intersections in the world. Prior to 1904, it was called Longacre Square until the New York Times moved its headquarters to the newly constructed Times Building on West Forty-Third Street just off Seventh Avenue. Over 300,000 people visit Times Square daily. Underneath Times Square, to the depth of about sixty feet, is Times Square Station. It is one of the most active stations in the world. Over 60,000 people used the station every day.

Using a syringe, Ahmed injected a few cc's of sarin into the bases of ten incandescent light bulbs. His plan was to throw the bulbs, from a distance, down a flight of stairs into a crowd. He had antidotes ready to inject himself and his confederate if needed.

Ahmed and Mohamed synchronized their watches and left the warehouse at 7:45 a.m. They drove the short distance south to Joralemon Street and Court Street and found parking. They would have walked, but it was cold in February.

Exiting the car, they separated. A few minutes later, they entered the subway system on Court Street and got onto a number Two-train heading toward 241st Street - Wakefield. Twenty minutes later, they alighted in the Forty-Second Street - Times Square Station. They were on opposite ends of the train and heard the clackity-clack of the subway moving through the tunnel.

Separately, they climbed the stairs on opposite ends of the platform to the Mezzanine level and waited while watching the throngs of unsuspecting people on their way to work or some other important destination. They were early and astonished with the number of people who filed past them with nary a glance.

At exactly 8:30 a.m., when hundreds of people were rushing through the station to get to work, Ahmed and Mohamed reached into their knapsacks and each extracted five light bulbs. They proceeded to toss them down the stairs to the platform and listened excitedly as the bulbs broke on their way down, then they ran. Seconds later, they were exiting the station onto Forty-Second Street and they turned left to Eighth Avenue.

The terrorists quickly caught a cab that dropped them off one block from their car in Brooklyn, which they then drove to the bunker.

At first, the passengers of the subway system were confused when they saw broken light bulbs on the stairs. It was no big deal and would easily be cleaned up in a few minutes by a custodian. After a few minutes, people started to feel ill and realized that another terrorist attack was taking place. Suddenly there was massive panic and pandemonium in the station from people who did not want to get sick. In the mad dash to exit the station for fresh air, many people were screaming, being trampled and severely injured; some were killed in the fracas. First responders were immediately dispatched and the hospitals were inundated with the sick and dying. People were rushed to area hospitals with varied symptoms of being poisoned by sarin, depending on how much they inhaled of the poison. Tragically, about three dozen people died and hundreds became sick. The CDC was called in and they closed the subway station for several days for cleanup and decontamination.

The Palestine Liberation Group claimed responsibility via WABC. Even more panic ensued and people were demanding action and answers. Who was this terrorist group and why had the authorities not caught them? How were they so successful on United States soil? How did they get here? Where were they from?

# March 1986
## Queens, New York

Yaakov and Rivkah were saddened by the news and attended the funeral of the late Mrs. Justin in the chilly March weather. They noticed each other but did not greet, as it was not the time or place, they would talk more on their next date or on the phone. Unfortunately, their desire to share their dating situation with their former teacher would never be realized.

There were not many people at the funeral, mostly some of her former students and a few friends. She was a widow and her only son was on the lam so he was not in attendance. There were no other heirs and Mrs. Justin's house lay uninhabited.

Because the house was vacant and no one was around to pay the mortgage, utilities or taxes, the house went into foreclosure and was repossessed by the bank. The bank took possession of the house to cover the outstanding debt and mortgage. Eventually, Steve Henderson and his wife Vanessa bought the house from the bank for a good price.

Steve was a highly skilled and popular commercial photographer and was considered an expert in photography by the Brooklyn Courts.

There were a number of times Henderson had been called as an expert witness in court. This was a tremendous honor and huge responsibility of which he took seriously. For most of these cases, he was asked to verify the authenticity of a photograph that it was not doctored in any way. (This was before Adobe Photoshop existed and doctoring was done by hand in a darkroom.) A trained and skilled eye was needed to discern the details of a doctored photograph. Steve had significant experience and training in custom black-and-white and color darkroom work.

ONE PARTICULAR CRIMINAL CASE WAS a dire one and would be a first for Steve and would go down in the annals of Brooklyn court history. A woman was in court accused of murdering her late husband and her life depended on his accurate depiction of his observations.

Because of the seriousness of the situation, when he walked into the courtroom, he entered with a bit more trepidation than usual. Due to the notoriety of the case, the hushed courtroom was pack with standing room only. As per protocol, at this point, he had no idea what the trial was about except that it was a murder case.

Steve went to the stand, was sworn in and sat down in the polished witness stand and waited. He was not sure of the exact capacity in which he would be needed, but he was about to find out.

The court officer read off his credentials to establish for the jury that he was considered an expert in the field in which he was about to testify, in the court system of that jurisdiction.

The defense attorney gave him a brief synopsis of how his expert services would be needed.

"I'm about to show you a photograph of the defendant that was taken at a ball. We want your determination that the picture is real."

The photograph was the sole alibi of the defendant who proclaimed her innocence saying that she was at a ball, but no one remembered her being there. However, there was one photograph of her at the ball. Also in the photograph were three other individuals who already testified they were at the event, remember having their pictures taken, but did not remember the defendant being there. Still, there was this picture of her. That was clear evidence of her presence at the event. Or was it? It was up to Steve to decide if her evidence was real or fabricated.

The defense attorney handed Steve the photograph, he briefly glanced at it and handed it back. Once the photograph was safely out of his hands, he emphatically and unemotionally declared, "It's a fake."

The defense attorney was in shock and did a double-take. "There is no way you could have seen the picture that quickly. You had the picture in your sights for only one or two seconds. How dare you declare it a fake? What type of expert are you? Did you even see the picture? Do you even know anything about photography?"

"Objection. Badgering," interrupted the prosecutor.

"Sustained," said the judge. Turning to the defense attorney, "This man is considered an expert in this court and he will be treated with respect."

"Yes, your Honor. I apologize to the witness and the court."

Steve had been in this judge's courtroom on several prior occasions and he knew the judge was not interested in hype or accretion, but in the truth to make sure everyone received a fair trial.

Steve turned to the judge, which was not proper protocol, and said, "I know that your Honor is not interested in histrionics, but the truth. With your Honor's permission, I will describe exactly what I saw in the photograph."

The judge said, "Proceed."

"I don't have the photograph in my hand, but I will describe exactly what I saw.". He proceeded to describe the appearance of the four individuals in the photograph including their clothes. He described the background. He mentioned that the individual second from the right was the defendant.

The judge responded, "You obviously saw the photograph, although briefly, well enough to describe the photograph and the four people in detail. How do you know it's a fake?"

"Persons one, two and four, the light is coming from the left. Person three, the defendant who is in the middle, the light is coming from the right," he said while gesticulating with his hands to make his point. "According to the laws of physics, that's impossible. The photograph has to be doctored or altered in some way."

The judge leaned over and said, "Show me."

Steve leaned over, addressed the judge, and while pointing, showed him the light patterns he saw. He explained how the light was talking to him in ways the layperson would not see. The judge did see now that it was pointed out to him.

The so-called photographic "evidence" was thrown out and the defendant went to prison for murder. There was also a question raised if the defendant's attorney was suborning perjury.

ANOTHER TIME HENDERSON WAS IN the courthouse waiting for another person to show up for a meeting. While lingering, he went into a courtroom to watch a trial already in progress.

A witness who looked out of place in the suit he was wearing for court, claimed that on one cool evening he was outside of a house and heard some commotion from inside. He wiped condensation off the outside of a window and looked inside. That is when, he said, he witnessed the murder.

Steve sent a note forward to the prosecutor that condensation only develops on the inside of a window.

The witness was arrested.

ONE TIME A WITNESS TESTIFIED that he was at Glatt Chow restaurant on Thirteenth Avenue having a lobster. Steve happened to be in the court while waiting for something else and privately mentioned to the prosecutor that it is a kosher restaurant.

The witness was arrested for perjury.

THE HENDERSON FAMILY WERE PREPPERS with about three months of supplies stocked on shelves in their cramped basement in Borough Park, N.Y. It was a good stock for their small family. They had food, water, medical supplies, batteries and more. They wanted to eventually have about a year's worth of supplies. They had even thought about making a bunker in their house but it was not a viable option since space was at a premium in their small house.

In addition to the space required for the family and prepping, Steve ran his successful and busy photography business from home. The small but growing family needed a larger house and Steve wanted to add a small darkroom to his office space. They found a great deal on a nice house in a great neighborhood in Kew Gardens, Queens, New York.

They purchased the house vacated by the passing of Mrs. Justin. They felt bad as there was no one left in her family to pay the balance of the mortgage and they were, therefore, able to get the house for a great deal. They knew there was a son, but no one knew where he was: he seemed to have disappeared off the face of the earth. The Hendersons were not concerned with Tuvya Justin returning for the house as he was eluding the law. When Steve bought the house, he was aware the former owner had been a prepper.

It took them several months to unpack in their new house and they were quickly turning it into a home. This house was much larger and more comfortable than their previous abode and they could live comfortably here with his business and their prepping needs.

One of the characteristics of a good photographer is attention to detail. Mr. Henderson, having been an expert in court cases was exceptionally detail-oriented and easily noticed when things were out of place. Sometimes his attention to detail was so severe that it caused problems in the home with him needing things to be in their proper place. He also noticed every detail about his children's activities and behaviors and that put added stress on the family. His wife felt he had obsessive-compulsive-disorder and he was inclined to agree with her.

"When we left, the curtains were open, now they're closed. Did you notice this?" he asked on a few occasions.

"I remember pushing these chairs in to the table before we went to sleep. Did you pull them out?"

"Who moved my book? I know I left it on the coffee table."

"Who used my bath towel?" was a common refrain.

"Who finished the box of crackers?"

"No one? So what happened to the box? We just bought it yesterday."

In the middle of the night, "Did you hear that noise?" his wife asked.

"I didn't hear anything."

"Go check."

They found nothing amiss. These strange happenings also occurred during the day, almost as if a poltergeist was living in their house. They even considered getting a few weapons in case they ever found someone breaking in or something to explain the mysterious goings-on in their new home.

They kept an accurate and detailed accounting of the inventory in their emergency supplies, and over time noticed that some of the food items did not correspond with their tabulation. They had fewer items than what was listed and there was no explanation.

These strange chants were commonly heard in their home and sometimes they felt there was a ghost inhabiting their house. On occasion, they teased each other about the eerie and strange weekly, and sometimes daily events; it was almost as if their house was haunted.

The police were called several times, especially after they were awoken by some strange noise. The police searched the house but found nothing amiss. It was bizarre as there was never a sign of an intruder or a break-in. The windows and doors were always locked with no indication someone had tried to enter.

Except for the strange happenings in their home, they loved the house. They were doing well and for the most part, the family was happy and comfortable.

Steve eventually went to Rabbi Mishovsky for an explanation and help. They explained to the *Rav* everything they knew. They described the missing food, moved furniture, strange sounds and more.

The *Rav* was surprised at what he heard and closed his eyes for a few minutes in deep thought. "The *Gemara Yoma* 21a, and Rashi in several places quote Rabbi Levi that our tradition states the Holy Ark in the *Mishkan* was not included in the measurements of the Holy of Holies. The *Aron* was the only thing in this world that did not take up any space."

It was an ambiguous and enigmatic statement that seemed to have nothing to do with their current situation. The Hendersons asked, "What does the Holy Ark have to do with our humble home? The *Mishkan* was only in use for the forty years in the Desert. How does any of this help us?"

The *Rav* only repeated himself and would not clarify. They did not know what to do and they were no closer to an answer than they were a few minutes ago. They had no clue what he meant; it was an additional mystery to add to the enigma in which they were living.

They spent the next several weeks trying to figure out what

the Rabbi meant.

MORE ROOM WAS NEEDED FOR their emergency supplies, but they did not want to bug-out to another location. In case of emergency, they wanted to stay in their own home so they started to fortify their home.

They happened upon _Doomsday Bunker Book_, by Jake Benjamin. For them, this book was a great resource of information on prepping and fortification.

Over time, they replaced the windows of their house with unbreakable glass. Technically, there is no such thing as unbreakable glass, but several sheets of glass sandwiched together tightly with a sheet of plastic of high sheen will come close. They also made shutters for the inside of the windows so they would be able to seal them up from the inside for even more security.

The previous owner had already replaced all exterior doors with heavy-duty reinforced steel doors. The new owners put bars across the doorways to prevent the doors from being forced open.

Most interior doors are hollow and easily penetrated, so the Hendersons replaced them with stronger solid wood doors.

They went into the attic and poured small stones and sand into the space of every exterior wall. This had the added benefit of extra insulation and fireproofing the structure. They then fortified the roof.

After all this fortification work, they felt more secure in case of a catastrophe, however, they were still feeling vulnerable in their own home. If not for all of their fortifications and expenditures, they even considered moving to a house that did not seem to be possessed.

The strange and unusual occurrences in their home were disturbing and upsetting, and the unusual sounds they heard at strange hours did not help the situation. There was no letup with the mysterious happenings that occurred too frequently. There was no explanation they could find and they needed help. It was bizarre that the only items that were missing were foodstuffs and toiletries. Nothing of value was ever taken.

As the family was no longer living out of boxes, the house seemed much larger than it was when the first moved in and they appreciated the extra space in their home. However, it was perplexing that their house was still haunted. It was a conundrum living in a house they liked so much, with so many strange things going on, and it gave them risibility. If it were not so discomforting living in a spooky house, it would have been humorous.

As Steve was perceptive, he eventually realized that

something was off with the structure of his house. He felt it was enigmatic that the upstairs seemed slightly larger than the main floor.

While the haunting continued, they decided to measure their house and came to realize the square footage of the floors did not compute. There was missing space somewhere in the house. They started doing careful measurements of each room. They sketched out each room and came to the realization there was missing space; maybe a hidden room on the first floor. Over the next few weeks, they started knocking and pushing on each panel of every wall in every single room on every floor. Eventually, a wall in the hallway on the first floor gave way and they found a hidden safe room. They were excited and scared at the same time. When they opened the panel to the safe room, they saw a man in tattered clothing cowering in the corner. Steve sent his wife to call the police while he made sure the intruder did not escape. Police Officers Connors and Jackson showed up and Tuvya Justin was arrested.

Suddenly, the haunting stopped and now they had a bunker already built into their house. It was perfect and they were relieved. They finally understood what Rabbi Mishovsky meant by his enigmatic response.


# March 1986
## New York City, New York

As is customary for many *Yeshivish* couples, Rivkah and Yaakov had many of their dates in a hotel lobby. On one such date, when they were at the newly built Trump Plaza Hotel, the couple played piano together - Heart and Soul duet. Yaakov played the lower half of the piano while Rivkah used the upper half. It was beautiful and guests at the hotel watched their four-minute performance which ended as Yaakov ran his fingers up the entire length of the piano playing all the keys. The young couple, not yet a couple, received a hearty ovation for their impromptu concert. They looked at each other fondly and smiled while their audience looked on. They were happy and things seemed to be going well for them as they had become close during their courtship.

After this date, they decided it was time to meet their respective parents. They were both excited and nervous at the same time. They were getting close to the point of making a commitment to each other.

Yaakov spent the next *Shabbos* with Mr. and Mrs. Somers

and family in their welcoming home. They were originally from London but had moved to the United States in the early 1960s and lived in Kensington, Brooklyn. Yaakov slept at a neighbor's home but spent all waking hours with Rivkah and her family. He had beautiful *divrei* Torah prepared and sang *zemiros* with the family. It was a wonderful *Shabbos* all around and he was treated as part of the family. Everyone immediately took a liking to him. Surprisingly, Rivkah's sister, Shoshanna, also took a shine to Yaakov and more astonishing was that when she conversed with Yaakov, she did not stutter. Shoshanna was comfortable with Yaakov and completely approved of him joining the family.

The following *Shabbos*, Rivkah enjoyed the welcoming hospitality of Yaakov's family while he again slept at a neighbor's abode. The couple *davened* by Rabbi Mishovsky's *shul*; after all, they both knew him. Everyone in the Applebaum family loved Rivkah and after she returned home, Yaakov's family gently poked fun of him and his naivete for taking so long to ask her on a date. It was a wonderful, exultant time for both families.

# March 1986
## Flatbush, New York

It had been a while since Yaakov discussed his investment accounts with his broker David Anderson and he had a few questions and also wanted to discuss his recent business trip to London.

Yaakov called David to discuss further investment strategies. During the course of their phone conversation, Yaakov asked, "I heard a rumor that your ex-wife has not yet received her *get*. Is that true?"

David confirmed, "Yeah, it's just... I just don't have the time to deal with it." In his own mind, he was trying to justify his cruel actions.

"Oh. Okay," he responded and then continued to discuss his London trip with David. The conversation was not long but was necessary. Yaakov had gone to London to investigate a particular investment opportunity and was pleased with what he learned and shared that information with his broker with a mind to make some modifications to his portfolio.

As they were about to end the phone conversation, almost as an afterthought, Yaakov asked, "Oh, by the way, I almost forgot, I was wondering if maybe you have some time to do a personal favor for me. It won't cost you anything and will only take a few minutes. It would really mean so much to me. Just tell me when and where."

"Sure. Let me get my calendar." Through the phone, Yaakov could hear him turning some pages in his datebook.

They made an appointment at David's office for two weeks hence.

YAAKOV WENT TO RABBI STARR'S house and told the rabbi of his idea. The plan was a great concept if they could pull it off. They made detailed arrangements, including setting up witnesses for the event. The day prior to their appointment with the recalcitrant husband, Yaakov, Rabbi Starr, and two witnesses, one being Chaim Outterbridge, went to Yehudis Anderson's apartment and told her their plans. Both of the witnesses were unusually large men. At the behest of Rabbi Starr, in front of the witnesses, Yehudis appointed Yaakov as her messenger to receive the *get* on her behalf.

"Don't get your hopes up," Yaakov said. "I don't know if this is going to work, but it is something I have to try. I couldn't stand by while you suffered."

Yehudis was touched by the kindness of these men: it brought tears to her eyes. "Either way," she said, "I appreciate your efforts on my behalf. May HaShem show you *chessed* as you have shown me."

"Amen," they all responded to her heartfelt blessing. The foursome left her presence feeling humbled by the woman's strength.

The following day, found the foursome at David's busy office. "What's the meaning of this?" he demanded angrily, surprised by the large group of men intruding in his space. David had immediately understood what they had in mind and felt trapped; he was not going to let himself be bullied into something he did not want to do.

"You are going to give your wife a *get*. You said that you just didn't have the time to deal with it. Now you do. You made time for me and this is the favor I want. It's long overdue." Yaakov understood that in actuality he should not be doing business with David since he was not following the dictates of the *bais din*, however, if he could use the time to influence David to give the *get*, he felt it was appropriate. If today did not result in a positive outcome, then he would definitely take his business elsewhere. In the meantime, he felt it inappropriate to mention that fact to David.

"How dare you?" Anderson fumed at the gall and effrontery of the young man in front of him.

The two large witnesses stepped forward and folded their arms across their massive chests. They did not say anything, but their presence was quite intimidating.

"My friend," Yaakov said softly, "it's high time that you freed your wife. Both of you need to get on with your lives. It's not appropriate for you to behave like this." His words were kind and gentle, trying to influence the older man to do the right thing by his own volition.

David was livid with rage, turned red and was shaking in anger at the unmitigated gall taking place in front of him, in his own office. He was glad that the office door was closed and Yaakov was speaking softly so that no one in the outer office heard or saw anything. He balked but he soon came to the realization that he did not have a choice in the matter. He sat down in his chair defeated and nodded his head, "Fine." He was not happy, but he was cornered. He covered his face in shame, fighting the tears that were trying to emerge. He did not want these strangers, especially Yaakov, to see him with tears on his face.

Rabbi Starr stepped forward and started the legal proceedings. "You agree to give your wife a *get* of your own free will?"

"Yes."

About half an hour later, when the *get* hit Yaakov's hand, Yehudis became a free woman. Yaakov, Rabbi Starr, and the two witnesses went directly to Yehudis' apartment with the good news and to finish up the *halacha* issues. All this time, Yehudis was trying not to get her hopes up while anxiously waiting for news about her status and pacing the floor. In quite a long time, no one had tried to help her from her predicament until this young man and rabbi showed up at her door. When Yehudis opened the door to four men with huge smiles on their faces, they did not need to tell her what happened — she knew immediately and was overjoyed. However, they wished her a hearty *mazal tov* and she was so ecstatic she had a huge smile on her face and clapped her hands with the gleeful news. She could not believe it: she was now a free woman thanks to the ministrations of this virtual stranger. Rabbi Starr reminded her that she had to wait three months before she could remarry.

Yaakov refused any remuneration. "Having been able to be a small part of freeing you is reward enough. The Big Boss put me in a situation that I was able to help you, and doing His will is what we are here for. It was my honor and pleasure." There was a tear of happiness in his eye and he was unsuccessfully trying not to let the happiness and excitement go to his head.

"You did not have a small part. But I can at least give you a *beracha* to thank you for your *chessed*," Yehudis said.

"It's not necessary, but I will not refuse a *beracha*," Yaakov replied with a shy smile.

"May you soon find your *bashert* and have health and happiness for the rest of your life," she said, hopeful for a good future for him.

"Amen," everyone responded.

UNFORTUNATELY, THE MERCIFUL ONE DECIDED He wanted the *neshama* of Rafael Tzvi Weinblatt.

The *Yeshiva,* along with everyone else, had been *davening* for the precious child, but to no avail. The *tefilohs* were heard on High, but the answer was 'no' and everyone was heartbroken. The Weinblatts remained resolute in the faith that HaShem had His reasons and that everything He did was for the best. Although they were hurting and it was very painful, they accepted His decision with equanimity.

During *shivah*, Rabbi Mishovsky came over to comfort the family who was surprised to see him, as he almost never left the *bais medrash.* The great *Rav* walked in and sat down and the family thanked him for coming; he just nodded his head. He did not say anything; he just held Zev's hand and cried with bitter tears running down his face. After about fifteen minutes of genuine emotion, the *Rav* stood up, said the appropriate words of comfort and left without saying another word.

The family felt comforted by his presence and they appreciated his coming. He had not said anything, but they felt uplifted and comforted by him.

# April 1986
## Fort Dix, New Jersey

Officer Connors gruffly said to Atkins, "You have the right to remain silent. Anything you say can be used against you in a court of law. You have the right to an attorney. If you cannot afford an attorney, one will be provided for you at no cost. Do you understand these rights as I have read them to you?"

"Yeah, I know my rights. What are the charges?" he demanded, trying to act macho. He was scared knowing that his house of cards was collapsing in on him and there was no one to help him. He suddenly realized that he was completely alone. He did not even hear the curious commotion that was going on outside his office from the inmates wanting to know what was going on.

"Conspiracy to commit murder, fraud, corruption, theft, abuse of power and more. The investigation has just begun and there are going to be many charges leveled against you. You're going away for a long time. I just hope it's to this prison." Connors hated crooked cops and here was a majorly bad case. "Turn around and put your hands on the wall. Do you have anything in your pockets that is sharp or that would hurt me when I frisk you?"

Atkins wanted to resist, but knew better: to where could he run? He was already in a prison with three sets of fencing, and no inmate was going to hide or help him. With shaking hands, Atkins gently took off his badge and keys and handed them to Connors. "I will not resist. I have a pen in my shirt pocket." He wanted to find a hole into which he could run and hide. Suddenly he realized his gig was up and he was in serious trouble, a bad predicament, especially for a law enforcement officer. He was shaking in fright as it suddenly dawned on him he was going to be a convict in prison. He was going to be one of the charges he used to control – the shoe was about to be on the other foot and he was petrified.

Dejectedly, Atkins turned around and put his hands on the wall. He was frisked and placed in steel handcuffs and was led away with the two arresting officers. They were each holding one of Atkins' arms, who hung his head in shame while they escorted him through the prison toward the exit. They also needed to protect him from any of the inmates who would want to take vengeance.

Some of the inmates noticed the arrest of Atkins and started cheering that their nemesis was in handcuffs. Word spread quickly and even before Atkins was out of the prison, the inmates started to riot. They were both angry that they had been mistreated all this time by a Correction's Officer, but happy that this buzzard was under arrest. The inmates refused to cooperate with the authorities; they destroyed prison property, stormed the fences and did serious damage to the buildings and property. The cons threw paper, trash, books and more all over the campus. They destroyed the landscaping and broke many windows. It was havoc as the prisoners ran amuck completely out of control.

In order to get control over the prison, the warden put the whole prison in complete lockdown for five days. The inmates were only allowed out of their cells for work detail and chow. All the inmates were responsible for cleaning up from the mayhem and destruction they caused. After a few more days, things in the prison started to return to normal. It took more than a week for things calmed down enough for the warden to restore commissary privileges.

It was reported back to the inmates that Atkins took a plea bargain. The evidence against him was overwhelming and due to the severity of his multiple crimes for many years, plus the attempt on the judge's daughter, he was sentenced to life without the possibility of parole at a super maximum-security facility. The residents of Fort Dix were hoping that Atkins would be doing his time with them. They were bitterly disappointed, as the law did not allow that to happen, for the protection of the convict.

JUDGE ARCHER SAT DOWN TO write a petition to the governor of New York, for the clemency of Bert Sobol.

When Judge Archer picked up his pen to write the petition, he lost his grip of the pen and it rolled a few inches away. Archer tilted his head slightly and looked at the pen laying on his desk and then looked at his hand. He could not imagine what caused the sudden weakness in his hand. With his left hand, he massaged his right and did not discern anything wrong.

Ignoring the incident, Archer retrieved the pen and started to write the petition.

It was unheard of for a judge to write such a petition on behalf of a convict. However, Archer felt that he owed it to Bert for saving his daughter's life. It was something he wanted to do even though Bert did not ask for recompense.

The Governor of New York, the chief executive of the state, granted said clemency, Bert was to be released immediately with no preamble.

The paperwork for the clemency and release came across the warden's desk the following morning; he was expecting it. The moment the documents were on his desk, it brought a smile to his face and he had Bert brought to his office. Bert was nervous about being called to the warden as a meeting between the warden and an inmate never portended good news but this was going to be an exception. Bert had never met the warden and when he was escorted to the warden's office, he was taken aback. The warden was not what he expected. He was short and stocky and solidly built. It was obvious he worked out regularly and could easily handle himself in a fight.

"Bert Sobol," the warden said looking up to the tall inmate, "I have in my hands an interesting document."

"Yes sir," Bert was uncomfortable and apprehensive, not sure what to expect from this unusual encounter.

"This is a letter from the Governor of the great state of New York. Although you are incarcerated in a federal prison in New Jersey, technically, you are a ward of the state of New York. It is a bit complicated."

"Yes, sir. But what does that have to do with me?" Bert asked.

"Why did you want to see me?" He asked more curious than concerned when he realized that the warden was talking to him as more of an equal than a charge.

"It seems that you were directly responsible for saving the life of a federal judge's daughter, and weeding out serious corruption here in my prison. Individually, those are no small matters. Coupled, both the state of New York and the state of New Jersey owe you their thanks.

"As a way of showing appreciation, the Governor of New York has granted you clemency."

It took a few moments for Bert to digest the news. "Are you saying I'm a free man?" he asked incredulously. He was afraid to hope this was true.

"Well, it will take a few hours, but by lunchtime, you should be on your way home."

Bert was in shock: his heart was beating so fast he could barely catch his breath. He was not expecting any thanks for what he did, let alone freedom.

With a huge smile on his face, Bert said, "Thank you so much! What do I need to do?"

"In order to expedite your leaving, use the phone in the outer office and call someone to pick you up. Have someone collect you at noon at the front entrance of Fort Dix, where you were dropped off. After you make the arrangements, you and I will start the process."

"Thank you, Warden."

Bert was so excited he wanted to pinch himself to make sure he was not dreaming. Due to the elation he was feeling about his impending release, he had a difficult time dialing the phone. At first, his family thought he was joking with them about his needing a ride, but he was able to convince them he was serious. Since he was about to be a free man, he briefly told them about the circumstances that led to the letter of clemency from the Governor.

After taking care of the initial paperwork, Bert went back to his cell to start packing.

"What are you doing? Where are you going?" he was asked.

"It seems that since I was responsible for Atkins being arrested and some other issues, I was given clemency by the Governor and I'm going home." He still had a difficult time processing the news about his imminent release.

Most of the inmates were happy for him; a few were jealous.

A few hours later, he was escorted to the I/O (Intake and Out) building for the processing of paperwork. Then he was given a ride to the security building at the front gate to await a ride home from his family. He had been given only a few hours notice of his pending release and it was difficult to fathom the news. He would be able to start over with a clean slate, as his record would be expunged.

Bert was happy and had someone in his family come to Fort Dix to retrieve him and escort him home. Bert had only been in prison for about five months, but for him, it seemed much longer.

He wanted to redirect his life and goals. He decided he would attend the *Yeshiva* of Rabbi Horowitz in New York. He also wanted to meet with Judge Archer to thank him for his freedom.

# May 1986
## Manhattan, New York

Yaakov was a wealthy man with a diverse portfolio and some real estate holdings. However, he did not tell many people since he preferred to live a quiet and low-key life. He decided this was information that could wait and had not even told the woman he was dating. He wanted to make sure she liked him for who he was and not be distracted by his wealth. He heard of many people getting married just for money and those marriages never lasted. The Mishneh (Pirkey Avos 5:19) states that any love that is dependent on something physical, when that physical thing goes away, then so does the love. If she got angry with him for not disclosing his wealth, so be it. He was not going to let money get in the way of his future happiness.

ON A BEAUTIFUL SUNNY SUNDAY in May, Yaakov and Rivkah took an early afternoon boat tour of the Hudson River. It was an almost cloudless sky with a temperature of about seventy-five degrees, the perfect weather for a date. The tour was three hours and circumvented the Island. There were not many people on the boat and they were standing alone in the forecastle watching the coastline pass to their right. It was turning out to be a perfect day and the couple was happy together and happily conversing. Just past the George Washington Bridge, the boat turned east on the Spuyten Duyvil Creek and then turned south into the Harlem River. As the boat headed south, it passed Randalis Island and then Roosevelt Island. The Harlem River dumped into the East River which took the sightseers to the foot of Manhattan and out to the Hudson River again where it headed north back to Pier Eighty-Three. Yaakov was apprehensive because of what he had planned for the end of their date. Rivkah was excited because her intuition told her something special was in the offing - she was sanguine.

After the boat tour, they went to Schmulka Bernstein's Chinese Restaurant at 135 Essex Street in Lower Manhattan for dinner. The waiters wore black Chinese *yarmulkes* with red tassels, and even the non-Jewish waiters spoke Yiddish. This was the original kosher Chinese restaurant.

The couple had a pleasant dinner together. Yaakov was nervous; "What will she say? Is it too soon? Will she like the ring?" his mind was racing and he was getting more apprehensive as their meal progressed. Rivkah was a sensitive soul, discerned his discomfiture, and felt bad for him, but there was nothing she could do at this point. At the next tables were both sets of their parents, Rivkah did not notice because of the way they had been purposely seated. There was a special bouquet of red roses on the couple's table: it was a nice and romantic dinner.

After their server cleared away the main course, Yaakov's parents came over and joined them. Rivkah was surprised to see them, was about to say something when just as dessert was about to be served, Rivkah's parents came over, and also joined them. It all happened so quickly that Rivkah was discombobulated and barely had time to react.

"What are you all doing here," she asked her parents.

"We are here for an engagement," they said elusively.

"Whose?" she asked bashfully? She was already thinking that her beau was planning something for her. "I sure hope it's mine," she thought to herself. She smiled shyly.

Before her parents even had a chance to answer, the waiter brought out a tiramisu cake with a candle and an open ring box, sitting on a bed of multi-color rose petals. It was a beautiful diamond ring. Tears came to Rivkah's eyes. She dabbed her eyes with her cloth napkin, looked up, and saw Yaakov on a knee looking up hopefully at her.

"Will you honor me by allowing me to marry you and try to make you happy for the rest of your life?" he asked nervously.

Rivkah blushed and looked around at her parents who were standing there watching, hopeful. Then she noticed the Applebaums also watching with bated breath. The waiters faded into the background knowing their presence would be an intrusion at this juncture.

The sounds of *"Mazal Tov"* abounded the restaurant. Everyone was so happy for the young couple. The men shook hands and the women hugged each other. Yaakov and Rivkah were so happy and the release of tension made them feel so much better.

A few days later, they had a small engagement party with a few of their friends. Everyone was happy for the engaged couple planning their nuptials and their future together.

Bert and Emily were among the invitees and the two of them noticed each other. They did not know it yet, but they were already acquainted. Emily went to Rivkah, and independently Bert went to Yaakov and each asked about one another.

After the engagement party, the happy couple conferred and were ecstatic to set Emily and Bert up on a *shidduch*. At first, Richard Archer was appalled by the idea of his daughter dating a former convict. However, since Bert saved Emily's life, he decided to bite his tongue, for the time being. When he saw how Bert treated his daughter, he had to agree that he was a good man.

Rivkah was planning to continue computer programming and teaching. Yaakov was considering teaching in the *Talmud Torah* where he went to *Yeshiva* high school and working with his fiancée with her business.

# June 1986
## Borough Park, New York

After Yaakov and Rivkah committed to spending the rest of their lives together, they started making plans. Yaakov came clean about the size of his investments and holdings and Rivkah was shocked at the enormity of it. She was not upset at him for withholding this information; she thought it prudent of him. They both agreed they would not live on the money Yaakov had. They would be productive in society and hold down jobs but keep their financial state private.

They formulated and discussed an idea for a joint business venture that would suit both of their talents. Together, they would open a computer store where they would build, repair and teach computers to others. They would engage Emily Archer to work with them as a sub-contractor and teacher as needed and as her time allowed. Since Shoshanna also showed a propensity for computers, maybe they would be able to use her help in the programming end of the business.

"I would like to live in Borough Park, preferably near Rabbi Mishovsky." Rivkah was excited that they were planning their future together. She was so happy and her eyes sparkled as she smiled.

"I agree," Yaakov said. "I have a few ideas I would like to run by you and I welcome your thoughts and any ideas you have."

"Great, what are your ideas?" she asked.

"The lease on the apartment in the basement of Rabbi Mishovsky's *shul* is about to come due. We can ask them to move out and we can live there until we are ready to buy a house.

"Or we can find another apartment in the neighborhood.

"In either case, we start your computer business in our apartment and as it grows, we consider moving into a house and bring the business with us, or move the business into another location. Time will dictate that."

"It's 'our' business," she corrected him. "What would you prefer?" she asked shyly.

Yaakov hesitated a moment. "I would like to answer by telling you a *d'var* Torah."

"That's perfect. Finding answers to our questions in the Torah is the only way for us to live," she said clapping her hands with excitement.

Smiling at his *kallah*, he said, "What was Adam *Harishon** punished for?"

"That's easy, for eating from the forbidden tree."

"That's a common misnomer. The *passuk* says differently; 'Because you listened to the voice of your wife.' " Yaakov paused to let his words sink in. "Since we are supposed to learn from and duplicate the words and actions of our antecedents, that's great! That means I don't have to listen to what you say, in fact, according to this, I should not listen to you."

"You dare try," she teased with a sly smile. They both laughed.

"Please allow me to continue." He smiled at his wise betrothed and she nodded her head graciously. "Let's look a bit further. On the other hand, Avraham *Avinu** was told 'All that your wife Sarah* tells you, listen to her voice'.

"Now I'm confused. Adam was punished for listening to his wife and Avraham was told to listen to everything his wife said. Which is it? What am I, a mere mortal, to do? Do I follow Adam *Harishon or* Avraham *Avinu?* We have to solve this seeming contradiction."

"That's an excellent question. I never noticed the contradiction. I don't know, but as a woman, I would say to listen to your wife." Rivkah was impressed with Yaakov's question.

"As always, you are wise. I digress a moment, but there is a famous expression that is apropos, 'Happy wife, happy life.' However, we still have difficulty with Adam being punished for listening to his wife. It's a conundrum and we somehow have to resolve the seeming dichotomy.

"I would like to suggest the following possible solution. There is a difference between the two episodes. With Adam, it was a spiritual issue; God said don't eat, Chavah* said eat. However, with Avraham, it was a domestic situation with Hagar* and Yishmael*.

"By Adam, it was a spiritual issue of HaShem said no, and Chavah said yes. With a spiritual issue, that is the husband's domain and Adam should not have listened to Chavah. We also see that with other areas in *halacha*. For example, the man does Chanukah lighting since it is to spread the word of the miracle of Chanukah and that is a spiritual issue. On the other hand, with Avraham, it was a domestic issue and that is the wife's domain. That is why the wife always lights *Shabbos* candles since they are lit for *shalom bayis.*"

"That makes perfect sense. I like that. Thank you so much for sharing. I guess what you are saying that when it comes to issues of spirituality and growth in Torah, etcetera, that is your area of expertise. In areas of domestic tranquility, that's my domain."

"Exactly! I'm proud of you for easily comprehending my intention." He smiled at her.

She smiled coyly. "Thank you."

"As an aside, I do have one request. When I have an opinion on a domestic issue, at least consider my point of view before you make a decision. Not that you have to follow my thoughts, but at least pay me the respect of considering them."

"Of course, that's perfect."

"Now to answer your question; where we live, is a domestic question. You decide."

"From the way you described the basement apartment of the *shul*, I would not have a problem living there and living in such close proximity of the *Rav* would be wonderful. However, I am not comfortable with just evicting the tenants."

"I think I have a solution that will benefit all parties. First, I greatly admire your sensitivity to the current tenants. That is commendable. My solution is that we give the current tenants three months' notice and they can use the last month's rent for moving expenses. If they are still there by the time of our *chassunah*, we will stay by your parents or mine until the time they can vacate. We won't rush them. Our wedding is in just under three months, so that would probably work well."

"That sounds absolutely perfect. Three months should be more than enough time for them to find a new place to live and using the last month's rent for moving expenses is generous."

"I'll call them today to let them know."

"In the meantime, we can start working on building our business. I will talk with Emily and Shoshanna and see what we can arrange."

"We will have to go to the bank to set up bank accounts, including for the business. I already have an account with a bank on Thirteenth Avenue and I know the manager. I am sure he'll be happy to assist us."

In the meantime, the couple would do everything they could to help others. They would base their future on *chessed*.

On the first Thursday of every month, Yaakov and Rivkah would go to Rabbi Starr's house. After Yaakov wrote a check for the poor, the Rabbi and *Rebbetzin* handed the young couple, bags of food and addresses.

The couple, who was starting their lives together, would take the bags of food and deliver them to indigent families. They did not have names, just addresses. They would deposit a bag of food in front of the door of someone's apartment, knock on the door and run.

"I never realized how many people were struggling to put food on the table," Rivkah said.

"It is significantly more than just the few we are able to help."

"I wish we could do more."

"I agree," he said with an appreciation for her sensitivity. "We have to make sure to use our money in the ways that the Big Boss wants, or He will give it to others. We have to remember that any money we have is on loan from Him." He admired her sensitivity to others and their needs.

"I completely agree." Rivkah appreciated his faith in HaShem. It warmed her heart that she was marrying someone who was on the same wavelength as herself.

They smiled at each other as they went about their awesome *mitzvah*.

On more than one occasion, they were almost caught in the act of their *chessed*, but that did not deter them from their great *mitzvah*. On one occasion the recipient was coming down the hallway at the same time they were heading to their door. To cover their tracks, they just continued up to another floor, waited a few minutes and continued with their original plan. Another episode found the beneficiary opening the door before they had a chance to run away. Most of the time, they were able to get away before the conferee discovered them.

# August 1986
## Brooklyn, New York

Rafe Bradford and Alesha Bates were tow truck drivers working anywhere in the five boroughs and beyond. They were not the smartest people in the world, but they were dedicated to each other. They worked hard and lived quiet lives.

Rafe graduated public high school in 1974. In actuality, he graduated only because his teachers felt bad for him and passed him from one year to the next until he completed high school. The only classes he excelled in were shop and recess, not necessarily in that order. The rest of the subjects he barely scraped by with a D-. At least he had his high school diploma.

His girlfriend, Alesha, was in his classes and they always hung out together. They had been together since they were juniors in high school and she did not fare much better in class than he.

Although Rafe was good with his hands and he could have been an auto mechanic, he was not interested in that type of work. He wanted to do something where he was on the road and moved around the city and could be with his girlfriend. He did not like the thought of being cooped up inside working all day.

They liked the idea of being tow truck drivers. They were able to work on cars and be mobile at the same time. They could also work whatever hours they wanted. There were not any specific requirements to become a tow truck driver, except a clean driver's license, which they both had. They applied for and were able to secure jobs as a team to drive a tow truck. They received on-the-job training and were gainfully employed.

They both had some basic automotive skills they had learned in shop class. Rafe and Alesha already knew how to jump-start dead batteries and change flat tires. They learned where to hook up the chains to tow cars without causing damage, and how to do minor roadside repairs.

They did a good job and after a few years had saved up enough to buy their own used tow truck. They were happy and doing well for themselves and were hoping to eventually purchase a second truck. Maybe they would be able to hire others to work for them, but that was much further down the road.

After they purchased their tow truck, they were able to take on more jobs, but finding those jobs became a challenge. They were in contact with companies that required tow trucks to repossess vehicles from people who were not paying for their cars, or they were needed because of accidents or vehicles that broke down and had to get to their mechanic. They had quite a bit of competition from other tow truck drivers and after a time, they were struggling to make ends meet. Things were difficult for them and they had to do something.

Rafe had an idea. They hired Alexander Bently to make some "No Parking, Tow Away Zone" signs. The signs also had the address of a lot they were renting for their swindle.

They would canvas a target zone for a decent middle price-range car. They made sure to vary their target zone regularly and they did not do this scam every day. Once they found a car, Alesha, dressed in dark blue to make herself look official, would get out of the truck. She would quickly post one of their signs by the car and walk away.

About ten minutes later, Rafe would drive up in his tow truck and start to hook up the car. He would do this slowly, hoping the victim would emerge before he drove off. If the owner of the car came out before he left the scene, he would offer them to ransom back their car before being towed. The inconvenience of having to get their vehicle from his lot was worth the expense.

Most often, the owner of the vehicle would be happy with the arrangement and gladly pay to redeem their car. This way the victim did not have to find a way to locate wherever his car was being held and pay the higher fine.

After the vehicle owner would drive away, Alesha would go back and collect the sign for future use.

If he drove off before the owner returned to their car, they would see the sign and go to Rafe's lot to reclaim their car. He would collect a significant fine for them to redeem their car.

Because they did not commit this fraud in the same area twice, and they waited a fortnight between extortions, it seemed to be going well for them.

They still did their regular towing to earn a living but committed this scam to supplement their income.

# August 2, 1986
## Brooklyn, New York

Ahmed decided he wanted some help on his next criminal venture as there were a number of parts to this plan that needed to be filled. Part of his plan included the hope that Mohamed would be arrested and this would be the end of having to deal with the Jew lover.

He needed a driver with less than stellar ethics; someone who could help with more than just transportation. After contacting Rafe, who he had used in the past, they all met on Friday, August 2, on the south side of Prospect Park Lake, Brooklyn, to discuss their ideas. It was a public place where they could meet and have privacy, in the warm August afternoon while listening to the birds chirping in the trees and watching toddlers running around in the park. This had the advantage of keeping their warehouse address private, in case things did not work out.

After exchanging social pleasantries, Ahmed started the conversation, "Have you guys heard of the Palestine Freedom Group?"

"Sure, who hasn't?" Alesha said. "They've taken responsibility for a number of terrorist attacks in the New York area recently."

Ahmed noticed they were not reviled by the question so he thought he would try them. "Yeah. That's us," he said.

"No. Get out!" said a surprised Rafe.

"It really is us and we're planning our next event and we need someone with your talents and abilities." He was a bit nervous about broaching the subject, but he decided he had to take a risk.

"We're not terrorists, we are low-level scammers. I doubt we could be of any help to you."

Ahmed saw the hesitation in their attitude and decided to hone in. "I will give you a brief synopsis of the idea and how you could help. If you're interested, fine. If not, then we go our separate ways. No harm, no foul."

Alesha and Rafe glanced at each other. "We'll listen," Alesha said. "We're not doing anything for free." She was desperate for money and maybe this would supply some needed cash.

That was his open and he jumped on it. "We are going to rob a bank and need your help in both the robbery and a getaway vehicle. That's the short of it. We will split the take evenly between the four of us. Are you interested?"

"When do you want to do this?" the couple asked.

"We haven't done much planning yet. It sounds as if you are interested."

They looked at each other and nodded their heads, "Yeah; money is tight right now."

Mohamed handed them a piece of paper. "That's our address. It's a warehouse in Brooklyn. Be there tomorrow at 6:00 p.m. and we will start making plans."

A few days later, Rafe walked into a bank on Thirteenth Avenue and Fiftieth Street in Borough Park, Brooklyn. Ostensibly, he was planning to open a bank account; however, he had a hidden agenda. Rafe had a good spatial memory and when he walked into the bank, he started to look around carefully. He made mental notes of where the security guard stood. He measured the number of steps from the door to the tellers and counted the tiles from one wall to the other.

Rafe walked into the bank a few more times to scout out the security and to make sure of the location of the security cameras and the routine of the guard.

After each visit to the bank, he made copious notes. He even went as far as sketching out the bank, including the vault location and offices of the bankers.

Mohamed also visited the bank a few times to acquaint himself with its layout.

Additionally, Alesha went to the bank with a different role. Of course, she wanted to familiarize herself with the bank; however, she started flirting with the guard to be able to distract him at the right time.

"Are the two of you ready yet?" asked Ahmed, his voice echoing slightly off the warehouse walls.

"I think so," said Mohamed. "I just want to review the plans with everyone one more time."

They sat at the table in their warehouse hideout and went over every detail and who would be doing what. They were not leaving anything to chance. Every nuance was meticulously planned.

Not wanting to use their truck for the heist, a few days before the job, Rafe pilfered a vehicle that they would use for their getaway. They stored it safely out of sight in the warehouse.

# August 18, 1986
## Borough Park, New York

Monday morning, Yaakov and Rivkah went into the bank on Thirteenth Avenue and Fiftieth Street to open an account in both of their names. They also wanted to talk with the manager about opening a business account in the near future. Before long, they would start to put together a business plan for their upcoming enterprise.

Yaakov introduced the bank manager to his fiancée, and he was happy for the young couple. When they started their vocation, they would also need a bank account and papers for incorporation.

They already had a pre-nuptial agreement in place that included a guarantee for a *get* they hoped would never be needed.

Rabbi Starr worked out the details for the assurance of the issuance of a *get* if Heaven forefend the need arose. "If more people made this type of prenuptial agreement there would be fewer problems in the world."

"I would consider it an honor if others will learn from this," Yaakov said sincerely. "As the Rabbi knows, I have had some minor involvement with one or two *agunahs* and if this will help prevent even one *agunah* in the future, I will be happy."

"You've had more than a minor involvement in helping a number of *agunahs*. What you have done to help free *agunahs* is commendable." Rabbi Starr was impressed with his protégé and his modesty.

Yaakov just brushed off the compliment.


IN ORDER NOT TO DRAW attention to themselves, Ahmed, Rafe, and Alesha individually entered the bank with ski masks in hand and armed to the teeth while Mohamed waited outside as a lookout. They each had two Glock 9mm guns with extra clips, as well as knives, and bags to carry their loot.

When the three criminals walked into the bank, they walked to their prearranged locations. Alesha started up a conversation with the security guard to distract him from the machinations of her conspirators. With a deceptive smile on his face, Ahmed went up to a teller wearing a nametag identifying herself as Melody. With a nod of his head, Ahmed, Rafe, and Alesha put their masks on to obscure their faces. Belatedly, they were hoping to hide their identity. When the security guard saw Alesha put on a mask, he reached for his weapon. Since Alesha worked a physically demanding job on a tow truck and was strong, she was prepared, and punched him hard in the stomach causing him to double over and then she swiftly drew her knee to his stomach. As the guard was trying to catch his breath from the impacts, she quickly grabbed his gun and pushed him away and down to the ground.

As this was transpiring, Rafe fired one shot in the air to get everyone's attention while Alesha turned and locked the door of the bank and flipped the "open" sign to "closed".

There was general panic among the bank employees and customers. Many screamed but Yaakov, who was in the same bank at that moment, jumped up alert and remained calm. Rivkah was anxious, but because her man was calm, it helped her to remain composed. Yaakov instinctively positioned himself in front of his fiancé to protect her while he quickly assessed the situation to determine if he had any options. They quickly ducked behind the desk of the bank manager to protect themselves while Yaakov was carefully observing all the actions of the criminals waiting for an opportunity. The customers and employees of the bank were frightened for their lives and whimpering as they knew that bank robberies rarely worked out well for either the robbers or the innocent bystanders inside the financial institution.

Ahmed quickly instructed one of the bank employees to close all the blinds. With Alesha guarding their backs and Mohamed guarding from the outside, Rafe and Ahmed went over and demanded the tellers fill their bags with all the money. They were not going to go for the safe, as they did not want to take that much time while the police came.

"Everyone on the floor," Ahmed yelled! "Now!"

"Move it! Quickly!" emphasized Rafe.

They yelled at the tellers to fill their bags with all the money in the tills. "Faster!" they yelled, trying to maintain control over their victims and keep them on edge. Things were going as planned and they were happy, expecting to be out of there momentarily with their ill-gotten loot.

From his perspective on the outside of the bank, Mohamed glanced inside to make sure everything was going according to plan. He could not see anything due to the blinds being closed. He just waited outside in the August heat.

Alesha was watching the goings-on with her head turned away from where Yaakov was crouching on the floor. Rafe and Ahmed had their backs to the center of the bank floor. Surreptitiously, Yaakov quietly reached onto the bank manager's desk and grabbed a pen and paperweight, the only viable items he could reach. It was the best he could grab at the moment; his martial arts training taught him that anything could be used as a weapon. Rivkah could not divine what her beau was planning or thinking. She was nervous and scared, and the actions of her man confused her.

"What are you doing?" she whispered concernedly.

He put his index finger to his lips, "Shhh." He smiled at Rivkah to reassure her, trying to help her stay calm.

Yaakov had three targets and only two projectiles; he had to choose his targets wisely and bide his time. His instincts made him want to protect everyone in the bank, especially his fiancée.

Because of the positions and demeanors of the criminals, Yaakov assumed that Rafe, the larger of the two men, was the leader. He was the closest to the tellers while the woman was standing guard by the door. He was not aware of Mohamed watching from the outside of the bank.

Yaakov waited for just the right moment and threw the pen hard at Rafe. Clutching his chest in shock, he looked down to see a pen sticking out of his chest. A moment after the pen left his hand, Yaakov threw the paperweight aimed at Alisha's head. Yaakov chose her because of her size. It struck her head broadside and she went down.

Shocked, Rafe looked down at the pen protruding from his chest with a small pool of blood forming on his shirt and was confused; it took a moment for the pain to register. In that moment of confusion and hesitation, Yaakov bolted forward. He jumped up and forward while cocking his right hand back, and came down leading by his right fist striking forward. Ahmed was just turning to see what all the commotion was about when a fist landed on his face from above breaking his nose. Ahmed went down clutching his bleeding face in a tremendous bout of pain.

Yaakov turned his attention to Rafe and turned around quickly striking a roundhouse kick to Rafe's stomach. He fell back and his head hit the counter with a thud.

Yaakov glanced at Alisha to asses her ability to return to the fray. She was sitting on the floor cowering and whimpering, with her hands covering her head. She had dropped her gun and clearly was no immediate threat. Yaakov ran over and kicked the gun away to be out of her immediate reach.

Ahmed panicked and ran out the door and looked for Mohamed, but he was long gone. "He must have run off when that man attacked. He's a coward," he growled angrily.

From the outside, when Mohamed heard a scuffle, he cracked open the door and saw Yaakov intervening, he panicked and ran a few blocks and grabbed a cab back to the warehouse. He did not want to use the stolen vehicle. He did not want to take a chance with the police, especially with the heist having just failed miserably.

Rafe gathered his wits, removed the pen from his chest and lunged at Yaakov. Because of his job towing vehicles, he was a rather large man and threw a right roundhouse punch toward Yaakov's face.

Yaakov placed his right foot forward into a right neutral bow checking the inside of Rafe's right knee with his own knee. At that same moment, Yaakov executed a right inward block to the inside of Rafe's right upper arm, hitting the bicep hard. He used his left hand to check the forearm.

Yaakov immediately struck to the right side of Rafe's neck

with a right outward hand-sword.

Yaakov then pivoted into a right forward bow and executed a left five-finger thrust to Rafe's eyes while he cocked his right fist to his right hip. Due to the thrust to his eyes, Rafe snapped his head back jutting his midsection forward.

Yaakov pivoted into a right neutral bow and struck a right uppercut punch to Rafe's stomach. While doing this, Yaakov's left arm became a cocking check guarding his right bicep.

Rafe was now bending over at the waist. Yaakov slid his left foot counterclockwise into a right forward bow and struck the back of Rafe's neck with a left outward hand-sword.

While doing that, Yaakov brought his right knee up into Rafe's chest.

Yaakov covered as he stepped away from the falling criminal. The whole process took fewer than five seconds and Rafe was completely spent and barely conscious. There was no fight left in him.

Yaakov looked around for the other two. Alesha was surrendering on the floor; she was not a seasoned criminal. Ahmed and Mohamed had both absconded.

Yaakov quickly kicked all the guns he saw to the side, out of reach of the criminals.

Rivkah's heart was racing but she could not believe her eyes. She was so proud of her *chassan.* Everything happened so quickly that she would have to ask him later what he did and where he learned to fight like that. She could not follow his movements due to the speed of execution of his moves.

Everyone at the bank stood up and gave Yaakov a standing ovation for his heroics. Yaakov blushed.

One of the tellers had triggered the silent alarm and a few moments after calm had been restored, the police arrive on the scene. They were not used to appearing at a bank robbery with everything under control and the perpetrators disarmed.

The police took custody of the two criminals and found the rest of their weapons. Thankfully, the only people hurt in the malaise were Alesha and Rafe, however, their wounds were not serious. The police put out an all-points-bulletin for Ahmed, who was now on the lam. They were not aware of another person's involvement.

Ahmed ran and ran; he did not know and was indifferent to where he was running. He was in pain and bleeding while panicking and running down Thirteenth Avenue which was a complete blur to him. As he ran, he bumped into people walking up and down the street. He did not care; he was frightened and did not know where to go. He turned left and ran; he turned right and ran; he stopped for a moment to catch his breath. Some people were looking at the strange man with a ski mask in August running as if he were a lunatic. He looked around and realized he was lost. He looked behind him and was thankful that no one seemed to be paying any attention to him. Quickly, he doffed the mask and continued walking, but this time at a more leisurely, if not nervous, pace. He looked around him but did not recognize the area; it was new to him. He could not have gone far on foot and he knew the streets followed a numerical progression. He quickly approached a street corner and saw that he was on Fort Hamilton Parkway. That did not help him much.

"How did I end up here," he wondered to himself. He was afraid to go to the hospital with a broken nose. He was sure the police would be on the alert for him and the hospital staff would ask too many questions.

He found a cemetery on the corner of Fort Hamilton Parkway and Thirty-Seventh Street. It was right next to a known drug lair, but he did not care. He did not expect much of a police presence there. About a quarter of a mile inside the corner fence, there were a few crypts in which he was able to hide. He needed time to think and rest from his exertions.

The police were able to trail the perpetrator for a while due to him making himself known by his strange appearance and bumping into people. After a while, the trail went cold and the police fanned out looking for him. They did not have a clear description at first, but after they reviewed the security camera footage, they were able to make a composite sketch.

"Is there ever anything not exciting with you?" Rivkah asked her fiancé. She had a sly smile on her face but was only half-joking.

Yaakov lifted his face, looked up, and brought his hand to his chin. He thought for a minute and then responded, "Nah! That would be no fun." They smiled at each other knowing they could expect more excitement in the future, and hopefully a long and happy life together.

# August 20, 1986
## Brooklyn, New York

Both local and federal law enforcement were out looking for Ahmed for several days, without success. Ahmed was hiding in a crypt in the cemetery barely venturing out at night in search of food and water; he was scared and in pain from his broken nose. He did not know what to do: he was tired, hungry, thirsty and alone and afraid of ghosts in the cemetery. At the darkest hours of the night, he cautiously snuck out and foraged for food scraps in some trashcans in the area. He was frightened and quickly retreated to his hideout where every little sound scared him. He wanted to return to the bunker, get a good meal and a drink. He barely slept while he was on the lam. Who could sleep in a crypt where even the flutter of birds or a slight breeze startled him?

He assumed the police had impounded the getaway vehicle, so that was not an option, besides, it was so far away. He had no idea what had happened to his conspirators. Were they all right? Who was that fighting machine who caught them off guard? Where did he come from? He knew the robbery attempt had failed miserably, even with all of their planning he had not thought of meeting resistance in the bank. He was angry and felt as if all of their criminal escapades were failures. He was sure he was going to prison. He had a significant amount of time to consider his predicament and he did not like the situation in which he found himself.

Flyers were hung all around the neighborhood with the likeness of the perpetrator. There were notices on TV and a large reward was offered for information leading to the arrest of the criminal. The man seemed to have just disappeared into thin air.

Bert had a few ideas where he could start looking for the missing bank robber. He had experience and contacts in searching out perpetrators.

After two days, Ahmed had enough and could not stand being cooped up in the cold and damp crypt any longer. During the day he had to keep the crypt closed which caused it to be hot with the air completely still and at night, he could open it to let in some air, but it was still dark.

Tentatively, he stepped outside into the cool night air and started walking toward the closest intersection. He was dirty and smelled. He was parched, famished, lost and not sure in which direction to go. He felt completely miserable and wanted to curl up somewhere and cry and then end it all.

He needed to get his bearings so he would know which direction he needed to go to get to the warehouse. He was on Thirty-Seventh Street and started walking down Fort Hamilton Parkway. A block later, he came to Thirty-Eighth Street and realized he was heading in the right direction. He kept walking trying to stay in the shadows as much as possible.

At Forty-Second Street, he saw a fast-food restaurant on his right that was well-lit. He was tempted to go inside for something to eat, but he had no money on him.

He did not want to walk past the well-lit restaurant lest he was seen, but he had no choice. "If I can get past it quickly enough, I may be able to hide for a few minutes by the school before passing the gas station. I've got to get off the main street."

As he was passing the restaurant, the inevitable happened: he was recognized.

Bert stepped in front of Ahmed, raised his hand, and said, "Stop!"

Ahmed panicked and tried to run across the asphalt of the restaurant to the back. He had not eaten or drunk anything in two days, nor had he slept well, so he could not run quickly. Bert, being in excellent physical condition, easily overtook and caught Ahmed.

Bert grabbed Ahmed's shirt from behind to restrain him. Ahmed balled his fist and turned around quickly to fend off his captor. Bert was too quick and he easily blocked the punch. Bert grabbed Ahmed's hand, placed his thumb firmly on the pressure point on the back of Ahmed's hand and quickly bent his wrist back. Ahmed was easily forced into submission.

A passerby noticed the commotion and Bert called out, "Please call the police, this man is a wanted criminal."

"What are the chances?" Ahmed thought to himself."Twice in a row, I meet a fighting machine. I need to learn how to fight."

Bert subdued the perp until Officers Connors and Jackson arrived on the scene. The officers immediately recognized everyone involved and promptly took control of the situation. Ahmed was put in handcuffs and read his rights.

"Are there no other police officers in the city? Why does it always have to be them?" Exasperatingly Bert thought to himself.

"I thought you were in prison for your crimes."

"I was, but the governor pardoned me."

"The governor did what?" they asked incredulously.

"I was pardoned by the governor of New York. You are more than welcome to check it out. In fact, my record was expunged, I am a free man.

"I am living a clean and respectable life now. I just happen to be out and recognized this perpetrator from the bank robbery sketches. I was not looking to be a vigilante again. I'm over that," Bert said.

Connors said, "We'll see; once a criminal, always a criminal."

Bert did not bother to respond. "Am I free to go?"

"For now; just stay out of trouble."

Bert shook his head. "No wonder people don't trust cops," he thought in disgust as he was leaving the scene.

# EPILOGUE

## September 28, 1986
## Throgs Neck, New York

**Rivkah** and Yaakov chose Sunday, September 28, 1986 (24 Elul, 5746), to start their married life together. There was not a cloud in the sky and the temperature was perfect; the day was impeccable in every way. It was a beautiful wedding in a large hall on the marina with awesome views of the Whitestone and Throgs Neck bridges. With sparkles in each of their eyes, they walked to the *chuppah*.

Rivkah looked elegant and regal in her flowing white wedding gown while walking down the aisle to meet Yaakov who appeared princely in a fine black suit awaiting her under the *chuppah*.

The ceremony took place outside in the gazebo with many friends and family in attendance. Rabbi Mishovsky was the *mesader kedushin* and Rabbi Horowitz came in from Israel and said the last *beracha* while Yaakov's *chavrusah* was one of the witnesses. The dancing and merriment continued unabated for hours.

At the conclusion of their wedding, they made sure that any leftover food was distributed to the poor at their own expense.

The newly married couple was so happy to start their married life together in the basement apartment of Rabbi Mishovsky's shul. All of their family and friends were excited for the newlyweds.

# October 4 & 5, 1986

Rosh HaShanah that year fell on Shabbos and Sunday and it was special for the newly married young couple. It was their inaugural *yom tov* together, the first of many new wonderful beginnings. They were still living in the basement of Rabbi Mishovskys *shul* in the building that Yaakov and Rivkah owned. They were always close at hand for the great man and they benefited from the closeness of the relationship and proximity.

With the blessings of the *Rav*, they started their computer business together in their apartment. Yaakov started substitute teaching in several of the local boy's Jewish day schools. He was able to control his hours to be available to assist his wife in their business. Being a brilliant man, Yaakov picked up computers easily and would be an asset to the enterprise.

Yaakov made sure to learn Torah for several hours every day in *Rav* Mishovskys *bais medrash*. Rabbi Mishovsky was so happy for Rivkah and Yaakov living a Torah true life. Yaakov noticed that whenever the *Rav* would see Rivkah, there was a faraway look of sadness in his wise eyes. Yaakov asked about it, but the *Rav* said nothing.

Emily Archer was busy teaching computers in college and helping with Rivkah's business on the side. Shoshanna was also available to help with the business while teaching children part-time. The more time she spent with her sister and brother-in-law with computers, the more she liked the idea and considered joining them in their business full time. However, with her disability, she would be more behind the scenes than dealing with customers.

Bert and Emily were dating, much to the consternation of her father.

Mohamed was still alive and free hidden in his bunker and was very confused about his own life and the nightmares that were disturbing his sleep. He was not sure what happened to Ahmed and not even sure if he cared. "Should I reach out to him? Or should I ignore him and let him suffer the consequences in prison. I hate the way he treated me for the last few months, but we used to be close."

Despite being in prison, Ahmed was planning his *coup d'état* with a massive computer virus that would take down the communication system in New York and beyond. He had some ideas of maybe forming an organization to hide his terrorist activities right under the noses of the authorities. He needed to recruit a new cadre

EPILOGUE

of terrorists, which would take time and effort. In the meantime, he would live out his time languishing in prison while waiting for his trial and probably a long sentence.

Palestine Freedom Group went underground, but it was not dead; far from it.

To be continued…

# INDEX OF HISTORICAL FIGURES

**ADAM HARISHON**: The first man, he was created on the sixth day of creation.

**ALLEN, BARRY**: Born 1965. Subway mugger who was shot by Bernhard Goetz in 1984

**AMNON, RABBI**: Eleventh-century rabbi, Mainz, Germany

**AVRAHAM AVINU**: The Patriarch Abraham

**BABA SALI ABUCHATZAYRAH, RABBI**: 1889-1984. Rabbi Israel Abuchatzayrah was a leading Moroccan Sephardic rabbi and kabbalist known for his prayers and ability to work miracles.

**BEHR, FRITZ**: 1933-2012. A police officer who tried to deactivate a terrorist bomb at Grand Central Station in 1976. He was injured in the explosion.

**BUŠIĆ, JULIENNE**: Born 1948. American writer and activist; she was the wife of Zvonko Bušić. Both were arrested in 1976 after hijacking TWA Flight 355.

**BUŠIĆ, ZVONKO**: 1946-2013. A Croatian immigrant who hijacked TWA Flight 355. Convicted of air piracy and spent thirty-two years in prison.

**CABEY, DARRELL**: Born 1965. Subway mugger who was shot by Bernhard Goetz in 1984

**CANTY, TROY**: Born 1965. Subway mugger who was shot by Bernhard Goetz in 1984

**CHAVAH**: The first woman, Eve, was created on the sixth day of creation from one of Adam's ribs.

**CUTINGA**: Paramour of Adolf Leipzig

**DWORKIN, HENRY**: Born 1936. A police officer who tried to deactivate a terrorist bomb at Grand Central Station in 1976. He was injured in the explosion.

**FEINSTEIN, RABBI MOSHE**: 1895-1986. Orthodox Rabbi, scholar, and writer of Jewish law. He was regarded by most as the supreme *halachic* authority of his time and beyond.

**GOETZ, BERNHARD HUGO**: Born 1947. New York City man was known for shooting four young men on a subway train in Manhattan in 1984

**HAGAR**: Concubine of the Patriarch Abraham

**HALBERSTAM,** *HARAV* **YEKUSIEL YEHUDAH - THE KLAUSENBERGER** *REBBI*: 1905-1994. An Orthodox rabbi and founder of the Sanz-Klausenburg Chasidic dynasty

**KLONIMOS** *BEN* **MESHULLAM, RABBI**: Head of the Jewish community in Mainz, Germany during the eleventh century

**HERMAN, RABBI YAAKOV YOSEF**: 1880-1967. Jewish rabbi who lived in New York and Israel. He is the subject of the book, *All for the Boss* by one of his daughter's Rebbetzin Ruchoma Shain.

**HITLER, ADOLF**: Born 1889-?. Leader of the Nazi party, Chancellor of Germany, dictator, responsible for the murder of millions of people

**HUSSEIN, SADDAM ABD AL-MAJID AL-TIKRIT**: 1937-2006. Fifth President of Iraq; murdered millions of people; also called the "Butcher of Baghdad".

**KADURI, RABBI YITZCHAK**: 1898?-2006. Great rabbi and Kabbalist of the Jewish people

**LEE, BRUCE**: 1940-1973. World-renowned martial arts expert

**LEIPZIG, ADOLF**: Died 1984. Some say this was really Adolf Hitler who escaped Germany and lived in South America.

**MCTIGUE, SERGEANT TERENCE**: Born 1949. A police officer who tried to deactivate a terrorist bomb at Grand Central Station in 1976. He lost an eye in the explosion.

**MURRAY, BRIAN J.**: 1949-1976. A police officer who tried to deactivate a terrorist bomb at Grand Central Station. He was killed in the subsequent explosion.

**NA'AMAH**: Wife of Noach

**NOACH**: From the Torah, he built the ark

**PARKER, ED**: 1931-1990. Martial arts expert and founder of the American Kenpo Karate system

**PRESLEY, ELVIS AARON**: 1935-1977. American singer and actor often referred to as "The king of Rock and Roll."

**RAMSEUR, JAMES**: 1966-2011. Subway mugger shot by Bernhard Goetz in 1984

**SARAH (IMAYNU)**: The first matriarch, wife of Abraham

**SILVER, RABBI DAVID L.**: 1907-2001. Rabbi and spiritual leader of Kesher Israel Congregation in Harrisburg, Pennsylvania for over fifty years.
**VILNA GAON**: 1720-1797. Elijah ben Solomon Zalman, known as the Vilna Gaon or Elijah of Vilna, or by his Hebrew acronym HaGra
**YISHMAEL**: Son of Abraham and Hagar

# GLOSSARY

**ACHARONIM**: Later rabbis
**AGUNAH**: A woman whose husband is withholding a *get* (Jewish divorce). She may not remarry.
**ALIYA**: Literally "To go up." 1. This refers to moving to Israel. 2. Being called up to the Torah for the reading of a portion.
**AMUD**: The lectern where the leader of the prayers stands
**ARON KODESH:** Holy ark in a synagogue
**BA'ALEI CHESSED:** Doers of good deeds
**BAAL TESHUVAH**: Someone new to the fold of observant Judaism
**BACHURIM**: Young men, students
**BAIS DIN**: Jewish court
**BAIS MEDRASH**: Jewish study hall or synagogue
**BARUCH HU UVARUCH SHEMO**: Blessed is He and blessed is His Name. This is said by someone hearing another person making a blessing, after hearing the Name of HaShem.
**BAVLI**: Babylonian Talmud
**BASHERT**: Preordained or destined match
**BECHINA(S)**: Test(s)
**BEN**: The son of
**BERACHA**: Blessing
**BERACHA ACHARONA:** A blessing that is said after consuming cakes, fruits or wines
**BESHA'AH TOVAH UMUTZLACHAS**: In a good and auspicious time
**BIMA:** Central podium from which the Torah is read in the synagogue

**CHASIDIC**: From being a *chasid*. A *chasid* is a pious person - one who goes "beyond the letter of the law" in his duties toward God and man.

**CHASSAN**: Groom

**CHASSUNAH**: Jewish wedding

**CHAVRUSAH**: Study partner

**CHAYN**: Inner beauty

**CHEDER**: Jewish day school

**CHESSED**: An act of kindness or charity

**CHOMETZ**: Leavened bread that is forbidden on Passover

**CHUMASH**: Scriptures of the Five Books of Moses

**CHUPPAH**: Wedding ceremony or canopy

**COYOTES**: (Spanish) Smugglers

**D'VAR TORAH**: Words of Torah

**DAF YOMI**: A cycle of *Gemara* learning one folio a day completing the entire Talmud in seven and a half years.

**DAN**: Level of accomplishment in karate, often called a belt or level

**DAVEN**: Pray

**DAVENED**: Prayed

**DAVENING**: Prayer service, or the act of praying

**DIRAH**: Apartment

**DOJO**: Karate classroom or studio

**ELUL**: Lunar month leading up to the Jewish New Year

**EMA:** (Hebrew) Mother

**EMUNAH**: Faith

**FAHAIR**: (Yiddish) Test

**FRUM**: Religious

**GABBAI***:* Sexton in a synagogue, someone who distributes the honors

**GADOL**: Literally "Big" refers to a great rabbi

**GADOL HADOR**: Leading rabbi of the generation

**GEMARA**: Talmud

**GER TZEDEK**: Righteous convert

**GET**: Jewish divorce

**GI**: Karate uniform

**HAMAPIL**: A prayer one says before retiring for the night

**HATZLACHA**: Good luck

**HAVDALAH**: A small ceremony that marking the symbolic end of Shabbos and holidays, and ushers in the new week.

**HETER**: Permission

**HIJAB**: A square piece of fabric, which is folded, placed over the head, and fastened under the chin as a headscarf, worn by Muslim women

**HISHTADLUS**: Effort

**IM YIRTZEH HASHEM**: If God wants

**JIHAD**: Islamic term referring to the religious duty of Muslims to spread their religion, even by force.

**KADISH**: A prayer said by mourners

**KALLAH**: Bride

**KAPARAH**: Atonement for sins

**KAVANA**: Intent

**KEDUSHA**: Literally "Holiness." This is a special prayer that is added during the repetition of the morning, afternoon and *musaf shemoneh esray* (eighteen-benediction prayer). It is a short prayer added to the third blessing when there is a quorum present.

**KESUBAH**: Jewish marriage contract

**KOLLEL**: Jewish college of higher learning for married men

**KOS SHEL ELIYAHU**: Cup of Elijah from Passover

**KOSSEL**: Western Wall in Jerusalem

**KRIYAS SHEMA**: See Shema

**LASHON HARAH**: Gossip

**LECHAYIM**: Literally "To life." When two people have a drink to thank HaShem for a special kindness

**MAASER**: Tithe

**MACHZORS**: Prayer books that are used for the holidays

**MAMZERET**: A bastard according to Jewish law (someone born from a prohibited levirate marriage) and cannot marry another Jew

**MASMID**: Diligent student who is always in the *bais medrash* when he was supposed to be there

**MAYIM SHELANU**: The water used to make matzah for Passover

**MEKUBAL**: Jewish Rabbi who is an expert in Jewish mysticism

**MENTCH**: A decent human being

**MESADER KEDUSHIN**: Officiate at a Jewish wedding.

**MEZUZOS**: (Plural of mezuzah) A piece of parchment (often contained in a decorative case) inscribed with specific Hebrew verses from the Torah (Deuteronomy 6:4-9 and 11:13-21). This is found on the doorposts of the home of Jews.

**MIDDAH**: Character trait

**MIDDOS**: Character traits

**MIKVAH**: Ritual bath

**MINCHA**: Afternoon prayers

**MINCHA GEDOLAH**: Afternoon prayers said at the earliest possible time

**MINYAN**: Quorum of ten men for prayer services

**MISHLOACH MANOS**: Literally "The sending of portions." On Purim, there is a custom to send two prepared foods to another person.

**MITZVAH**: Commandment from the Torah

**MUSAF**: Additional prayer said on *Shabbos* and holidays

**MUSAR**: Ethical teaching

**NACHAS**: Pride over the achievements, specifically of one's children.

**NESHAMA**: Soul

**PARNASSAH**: Income

**PESSACH**: Passover

**POSEK (POSKIM, PLURAL)**: Rabbi who is a decider of difficult Jewish law

**PUSHKA**: Charity box

**RABAYNU**: Our teacher, usually referring to Moshe (Moses) who took the Jewish people out of Egypt

**RACHAMIM**: Mercy

*RAV*: Rabbi

**REB**: Respectful title for Mr.

**REBBETZIN**: A rabbi's wife

**REBBI**: A rabbi

**RISHONIM**: Early rabbis

**ROSH HASHANA**: Start of the Jewish calendar year

**ROSH HAYESHIVA**: Dean of a Yeshiva

**SEDER**: Literally "Order." In this context, refers to the order of the day of the study program.

**SEFER, SEFARIM**: Jewish book(s)

**SEMACHOS**: Celebrations

**SEMICHA**: Rabbinic ordination

**SENSI**: Karate instructor

**SEUDAH**: Meal

**SHAATNEZ**: A Biblically prohibited mixture of wool and linen.

**SHABBOS**: Sabbath

**SHACHARIS**: Morning prayers

**SHADCHAN**: Matchmaker

**SHAITEL**: Wig

**SHALIACH TZIBUR**: Literally, "The messenger of the congregation." This refers to the person leading the services

**SHALOM BAYIS**: Peace in the home

**SHAMASH**: Sexton, assistant

**SHAMAYIM**: Heaven

**SHECHINAH**: Divine presence

**SHEMA**: Prayer of affirmation recited thrice daily. It is also said on the deathbed. It is comprised of three paragraphs from the Torah.

**SHEMURAH MATZAH**: Hand-baked matzah for Passover that is made from grain that is watched from the time of the harvesting of the wheat

**SHEPPING NACHAS**: Deriving pride (see *nachas*)

**SHEVA BERACHOS**: The Seven Blessings said both under the wedding canopy and during every meal for a week after a wedding.

**SHIRAYIM**: Literally "Leftovers." During a *tish*, the rabbi passes around food for his followers to taste.

**SHIDDUCH**: A matrimonial match

**SHIMUSH**: Literally "Serving." This is where a student is serving his teacher/rabbi to learn the intricacies of being a rabbi. This is the final step before receiving ordination.

**SHIR HASHIRIM**: Song of Songs

**SHIUR**: Class or lecture

**SHIURIM**: Classes or lectures

**SHIVAH**: Literally, "Seven." Refers to the seven days of mourning after someone dies

**SHTEIGING**: (Yiddish) Studying hard and growing

**SHUL**: Synagogue

**SIDDUR**: Jewish prayer book

**SIMCHA**: Joyous event

**SIYATA DISHMAYA**: Aramaic, Help from Heaven

**SOFER**: Scribe

**STENDER**: Lectern

**SUCCAH**: A temporary shelter used during the festival of Succoth (Tabernacles).

**SUGYA:** Section of Talmud

**TALMID**: Student

**TALMID CHACHAM**: Literally, "Student of wisdom", this usually refers to someone who is knowledgeable in Torah, most often a rabbi

**TALMIDIM**: Students

**TANACH**: Torah, Prophets, and Writings. The twenty-four books of the scriptures.

**TEFILAH**: Prayer

**TEFILLIN**: Phylacteries. These are two small black leather boxes with leather straps worn by men during the weekday morning prayers. One is worn on the forearm and the other on the head.

**TEHILLIM**: Psalms

**TESHUVA**: Repentance

**TISH**: Literally "Table." It is usually a Friday night event held by Chasidic Rabbis with Torah, song, and food.

**TORAH**: The Jewish Bible

**TZADIK**: Righteous person

**TZEDAKAH**: Charity

**TZEDEK**: Righteous

**TZITZIT**: Small four-cornered garment worn by men. Each corner of the garment is adorned by four strings doubled over and tied in a specific manner.

**VIDDUY**: Confessional prayer said on Yom Kippur and one's deathbed.

**YAHRZEIT**: The anniversary of someone's death

**YARMULKE**: Jewish skullcap worn by men.

**YERUSHALMI**: Jerusalem Talmud

**YESHIVA**: Jewish academy of higher learning

**YESHIVISH**: Either a dialect or behavior indicative of someone who learns or has learned in a *Yeshiva*.

**YIRAS**: Fear of

**YISBARACH**: May His Name be blessed

**ZECHUS**: Merit of

**ZEMIROS**: Spiritual songs sung on *Shabbos* and holidays. Mostly these are sung during the meals

**ZIVUG**: Marriage partner

**ZT'L**: *Zecher Tzadik Levracha*, Hebrew abbreviation: May the memory of the righteous person be remembered for a blessing.